... ER

BOO...
ON FATAL C...

"Intricately plotted, *Fatal Conv...* ...
with international overtones. In a... ...tal
information, realistic characters carry the act... ...sion."

FAITHFULREADER.COM

"Singer's legal knowledge is well matched by his stellar storytelling. Again,
he brings us to the brink and lets us hang before skillfully pulling us back."

ROMANTIC TIMES
ON *FATAL CONVICTIONS*

"Get ready to wrestle with larger themes of truth, justice,
and courage. Between the legal tension in the courtroom
scenes and the emotional tension between the characters,
readers will be riveted to the final few chapters."

CROSSWALK.COM
ON *FATAL CONVICTIONS*

"Great suspense; gritty, believable action . . . make [*False Witness*]
Singer's best yet."

BOOKLIST
STARRED REVIEW

"Randy Singer never disappoints, [and] *False Witness* is not just your
typical legal thriller. Singer expertly combines elements of suspense,
action, and intrigue into an explosive combination that really delivers."

FICTIONADDICT.COM

"Randy Singer is masterful at combining the action and suspense aspects
of the novel with the scenes of legal maneuvering."

CBA RETAILERS + RESOURCES
ON *FALSE WITNESS*

"A book that will entertain readers and make them think—
what more can one ask?"

PUBLISHERS WEEKLY

ON *THE JUSTICE GAME*

"Singer artfully crafts a novel that is the perfect mix of faith
and suspense. . . . [*The Justice Game* is] fast-paced from
the start to the surprising conclusion."

ROMANTIC TIMES

"At the center of the heart-pounding action are the moral dilemmas that
have become Singer's stock-in-trade. . . . An exciting thriller."

BOOKLIST

ON *BY REASON OF INSANITY*

"Readers will be left on the edge of their seats by
Singer's latest suspense-filled thriller."

CHRISTIAN RETAILING

ON *BY REASON OF INSANITY*

"Singer hooks readers from the opening courtroom scene of
this tasty thriller, then spurs them through a fast trot across
a story line that just keeps delivering."

PUBLISHERS WEEKLY

ON *BY REASON OF INSANITY*

"[A] legal thriller that matches up easily with the best of Grisham."

CHRISTIAN FICTION REVIEW

ON *IRREPARABLE HARM*

"*Directed Verdict* is a well-crafted courtroom drama with strong
characters, surprising twists, and a compelling theme."

RANDY ALCORN

BESTSELLING AUTHOR OF *SAFELY HOME*

THE
LAST PLEA
BARGAIN

TYNDALE HOUSE PUBLISHERS, INC., CAROL STREAM, ILLINOIS

RANDY
SINGER

Visit Tyndale online at www.tyndale.com.

Visit Randy Singer's website at www.randysinger.net.

TYNDALE and Tyndale's quill logo are registered trademarks of Tyndale House Publishers, Inc.

The Last Plea Bargain

Designed by Dean H. Renninger

Published in association with the literary agency of Alive Communications, Inc., 7680 Goddard St., Suite 200, Colorado Springs, CO 80920, www.alivecommunications.com.

Scripture taken from the Holy Bible, *New International Version,*® *NIV.*® Copyright © 1973, 1978, 1984, 2011 by Biblica, Inc.™ Used by permission of Zondervan. All rights reserved worldwide. www.zondervan.com.

Library of Congress Cataloging-in-Publication Data

Singer, Randy (Randy D.)
 The last plea bargain / Randy Singer.
  p. cm.
 ISBN 978-1-4143-3321-2 (sc)
 1. Women lawyers—Fiction. I. Title.
PS3619.I5725L37 2012
813'.6—dc23   2011040307

Printed in the United States of America

18   17   16   15   14   13   12
7   6   5   4   3   2   1

To the Somerville girls—Ginger, Alita, and Sara—
whose unrelenting pursuit of justice inspired this book.
Your father was a good man.

PROLOGUE

THE PARAMEDICS ARRIVED with a speed that surprised Caleb Tate. He met them at the front door of his seventy-five-hundred-square-foot mansion, a house on a large hill in the middle of Atlanta's illustrious Buckhead area. His friends called it "the house that murder built." Caleb Tate was, after all, one of the most notorious defense attorneys in the city of Atlanta—a reputation he had carefully nurtured his entire professional career.

He let the team in and breathlessly provided them with details as they followed him up the winding staircase, two steps at a time. The paramedics struggled to keep up, dragging their oxygen masks and defibrillators and other life-sustaining equipment. Adrenaline pumped through Caleb's body, and he felt as if this whole thing were a nightmare, a scene from a horror movie.

He rushed through the door of the bedroom and stepped aside, his body trembling as he took in the scene as if seeing it for the first time. His wife was sprawled in the middle of the floor, a scoop-neck sleepshirt twisted around her body.

He had lifted her from the bed, placed her on the carpet, and started CPR, tilting her head back and blowing in a breath. She had gurgled and vomited, the night's supper spilling down her cheek and matting her brown hair. He had cleaned her face with her sleepshirt, moved her head to the side, and used two fingers to clear out her throat. Then he'd tilted her head back again and resumed CPR, frantically pumping her chest with the heels of his hands and blowing deep breaths into her lungs. He'd counted out loud, slowing himself down. He kept checking for a pulse. He fought the urge to panic.

When his efforts proved unavailing, he had called 911. He knew it would be too late.

"You might want to step out in the hallway," an older paramedic said. He was kneeling next to Rikki and had a calm and efficient way about him, as if he might simply be putting a splint on a broken leg.

The team hooked up the defibrillator, but the readout said, "No shock advised." They stuck a tube down Rikki's throat, and a machine began pumping breath into her.

"You really need to wait outside." The man was more emphatic this time. He was a big guy with receding gray hair.

But Caleb *couldn't* move. His feet were in concrete, and the room was starting to spin.

"I need to stay," he insisted, his voice soft and distant. He could hear the sirens from other vehicles pulling into the driveway. Blue strobe lights pulsed through the windows. Police officers rushed up the stairs, and another set of paramedics arrived. Before Caleb knew what was happening, the house was swarming with rescue personnel. Somebody gently led him into the hallway, and the questions started flying. When did you find her? Has she had any health problems? What medications was she taking? How long were you gone?

Haltingly, Caleb explained that he had been at a friend's house to watch a couple of March Madness games. He had crawled into bed next to Rikki and asked her a question, jostling her when he received no answer. He had reached over and touched her again and realized that her skin was cold and she wasn't breathing. From there it was all a blur—jumping out of bed, doing CPR, calling for help.

He didn't know how long the paramedics worked on her before the older gentleman came into the hallway with a grim look. "I'm sorry," he said. "We've done everything we can."

Caleb felt his legs start to buckle, and he grabbed a police officer's arm. They helped him to the floor, and he placed his head between his knees to catch his breath.

"This can't be happening," he said.

"I'm sorry," one of the officers mumbled.

After a few moments, Caleb managed to rise slowly to his feet and regain some semblance of the composure that made him such a formidable force in the courtroom. He glanced toward the bedroom door and headed for it.

A female officer stepped in front of him. "I don't think you should go in there," she said.

He pushed her gently aside. "It's my house."

He stopped at the door—the room was littered with medical equipment. Police officers were taking pictures and milling around as if it were a crime scene. At least a half-dozen people froze and looked at him.

"I need a moment alone with my wife."

The officers and paramedics looked at each other, and a senior officer nodded. "Please don't disturb anything," the man said. "It's just routine, but we need to have things exactly as we found them." The officers and paramedics left without shutting the door. Two of them stood next to the doorway, engaged in casual conversation. Caleb knew they were watching.

He walked to his wife and straightened her sleepshirt, covering more of her exposed body. He pulled the comforter from the bed and laid it over her, tucking it in around her shoulders and underneath her heels. He pushed her hair out of her face and was shocked at how much she had already changed. The pallor of her skin. The lifeless stare of her eyes. Her mouth open in what seemed like an awkward grasp for a final breath. The paramedics had already removed the tubes.

He thought about the pictures the police had taken, and he knew that the pictures would be leaked and would make their rounds on the Internet. But there was nothing he could do about that now.

Rikki Tate, wife of infamous criminal-defense attorney Caleb Tate. A showgirl in life. She would also be a showgirl in death.

Caleb felt a hand on his shoulder. "I'm sorry, Mr. Tate, but we need to ask you a few more questions."

Caleb stood and met the officer's stare. He couldn't remember the guy's name, but he had cross-examined this man at least once or twice. Now the shoe would be on the other foot.

Caleb was a realist. He knew he had enemies at every level of law enforcement in the city of Atlanta. And he also knew that as soon as the autopsy results came in, he would be their first and only suspect.

Caleb would cooperate fully. He followed the officer into the hallway and down the stairs to the dining room. He answered every question, fighting off the numbness and fatigue as the reality of the night's events began to sink in. Rikki was dead, and she was never coming back. So young. So much potential. So relentlessly determined to make something of her life. So committed to her newfound faith.

None of that would matter now. It would all be lost in the swirl of rumors surrounding the drugs they would find in her body. It was an American tragedy, plain and simple.

Marilyn Monroe. Anna Nicole Smith. And now, Rikki Tate.

1

FOR THE FOURTH STRAIGHT DAY, I walked through the winding corridors of Piedmont Hospital, heels clicking on the tile floor. I had grown accustomed to the smell of antiseptics and the slow, lumbering elevators that carried me to the third floor. Outside my father's room, I squirted some disinfectant on my hands, just as I had done a few minutes earlier when I first entered the hospital. It had become something of a ritual.

There was no nurse in my father's room, no sign of anything that resembled life.

My name is Jamie Brock. Assistant DA for Milton County. Single and hardworking, with no time in my life for males other than my father, my black Lab, and the eighty-three defendants I am trying to put behind bars.

But at that moment, as I pulled a chair to the side of my father's bed and placed a hand on his forearm, I was also Jamie Brock, daddy's girl.

And at the age of twenty-eight, I would soon be an orphan.

My father had not spoken since his second stroke four days ago. The first stroke turned him into a man I did not recognize. The sharp mind and acid wit gave way to a tender and confused man who looked like my father but fumbled with complex ideas. Sometimes he didn't even recognize his family and friends. The second stroke left him comatose. He had been lying here in this same bed, hooked up to these same machines, attended by the same nurses and doctors, for the past four days. His primary physician, a competent Indian doctor named Kumar Guptara, told me that my dad would never recover. Never give me another reassuring hug. His eyes would never open and sparkle at the sight of his only daughter. He would never again tell me that he loved me.

Despite Guptara's pessimism, which was shared by every other doctor we consulted, I half expected my father to someday wake up, unhook the machines, change out of his hospital gown, and walk out of the room even as the nurses called after him to stop. My father was a fighter. It was a trait I had inherited.

My brother wanted to pull the plug. But my dad, like most lawyers, had taken care of his clients' affairs and not his own. Evan after his first stroke, he'd refused to consider his own mortality and sign a living will. Now the doctors were unwilling to cut the umbilical cord to the machines when there was a stalemate among the children. Especially when one of the children was a lawyer.

And so I rubbed his forearm and tried to ignore the fact that he was wasting away in front of me, losing weight even as nutrition was pumped into his body, the hairy arms becoming drier and more brittle every day.

"Hey, Dad, it's Jamie. They say you can't hear me, but who really knows—right?" The room was still, machines pulsating, my father's chest slowly rising and falling.

I lowered my voice. "Four more days, Dad. Can you hang in there for four more days?"

After eleven years of appeals, the experts said that this time the date would stick. Antoine Marshall, the man who broke into our home and killed my mother three months after my sixteenth birthday, was scheduled to get the needle. That same night, he'd shot my father and left him for dead. My dad had lost three pints of blood but lived to testify. How could I let him die now?

"We expect the lab results to be back on Rikki Tate tomorrow," I told my dad. I had been delivering reports on the Tate case every day. Rikki's death had occurred before my father's second stroke, and we both knew there was foul play. "Caleb Tate is already making excuses. Says that he knew Rikki was addicted to narcotics, but he couldn't stop her."

I leaned closer to my dad's ear. "You were right, Dad. He poisoned her. I can feel it in my bones."

Caleb Tate had represented Antoine Marshall at his trial. I would never forget the day he cross-examined my father, the only eyewitness to the crime. Dad was a great lawyer, but it's true what they say about the best lawyers making the worst witnesses. It was painful to watch Tate dissect my father's testimony piece by piece. If it hadn't been for Judge Snowden, the jury might have set Marshall free.

I took one of my father's hands in both of mine. "I'm going to nail Caleb Tate," I promised him. Antoine Marshall and Caleb Tate were responsible for putting my father in this bed. He had survived the shooting but never fully recovered emotionally. They were also the reason I had been working for three years in the district attorney's office and had never plea-bargained a case. Even now, as I looked at my father's pallid face and brushed his gray hair off his forehead, the bitterness ate at my soul like a cancer. My dream was to indict Caleb Tate within thirty days of his former client's execution.

My father would not be around to see his daughter avenge the memory of a woman we both loved. But I would do it to honor my father's memory. And I would swear to it on my mother's grave.

◁▷

At home that night, I waited for the latest news report about Antoine Marshall's appeal with a mixture of apprehension and disgust. A friend from the DA's office had alerted me to the story on WDKX. "Shows how desperate he is," my friend had said.

The story had run at six and was scheduled to air again at eleven. An anchor teased the report just before a commercial break, and my palms began to sweat. I braced myself, knowing that Marshall's defense team would stop at nothing.

After the break, the station cut to an interview with Professor Mason James from Southeastern Law School, Antoine Marshall's lead appellate lawyer.

The interview took place in James's cramped law school office. The man looked more like a UFC fighter than a professor. He wore a tight black T-shirt that showed off a bodybuilder's physique—thick neck, trapezius muscles that stood out like cables, huge biceps, and tattoo sleeves covering both arms. He was completely bald with a dark complexion, square chin, and broad nose that had been on the wrong end of too many fists.

He was, I knew, Southeastern's poster-boy faculty member—loved by most students but detested by law-and-order alumni like me. A convicted felon who saved a guard's life during a prison riot and was then granted a pardon by Georgia's Pardons and Paroles Board. One of only three former felons licensed to practice law in Georgia, he now headed Southeastern's Innocence Project, a clinic that filed truckloads of appellate motions for convicted felons.

The camera zoomed to a head-and-shoulders shot of James with a dry-erase board visible in the background. *4 more days* was written on it.

"Give me a break," I mumbled.

"You can't be serious," the reporter said. She was referencing James's latest appellate filing.

"Dead serious," James said. "No pun intended. There's a nation-wide shortage of sodium thiopental right now—part of the three-drug cocktail used to kill prisoners in Georgia. My sources tell me that the state is getting the drug from some fly-by-night supplier operating out of the back of a driving school in England."

James gave the camera a hard look. "You wouldn't put your dog down with drugs like that," he said. "We're just asking for thirty days to investigate."

I scoffed at the TV. It would be funny if it weren't so heart-breakingly sad. Antoine Marshall had shot my mother in the head without thinking twice, desperate for money to buy meth. And now, twelve years after the shooting, eleven years after his conviction, he was complaining about the pedigree of the drugs they would use to gently end his life.

I couldn't wait for Friday to be over.

2

THE DEBATE TOOK PLACE in the Milton High School auditorium. It was less than half-full, and I sat next to my friend and mentor, Regina Granger, the senior assistant district attorney for Milton County. Regina, a large and loud woman, had a boisterous belly laugh that made you think she was warm and cuddly. She was not. Regina was one of the toughest people I knew, an African American woman who earned her stripes thirty years ago in Milton County's good-ole-boy system.

If you were accused of a crime in our county, the worst news you could get was that Regina Granger was handling your case. In my three years at the prosecutor's office, I had never seen her lose.

We were watching the Republican candidates for attorney general of Georgia debate. I would rather have been getting a root canal or watching an opera. Regina and I were both there for the same reason—our boss was one of the candidates.

District Attorney William Masterson filled every inch of his chair in the middle seat at the table of candidates and a little more. He was the John Madden of the Milton County Courthouse—demonstrative, gruff, and down to earth. Everyone in the DA's office loved him or at least respected him. But he was also mired in third place in a five-candidate race with four months left before the primary.

The leader was the current chief assistant AG, a man named Andrew Thornton. In contrast to Masterson, Thornton was thin, bookish, and deadly serious. I had watched him argue twice before the Georgia Supreme Court, opposing Antoine Marshall's appeals, though he never returned my phone calls. Instead, he had junior members of the AG's office deal with bothersome victims like me.

Toward the end of the debate, the moderator asked a question about the death penalty, and Masterson pounced on it. "I will never apologize for seeking the death penalty for those members of our society who show such callous disregard for the lives of others. We hear a lot about the rights of defendants, but I can tell you this. . . ." Masterson paused and made sure he had everyone's full attention. "In every case where I've sought the death penalty, the victim suffered far more than any defendant executed by the state. I could tell you some gruesome stories about how these victims were tortured, raped, and killed. And unlike the defendants, the victims had no choice in the matter."

There was a smattering of applause from the archconservatives who had shown up for the debate. I found the whole thing a little unseemly.

"My biggest problem with the death penalty is that we allow these cases to drag on for years, costing the taxpayers millions," Masterson continued. "In the audience tonight is one of my assistant district attorneys, Jamie Brock."

I felt my face redden, and I knew what was coming next. I hated playing the victim card, and I hated having others play it for me.

"As many of you know, her mother was killed by a three-time felon named Antoine Marshall more than ten years ago. He's still sitting on death row, attacking everyone and everything involved in the process, even though Jamie's father, whom this man also shot, survived that night and ID'd him at trial. That's why Jamie is a prosecutor today."

Masterson motioned toward me in the audience. "Jamie, would you stand for a moment?"

I shot him a quick look to let him know that I wasn't happy, then stood and forced a smile. The crowd applauded politely.

"For me, being a prosecutor is not just a career," Masterson said. "I feel the same way Jamie does—what we do is a calling. Victims have rights, and they're entitled to justice."

◁▷

When the debate was over and Masterson had finished glad-handing every person who'd stuck around, he gave me a hug. "Hope I didn't embarrass you," he said.

"You did," I said. "But you can make it up to me. We need to talk."

Masterson raised an eyebrow. "This can't wait till tomorrow?"

"I only need five minutes."

He grunted his approval and then decided that if the conversation couldn't wait, we might as well get coffee and ice cream. Fifteen minutes later, we were sitting in an Applebee's, and Masterson was replaying the debate, asking for my perspective. When his ice cream finally came, he had two questions. "You sure you don't want some?"

"No thanks." I was sticking with just coffee.

"What do you want to talk about?"

"Rikki Tate."

"So talk." He took a bite of ice cream.

I had already formulated my negotiating strategy. I wanted to work on the Tate case. I knew it was the kind of high-profile case where Masterson would want someone from the DA's office working with the major felony squad detectives right from the start. I also knew Masterson would say I was too busy. I would tell him that I would work overtime and still handle my normal caseload. He would then say that I didn't have enough experience to handle the case, and I would offer to ride second chair. He would claim that I was too emotionally involved, and I would quote one of his answers from earlier that night when he said that, as prosecutors, we ought to be personally involved in every case. Like I did with every cross-examination, I had scripted the conversation in my head a hundred times and had a response for every objection, a counterpoint for every argument.

"I'd like to work on the Tate case," I said.

"I'm handling that one myself," Masterson responded, going for another bite. "But I could use a good second chair."

It took me a second to shift gears—I was expecting an argument, not capitulation. "Seriously?"

"On one condition."

"Anything," I said quickly. Maybe too quickly.

Masterson leaned forward, creating that hulking presence that intimidated defense attorneys. The look didn't bother me; I knew he was just a big teddy bear.

"I'm calling the shots," he said. "I'll ask for your input, but at the end of the day, I'm making all the strategic decisions. If we go to trial, you'll get to take a few witnesses and maybe even do the opening. Heck, I might have you try the whole case. But when it comes to whether we charge him and if so, what we charge him with—that's all up to me."

Masterson studied me for a moment and I knew I had no room to negotiate.

"Understood?"

"Anything you say, boss."

3

ON THE WAY HOME, I called Regina. "He didn't even put up a fight," I said excitedly. "He said I could ride second chair as long as he controlled the strategy."

There was silence on the other end as Regina processed the information. "I was afraid of that," she eventually said.

"Huh?"

"The boss could be planning on either not charging Tate or negotiating a quick plea. He knows that if he has you involved, the press will have a harder time attacking him for being soft because they know how much you hate Tate. You're his buffer, Jamie. Blunt any criticism in the midst of an election campaign."

I hadn't even thought of that. And for a moment I wondered if I would ever be half the lawyer my mentor was. Or Masterson either, for that matter.

"But the autopsy's not even done yet."

"When's the last time the boss reacted instead of being proactive?"

Regina had a point.

"So you're saying I shouldn't take it?"

"No; he wants you involved," Regina said. "And you know Bill. If he believes Tate poisoned his wife, he'll charge hell with a water pistol to convict him. He's just making sure he's covered if he decides to pull the plug."

"Nice to know I'm valued," I said.

◁▷

My spirits lifted when I walked in the front door of my house and was greeted like a rock star by my black Lab. We wrestled for a while on the floor and played tug-of-war with some well-worn interconnected rubber rings. He growled like a he-man and jerked his strong neck muscles back and forth to pull the toy out of my hands. I growled back and then loved on him and fixed him dinner. He'd been cooped up in the house for more than twelve hours and was starved for attention.

"It was a good day for the good guys," I said to Justice. He looked up at me with those adoring brown puppy-dog eyes and tilted his head to the side.

"We're going to get this guy," I promised him.

4

ON WEDNESDAY, my BlackBerry alarm went off at 5 a.m., a half hour earlier than normal, and Justice decided it was time to eat. Normal people could work their snooze alarms for a good fifteen or twenty minutes, but not me. Like one of Pavlov's dogs, Justice thought the unique alarm on the BlackBerry was designed solely for him and meant one thing and one thing only. He pawed at my hand until I reluctantly rolled out of bed and padded downstairs to the kitchen. I fixed a cup of coffee for me and breakfast for my housemate.

I lived in my parents' house, the same house where I had grown up. It was a nice place in the upscale Seven Oaks subdivision of Alpharetta, Georgia. The house was over three thousand square feet, and Justice and I used a grand total of about four rooms. A year ago, my brother and I had decided that my father could no longer live here alone. Chris, a pastor for a small church in northern Georgia, offered for Dad to move in with him. But my father's independent streak and stubbornness nixed that plan. We quickly realized that the only way my father would accept help was if Justice and I moved back home.

This was also the house where my mother was killed. For the first month after I returned home, I had nightmares every night. But my father had refused to move out, believing that he would be severing his last connection with my mom. And so I left the chic urban setting of my apartment at Atlantic Station to move to suburbia, to a neighborhood of families and married couples who embraced me and Justice warmly. And now, after a year in a house with a fenced-in backyard, I doubted whether I would ever be able to go back to the life of studio lofts.

I let Justice out the back door and started preparing mentally for the day's events. I put on my workout clothes—long running tights and a T-shirt for a brisk March morning. Justice and I would go for a run through the neighborhood, and then I would be on my way to work by seven.

I was the busiest prosecutor in Milton County, and I would have it no other way. When I interviewed with Bill Masterson, I explained to him that I was philosophically opposed to plea bargains—deals cut by prosecutors in 90 percent of their cases that usually allow the defendants to serve less time in exchange for a guilty plea. He explained that Milton County handled about eight thousand felony cases a year and that the system would shut down without plea bargains. We eventually agreed on a compromise—I could implement a no-plea-bargain strategy on my own cases as long as I got the job done and handled the same caseload as everyone else. To the surprise of most people in the office, my strategy worked. Many of my defendants pleaded guilty even without a deal, hoping the court might show some leniency.

Defense lawyers hated me for it. Even the judges thought I was a little crazy.

At seven o'clock, I left the calm of my home behind and started navigating traffic on the back roads to my office. On the way, I thought about the frantic appeals Mace James would be filing, and I thought about my dad. I also thought about the meeting that would be the highlight of my day. The autopsy had been completed on Rikki Tate.

◁▷

Milton County's top medical examiner, a feisty lady named Grace O'Leary, didn't look much like a distinguished doctor. She was short and plump with unruly black hair. She smelled like cigarettes, which I found ironic because I knew she had seen up close what cancer could do to a person's lungs. But she was unimpeachable on cross-examination, a bigger-than-life presence in the courtroom.

The first time I worked with Dr. O'Leary, she had made it clear who was boss. I was second chair on a murder case, and one of my jobs was to prepare O'Leary for cross-examination. She took this assignment as a personal insult and reminded me that she had been doing autopsies since before I was born.

In typical Jamie Brock fashion, I'd badgered her for a meeting anyway and she had finally relented. But she had terms. The meeting was to take place at her lab; every prosecuting attorney should understand exactly how an autopsy was performed, or they would never be able to ask intelligent questions about it. It just so happened that she could squeeze in our meeting right after a scheduled autopsy she had the next day. Why didn't I come by early so I could see it? I should have known it was a setup, but I am Jamie Brock, athlete and hard-nosed prosecutor who is not afraid of a little blood. So I'd agreed to the invitation as though we were going to lunch.

On the way downstairs to the lab that day, O'Leary was talkative and upbeat. "Did you know that *autopsy* is a Greek word that means 'see for yourself'?"

"Not really."

"I'm just like every other doctor," she explained. "It's just that my patients happen to be dead. Still, they have a story to tell, and it's my job on the witness stand to help them tell that story."

I could already see why the prosecutors all said O'Leary was the best secret weapon we had in Milton County.

I held up pretty well during the external examination—O'Leary recording the height and weight of the naked, blue body and dictating notes about identifying marks, scars, and tattoos. As she chatted, I started getting a little nauseated just thinking about the fact that the man in front of us had stopped breathing nearly forty-eight hours ago. Rigor mortis had set in, and O'Leary treated him like a slab of beef.

My knees went weak when she performed the Y-shaped incision from both shoulders down through the sternum and then pulled back the skin and underlying tissues. I passed out before she got around to removing the brain.

When I returned to my office that day, I found out that only three ADAs had made it through an entire autopsy. But I was a little embarrassed to learn that nine out of ten made it further than I had. From then on, I decided O'Leary didn't require the kind of trial prep that most witnesses did.

"Jamie, great to see you again," O'Leary said when I showed up to discuss Rikki Tate's autopsy. Thankfully, we were in her office. On the way over, I had been dreading the thought of her inviting me to the lab so we could talk while she carved up another dead person.

"Do you want to sit down before I show you the photos?" she asked.

"Thanks," I said and took a seat. There was no sense trying to play macho with somebody who had already made me faint.

For the next few minutes Dr. O'Leary walked me through the autopsy, illustrating each step with graphic photos, inserting a few stories about other autopsy victims along the way. O'Leary had found no signs of trauma, choking, or any possible cause of death apart from the drug overdose. She had ruled out congestive heart failure and sudden acute heart failure.

"Rikki's lungs had pulmonary congestive edema, which is a very common finding in people who die of drug overdoses. It means her lungs were filled with fluid and that she basically suffocated. It's not a common finding in people who die of a heart arrhythmia."

She explained that she had taken blood from a femoral artery and had sent that blood and Rikki's stomach contents to the state's toxicology lab. She checked the exact numbers on the tox report. "We sent 134 grams of gastric contents. The lab found 16 milligrams of oxycodone and 9 milligrams of codeine. In the blood they found .74 milligrams per liter of oxycodone and .27 milligrams per liter of codeine."

"How do those levels compare with other levels you've seen?"

"They're toxic," O'Leary said confidently. "The codeine alone would kill her. The oxycodone alone would kill her. Combined, they have an additive effect and are clearly the cause of death. You might see higher levels than these in hospice patients, but even for addicts, these levels are elevated."

I had already heard by way of the grapevine that the tox lab had found elevated levels of drugs. But that didn't answer the most important question: "Is there any way to tell whether this is an accidental overdose or whether she was poisoned?"

O'Leary reorganized her papers and put them in a neat little stack. We were done with the hard data. Now for the analysis. "That's the question, isn't it?" Without waiting for me to answer, she launched into her theory.

"The best way to tell would be to send her hair to the lab for testing.

Drugs in the blood bond to the roots of the hair. As the hair grows out, the drugs become an integral part of the hair shaft. Hair grows at a rate of about one centimeter per month, so depending on how long someone's hair is, you can sometimes determine how long they've been exposed to the drugs. Rikki had short hair, but you could still probably get six months of data." Before I could ask any questions about the hair testing, she moved on to her second point.

"Another curious thing is that I found promethazine in Rikki Tate's stomach contents and blood. That's an antinausea drug that helps somebody absorb narcotics into their system. You usually don't see this unless it's a pretty sophisticated addict or a doctor prescribes promethazine along with oxycodone. When I checked Rikki's medical records, I didn't find any prescriptions for these drugs."

O'Leary paused and studied my expression. She apparently wanted me to absorb this and consider the implications, which were not good for our case.

"If you're thinking that Caleb Tate poisoned his wife, he would have to be pretty sophisticated to stick promethazine in there as well. And if he were that sophisticated, he probably would have used drugs that would be more difficult to detect."

"Where could we have the hair analyzed?"

O'Leary stuffed the pictures and autopsy report back in her folder. "There's a lab in Washington, DC, called National Toxicology Testing. They're the best in the business. They should be able to tell us how long Rikki Tate had been ingesting these drugs."

"Let's give it a shot," I said. But I didn't hold out much hope. Caleb Tate was not stupid. If he was cold-blooded and cunning enough to poison his wife, he would have done his research. He would have slipped the drugs into her food gradually, over time, culminating with one massive overdose. He would know all about hair testing. And he would use it to prove that Rikki Tate had been taking these drugs for a very long time.

5

ON THURSDAY AFTERNOON, one day after the autopsy results were released, I settled into one of the leather chairs in our main conference room to watch the Caleb Tate news conference. Other ADAs were busy in court, but I had talked a friend into handling my afternoon docket. Two office assistants joined me as we waited for the channel to break from its regularly scheduled programming.

Rikki Tate's death had already dominated the local 24-7 news coverage and even garnered a few mentions nationally. Before moving to Atlanta, Rikki had worked in Vegas as a showgirl. In Atlanta, she'd done some modeling and worked for a high-end escort service. When the Milton County vice squad had leaned on Rikki to testify against those running the service, she'd hired Caleb Tate. He cut a deal. Rikki worked closely with Bill Masterson and others, testified against the pimps and johns, including many of her own clients, and avoided jail time. Less than a year later, she became Caleb Tate's trophy wife. And now, after twelve years of marriage, she was dead.

What made it even more intriguing was that Rikki had experienced a high-profile religious conversion about eighteen months earlier that was touted by Christian groups throughout the country. She had sued websites that displayed topless pictures of her, asking courts for injunctions because the contracts she had signed when the pictures were taken violated public policy. Porn companies sounded the alarm, claiming that the same justification could allow any of their actresses to renege on contracts whenever they wanted. There was a lot riding on Rikki's case, which was still in the discovery phase.

The autopsy results fueled the controversy. Some claimed it was proof that Rikki Tate had never really changed, that her conversion and the lawsuits were just publicity stunts. Others claimed that her change was real and had created problems in the marriage, eventually leading to her murder. I was in that camp. And then there were the conspiracy buffs, who were convinced that Rikki had somehow been poisoned by hit men from the porn industry.

Tate held his press conference in an elegant conference room at his law firm. The wall behind him served as a billboard for his services—the words *Tate and Associates* were embossed there in large gold lettering. The room was trimmed in dark wood and decorated with original oil paintings from an impressionistic artist. Tate had set up a podium at the end of a polished oak table.

He wore his latest Brooks Brothers suit; every hair was in place, and he looked tanned, as if he had just come home from a Hawaiian vacation. He knew enough to appear somber and heartbroken, and I was reminded of what a great actor he had been throughout the trial of Antoine Marshall.

"My name is Caleb Tate, and I called this press conference to address rumors about my wife and the circumstances surrounding her death." Tate looked up and faced the cameras with bloodshot eyes underscored by dark circles. Either the man had been sleepless and crying, or he had a good makeup artist. "I do not intend to take questions today. The death of my beloved wife has shaken me to the core, and I'm still trying to grasp the reality of it. However, that pain has been increased by rumors that I need to address."

Tate had no notes and made it appear as if he were speaking off the cuff. But I had watched him before. I knew that every word had been carefully chosen and repeatedly rehearsed.

"As the autopsy results yesterday proved, my wife died from an overdose of certain narcotics, including oxycodone. Given the toxic levels of these drugs in her system, the Internet has exploded with rumors about the possibility of foul play. To put these irresponsible and unfounded rumors to bed, I want to make a few things abundantly clear."

As he talked, I was struck by his careful selection of words. The allegations of foul play were just "Internet rumors." And even then, according to Tate, they were only rumors about the "possibility of foul play." It seemed to me that the type of man who could choose his words this carefully and stage this kind of performance might be the same kind of man who could carefully plan and execute murder by poison.

"I loved Rikki very much. We had never been happier in our marriage than we were this past year, and it was our hope and dream to grow old together."

Tate paused for a moment to regather his composure. I noticed that his eyes stayed dry.

"It is true that Rikki struggled with an addiction to certain narcotics, including oxycodone. As any doctor will tell you, over time you end up taking more and more of the same narcotic in order to achieve the desired result. This explains the high levels of both oxycodone and codeine in Rikki's blood.

"Some will want to blame me for what happened. If that's your desire, then get in line. At the front of that line is me. Nobody is more devastated by what happened than I am, and nobody will be harder on me than I will be on myself. I should have done more to help Rikki kick her addiction."

Tate's voice had become hoarse, and he swallowed hard. "I tried.... I *really* tried. . . . But after a while, I just learned to live with it. Rikki changed as a result of the drugs, but I still loved her. Since she died, I've been second-guessing everything I did or didn't do. I am especially distraught that my preoccupation with work caused me not to be there for Rikki when she needed me most.

"So if you want to blame me—go ahead. But don't blame Rikki. Growing up, she was abused by both her stepfather and an uncle. When she finally escaped that environment, she ended up in Vegas, where they used her as eye candy for their shows, and then here in Atlanta, where she was again abused by a high-end prostitution ring. When I first met Rikki, I saw something more, something deeper than just the surface beauty that drew others to her. She was full of grace and class and a desire to love and be loved. She finally found that love in our marriage and recently through her conversion to Christianity."

Tate paused again as if considering what to say next. The conference room was quiet, and I could tell, even without seeing their faces, that the reporters were mesmerized.

"If you've never had to take drugs in order to escape the memories of those who abused you, you have no right to judge Rikki," Tate continued. He had more force in his voice now, defending the woman he loved. "You have no idea what she went through. She was a wonderful wife and a good woman who loved a world that in turn used her only for her body. So please stop passing judgment on my wife. You can take shots at me all you want, but let Rikki rest in peace."

Tate surveyed his captive audience one face at a time, the same way he did a jury during closing arguments. "Thank you," he said and walked out of his conference room.

I was frustrated by the effectiveness of his performance. He had somehow managed to change his role—from number one suspect to the protector of Rikki Tate. How chivalrous!

What a jerk!

The commentators started talking about how compelling Tate's statement had been. As I got up to leave, one of the assistants near me in the conference room sighed. "I hate to say it," she said, "but I actually feel a little sorry for the guy."

◁▷

I went home and let Justice outside. After he ate a quick dinner, I asked him if he wanted to go on a field trip. His tail wagged as he pranced around and waited impatiently by the door. On the way to the hospital, he sat in the front passenger seat of my 4Runner, barking a few times at pedestrians and enjoying himself immensely.

I found a spot in the parking garage, cracked the windows, and ordered Justice to stay in his seat. I closed the door, beeped it locked, and knew that Justice would be in the driver's seat within five seconds. He would sit there like a little sentry until I came back from visiting my dad, and then he would stand up, get excited, and slobber all over me when I climbed into the vehicle.

It's nice to be loved.

I talked to the nurses for a few minutes before entering my dad's room, getting an update about his lack of progress. The machines beeped steadily along, and my father's only movement was the slow rise and fall of his chest. I didn't know if I was just imagining things, but he still seemed to be losing weight, shrinking to a mere fraction of the person I used to know.

I sat next to his bed and put a hand on his forearm.

"Hey, Dad. I don't know if you can hear me, but we're making progress in the Tate investigation. Your old friend Bill Masterson is working the campaign trail hard. And I think Antoine Marshall's execution is actually going to happen tomorrow. Twenty-four more hours, Dad; can you believe it?"

Before my dad suffered his second stroke, these were the things we talked about. Things we had to do. Current events. Cases, judges, and trial tactics. But for some reason, now that he was lying here in this hospital bed unable to respond, I felt the freedom to go deeper, to talk about things we should have talked about my entire life. Things I wished we had talked about. Things that really mattered.

"I really miss Mom," I said softly. "And to be honest, with what happened to Mom and now you, I've got this fear that as soon as I start loving someone, they'll be taken away."

I looked at my dad's expressionless face, the closed eyes, tubes coming from his nose and mouth. "Chris is doing good, Dad. He says he's leaning into God even though he'll never understand why any of this happened."

I hesitated and wondered if I should say this next sentence out loud. But I was tired of pretending. "I guess you could say I'm leaning the other way. I know in my mind that God still loves me, but it doesn't always feel that way."

I sighed and looked around the room. Tonight, more than any other night since I'd started visiting my father, I sensed that he was no longer here. It was as if he had already left this shell of a body behind. I squeezed his arm, told my father that I loved him, and stood to leave.

As I walked to the door, I sensed that something was different, but I couldn't quite put my finger on it. Everything about the room looked the same. The same machines with the same readouts. The same get-well cards on the tables. The television hanging from one wall and the small window to the outside world.

I shrugged and was almost out the door before I realized what it was. For the first time since I'd started visiting my father, I realized that I had lost all hope. He wasn't coming back. And strangely, the thought didn't break me or drive me to my knees or cause me to sob uncontrollably. It was as if I had begun to accept this reality slowly, each day unraveling a few more threads of my hope that he would ever come out of this coma. And today, that final strand had simply disappeared.

In two more days, after Antoine Marshall's execution, I would let my father die in peace. That would still give God time to work a miracle. And if no miracle came, it would give me time to prepare for the loneliness.

6

MACE JAMES SAT in his pickup truck, parked outside the Flying Saucer in Nashville, Tennessee. It was one of Nashville's trendiest bars, located on the back side of the old Union Station train depot. Despite the futuristic name, the building was old-style stone with arched windows and a canopy out front. It made you feel like you were stepping back into the 1950s and might bump into James Cagney inside.

Mace had a bad feeling about this, but he could think of no better alternative. He flashed back fifteen years to the night that had changed his life. A friend had picked a fight in a Buckhead bar and was getting pummeled. Without thinking, Mace and a few buddies had jumped in, evening the odds. Fueled by adrenaline and alcohol, Mace put two men in the hospital. One of them was an off-duty police officer who had flashed a badge (or so he claimed) and was shouting orders just before Mace caught him with a right hook that broke his jaw. The man's partner tackled Mace and had him cuffed before Mace knew what was happening.

A few minutes later, when Mace was frisked, they discovered a small bag of cocaine in the back pocket of his jeans. To this day, Mace didn't know whether it was planted by one of the cops or one of the men he'd been fighting.

Either way, he was facing two felonies and a misdemeanor. His lawyer didn't waste any time cutting a deal—battery against a police officer and resisting arrest. The possession charge was dropped.

Two years later, when Mace saved the life of a guard in a prison riot, he was granted a pardon. He always found it ironic that the same

conduct that had landed him in jail—sticking up for the underdog—
also got him out. It all depended, Mace knew, on who wore the badge.

He also knew that his plan tonight smacked of desperation. If it
backfired, he would lose his reputation and quite possibly his law
license. Another bar brawl. They would say he never learned.

But he *had* learned. He had changed in prison, a spiritual conversion that was real, not just window dressing for the parole board. So
why was he sitting here contemplating another bar fight? Because he
had also learned one other thing: innocent men could get framed.
Somebody had planted cocaine on him. How easy would it have been
to set up Antoine Marshall for murder?

Before entering the bar, Mace listened to the recording on his
BlackBerry one last time. It had been sent by a PI Mace had hired,
and the quality was not good. You could make out the garbled voice
of Freddie Cooper, but even with the best digital enhancement, his
words would barely be discernible. Mace could tell Freddie had been
drinking, his thoughts incoherent. It surely wouldn't convince the
judges on the Georgia Supreme Court.

Mace stretched his neck, blew out a deep breath, and climbed out
of his truck. It was a warm March night with a full moon and an omi-
nous wind blowing from the north. Mace wore jeans and a tight black
T-shirt, looking the part of a bouncer.

People were lined up two deep at the bar, ordering one of the eighty
beers prominently listed on a blackboard high above the bartenders.
Mixed drinks were a rare sight in this Nashville crowd. Mace pushed
his way through the bodies to the poolroom, where groups of men and
a few women lounged around six red-felt pool tables. Barstools lined
the walls, and green lamps hung low over the tables. The only thing
missing was cigarette smoke.

At the far end of the room was an outdoor lamppost, vintage 1950.
Junior Watts leaned against it, holding a pool cue and eyeing the table.
Junior was a short, pudgy man with jowls and gray hair that made him
look every bit of fifty. The poolroom featured a younger crowd, and
Junior stood out like a teenager in a Santa Claus line.

He looked up and nodded at Mace.

Mace edged closer to the last table while Junior circled it, preparing for his next shot, eyeing the layout of the balls from this angle and that. As he plotted, Junior talked trash with a group of friends until things got heated. He put down his cue and got in the face of the tallest and skinniest member of the group. More words were exchanged and then Junior knocked a beer out of the guy's hand. Curses followed, and the man took a swing. Junior ducked the blow, landed a right cross, and the fight was on.

Others in the poolroom gawked at the sudden outbreak of violence and backed away from the maniacs throwing punches. A man jumped Junior from behind. The fight might have stayed confined to those first few participants if the three men Junior had earlier paid off had stayed out of the fray. But they wanted to earn their hundred bucks. One of them cracked a pool cue across the shoulders of a man fighting with Junior, and the melee escalated. Wild roundhouse punches were thrown, pool sticks turned into clubs, and a few bodies got tossed across the pool table.

Like most fights, the action separated the pool hall into two groups—those who inched away and those who couldn't resist a good scuffle. Mace managed to push his way into the action just before the bouncers arrived to pull the participants off each other, flinging bodies this way and that.

Mace went straight for the man Junior had first attacked—a skinny guy with yellow teeth, matching dirty-blond hair, and a scraggly goatee. Playing the part of a good bouncer, Mace got in the man's face and started pushing him away from the crowd. The guy was cursing and screaming at Junior, telling Junior and the others that they were all crazy, that he would meet them outside in the parking lot.

"Calm down," Mace warned. "No need to get arrested here."

As Mace backed the man away, he tried to lunge around Mace and get in a few more licks. But Mace put him in a bear hug and dragged him toward the door. "Let's get you outta here," Mace said. The bouncers were still separating the other combatants, trying to figure out who had started what.

"Come on, Coop." Mace wrestled the man toward the exit door. "They're calling the cops, and you don't want to be in the middle of it when they show up."

The words seemed to calm Freddie Cooper, and he gave Mace a glazed look as if wondering how the big man knew his nickname. Mace pulled him outside, and Freddie stumbled. He regained his balance, swaying a little, and shook his head, trying to focus his vision.

"They're lucky you pulled me outta there," Freddie said. He then proceeded to curse Junior. "I was fixin' to kill that man."

"Yeah," Mace said. He grabbed Freddie's arm and wedged him toward the pickup. "We've got to get you sobered up before the police start asking questions."

"What are you talking about?" Freddie stiffened; he clearly thought he had gone far enough.

Mace didn't ask a second time. He drove his fist into Freddie's midsection, doubling the man over as the air left his lungs. Mace stood him up, grabbed him by the collar, and practically lifted him off the ground. His nose was inches from Freddie's. "You're coming with me. Okay?"

Freddie nodded, his eyes darting with fright. He looked like he didn't have a clue what was going on but probably figured it couldn't be good.

On that point, Freddie was right.

7

IN THE HOTEL ROOM, Mace guarded the door while Freddie sat on the bed, rubbing his jaw, nursing his left eye with ice wrapped in a wet washcloth. They had cleaned up most of the blood, but a small cut was visible. Mace hadn't landed that particular blow, but it still wouldn't look good.

Junior arrived five minutes later and fired up his video recorder.

"What's he doing here?" Freddie demanded. When he stood, Mace pushed him back onto the bed.

"Sit down and shut up."

Mace turned toward the camera and waited for Junior to start recording. "My name is Mason James, and I'm here at the Union Station Hotel in Nashville, Tennessee, room 521, with a man by the name of Freddie Cooper whose friends call him Coop."

Junior trained the camera on Freddie, who sat on the bed, frowning.

"I just rescued Mr. Cooper from a fight in the poolroom at the Flying Saucer bar," Mace continued. "It just so happens that I recognized Mr. Cooper as a man with three prior felony convictions for various drug offenses. It could have been four, and he could be serving time right now, but he managed to get the fourth one dismissed when he turned jailhouse snitch against my client Antoine Marshall about eleven years ago."

Mace moved to the bed and towered over Freddie. "I also happen to believe that Mr. Cooper is in possession of cocaine again."

Junior panned out to a wide-angle shot.

"Empty your pockets," Mace demanded.

"Kiss my—"

Mace pounced and pulled Freddie up from the bed by his collar. "Empty your pockets," he hissed.

"Oops," Junior said from his perch next to the door. "The camera cut off. It will be a few seconds before I can turn it back on."

Freddie's eyes were wide with fright. "Don't hit me, man," he said to Mace. He held up his palms and glanced at the camera to see if the recording light was on. He quickly reached into his pocket and threw a package of white powder on the bed.

"Did you get that?" Mace asked Junior.

"Yep. Hidden camera next to the TV. Installed it this afternoon."

Mace let go of Freddie, pulled a pair of gloves from his pocket, put them on, and picked up the bag. "Don't want to confuse the fingerprints," he said to Freddie.

Freddie looked dazed by the events taking place. The booze was apparently clouding his judgment. "What do you want?" he asked.

"I want you to smile for the camera and repeat what you told my buddy last night."

Mace was referring to the conversation that Junior had taped. It had taken Junior a week to befriend Freddie and manipulate the conversation around to the role Freddie played in the trial of Antoine Marshall. Finally, last night, after more than a few beers, Freddie had bragged about the deal he had cut with prosecutors and how he had played fast and loose with the truth. But the tape was indecipherable. And when Junior tried to pry the same information out of Freddie tonight, Freddie didn't want to talk.

"We've already got you on tape," Mace said. "And the way I see it, you've got two choices. One, you repeat what you said last night for the video camera. You also sign an affidavit stating under oath that you lied eleven years ago. Then I'll file it with the court. Under that scenario, the prosecutors and courts will try to minimize your testimony because they don't want to upset the conviction of Antoine Marshall. There's not a chance in the world that you'd be prosecuted for perjury."

Mace could see the sweat breaking out on Freddie's brow, and he knew he had him.

"The second choice is that you refuse to clear this up, and you stand by your original testimony. Under that scenario, I'll turn this videotape and bag of cocaine over to the Nashville police and, after Antoine Marshall is executed, I'll send the tape from last night's confession to the prosecutors in Atlanta. With Antoine Marshall dead, they'll have no reason to minimize your lies, and you'll get prosecuted for both perjury *and* possession of drugs. You've got ten seconds. Which one will it be?"

Freddie stared blankly at Mace and blinked a few times as if this were all just a bad dream. He looked at the small package of cocaine that Mace had placed on the dresser and then glanced at the video camera.

Mace crossed his arms. "Five seconds."

"They put me in a cell with your boy," Freddie said. "I told them I didn't want to room with no . . ." Freddie stole another glance at the video camera. "With no Afro American."

He shifted his feet and continued. "Um . . . they told me it would only be for a few days and if I knew what was good for me, I'd shut up and do it. They told me your boy was up for murder and that maybe he'd talk to me. They didn't give me no promises or nothing like that, but I'm not stupid."

Mace could have debated that point, but he let it slide. Junior circled around behind Mace's shoulder to get a better angle on Freddie. Mace listened stone-faced as Freddie gave a rambling and at times incoherent rendition of why he had lied. When the whole thing was on tape, Mace suggested that he make some coffee and they run through it again.

Three cups of coffee later, with more than a little coaching by Mace, Freddie turned in his best performance of the night. The left eye was now swollen, and both eyelids were heavy with sleep and inebriation. The bloodshot eyes darted away from the camera more frequently than Mace would have liked, and Freddie couldn't keep himself from slurring his words, which were sometimes incoherent. But this wasn't a Spielberg film. At 3 a.m., Mace allowed Freddie to lie down and take a short nap while Mace pounded out an affidavit on his computer. By 5 a.m., nap time was over, and Mace printed the affidavit on a portable printer that Junior had brought into the room and made Freddie sign it.

If all went according to plan, Freddie's face would soon be splashed all over the Atlanta TV stations. Mace went to the front desk and faxed the affidavit to an attorney at Knight and Joyner, a large firm in downtown Atlanta that was helping on the case as part of their pro bono program.

Mace checked his watch. Fourteen hours from now, if this plan didn't work, a medic at the Georgia Diagnostic and Classification Prison in Jackson would stick a needle in Antoine Marshall's arm, and Georgia would execute an innocent man.

8

I DON'T REMEMBER WAKING UP on the day of Antoine Marshall's scheduled execution because I don't remember falling asleep the night before. Instead, I slipped in and out of consciousness all night, interrupting my nightmares to jump awake and stare at the clock. After my heart calmed down, I would realize that I still had hours to go before the sun came up.

The sun never did come up. The morning was overcast and gray, and the weatherman was predicting showers all day. It was, I decided, an appropriate forecast for what promised to be a brutal day.

I got out of bed early and checked the paper online. There was no fresh news about Marshall's execution. I fixed a cup of coffee, fed Justice, and steeled myself for the onslaught of noise that would come out of Antoine Marshall's camp. Each filing would be more ridiculous than the last. Bill Masterson, who had been through this drill a time or two before, warned me not to read any of them. "They're desperate, Jamie. They'll say whatever they need to say to get the execution postponed."

I ignored his advice. For the past seven years—three years as a law student and four as a prosecutor—I had obsessively monitored each court system where Mason James and the lawyers from Knight and Joyner filed their various petitions and writs. Each word of their briefs would eat at me and fuel my frantic desire to get this final day of Marshall's fight behind me. Now, at last, the day had arrived.

To prepare myself, I had read a wide range of reactions from other victims who had viewed executions. Some ranted that the process seemed too humane for the monsters who had committed such despicable crimes. Others were stunned and speechless. A few said they regretted going. For most, it seemed that the process was strangely unsettling and created more questions than answers. Protesters treated the death-row inmates like heroes. The convicts received marriage proposals from crazy European women. Pastors who engaged in prison ministry would tell stories about last-minute conversions. Even the prison system catered to the murderers for most of the day, giving them whatever they wanted for a last meal. The condemned man's final words were circulated far and wide.

And the victims were once again forgotten.

I was so emotionally drained by the time Friday morning arrived that I didn't have the energy to go to the gym. I showered and dressed by seven and then changed my outfit three times. I didn't want to wear black as if I were in mourning. Nor did I want to look too much like a lawyer. I finally settled on a skirt-and-blouse combination with a sweater that my mother once wore. I put on a topaz necklace and matching earrings that had belonged to her.

Legally, I didn't have to go to the execution. But morally . . . that was a different issue. How could I advocate for the ultimate punishment in my cases at the office and not show up to see it through in my personal life? I told myself I wasn't bloodthirsty or seeking revenge. This was the way I paid tribute to the memory of my mom. This was the way I stood for justice.

I wondered what Antoine Marshall would say when the time came. He had written letters to my brother, Chris, talking about how he had found Jesus in prison and how religion had changed his life. He said he prayed for us every day. But he never admitted that he had killed my mom, and I knew he would deny it to the grave. I tried to brace myself for seeing the man who had made me an orphan boldly proclaiming his innocence one last time. I would stare through the one-way glass and shake my head in defiance.

Chris woke up at eight and came down to fix oatmeal. He had left Amanda and their two young girls at home in northern Georgia so the girls could stay in their routines, impacted as little as possible by Marshall's execution. Even Chris had originally said he wasn't going to the execution, but after Dad's stroke, he'd changed his mind.

Chris was fundamentally opposed to the death penalty because he thought the system too often got it wrong. African Americans were disproportionately executed, and DNA evidence too frequently exonerated men who had served long stretches in prison. But Chris was the passive one in the family, and I had convinced him not to share those views publicly. I knew the system wasn't perfect, but I also knew the system had gotten it right this time. We didn't need the press playing one sibling against the other.

"Good morning," Chris said. "What time are we leaving?" He was still wearing pajama bottoms and a T-shirt. His blond hair stuck out in a number of random directions.

"I thought I'd go to work for a while first," I said. "We probably need to leave here by three."

We ate in silence for a few minutes while I checked some websites, then shut down my computer. "Thanks for doing this, Chris," I said softly.

"I'm not looking forward to it."

"Neither am I."

He continued eating, concentrating on his oatmeal, while I packed my briefcase. We each had a thousand thoughts but no words to express them. We had talked for hours about this moment, but now that it had arrived, it seemed the only thing to do was march stoically ahead and accept whatever life threw at us.

"Any chance he'll get a stay?" Chris asked. He took a swig of milk. I didn't think he would be so calm this morning, just wolfing down breakfast as if it were any other day. My stomach was already in knots.

I shrugged. "Doesn't look like it. But who knows? We need to be ready for anything."

Chris looked at me, and I saw the apprehension in his eyes. I had misread his silence as nonchalance. But at that moment, I realized it was something else—uncertainty, nerves, even fear. My brother was older, the pastor in the family. But I would have to be the steadfast one. I could tell he didn't want to face this day; he didn't want to be a silent accomplice to a state-sanctioned killing. I had no such reservations.

"I just want it to be over," Chris said.

9

MACE JAMES RACED from Nashville to Atlanta, working his cell phone the entire trip. While he drove, nine attorneys at Knight and Joyner worked on the last-minute filings. In the less-frantic weeks and months leading up to this day, Mace had taken the lead. He had argued before the Georgia Supreme Court and the Eleventh Circuit Court of Appeals. He had personally written most of the briefs and had filed, at last count, sixteen habeas petitions. But now, on the final day, he let the big firm take care of the details. His job was twofold: get the press involved and, if all else failed, be there for Antoine.

There were only three chances left—all long shots. They had just filed a habeas petition with the US Supreme Court based on the shortage of sodium thiopental and concerns about where Georgia had obtained its supply. Mace figured he had better odds of becoming pope. They had also petitioned the Georgia State Board of Pardons and Paroles for clemency. The outlook there was dismal but not entirely hopeless. The board had granted clemency in seven cases since 1976, including a 1990 case where a death-row inmate's sentence was commuted based on an exemplary prison record, demonstrated remorse, a religious conversion, and pleas for clemency from the victim's family. Antoine had two out of four—a good prison record and a religious conversion. Mace doubted it was enough. Many prisoners claimed dramatic jailhouse conversions. Mace was one of a select few who had stayed the course after his release.

That left the habeas petition being filed that morning with the Georgia Supreme Court. Another Hail Mary, but the best of a meager lot. Mace had flipped Freddie Cooper, leaving only the eyewitness testimony of Robert Brock with no corroborating DNA or other scientific evidence. And Brock's testimony had been largely discredited on cross-examination.

Despite patches of rain, Mace pushed the speedometer to ninety miles per hour as he raced down I-75 in north Georgia. He held the speed until his truck started shaking and then backed off the accelerator just a little. A few times he saw the state police early enough to slow down to eighty. Once he probably would have been pulled over but got boxed in before passing a state trooper hiding in the median. None of that stopped him from sending text messages and making phone calls. One eye on the road. The other checking the Internet using his BlackBerry, wondering why the press had so little interest in an innocent man's execution.

Actually, Mace knew exactly why. His client was a three-time convicted felon. A black man convicted of killing a respected white woman in her own home. Antoine had no advocates other than his lawyers and a committed band of death penalty opponents who took up the cause of every death-row inmate. Antoine's mother had died five years ago, and there were no other family members who would attend the execution. For most of Georgia, Antoine Marshall was nothing more than prisoner 12452, a man destined to make headlines one last time—the local section—before he stopped getting room and board at taxpayer expense. Troy Davis, a former death row inmate, had been executed in 2011 despite recantations from seven of the nine witnesses against him. By comparison, Freddie Cooper's recantation was nothing special. Only one television station in all of Atlanta had any interest in airing taped footage of it.

Mace arrived at that station at nine thirty and checked in with the receptionist. He had thrown a gray suit coat over his black T-shirt because he hadn't had time to go home and change. He knew he looked like death, but maybe that was appropriate.

Staci Anderson, the reporter who would be asking the questions, was shorter than she appeared on television but every bit as striking. She had long dark hair and a subtle Latin American look. Like all anchors, she had layered on the makeup, and her teeth nearly sparkled.

Mace followed Staci inside and spent the next few minutes in makeup. A talkative woman dusted his bald head so it wouldn't create too much glare and caked on some blush. When he was finished, Mace showed Staci and her producer the tape, and the producer mumbled something about it being "good stuff." Before he knew it, Mace was sitting on the set with cameras rolling and Staci firing questions at him.

"Why did Freddie Cooper wait until the night before the execution to come forward?" Staci asked. "It seems awfully convenient."

Mace tried not to bristle at the question. He didn't want to seem like one of those crusaders who thought every death-row inmate should be turned loose on the streets. "We had been looking for him for a few weeks," Mace said. "He doesn't exactly have a hyperactive conscience, and if we hadn't found him, he probably wouldn't have said anything. I think he was hoping we would get the execution stopped by some other means."

"But as I understand it," Staci said, "there is still an eyewitness to this crime—Robert Brock, the husband of the victim, who was also shot by your client. How does Mr. Cooper's change of heart impact Mr. Brock's credibility?"

It was a good question, Mace knew. And it was the same question the Georgia Supreme Court would be asking. This might be Mace's best chance to convince the court. Justices watched television too.

Mace turned away from Staci and looked directly into the camera. "Mr. Brock is a victim of a horrible crime, and my sympathy goes out to him and his family. But he was in shock when he saw his wife bleeding on the floor. He had a moment's glance at the intruder before being shot himself. Later, the police used suggestive questioning and a faulty lineup to convince Mr. Brock that my client was the killer. At trial, the defense was not allowed to introduce expert testimony about the dangers of cross-racial eyewitness identifications nor about how the police officers, using a bad lineup and loaded questions, had planted false memories about the suspect's appearance."

"What happens next?" Staci asked.

"We've filed a petition for a stay with the Georgia Supreme Court," Mace said. "We'll get a ruling later today."

"Thank you, Professor James," Staci said. "I know you've got a busy day ahead of you, and we appreciate your time."

Mace knew he was expected to just mumble his own thanks. The cue cards behind the camera were down to five seconds. But he didn't have to play by their rules.

"Antoine Marshall, to my knowledge, is the only defendant on death row who's passed a lie detector test," Mace added.

The time card was up before Staci could tease the next segment. During the break, she thanked Mace, then started talking to her producer about what was coming up next.

Mace left a copy of the Freddie Cooper tape with the station and checked his watch. It was time to head south to death row.

◁▷

All morning long, I worked at my desk and, with sweaty palms, hit the button to refresh the various court sites I monitored. I saw the petition with the attached Freddie Cooper affidavit at ten thirty. I immediately called the AG's office, and they said they were on it. A response would be filed within two hours.

"This happens all the time," one of the lawyers assured me. "You've got nothing to worry about."

I got a text from a friend about the news report when it aired at noon. I watched a replay on my computer and caught myself grinding my teeth. Mace James had no shame. My dad was lying unconscious in a hospital bed, and James was taking shots at him.

They ran a clip from Cooper's recantation, and he looked like he had been beaten up. I called the AG's office a second time.

"Have you watched the video?" I asked. "It looks like they beat that statement out of him."

"We noticed that," they assured me. "We put it in our briefs."

A few hours later, just before I arrived home, I gave Chris a call. "I'll be there in a few minutes. Have you let Justice out?"

"About a dozen times."

I knew Justice was taking advantage of my brother and garnering some extra attention. The thought of it made me smile.

When I arrived home, I parked in the driveway, and Chris was out the front door before I even beeped the horn. The sky was still overcast, but it had stopped raining. When Chris reached the car, he took off his overcoat and tossed it in the backseat. My father was a few inches shorter than Chris and before his strokes had outweighed Chris by about twenty pounds. But for this occasion, Chris had decided to throw on one of my dad's sport coats and my dad's favorite tie. The tie looked great, but the coat was riding a few inches up Chris's arms and dwarfed him in the shoulders.

Chris had told me I looked good before I left for work that morning. I had told him that I was wearing Mom's earrings and necklace. Now, the sight of my brother wearing my dad's sport coat made me tear up.

Chris got in without saying a word.

"You look great," I said, my voice hoarse.

"I wish he could be here," Chris said.

I backed out of the driveway without saying another word.

10

MACE JAMES ARRIVED at the Diagnostic and Classification Prison in Jackson at three fifteen. There were 107 men on death row, all residing in the same wing of the facility, within yards of the execution chamber housed in a white building at the edge of the prison facility. Other states transported their prisoners to specially constructed execution rooms miles away from where the prisoners were held. But Georgia believed in efficiency.

A handful of demonstrators had already gathered outside the facility, and Mace took the time to shake everyone's hand. He was still amazed at how little public outcry this case had generated, even after his TV interview. The Troy Davis case, just a year earlier, had garnered widespread publicity. But nothing had changed. If anything, the public just grew more desensitized to last-minute desperation filings by death-row attorneys claiming that their clients were "truly innocent." Most people now greeted such filings with a yawn.

By midafternoon the Georgia Board of Pardons and Paroles had voted to deny clemency. The US Supreme Court had denied a stay based on the suspect nature of the sodium thiopental. The only hope left was the petition presently before the Georgia Supreme Court. If that petition was denied, the attorneys at Knight and Joyner would raise the same issue with a habeas filing in the federal courts—first with the Eleventh Circuit and ultimately with a single justice of the US Supreme Court.

It was never too late. Troy Davis held the record. He'd been convicted in the 1989 killing of a Savannah police officer. Twenty years later, the Supreme Court granted a stay less than two hours before his scheduled execution. Davis later presented new evidence to a Georgia federal judge who ruled that the evidence amounted to nothing more than "smoke and mirrors." Davis proclaimed his innocence with his last breath on September 21, 2011. How had Davis's lawyers managed to keep their client alive for twenty-two years, yet Mace couldn't keep Antoine alive for more than eleven?

The answer, Mace knew, was the 1996 enactment of the Anti-terrorism and Effective Death Penalty Act, which seriously curtailed the habeas corpus rights of death-row inmates convicted after the law's passage. But Mace also shouldered a fair share of the blame. A good lawyer would never allow an innocent man to die.

Before meeting with Antoine, Mace inspected the lethal-injection chamber, which had already been prepared for that evening's event. The room was small, cold, and sterile, about the size of an examination room at a doctor's office. It was so white that it was nearly disorienting—the white walls and white tile floor interrupted only by a four-inch black baseboard and a bright-yellow door. The "bed" where they would strap Antoine featured a two-inch mattress covered in a white disposable sheet. There were black straps for his arms, knees, and ankle, as well as one that would lie across his shoulders.

Mace had never witnessed an execution. But it was clear that the state wanted this to look like every other medical procedure. They would even swab Antoine's arm with alcohol before inserting the needle for the IV.

One wall of the execution chamber was a large window that allowed observers to watch the procedure. There were blinds on the inside that would be pulled back once Antoine was strapped in. Members of the victim's family and District Attorney Masterson would be in the observation room. Mace would be there too, along with the prison chaplain, who had taken quite a liking to Antoine. They would be joined by five reporters, selected to serve as witnesses for the media, along with a few prison guards.

Mace surveyed the execution chamber and shrugged at the prison guards. What was he supposed to do—complain that he wanted the walls painted a different color?

"I'd like to see my client now," he said.

A few minutes later, Mace walked into a small room in the main facility where Antoine was sitting at a bolted-down table, wearing shackles on his ankles and wrists. A guard stood just outside the door, staring in through a barred window.

As the door closed behind Mace, Antoine looked up at him, wide eyed. Before, the two had been separated by bulletproof glass. But today, Antoine's last scheduled day on earth, they were allowed to meet with no barriers between them.

Antoine stood, and Mace walked over and gave him a big hug. Mace felt his client's bony shoulder blades and was a little surprised at how much shorter Antoine was than he had looked when seated in the cubicle. The inmate smelled like he hadn't taken a shower in a couple of weeks, and his hair was matted and ratty, his breath enough to knock Mace over.

"Thanks for coming," Antoine said as if Mace were a hospital visitor after surgery.

"Yeah, I was thinking about going golfing instead but decided against it," Mace said.

Antoine didn't smile, and the two men took their places on opposite sides of the table. They both leaned forward on their elbows so they could keep their voices low. Antoine had a healthy sense of paranoia nurtured by eleven years inside the system and memories of Freddie Cooper turning on him. Mace tried to ignore his client's putrid breath.

"I don't have any good news," Mace said, getting right to the point. "The State Board of Pardons and Paroles has denied clemency. The Supreme Court ruled against our petition for cert. The only chance we have is the petition based on Cooper's affidavit."

Antoine's expression didn't change. "About what I expected."

"We basically get three strikes on that petition. The Georgia Supreme Court. The Eleventh Circuit. The Supremes."

"I'm not holding my breath."

Mace wished he would.

"I'm not either," Mace said. He had never tried to pump Antoine up with false expectations. There was no need to start now.

"I'm ready," Antoine proclaimed. "And I wanted you to look over something."

He reached into the pocket of his orange jumpsuit and handed Mace a folded piece of paper.

"What's this?" Mace asked.

"My last statement. I'll memorize it by seven."

Mace read the paper while Antoine watched:

> I want to say how sorry I am to the members of the Brock family. I have prayed for you every day, and I hope that my execution will allow you to close this chapter of your lives. To Jamie and Chris Brock: I am sorry that you lost a mother. To Robert Brock: I am sorry that you lost a wife.
>
> I am prepared to die. Those of you with power over me would have no power if it were not given to you from above.
>
> Forgive them, Father, for they know not what they do.
>
> Into your hands, Jesus, I commit my spirit.

Mace read the statement twice to give himself time to think. He didn't like it. The proclamation was confusing, and there was no clear declaration of innocence. Worse, Antoine was repeating the words of Jesus, which would make the victims furious.

"What do you think?" Antoine asked, his eyes lighting up for the first time since Mace had entered the room.

Mace made a slight grimace. "It's okay. Very biblical. But I think you could make a stronger claim of innocence."

Antoine had obviously thought about this. "Jesus could have insisted on his innocence too. But the Bible says he was silent, like a lamb at the slaughter."

"But that's different. Jesus had to die to save the world. This is just plain injustice."

Antoine reached across the table and took the paper, refolded it, and placed it in his pocket. "I appreciate your input. But the chaplain liked it. And I don't think I can go wrong quoting the words of Jesus."

Mace wanted to argue the point but decided against it. This was Antoine's final act of self-determination. The state had taken everything else away except his right to say whatever he wanted just prior to death. Who was Mace to criticize those words?

"It's a good statement, Antoine. Me, I would be too bitter to say something this gracious. You're a better man than I."

"Some might disagree," Antoine said, forcing a smile. Then he turned serious and narrowed his eyes. "Mace, are you going to stop working on this case once they kill me?"

"No," Mace said. "I'm going to stop working this case when I clear your name."

Antoine studied Mace for a moment as if ascertaining whether he could truly believe that promise. They both knew there would be other men on death row who needed Mace's help. "You've done everything you said you'd do," Antoine eventually said.

"I appreciate that," Mace said. "But I'm not giving up on saving you yet."

At this, Antoine leaned back in his chair. "Let's just get it over with."

11

CHRIS AND I were both lost in our thoughts as we drove south on Route 400, listening to country music. The trip to Jackson would take ninety minutes if traffic cooperated. But in Atlanta, that was a big *if*.

Things slowed down on the 285 loop just past the intersection with I-85. The road was six lanes wide in each direction with concrete barriers on each side. When traffic came to a complete stop, I knew there must have been some kind of accident.

Chris scanned the radio stations to see if he could pick up any traffic alerts. Since I was driving, I handed him my BlackBerry and asked him to check the traffic updates on the newspaper site.

Chris was the kind who liked to get places early. I could tell by his body language that he was simmering because I had picked him up fifteen minutes late.

"We should still be okay," I said. "We gave ourselves two extra hours."

"Except the traffic's not moving at all," Chris responded.

I was tempted to remind him that he hadn't even wanted to go in the first place, but I decided not to pick a fight. We would need each other today. Chris was the only family I had left.

"There's a tractor-trailer accident ten miles south of here," he said. He was reading the report on my BlackBerry, and the frustration was evident in his voice. "We'd better get off at the next exit and take the connector."

I knew everyone else would have the same idea. I also knew it would take forever just to get to the next exit. I jammed the car into park. "I can't believe this," I muttered.

"Maybe we're not supposed to be there," Chris said.

It was the wrong comment at the wrong time. "I'm sure that would make you happy," I snapped.

Chris scoffed. "I'm not the one who got to the house fifteen minutes late."

I could sense a full-scale sibling argument erupting with no clear winner in sight. Normally, I was more strong willed and would wear him down. Chris would go into his shell; I would feel bad and eventually apologize. This time, I decided to short-circuit the whole vicious cycle.

"We've still got plenty of time," I murmured.

He accepted my peace offering and didn't respond.

Twenty minutes later, after a few emergency vehicles made their way past us in the HOV lane and we still hadn't moved, I decided to call Bill Masterson.

"Have you heard about the loop?" I asked.

"No. What about it?"

"We're stuck in traffic. We haven't moved in half an hour. What's the latest we can check in at the prison?"

Masterson hesitated. "I don't know. It's not like I do this every day."

He promised to look into it and call me back. Five minutes later, I was on the phone with him again.

"Can you get the car over to the shoulder of the road?" he asked.

"Why?"

"I called in a few favors. The state police will be there to give you a ride in about ten minutes. When they come, they'll turn on their lights, and you can follow them down the shoulder of the road until you can get to an exit and find a place to leave your car."

It was now four thirty, and our cushion had diminished to less than an hour. I wondered if, in the history of Georgia executions, a victim's family members had ever been late.

I thanked Masterson and explained the strategy to Chris. Since we were in one of the middle lanes, I took some executive action.

"You drive," I told him. I hopped out of the car and walked up to drivers who were ahead of us in the right lanes. I explained the situation, and they all sized me up as if trying to figure out whether

I would invent something this crazy. Eventually, they squeezed together and created enough space for us to weave our car onto the right shoulder of the road. Ten minutes later, a squad car arrived. The officer told us we should let him pass and follow him down the shoulder to the next exit. After we parked my vehicle, we could ride in the police car to Jackson.

As we started down the shoulder, I was filled with a sense of gratitude. It felt good to be on the right side of justice. Prosecutors and cops could sometimes be at each other's throats, but we also had each other's backs. I had dedicated my professional life to helping officers like the ones in front of us by putting thugs in jail. Today the blue brotherhood was looking out for one of its own.

"I can't believe they're doing this for us," I said.

"Pretty cool," Chris agreed.

◁▷

We had cleared the traffic on the loop and were heading south on I-75, riding in the back of the state police car, when the next call from Bill Masterson came. As always, the boss was blunt, but I could hear concern in his voice.

"Jamie, I just got a call from the AG's office. The Georgia Supreme Court granted a stay of execution until August 7. They want time to reevaluate the case in light of the Cooper affidavit. They've sent out a briefing schedule and a date for oral arguments." He paused as I took the news in. "I'm sorry."

I stared straight ahead, feeling numb. I had thought I was ready for everything. I'd reminded myself a thousand times that this could happen. But the reality of it hit harder than I had imagined. I had marked this day months ago as a day when I would finally achieve closure. But here I was, getting abused by the system all over again.

"You okay?" Masterson asked.

"I don't believe it" was all I could manage.

"I know you're disappointed," Masterson said. "But I wouldn't read too much into this. They just want time to consider it. That affidavit won't invalidate your dad's testimony."

It helped to hear Masterson sounding so confident. But the gut punch had left me nearly breathless. I knew I had to get off the phone before I started crying.

"Okay. Thanks for letting me know."

Masterson apologized again before he hung up. Chris looked at me, and I could tell the blood had drained from my face. He slid next to me and put an arm around my shoulder. He had heard enough of the phone call to know.

"Officer Hartley, I hate to ask you to do this, but could you take us back to our car?" I asked. My voice held up, though I could feel my throat clenching, the tears starting. "The Georgia Supreme Court just granted a stay."

I leaned into my older brother, and the tears started pouring down my face. Before I could stop, I was sobbing, even though I tried to be quiet and stoic.

"I'm sorry," Officer Hartley said from the front seat.

At that moment I couldn't even respond. Instead, I lowered my head onto Chris's shoulder and allowed myself to cry.

◁▷

One of the prison guards found Mace talking on his cell phone in a conference room and handed him a single sheet of paper. Mace ended the call and quickly scanned the page.

"He's been a good prisoner," the guard said, his voice low. "He prob'ly deserves this."

"Can I be the one to break the news to Antoine?" Mace asked.

"Of course."

They met in the same room where Antoine had shown Mace his final statement just an hour or so earlier.

"Troy Davis still has the record," Mace said. "His stay came two hours before his scheduled execution." Mace looked at his watch, then back at Antoine. "Yours came with a generous three hours and three minutes to go."

Antoine stared like a man who had seen a ghost. Perhaps his own? "What are you saying?"

"The Georgia Supreme Court granted our stay. They're taking four months to reconsider the case."

For the longest second, a stunned Antoine Marshall just stared at his lawyer, absorbing the news. His lips started trembling, and his eyes brimmed with tears. "Glory to God," he said. Then he buried his face in his hands and started crying.

12

MY FATHER WAS THE ONE who taught me how to be tough. When I was in elementary school, some of the boys called my father names because he was defending a man accused of killing his wife and children. My father argued the insanity plea—his client believed that the gods required a blood sacrifice—and my mother provided the psychiatric testimony. I got in a fight at school, and my parents found out about it.

That night, my mother lectured me on why violence was never the answer. She grounded me and sent me to my room while my father stood by silently. Later, as I was stewing about being punished for defending my parents, my dad came in and sat down on my bed.

"Did you win?" he asked, his voice a conspiratorial whisper.

"Yes."

"Good. Tell me about it."

After I got done describing the fight and getting some pointers about the next one, he kissed me on the forehead and got up to leave. "For the record," he said, "I'm opposed to fighting too. But I do know this—if you're going to fight, you'd better get in the first blow, and you'd better make it a good one. And, Jamie . . ."

He waited, commanding my full attention.

"If you get the other guy down, don't let him up."

Maybe that's why it was so hard to take my father off life support. He was a fighter. I just knew I would come to the hospital and there would be a twitch in the arms, a blinking of the eyes, my father slowly but surely getting up off the canvas one last time. You could never count him out.

But after Antoine Marshall received his stay, I realized it was time to let Chris pull the plug. Even before Friday's disappointment, I had worked through the phase of grief that denies reality. I wasn't yet ready for my dad to die, but I knew I never would be. I had finally accepted the fact that he was never coming back.

By the time I got to the hospital on Saturday morning, I had cried so much that I felt like I didn't have any tears left. I was already weak from the grief of knowing what we had to do, as if somebody had squeezed all the energy and joy out of my heart. I met Chris and Amanda in the lobby, and we made our way to Dad's room, where we met with Dr. Guptara and a few nurses. We asked for some time alone.

I entered the room without using the hand sanitizer and stood on one side of the hospital bed while Chris and Amanda stood on the other. Holding Amanda's hand, Chris told my father how much he loved him.

"I'll miss just picking up the phone and hearing his voice," Chris said to Amanda and me. "I'll miss watching him get down on the floor to play with the girls."

He wiped his eyes and placed a hand on Dad's forehead. Tears rolled down his cheek as he closed his eyes and thanked God for giving us such a wonderful father. "I don't know what I did to deserve a father like you," he said to Dad after finishing the prayer. "And you deserve better than this." He paused and swallowed hard. "Give Mom a hug for me when you see her."

All day long, I had been thinking about what I might say to my dad during these last few moments with him. But now it all seemed so pointless. The tears had welled up in my eyes as I listened to Chris, and now sorrow choked my words.

I knew that the last words my dad had truly heard me say were the ones I'd said on the way out the door the morning of his second stroke. Because his first stroke had impacted his short-term memory, I had made a habit of writing things down so he could remember them. On the morning of his second stroke, I had reminded him to bring the trash can in after the city trucks came by. "Don't forget to take Justice for a walk. I'll probably be working late tonight, so don't worry if I'm not home for dinner."

There was no hug. No *I love you*. My dad was already in his study, pretending to be hard at work.

"See you later," I'd said. "Have a good day."

And now, as we stood at his bed one last time, it seemed futile to try to make up for that. I wiped the tears from my eyes with the back of my hand and looked at Chris. "I can't say anything."

Chris nodded. "It's okay. We'll see him again one day. You can tell him everything then."

I leaned down and kissed my dad on the cheek, my fresh tears wetting his face. The nurses shaved him every day, but I could still feel the stubble from his beard. When I was little, he would wrestle with Chris and me and sometimes pin us down and tickle us or rub that stubble gently against our cheeks.

The thought of it made my heart hurt. We hadn't been a picture-perfect family, but we were doing our best until Antoine Marshall came along and blew it all away. I straightened and held my fist over my mouth, trying to hold it together. I sniffed and nodded at Chris.

I don't remember him going out to get Dr. Guptara, but I remember the doctor taking my spot next to the bed, scribbling on his chart, telling us that this was the best thing for my dad, and unhooking the life-support machines.

When Dad passed, I was standing near the foot of his bed, watching the monitors. It was amazing to see how quickly and quietly my dad's heart stopped beating. A wave of grief and guilt washed over me as the finality of it sank in—we had just taken away all hope of a miraculous recovery. My knees buckled, and the room started spinning.

Chris came over and gave me a long hug. Neither of us spoke. Eventually I moved back to the bed and gave my dad one last kiss on the forehead.

Numb, I filled out the paperwork and assured Chris and Amanda that I would be all right.

I don't remember the drive home. I felt dead myself, as if someone had taken over my body and forced me to go through the motions of life while I floated outside myself in a pool of grief and despair. At home, Justice sensed immediately that something was wrong and tried his best to console me. He found a toy and nudged it against my leg—

Wanna play? When I refused, he lay down next to me, placing his head gently on my feet, occasionally glancing up at me to see if I was okay.

After a few hours, I put on my dry-wick running clothes and took Justice on a long run. I worked the hills hard until it felt like my lungs might explode. The pain helped dull some of the sorrow. When I finally arrived home, exhausted to the core, I sat on the steps of the front porch for a long time, my head down and Justice lying next to me. I remembered the good times with my dad, and the tears began to flow again, forming a little puddle between my feet. This time, I did nothing to stop them.

After I showered, I put on a pair of jeans, a T-shirt, and one of my dad's sweatshirts, then curled up on the couch. I had agreed to meet Chris at the funeral home at five. We had a memorial service to plan and burial details to discuss and an obituary to write, but I also knew that everything would get done with or without me.

The house seemed more lifeless than ever, and I struggled with the thought of having to clean out my dad's stuff and put the house on the market.

"It was his time," Chris had said at the hospital. "But nobody can take the memories."

On that point, Chris was right. So I went into my dad's study and pulled out the book that he had read to me as a little girl. I snuggled with it on the couch, and Justice looked up at me with pleading eyes. I patted the cushion beside me, and he jumped up and curled next to my legs.

For the next two hours, I was my daddy's girl again. He was Aslan, and I was Lucy, and whenever he would try to put the book down and tell me it was time to go to bed, I would beg him to read just one more chapter of *The Lion, the Witch, and the Wardrobe.*

13

I SPENT THE NEXT FEW DAYS in a fog of grief and disbelief. In the South, we have lots of traditions that occupy our hands and minds in the days following a death that allow us to push the real mourning back by at least a week. On the day my dad died, Chris and I finalized the obituary and made plans for the funeral. The next day, Chris and Amanda helped clean the house so we could have a proper reception for family, friends, and well-wishers. Food arrived in massive quantities, as if the house were a staging area for disaster relief rather than the home of a family who had just lost a loved one.

The greatest torture was the two hours I spent in the receiving line at the viewing. The line snaked out the door of the funeral home and seemed interminable. When people finally got to the head of the line to shake my hand and hug Chris, Amanda, and their two girls, they would speak in hushed voices and tell me how sorry they were, as if they might have somehow caused my dad's death themselves. Everybody was ill at ease, and you could tell there were a million places they would rather be.

Well, not everybody. The few exceptions brightened my night. One was an old law school classmate of mine named Isaiah Haywood. He had always been irreverent, loud, and obnoxious, and he obviously saw no reason to make an exception just because my father had died.

"Thanks for coming," I told Isaiah. As usual, he had decided to be the best-dressed man at the occasion. He was now working as the in-house attorney for a sports agency and was apparently making enough money to afford five-hundred-dollar suits.

"I would have crawled here across broken glass just to see you in that black dress again," he said. The comment made me blush. Isaiah had made similar remarks all through law school. I had rebuffed him every time, but that didn't seem to bother him.

"I really am sorry for your loss," Isaiah said. "He must have been a great man to raise such a wonderful daughter."

I leaned in to give him a hug. It was one of the few that I judiciously parceled out that night.

Two days later, we staged a funeral that was attended by a large part of the Atlanta legal community. My dad had been a minor legend. Chris did an amazing job eulogizing him and somehow kept his composure throughout. We tried to make it a celebration of my father's life, and we generally succeeded. I cried only once, and that was when I saw Chris's girls, ten-year-old Lola and eight-year-old Sophie, each put a rose on their granddaddy's casket.

I was touched by the showing from the DA's office. Bill Masterson was there and had apparently decreed that every person not in trial should show up as well. They occupied two full rows, and it was heartwarming to see the prosecutors paying their respects to a defense attorney who had generally been a thorn in their sides.

By the time the funeral ended, I was drained from the pain and protocol and just wanted to be alone. But that wasn't possible, because I lived in my parents' house, where we held the reception. My aunts and uncles all came, along with my closest friends from law school and work. Justice made the rounds, working the crowd for scraps of food and scarfing down anything left on plates that had been abandoned on coffee tables.

When the crowd thinned out, Chris and I started telling stories about our dad, and everyone had a few good laughs.

My friends and relatives cleaned the place before they left, and finally, at eight that evening, I hugged Chris and his family, assured them again that I would be fine by myself, and waved at them from the front porch as they pulled away. When I went back inside, the house was deathly quiet. I felt the loneliness begin to descend and knew I needed a distraction. We had done a wonderful job of honoring my dad at the funeral, and putting that ceremony behind me seemed to alleviate some of the pressure that had been building in my chest.

I didn't believe for a minute that my dad would want me to sit around and wallow in self-pity. His solution to pretty much everything was to work a little harder. And even though Masterson had told me that I should take at least a week off, I was anxious to get back to the office and start wreaking havoc on the bad guys again.

I spent the evening organizing the Rikki Tate materials that I had. I took the burgundy tablecloth and silver candlesticks off our dining room table and spread the case file on it, converting the dining room into my Rikki Tate war room. As I'd hoped it would, the task temporarily took my mind off my loss. I needed to get back into a routine, and I was more determined than ever to see that Caleb Tate got what he deserved.

Justice responded to the uptick in my mood, and we played a game of tug-of-war before we went to bed. That night, for the first time since my dad's death, I kicked Justice off the bed and made him sleep in his traditional spot on a blanket on the floor.

Jamie Brock was back. And it was time to restore a little discipline.

14

OUR HOUSE SAT on a small hill at the end of a cul-de-sac. When I looked out the picture windows of my dad's study, I could see a good portion of the Seven Oaks neighborhood, and I felt like a queen in her medieval castle.

After my dad's first stroke, he would spend several hours a day in there, acting busy, though he could no longer practice law. Many times, when I walked by the study on my way out the front door, he would just be sitting at his desk, staring out the windows, deep in thought. There would be a half-full cup of coffee next to his computer, getting cold. When I got home that night, I would dump it down the sink and put the cup in the dishwasher. Sometimes there would be two or three half-full cups scattered around the study, all apparently forgotten and abandoned.

On the morning after my dad's funeral, I took his spot and drank coffee at his desk, gazing out the windows. Neighborhood kids were waiting for the school bus at the entrance to the cul-de-sac, their parents standing with them, chatting and enjoying the beautiful spring day. I yearned for a life of normalcy like that. And I wished my father were still sitting in this chair, even with the weakened mind and altered personality that had followed his first stroke. I struggled to grasp the finality of everything—the hard fact that I would never see him in this house again, never be able to gain courage and strength from just knowing he was here.

After I finished my coffee, I shook off the melancholy and moved to the Rikki Tate war room. I removed the pictures from the walls and set up an easel in the corner. There were some decorative tables lining the walls, and I cleared the tops of those as well.

I taped a few pictures of Rikki to a side wall and sat down at my computer to start outlining her biography. This was the unique perspective I brought to cases like this. I would look at things through the victim's eyes—study her habits, her friends, and her personality. I would practically become Rikki Tate so that I could understand what she was thinking and why someone might want her dead. Like others, I would also study the suspect. But big chunks of my time would be spent on the victim, something other law enforcement types didn't emphasize enough.

Rikki's life read like a Shakespearean tragedy—from an abusive childhood to Vegas to an Atlanta escort service and ultimately to her marriage to Caleb Tate. I reviewed the pleadings from the civil lawsuits she had filed trying to get her topless pictures removed from the Internet. I read online reports about the angst this created among the purveyors of porn. I searched for a connection between them and Caleb Tate.

The major felony squad detectives had spent a fair amount of time chasing down rumors that both Rikki and Caleb were involved in affairs. Caleb had allegedly been sneaking off with an office assistant. Two years ago, Rikki had been getting together with a guy she met at the gym. Rikki's affair ended just before her spiritual conversion. The current status of Caleb and his assistant was unknown.

With the help of another ADA, the detectives had already obtained and executed a search warrant at Tate's home and subpoenaed medical records. Most of Rikki's records consisted of plastic surgery and other unrelated matters. There was no indication she had ever obtained a prescription for oxycodone, codeine, or promethazine. Caleb Tate had been on OxyContin, a brand name for oxycodone, for a few months after rotator cuff surgery several years ago, but he had only filled the prescription twice.

Caleb and Rikki certainly had their problems. Friends reported fights, but the police were never called, and no one ever claimed that Caleb had laid a hand on Rikki. Her conversion, according to her church friends, only served to exacerbate the issues. Rikki would ask fellow church members to pray for her husband. He flippantly dismissed her faith, certain it was just a fad she would outgrow.

I read every police interview, every medical record, and every other document in the file. There was no way Bill Masterson would let me indict on the basis of *this* information. At the very least, we would need to show that Caleb Tate had access to the drugs found in Rikki's bloodstream, and we would have to put together a strong case of motive. Maybe Caleb's office assistant had demanded that he do something. Maybe Rikki had threatened to file for divorce. Maybe Caleb had just gotten tired of a washed-out former showgirl who was hooked on drugs.

I searched in vain for a hint of a smoking gun among the documents on the table, but I didn't find one. There was, however, one item in the file that provided a slight flicker of hope. Rikki Tate, not surprisingly, had been seeing an expensive psychiatrist. And not just any psychiatrist. Dr. Aaron Gillespie, an expert witness whom I had used as a forensic psychiatrist on a few insanity plea cases and a former colleague of my mother, had been the primary psychiatrist seeing Rikki for the past ten years.

I called to make an appointment, but his assistant asked so many questions that I politely ended the conversation and hung up. I dressed for work, googled his address, and headed off in my 4Runner to see if the doctor was in.

15

GILLESPIE WORKED in a cozy office complex nestled among the pine trees less than a mile from Johns Creek Hospital. The Georgian brick buildings were all brand new with perfectly manicured lawns and a small pond behind them. The pod of offices was set back from Johns Creek Parkway far enough that the setting presented an oasis of calm in the chaos of north-Georgia traffic.

Though I had been friends with Dr. Gillespie since my mother's death nearly twelve years ago, I'd never been to his new office. Like several other forensic psychiatrists, he considered my mother a mentor of sorts. But unlike the others, he had reached out to me in the days after her death, letting me know he would be there if I ever needed to talk.

I politely declined his offer, but he stayed in touch. Several years later, when I began working as a part-time trainer at a Gold's Gym during law school, Gillespie hired me to train him three times a week. He was happily married and one of the few men who didn't try to impress me during our workout sessions. In fact, he allowed me to do most of the talking, and I worked through some pretty serious issues while he lifted. Only later did I realize that he had come to the gym because he knew I needed counseling but would never set foot in his office.

I announced myself to his receptionist and took a seat in his plush waiting room. Gillespie was doing quite well for himself.

After a few minutes he came bounding out. The man was tall—about six-three—with a boyish face, black glasses, and dark hair that he combed to the side as if he didn't realize parts had gone out several years earlier. He was soft around the middle and showed no lasting effects from the training I had provided.

He bowed deeply when I rose from my chair, as if I were the queen of England. "To what do I owe this great honor?" he asked. He straightened and gave me a hug.

"Have you got a second?"

He looked around as if the office belonged to somebody else. "I'm actually seeing somebody right now. Is this about one of our cases?"

One of the reasons for my rapid rise in the district attorney's office was the man standing in front of me. Gillespie had become the DA's go-to guy for cases involving the insanity plea. Juries loved him, and we were now using him on three of our most prominent files.

"Can we talk in private for a moment?" I asked.

The receptionist frowned, but Gillespie got the idea. He led me to an office down the hall and closed the door.

"I'll be done with my client in about thirty minutes. I could cancel my next appointment if I need to," he said, concern registering on his face.

"No, no, it's nothing like that. I just didn't want to talk about this over the phone." I lowered my voice a little. "This has to stay confidential, okay?"

Gillespie gave me a sideways look. "Of course."

"I'm investigating the death of Rikki Tate. I understand she was one of your patients."

"You know I can't comment on that."

"I know. And I'm not asking you to violate her privacy rights. You know we can get the records through a grand jury subpoena, but that will take a while. I was hoping maybe you could tell me, hypothetically speaking, whether or not there might be anything of value in the records that might help our case."

Gillespie sat on the edge of a desk and sighed. He took off his glasses and rubbed his face before putting the glasses back on. "Hypothetically speaking, what types of things are you looking for?"

"Fights with her husband. Affairs. Access to drugs like oxycodone and codeine."

For a moment, Gillespie stared at the wall behind me. Then he turned back to me. "I'm not saying whether or not I had a counseling relationship with Rikki Tate because that would violate federal HIPAA laws. But I can tell you this—it's almost always worth your while to subpoena the records of a treating psychiatrist."

"Because that psychiatrist can prescribe medication?"

"Not necessarily. Because a psychiatrist is told things. Most people, except for a few prosecutors who think they're so tough that they don't need outlets for their emotions . . ." He gave me a slight nod of the head, a subtle scold. "Most people talk to psychiatrists about issues in their lives. About addictions they are trying to kick. About whether they've been faithful to their spouse. Those types of things."

"I see." I knew better than to push the matter any further. I'd have to issue a subpoena and get a judge to sign a qualified protective order so I could obtain the documents under seal. But the answer he had dropped so casually already provided a road map—*"addictions they are trying to kick . . . whether they've been faithful to their spouse."*

"We never had this conversation—right?"

"What conversation?" Gillespie rose from the desk. He walked to the door and put his hand on the knob, then turned in a moment of reflection. "Jamie, I really liked this girl. Sure, she had issues, but we've all got issues. The records may hurt you as much as they help. She'll be an easy target."

He hesitated, perhaps worrying that he might have said too much. "But she didn't kill herself. And she didn't deserve to die."

Now the man was speaking my language. In his own way, Gillespie was as much an advocate for victims as I was.

"And, Jamie, I'm also very fond of you. In all candor, I'm not sure what Masterson was thinking when he put you in charge of this investigation. This could reopen old wounds. You've got to separate your mother's death from Rikki Tate's death. You understand that?"

I didn't answer, but that didn't deter Gillespie. "This is not part of avenging your mom. Your mom was avenged when Antoine Marshall was sentenced to death."

I wanted to tell the good doctor that I didn't come here for a counseling session. But I bit my tongue. The man had my best interest at heart. "I get that," I said.

"I may need to get back on another exercise routine," Gillespie said as he opened the door. "You know any good trainers?"

I smiled. "I'll call you if I need to talk," I said. "But you're right; you probably should get back on an exercise routine."

He sucked in his stomach and puffed out his chest. "Glad to see you haven't lost your edge." He came over, gave me a hug, and sent me on my way.

16

I SPENT THURSDAY AFTERNOON in a cramped courtroom on the third floor of the Milton County Superior Court building, arguing bond hearings. I had the good fortune of having drawn Magistrate Simmons, a chubby blonde woman who looked like a kindergarten teacher but was tough as nails. She had a squeaky voice that engendered not one ounce of respect, but lawyers or defendants who tried to cross her found themselves on the short end of a lightning-quick temper.

I opposed two of the first three requests for bond modifications. On the third case, after Simmons ruled in my favor, the defense lawyer cursed under his breath on the way out of the courtroom. Simmons heard it, and the lawyer almost ended up joining his client in jail.

As a result, tension lingered in the courtroom when the clerk called the case for Rafael Rivera, a reputed gang member facing time for dealing based on the testimony of an undercover narcotics officer. In addition to his drug offenses, Rivera had been tried twice for murder, but witnesses had mysteriously disappeared or miraculously recanted their testimony. That's what made this third distribution charge so important. We might not get him for murder, but he would serve at least fifteen years under the three-strikes law.

Ironically, Rivera was represented by an associate from Caleb Tate's law firm, a hard-charging young woman who graduated one year ahead of me from Southeastern Law School. But when Rivera's case was called, the young attorney was nowhere to be found.

"She called in to say she got stuck in a motion-to-suppress hearing in Fulton," the clerk told Magistrate Simmons. "She's sending someone else to cover."

Simmons looked perturbed. "Did she say when her colleague might grace us with his or her presence?"

"Three o'clock, give or take."

Simmons didn't like it, but she realized that defense lawyers couldn't be in two places at once. Bond hearings didn't have a high priority.

Simmons banged her gavel. "We'll reconvene at 3:10," she said.

◁▷

I reentered Simmons's courtroom at three and was shocked to see that the great man himself—Caleb Tate—had taken a seat at the defense counsel table. "Slummin' today?" I asked.

He stood and extended a hand. "Good to see you too, Counselor."

I thought about extending condolences for the death of his wife but couldn't bring myself to be that hypocritical. "You're here for the bond hearing?"

Tate broke into his sleazy smile, showing off a mouth full of big white teeth, a smile that had wooed more than a few jurors—especially the women. "My man's innocent, Jamie. He needs to be out contributing to society."

"Save it for the magistrate."

Tate lowered his voice. "I don't really expect to get too far with Simmons. But after the hearing, could I get five minutes of your time?"

"For what?"

He took a step closer as if we were frat brothers ready to share a secret. "I've got a deal I'd like you to consider."

"I don't do deals, Caleb. Maybe if you came to court once in a while on some common felonies, you'd know that."

He snickered. "Didn't mean to hit a sore spot. But could I just have a few minutes? You might be glad we talked."

I wanted to spit on him, but I knew I couldn't refuse to even listen. I had enough of a reputation among the defense bar as it was.

"You're wasting your breath. But I'll give you five minutes after the hearing."

"Fair enough. That's three minutes more than I expected."

The hearing went according to form. Rivera made a sulking appearance, frowning at the judge and slumping in his chair. He had dreads and stringy facial hair and conveyed an attitude of superiority to everyone in the courtroom. Simmons listened skeptically, her hand on her chin, as Caleb Tate argued that the bond should be reduced from the three hundred thousand another magistrate had established shortly after Rivera's arrest. "I've represented murderers who got lower bonds," Tate said. "Alleged murderers," he added with a smile.

I responded with a passionate argument about how dangerous Rivera was and reminded Simmons that witnesses had disappeared in his prior cases. She nodded and checked her notes. When I finished, she told Rivera to stand. He stayed seated until a deputy moved behind him and gave him a hard nudge. Rivera shrugged it off and rose slowly to his feet, keeping his eyes fixed on Magistrate Simmons.

"I ought to increase your bond to half a million," she said, matching his stare with a hard look of her own. "I'm certainly not going to *decrease* it. And let me tell you something, Mr. Rivera: if I hear even a hint about witness tampering or intimidation, you're going to wish that you and I had never met. Is that clear?"

When Rivera didn't respond, Tate jumped in. "Your Honor, Ms. Brock's allegations about witness tampering are unfounded and—"

"Save it," Simmons snapped. "Mr. Rivera, your bond modification request is denied." She banged her gavel. "Court will stand adjourned."

Rivera sneered and let out a haughty chuckle as Simmons left the bench. Two deputies pushed him through the exit door and let it slam behind them.

Tate turned to me. "Another rousing success," he said. He packed up his stuff and asked if we could step into the hallway. I nodded and followed him out the door.

It had been eleven years since this man had defended my mother's killer and called my father a liar. The time had done nothing to lessen my contempt for him.

During my three years as a prosecutor, I'd never had the chance to try a case against Caleb Tate head to head. In fact, I'd never been this close to him. I'd learned to despise him from a distance. And now, standing toe to toe with him, I felt the old hatred bubbling up in me with new intensity.

I was five-eight, and Tate was only a few inches taller. In my mind, I would always recall him from eleven years earlier, strutting around the courtroom, making outrageous claims and pouring acid on the gaping wounds of our shattered family. But now, standing in front of me, he looked like a hollowed-out version of the man I remembered. It was like seeing a movie star up close where you could examine every wrinkle and pore and the red blood vessels in the tired eyes.

"Five minutes," I reminded him.

"Let's cut a deal on Rivera," Tate suggested. "You and I both have more important things to do. It's just a drug charge, Jamie. I'll talk him into seven years, all but two suspended on the condition of good behavior. Nail him again during that seven years, and you can send him away until I retire."

My briefcase was on the floor, and I had my arms folded across my chest. "Done?"

"With that part," he said.

"No," I said. "No way. Not now, not on the eve of trial. Not ever. This one's going to trial, Caleb. You're right—we're both too busy to waste time. So don't bother proposing any more deals."

Tate made a face. "Okay," he said. "I knew it was a long shot."

That felt good. I picked up my briefcase, feeling a little smug.

"I've still got two minutes," Tate said.

"For what?"

"The real reason I'm here." He lowered his voice and did a quick scan of the hall. "I know Bill Masterson has asked you to help with the investigation of my wife's death. I've tried to reach Bill, but he's busy on the campaign trail. I can imagine that you might find it a little hard to remain unbiased, and I can't really blame you for that. But, Jamie . . ." He paused and looked me dead in the eye. "I didn't kill Rikki. I'll answer any questions you want. I'll take a lie detector. But you've got to believe me—I loved that woman, and I would never have harmed her."

I didn't say a word. I learned early in my career that when a suspect was talking, you let him talk . . . even if you hated his guts. Even if you wanted to wrap your hands around his neck and strangle him.

So I said nothing.

"I've been around long enough to know that you can get an indict-ment for anything," Tate continued. "But tell your boss that if he indicts me on this, he won't get his conviction. The only way I can defend myself is to tell the world about the dark side of Rikki Tate. She had a hard-enough life, Jamie. Don't make me dissect her in public."

It was as close to begging as I would ever see the great Caleb Tate stoop. With another prosecutor, it might have triggered a tinge of sym-pathy. But this was the same man who had faked outrage at the police and accused them of trying to railroad Antoine Marshall. The same man who had oozed sincerity even as he challenged my father's testi-mony during a dramatic cross-examination.

Caleb Tate was an actor. And I wasn't buying it.

"I'll pass your message on to Mr. Masterson," I promised. "But the messages go both ways."

I paused for a second, gathering my thoughts. I kept my anger in check, my voice steady. "If you made one mistake when you poisoned your wife, if you forgot to cross one t or dot one i or gave us even the tiniest bit of rope . . . I promise you this: I'll use every inch of that rope to string you up from the first tree that I can find, and I won't think twice about it. You're right—Rikki had a hard life. And she deserved better than a man like you."

17

THURSDAY ENDED with an office meeting called by Bill Masterson. He assembled six other ADAs and me in our largest conference room and, in typical Masterson style, got right to the point.

"We've got four months before the primary, and things are getting kind of nasty on the campaign trail." Masterson was seated at the head of the table. Regina Granger sat at his right hand. From the look on her face, she probably knew the purpose of this meeting. The rest of us did not.

"My little RV tours of the state seem to be picking up momentum, and some of the front-runners are getting spooked," Masterson said.

For the last six weeks, Masterson had been touring around in an RV a supporter had loaned him, attending small events and church services while shaking hands with every Georgian he could find.

"One of my opponents just sent out a direct-mail hit piece." He passed around a glossy tri-fold that had some unflattering shots of a young Bill Masterson dancing with somebody other than his wife on a dark dance floor. There were pictures of three other women who alleged that Masterson had fostered a hostile work environment at the DA's office.

"Years ago, when I was the chief assistant, our illustrious DA would throw an office party every Christmas. Some of you were here and know that spouses weren't invited. Things sometimes got a bit out of hand. One of our ADAs got fired about ten years ago and filed a sexual-harassment lawsuit against my predecessor. But since I'm the one now running for office, this whole thing somehow becomes my fault."

I had heard stories about the office parties. I wrote off most of it as legend. Everybody who worked for Masterson knew that he was a fair boss who treated everyone the same. He was rough around the edges but never tolerated anything that remotely smacked of harassment.

His wife had filed for divorce six years ago because Bill was an incurable workaholic; she finally gave up trying to compete with his work. As far as I knew, there wasn't even a hint of an affair. He had dated a few women in the last couple of years but spent most of his time at the office, consumed by the job.

"They've quoted a few rape victims who claim I was less than enthusiastic about pursuing their cases. Same for three or four battered wives. Throw in a few anonymous sources who say I like dirty jokes around the office, and you've got yourself a pretty good piece."

Just hearing this reminded me of why I never wanted to go into politics. I liked the courtroom, where at least there were rules of evidence and, for the most part, impartial judges. Politics usually degenerated into something that resembled a middle school food fight more than the lofty democracy our founders envisioned.

"My political advisers asked me whether the women in my office would be willing to sign a petition stating what an enlightened and fair-minded boss I am," Masterson continued. "I told them you might do so as long as you didn't have to sign it under oath."

There were some nervous chuckles, and I got the sense that the other ADAs, like myself, were anxious to help. We all knew politics could get ugly, but it was hard to watch a good man like Masterson get slimed for something he didn't do. He had gone to the mat more than once for just about everybody around the table, and prosecutors had a way of sticking up for their own.

"My consultants want to put together a 'Women for Masterson' piece that we could distribute to the media and turn into a television ad as well. They'll be asking each of you individually, but I wanted to meet with you first and let you know that you don't have to get involved and, though it goes without saying, it won't affect your job evaluations either way. In fact, I was reluctant to drag any of you into this, and I'm sorry that I have to make this request. I would rather just ride it out. But I'm being told that if we don't respond aggressively, the public will assume it's all true."

"This is crap," Regina said as soon as Masterson took a breath. Bill's voice had been calm and measured, but Regina was fired up. "I'm sure every one of us would be willing to sign whatever you need. And you might as well have one done for 'African Americans for Masterson' too because that will probably be the next attack."

After Regina spoke, the brownnosing began in earnest, and all of us told the boss that we were on board. He thanked us for our support, told us not to believe everything we read in the papers, and apologized again that he had to make this request. A few of my coworkers started reminding each other of how Bill had stood up for them when they were attacked by this defense attorney or that defense attorney, but Bill cut them off. He said he didn't want to waste our valuable time eliciting pats on the back. "The streets aren't getting any safer while we sit around singing 'Kumbaya,'" he said. "Let's get back to work."

I got up to leave with the rest of the women, but Masterson had other ideas. "Brock, can I see you a minute?" he growled.

Regina stayed behind as well and listened as Bill made his request. "I've asked Regina to be part of our television commercial," he said. "It would help me a lot if you'd be willing to say a few words as well. Maybe remind folks that I prosecuted your mother's killer and that's part of the reason you're working for me now." Masterson shrugged. "It would probably take some of the sting out of the claims by these victims."

"Plus, you're photogenic," Regina said. "I've got a face for radio, but you've got a face for TV."

I agreed to do the TV spot and then gave Bill and Regina an update on the Tate investigation. I reported that we were making progress, though we couldn't yet prove that Tate had access to the drugs.

"A minor point," Masterson said sarcastically. "Other than that, Mrs. Lincoln, how'd you enjoy the play?"

I just agreed to do you a favor, I wanted to say. But things didn't work that way with Masterson. He was always straight up, a man who didn't believe in owing people.

"I understand," I said. "But Tate is already acting guilty." I detailed my conversation with Tate after the bond hearing—everything except my threat at the end.

"Definitely guilty," Masterson responded. "Wants to take a polygraph, answer police questions, and cooperate fully. Basically a confession."

I hated it when Masterson slipped into his sarcastic mode. But the man had a point. "I didn't say I was ready to indict yet."

"The queen of understatement," Masterson replied.

◁▷

The next day, film crews were at our office. Regina Granger, big and boisterous, looked straight into the eye of the camera and confidently proclaimed her support for her boss and trusted friend, Bill Masterson. She did it on the first take while I watched nervously. The camera crew decided to do a second take with Regina just to be on the safe side.

After she finished, it took me five tries to get the right amount of intensity and enthusiasm. Everybody kept encouraging me, telling me I was a natural, but then they would suggest another try and give me some coaching on how to change my facial expression or hold my hands or talk slower or faster or look toward a different spot. When they finally said, "It's a wrap," I couldn't get out of there fast enough.

The mudslinging commercials from the other candidates started running on Saturday, and "Women for Masterson" responded on Sunday. Despite the counterpunch, Masterson's consultants worried that he had dipped in the polls. "Negative ads work," they told him. "Positive commercials are just damage control. We need to think of something more creative. We need a game changer."

18

ON THE THREE-HOUR TRIP from death row to Rabun County, Mace kept himself occupied with thoughts about Antoine Marshall's living conditions. Because of two attempted death-row suicides last year, Marshall and the other inmates were being held in solitary confinement for twenty-three hours a day and were limited to noncontact visits from lawyers, clergy, and family members. Antoine had no family, and his only occasional visitor was Mace.

Over the past eleven years, Mace had watched his client go through cycles of despair and hope. Sometimes Antoine would stay depressed for months. But when he was in a manic phase, he would furiously scribble notes of future sermons he intended to preach once his innocence was finally established. He was studying to be a pastor, and he had visions of leading the down-and-out to Christ. His slant on the New Testament, which Mace found refreshing and entirely consistent with his own, saw Jesus as a defender of the oppressed and powerless. And Antoine was ready to be his wingman.

Antoine also spent time writing letters. He had some female pen pals from the more liberal European countries, two of whom had proposed to Antoine. He had also written letters to the Brock family, though only Chris had bothered to respond.

It was late Friday afternoon when Mace pulled into the parking lot of Chris Brock's church—First Baptist Church of Rabun, Georgia. Driving his truck, Mace felt right at home in the Georgia mountains. Normally, Mace would ride his Harley on a beautiful spring day like this one. But he would have enough stereotypes to overcome as Antoine Walker's defense lawyer, so he'd left the Harley at home.

The church was small and nondescript, like a thousand other Baptist churches in rural Georgia. Pastor Brock ministered to about a hundred salt-of-the-earth types, true conservative believers devoted to God, guns, and the Georgia Bulldogs, though not necessarily in that order.

A receptionist whose nameplate identified her as Diane greeted Mace suspiciously, probably thinking he was looking for a handout. Mace explained who he was, and her skepticism turned into thinly masked hostility. "Pastor Brock is at the parsonage this afternoon," she said. "Perhaps next time you could call for an appointment."

"Could you call him and ask if I could stop by?" Mace asked. "I promise I won't take more than a half hour of his time."

Diane frowned. Pastor Brock's time was apparently very important, especially when the lawyer representing his mother's killer was asking. Mace could see her mind formulating excuses. She looked like she was regretting the fact that she already told him the pastor was at the parsonage. "He's probably studying for Sunday's sermon," Diane said. "He doesn't like to be disturbed when he's in the middle of Sunday prep."

"You're very good. And I appreciate what you're doing for the reverend. But, ma'am, I could find out from a hundred different people here in Rabun where the pastor lives. I'd rather not show up unannounced on his doorstep, but I've driven more than three hours, and I really need to talk to him for just a few minutes. If I were him, I'd want you to call and let me know."

Diane shook her head and let out a big sigh. What could one expect from a criminal-defense lawyer? She dialed a number and, after talking to Pastor Brock, told Mace to take a seat. She even asked if he wanted coffee.

◁▷

When the reverend arrived, he greeted Mace with a smile and a firm handshake. Mace had always been struck with how alike the Brock kids looked. They both had bright, expressive eyes and dimples when they smiled. Jamie had a firmer set to the jaw and high cheekbones, a hard-edged beauty that attracted lots of attention. Chris looked more wholesome and good-natured, a few added pounds bringing a softness to his face that Jamie's features lacked.

"They're painting my office, so maybe we could talk for a few minutes in the sanctuary," Chris suggested. "Did Diane offer you anything to drink?"

"Yes, thanks."

Mace followed Chris into the sanctuary, and the silence increased his nervousness. In his letter to Antoine, Chris had said he'd forgiven the condemned man. He'd even expressed gratefulness that Antoine had come to Christ. Yet Chris had still planned to be there to watch the scheduled execution. Now, with the new evidence of Antoine's innocence before the Georgia Supreme Court, Mace was hopeful that Chris might be having second thoughts about the next execution date.

The two men sat on a padded front pew, a few feet apart, looking at the altar in front of them.

"I appreciate your seeing me, Pastor. And on behalf of my client, I can't tell you how much your forgiveness means to him."

"I wouldn't be much of a pastor if I preached about it but didn't extend it myself. I've seen how bitterness and revenge can shrink a man's soul," Chris said. He spoke softly and seemed entirely at ease in this situation. Mace wondered if he might be talking about Jamie—or maybe their father.

"How does a Christian's duty to forgive square with the death penalty?" Mace asked. He knew the question was blunt, but he thought it would be a greater insult to beat around the bush when it was obvious why he had come.

Chris thought about it for a minute. He had undoubtedly wrestled with the question before, but he probably wanted to choose his words carefully. He might have been worried that Mace would try to use his answer against him. "Individuals should forgive. But the government's role is to restrain evil, and sometimes that requires using the death penalty. I'm not against capital punishment in general. It's just that if there's any doubt about guilt, it should be off the table."

"Do you believe in second chances?"

This brought another pause from Chris, his eyes fixed on the altar. "I don't believe that anybody is beyond redemption, if that's what you mean. But our actions have consequences. So in that respect, no, I don't believe that a guy like Antoine Marshall should be released so he can have another chance to kill."

"What about King David? What about Moses?"

This time Chris responded with an irritated grunt. "What do you want from me?"

Mace turned to look at the pastor. "I've spent the last several years in prison ministry. You probably know this, but I've also spent some time in prison myself, prior to law school. I'm one of maybe three or four lawyers in the entire state with a felony conviction. If anybody knows how to sniff out a fake jailhouse conversion, it's me.

"I just want you to know that Antoine Marshall really is a changed man. Whoever he was before . . . that's not who he is now. As you know, the Scriptures say that the old man is gone and that everything becomes new.

"What I'm asking is for you to meet with him, Pastor. Judge for yourself. If you still want to support his execution after doing that, I'll never bother you again. But you can't judge a man from his letters or know his heart unless you look into his eyes. I'm asking you to go down to Jackson and meet my client."

Chris shifted in his seat. "Professor James—"

"Please . . . call me Mace. Everybody else does."

"Okay . . . Mace. My problem with your request is simply this: Every believer needs to learn how to extend forgiveness. If somebody slaps me on one cheek, I need to turn the other. But before absolution can be granted, the person who commits the wrong must repent. You sound like you've read through the Bible a few times. So you know that John the Baptist and Jesus and all of Jesus' disciples had one thing in common—they told people everywhere to repent. And repentance begins with acknowledging what we've done wrong."

Chris stood, signaling an end to the meeting. His voice was still soft, but it was also firm. "I'll go down there and meet with your guy," Chris said. "But the first thing I'm going to ask him is whether he killed my mother and whether he's sorry for what he did. Changed hearts begin with repentance. And if he's truly repentant, he'll have no greater champion than me. But if he's not, I can't help him."

"Fair enough," Mace said. "I'll set it up."

19

AT THE BEGINNING of the Caleb Tate investigation, I had asked Bill Masterson to use his influence to get a couple of senior homicide detectives I knew from the major felony squad assigned to the case. But Masterson reminded me that he didn't let the cops run the DA's office, and they didn't let him run theirs.

So instead, the case got assigned to Tyler Finnegan, a young detective who had moved from Los Angeles to Atlanta just three years ago and had consequently been tagged with the unimaginative nickname "LA." He was only in his early thirties and had none of the hard-edged demeanor I thought we needed in dealing with a slimeball like Caleb Tate.

LA was more surfer than cop, with an unruly shock of blond hair and bright-blue eyes. He sometimes came across as clueless or disinterested, but according to a few ADAs who had worked with him in the past, he had an uncanny way of making suspects open up. He also noticed things that nobody else caught. Sometimes it was a gesture of discomfort, sometimes a microexpression of anger, sometimes a change in vocabulary. Many times, according to my sources, LA couldn't even explain it himself. But he had been one of fifteen thousand people tested by California researchers in a project concerning social intelligence for law enforcement officers. Among the candidates, only fifty had been able to score at least 80 percent on two separate lie-detecting exercises. LA was one of them and had been ostentatiously labeled a "truth wizard."

He had also worked a few celebrity crimes in Hollywood and supposedly knew how to deal with the press. And after a few weeks of working with the man, I began to appreciate the fact that he had a blue-collar work ethic, even if he tried to disguise it with a laid-back attitude.

But most important, he was a fellow believer in the guilt of Caleb Tate. For both of us, it wasn't a matter of *if*; it was only *whether* we could prove it. All in all, by the third week of the investigation, I had pretty much concluded that LA was the right guy for the job, even if we did tend to rub each other the wrong way.

I admired LA's ability to keep the press churning out pro-prosecution stories on an almost-daily basis. He made very few comments on the record, but on the side he would feed juicy tidbits to favored reporters, and the stories then cited "unnamed sources familiar with the investigation." The Tate story had legs because it hit all the hot-button issues. There was the *Pretty Woman* angle of a girl working for an escort service and then marrying a rich guy. There was marital strife with rumors of affairs. There was a high-profile conversion to Christianity and a disapproving husband. And there was the creep factor. An "anonymous source" leaked information that Caleb Tate habitually recorded his wife's phone calls and made her get his approval anytime she spent more than fifty dollars. Not only that, but Caleb Tate had publicly disagreed with his wife's decision to file suit against the websites that displayed topless pictures of her.

If the good folks in my county who attended church on Sunday could have rendered a verdict based solely on the press reports, they would have viewed lethal injection as too merciful.

I didn't normally like to try my cases in the press, but on this one, I was willing to make an exception. Besides, when I confronted LA about the leaks, he just smiled and agreed that it was a terrible thing for the press to have so many moles inside the police department. Then he would turn around and leak another story.

The downside of LA's tactics was that he had the public howling for an arrest, but we still had a big evidentiary problem. We couldn't prove Caleb Tate's access to the drugs. Nor did we have a solid motive. As our case stood, I doubted that we could get an indictment, much less a conviction.

◁▷

I received Rikki Tate's subpoenaed psychiatric records on the first Thursday in April. I took the records home and immediately began going through them. I went to bed at midnight and stared at the ceiling for an hour, thinking about my father. The emotions would come like a flash flood, unpredictable and overwhelming, receding to leave behind the muck of despondency. For some reason, the house pulsed with loneliness that night, and I found myself reminiscing about my childhood, tears dampening my pillow.

After a good cry, I turned on the light and decided to get up and do some work. Two hours later, I was still poring over the documents in the war room, wearing my pajama bottoms, a sweatshirt, and a pair of running socks. Justice had moved from the bedroom to the war room with me, but not until he had given me one of those *How long are we going to be acting crazy like this?* looks.

Reading through Rikki's counseling records on an emotional night like this only exacerbated my melancholy and depression. Identifying with the victim came at an emotional price.

Rikki was a sporadic patient who seemed to show up for counseling only when she was in the middle of one crisis or another. Her appointments had been much more frequent in the six months prior to her death. The counseling notes tended to ramble and jump around, and I did my best to integrate the information into the timeline of Rikki's life I had already established.

Hers was the all-too-familiar story of childhood abuse destroying a beautiful young woman's sense of self-worth and identity. Rikki's father left the family when she was in elementary school. During her early teenage years, she was abused by her stepfather. She ran away two months after she turned sixteen. Her sad home life made me ache even more for one of my father's hugs.

Rikki eventually landed in Las Vegas and moved in with one boyfriend after another. She got her first break when she put pictures of herself on a modeling website and before long started getting offers for modeling, some of it topless. When she turned twenty-one, she began working the Vegas shows—first as a crowd plant for a comedy hypnotist, then as an assistant to a well-known magician, and finally as a showgirl in one of the biggest musicals on the Strip.

Unfortunately, as her career continued its upward trajectory, her relationships spiraled downward. She was arrested twice for drugs. A boyfriend beat her up, and she pressed charges. The casino fired her for missing work, and she got blacklisted on the Strip.

At twenty-six, Rikki moved to Atlanta to start over.

She landed with a high-end escort service and promptly got busted for prostitution and possession. When she retained Caleb Tate as her defense attorney, her life took a dramatic turn.

Tate cut two deals, one of which he claimed was the best deal of his life. The first was a plea agreement with Masterson. Rikki had a high-profile client list and agreed to testify against her pimps and her johns. In exchange, the DA dropped all charges against Rikki.

The second deal was one proposed by Caleb, who was twelve years older than his ravishing client. After the smoke of the investigation had cleared, Caleb and Rikki took a trip together to Vegas, where Rikki enjoyed her old stomping grounds on the arm of a man who had lots of money. They returned to Atlanta as Mr. and Mrs. Tate. According to Gillespie's notes, Rikki claimed that Caleb Tate was the first man who had ever treated her like a lady. He loved her for who she was, not for what she could do for him. It was Caleb's third marriage and Rikki's first.

The honeymoon lasted two years.

After that, Rikki felt out of place in the circles that Tate inhabited. Only in the movies could a Vegas showgirl fit in with the debutantes of Atlanta. She turned back to drugs for a year or two and then, when Caleb seemed to be more interested in work than paying attention to her, she began a series of affairs with at least three different men. She only used first names in her counseling sessions, and it was hard to tell if those names were real or fictitious. Gillespie never pressed for details about their identities.

According to Gillespie's notes, Caleb Tate found out about two of the affairs, and both times Rikki promised that it would be the last. About nineteen months before her death, just after Caleb had uncovered the second affair he learned about, Rikki began attending a neighborhood Bible study. She eventually went to a charismatic church service with one of the women in the study and, in the sort of high drama that characterized Rikki's life, went through a radical salvation experience. From what she told Dr. Gillespie, she thought her new faith would solve the marital strife, but it only made things worse.

In the year prior to her death, she had fights with Caleb about how vocal she should be about her faith. When she decided to sue the owners of Internet sites still displaying her topless pictures, Caleb advised against it.

The one entry that I found the most disconcerting from a prosecutor's perspective was a note from about three months prior to Rikki's death. It reflected a phone call from Caleb Tate to Dr. Gillespie, expressing a concern that Rikki was back into her drug habit. She seemed, according to Caleb Tate, to be out of it all the time and more lethargic than ever. Gillespie confronted Rikki about it, and though she denied any drug use, he suspected she might have been lying.

As I read the notes, I was surprised at Caleb Tate's response to Rikki's affairs. He had forgiven her not once but twice. And I had a hard time reconciling Caleb's phone call with my theory of the case. Maybe he had already started drugging his wife and was setting up a sophisticated alibi, but that seemed a bit reckless for a man who planned as meticulously as Caleb. If nothing else, it would make Gillespie more sensitive to signs of drug abuse. And what if Gillespie talked Rikki into rehab?

On the plus side, there were no suicidal thoughts by Rikki reflected in the notes. And Rikki's affairs could cut both ways. Yes, they showed Caleb to be a forgiving husband. But they also helped establish motive. Rikki and Caleb had been sleeping in separate rooms for two years. Their marriage was one of convenience. Caleb liked having a trophy wife on his arm when he went to his high-society events. Rikki liked the creature comforts Caleb provided and enjoyed living the good life of an Atlanta housewife.

Maybe Rikki had become too expensive a trophy. Maybe Caleb had found somebody else and didn't want to pay a fortune in alimony to a third ex-spouse. His second divorce had cost him a king's ransom.

It was nearly four in the morning when I finished reviewing the records. Since I had given LA a copy of them, I sent him an e-mail reminding him that the records were confidential and to make sure the press didn't get their hands on them. **Frankly, they don't help our case, and they paint Rikki in a bad light. She had a hard life, and I want to make sure we don't tarnish her reputation any more than we have to.**

I was surprised to get a reply before I had even shut down my computer.

I agree. Now get some sleep.

I fired back another e-mail. **You should talk.**

Three hours later, when I woke up and turned on my computer, the *Atlanta Times* already had the story prominently featured on its website: "Tate's Psychiatric Records Reflect a Troubled Marriage."

20

MACE JAMES STOOD BEHIND Chris Brock, arms folded across his chest. On the other side of the bulletproof glass was Antoine Marshall, speaking into the telephone, his face less than two feet from the son of the woman he was convicted of killing. Antoine thanked Chris for coming and told Chris he was sorry to hear that his father had passed away. He said it without the least bit of irony, but all three men knew that if not for Chris's father, Antoine would not be facing his own execution in 123 days.

Mace had done everything possible to attack Robert Brock's credibility on appeal. At the trial, Caleb Tate had tried to introduce an expert witness to talk about the reliability of cross-racial identifications, but Judge Snowden hadn't allowed the testimony. To make his point another way, Tate had kept his client out of the courtroom the morning that Robert Brock took the stand. In an effort to show how suggestive the police lineup had been, Tate put together his own lineup, but he used men who more closely resembled Antoine Marshall. In addition to a year-old picture of Marshall, Tate's lineup included four other convicted felons who had been out on probation when Laura Brock was killed. After staring at the photos for an inordinately long time, Robert Brock admitted that he wasn't 100 percent certain which of the men was the intruder.

From there, Tate had attempted to hang Robert Brock with his own words. He started asking questions about closing arguments Robert Brock had given in other cases, stressing the unreliability of cross-racial eyewitness identifications. But Masterson had objected, and Judge Snowden had quickly sustained the objection.

When Tate sat down, Judge Snowden undermined the entire cross-examination by asking some pointed questions of her own. Mace had made this conduct a linchpin of his appeals, but four separate appellate courts had found nothing wrong with it. Nevertheless, Mace had practically memorized the exchange.

Judge Snowden: It's been more than a year since your wife's murder, Mr. Brock. Do you think your memory of the defendant's face was better on the night that it happened or as we sit here in court a year later?

The Witness: It was definitely better then. In fact, every time I closed my eyes that night, I saw his face.

Judge Snowden: Mr. Tate seems to be implying that you have very little exposure to or interaction with the African American community. Can you tell the court what percentage of your clients are African American?

Caleb Tate: Your Honor, I have to object to the court's questions. Cross-racial identifications are problematic regardless of how much exposure we might have to other races.

Judge Snowden: As you know, Mr. Tate, the jury will decide the reliability of Mr. Brock's eyewitness identification. I just thought it might be helpful if we provide them with all the relevant information.

Caleb Tate: I believe Your Honor ought to allow the district attorney to try his own case.

Judge Snowden: Overruled, Mr. Tate. Now sit down. If you want to ask follow-up questions, you may do so when I'm done.

Caleb Tate: Just note my objection, Judge. And I'd like the record to reflect that the court is raising her voice at me in front of the jury.

Judge Snowden: Sit down, Mr. Tate!

Caleb Tate: Yes, Your Honor.

Judge Snowden: Now, Mr. Brock, you may answer the question.

The Witness: I don't know the exact percentage, Your Honor. But I would say the majority of my clients are African American.

Mace hadn't been there, but Caleb Tate told him that the jurors, most of whom were black, had seemed particularly attentive during the court's questioning.

All of that was history now. And it wouldn't help to criticize Chris Brock's dead father at this meeting.

"He was a good man," Chris said.

Antoine nodded but didn't say anything.

"Why don't you tell Mr. Brock how your life has changed in jail?" Mace prompted. He tried to talk loud enough that his voice could be heard through the phone Chris was holding.

Antoine collected his thoughts and started his story. He and Mace had actually rehearsed this part, not because the narrative wasn't genuine but because Mace wanted to make sure his client hit all the right notes. Antoine's voice was tight and hoarse as he described his childhood—the father he never knew, the gangs where he found a sense of belonging, the drugs he started experimenting with before his fourteenth birthday. Crack and meth became his drugs of choice, and they were not cheap. He would move from mall to mall, shoplifting and pawning the merchandise. He tried part-time work but found he could make more money by breaking and entering people's homes. He started packing heat not because he ever intended to shoot anybody but because he had lost too many friends to gang violence.

Chris listened intently, never taking his eyes off Antoine. As the prisoner warmed to his story, he slowed down and became more animated.

"As you know, I was out on bond the night your mom got murdered. I was facing my third strike in ten years and a lot of hard time. You ever been high?"

Chris shook his head. "I never got into drugs."

"Man, it's all you can think about. I mean, if I didn't get my fix, I went berserk. I'd do *anything* to get my hands on more crack. I didn't even try holdin' down no job because I couldn't make money fast enough the way I was smokin' it and snortin' it up my nose. I had to steal stuff so I could keep the crack coming."

Antoine looked down, clearly ashamed of what he had done. Other inmates liked to brag about their past. Antoine wasn't one of them.

"I don't know. . . . I'm not trying to make no excuses. I'm just saying—it wasn't me. It was like some other brother just took over my body. I didn't even know when I woke up where I had been the night before."

Mace could tell that Antoine was doing his best to walk a tightrope. He would never admit to killing Laura Brock, but Mace had emphasized how important it was to have a repentant attitude. It seemed to Mace that Antoine was overdoing it, making it seem like he had done things he couldn't remember.

Antoine talked about the drugs some more, frequently slipping into language that would prompt an apology—"Sorry, Pastor."

"No problem," Chris would say.

Eventually Antoine worked his way around to the despair and depression that he had felt in prison. It had been hard quitting the drugs cold turkey, but it was one of the best things that ever happened to him.

At this point, Antoine nodded at Mace. "That man back there saved me," he said. "All these other dudes on death row are always complaining about their lawyers. Their lawyers don't take collect calls. They don't care about their cases. They're just trying to grab the headlines. But that man—he cares about me."

This wasn't exactly how they had practiced it. But Antoine had gone off script and was speaking from the heart. He swallowed, choked up, and paused to get his composure.

"One day I just asked the man: 'Why do you care about me?' You know what he said?"

Chris shook his head.

"He told me that Jesus Christ cared about him when he was guilty. He told me that he wanted to be the same kind of defender for me that Christ was for him. And you know what? That . . . blew me away." Antoine shook his head like he still couldn't believe it. "I mean, it was like, *man*, I never thought nobody would care about me after everything I'd done. But Mace showed me that was just the devil's lie."

Antoine had a few pieces of paper sitting next to him, and he showed them to Chris. "I prayed for Christ to forgive me, and I pray every night for you and your family." He held one paper so Chris could see it. Every inch of it was covered with tiny handwritten notes. Paper was a precious resource in prison.

"These are the things I pray for. You're on here. Your sister's on here. Your dad was too. . . ." Antoine couldn't bring himself to look at Chris, and the paper trembled a little in his hand. "You don't know how much it meant getting that letter saying you forgave me."

Antoine pursed his lips and put the paper down. He opened a Bible that was literally falling apart at the binding. "I want to be a preacher like you someday," Antoine said. "I think I've got the gift."

He showed Chris some pages in the Bible where he had made notes in the margins. "This is a sermon I put together on the woman at the well," he said. In small handwriting, covering all the margins on the page where John 4 was located, Antoine had written a sermon outline.

"I was going to ask you—but don't feel like you've got to do this—if maybe you could send me some of your sermon notes."

"Sure, I could do that."

"Thanks. Anyway . . ." Antoine seemed to be running out of steam. He furrowed his brow and then remembered something. "Oh yeah. Almost forgot. I get an hour a day with the other inmates. One of them figured out a way to do some tats with a—" Antoine suddenly remembered that he had a guard standing behind him. He cupped his hand over the phone and lowered his voice. "Anyway, I'll tell you some other time how we do it. But I knew that what Mace was saying was right. That Christ didn't just go to the *cross* for me, but he got beat up for me too. He got whipped. Well . . . you know."

At this, Antoine placed the phone down and stood slowly. The guard took a step forward. Antoine unzipped the front of his jumpsuit and shrugged the suit off his shoulders so that it hung from his waist.

Mace had not seen him without the jumpsuit on in a long time. The man had become shockingly thin. Mace could count every rib; Antoine's bony shoulders protruded like a prisoner of war's. At one time, his arms had had some definition, but now they were just skin and bones.

Mace knew what was coming.

Antoine turned so that Chris could see his back. Not surprisingly, he had tattoos on his neck, shoulders, and triceps. But there was one tattoo across the middle of his back that covered him from shoulder blade to shoulder blade. It was five letters scrawled out in a cursive style by the inmate who controlled the tattoo needle. It read simply: *Jesus*.

"Nice," Chris said.

21

AFTER ANTOINE PUT HIS jumpsuit back on and sat down, he shrugged. "Guess that's about it. I'm just trying to live for Jesus now. And if I die—I pray he'll help me get ready for that, too."

There was an awkward silence, and Antoine snuck a glance at Mace. Mace stared back at him with a silent message. *Let the pastor process this. It's his turn to speak now.*

Chris had brought his own Bible, and he had it out on the ledge on his side of the window. "I really appreciate your sharing the story of your conversion," he said. "If I didn't believe that God could save the worst of sinners, then I wouldn't be a pastor. In fact, God tells me that if I have hatred in my heart toward my brother, it's the same as if I've killed him. So in that regard, I've been convicted of murder too."

Though Chris didn't expand on that statement, the implications couldn't have been more clear. The person Chris had once hated—hated strongly enough for it to qualify as murder—was sitting right in front of him.

"And it's not only hatred," Chris continued. "I've struggled my whole life with things like pride and greed. So, Antoine, it looks like you're wearing that Bible of yours out. I'm going to read something that will probably sound familiar to you, and then I want to ask you a question. Is that okay?"

"Yes."

Chris flipped to a page toward the back of his Bible. "First John 1:8-10," he said, pointing to the verses. "'If we claim to be without sin, we deceive ourselves and the truth is not in us. If we confess our sins, he is faithful and just and will forgive us our sins and purify us from all unrighteousness. If we claim we have not sinned, we make him out to be a liar and his word is not in us.'"

Chris stared at Antoine for a moment, and the convict's eyes started darting around a little. He was always fidgeting, his nervous energy preventing him from sitting still. But it was more noticeable now.

"Antoine, I need to know and I need to hear it from you. Did you kill my mother? And are you asking me to forgive you for that? Because if you confess that and pray for forgiveness—not to me but to God—he *will* forgive you. But if we don't own our sin, how can we ask God to forgive us? It says right here—" Chris tapped his Bible with his finger like a good preacher, though the softness and urgency in his voice signaled a genuine concern for Antoine—"that his Word is not in us if we claim we have not sinned."

Antoine looked down, then turned in his own Bible to the same passage as if checking it out just to be sure. He shook his head a little, a nervous tic, and looked straight at Chris. "I can't say I did something I didn't do. That right there is what would make me a liar. I can't lie to you, Pastor. You're a man of God."

Chris kept his gaze steady, his voice soft. "Are you denying that you killed my mother?"

Antoine rubbed his hand over his forehead, down his dreads. "I'm saying I don't remember nothin' from that time in my life. God as my witness, Preacher, I don't remember killing nobody. I don't remember breaking into your house. I swear to you, man—I never shot a gun in anger at anyone. That just wasn't me. I couldn't have done it. Not me, man. I *didn't* do it." Antoine's voice was getting sharper, more tense. Mace gave the slash sign across his throat but Antoine ignored him.

"I've been sitting in here for eleven years for something somebody else did. Pastor, you've got to believe that. I didn't shoot that woman. I never even been in your house. I know if I say I did it and start bawlin' and telling you how sorry I am, you would probably try to help me out. But I can't tell you something I didn't do. C'mon, man. I can't lie to you. I can't lie to God."

Mace took a step forward. "Antoine," he said, his voice firm. "Chris is not accusing you. But he's got to believe his own father's testimony. And if it were you sitting in his seat, you'd do the same thing."

"Sorry, Pastor," Antoine said, his voice more subdued. The humility was back. "I just—you don't know what it's like sitting in this same cramped room all day, no windows, praying for God to somehow make the truth come out."

Antoine opened his mouth as if to say more but decided against it. All three men let the silence hang there for a moment.

"I prayed for the same thing all the way through the trial," Chris said softly. "I only wanted the truth to come out. And I believe my prayers were answered."

"I'm sorry you don't believe me," Antoine replied. "And I'm going to keep praying for you every day." His fidgeting had become a full-blown tic, sporadic little movements of the head. Mace had seen it a few times before when his client was under pressure. "But I didn't kill your mama. And I can't say that I did."

◁▷

In the parking lot, Mace tried to do some damage control. "He's never wavered on the issue of his innocence," Mace said. "But don't forget what he said before. He doesn't remember half the stuff he did because he was high most of the time."

"I understand that," Chris said. "And I've lost a lot of sleep about today's meeting, praying about what I should do. But I can't write a letter asking the parole board for mercy if I don't think your client is repentant."

It was a gut punch for Mace. He had anticipated this result, but he had always held out hope. "I understand," he said.

Chris handed Mace his Bible. "Looks like your client could use a new one," Chris said. "Could you make sure he gets this? And let him know that I'm praying for him, too."

22

ON MONDAY, APRIL 9, Detective LA Finnegan and a tribe of four Milton County police officers and evidence techs executed a second search warrant on Caleb Tate's mansion. They wanted to see if they could find strands of Rikki's hair for testing—perhaps from an old brush—that might generate results different from the hair on her head when she died. They also needed detailed information from Tate's computer. The court had authorized the warrant on the condition that a special master oversee the retrieval of data. The court was worried that there might be information on the hard drive pertaining to Tate's other cases that was protected by the attorney-client privilege.

Somebody—and I was pretty sure I knew who it was—had tipped off the media so the local TV stations could show live footage of the police swarming Tate's home. They also ran excerpts from the affidavit we'd filed in support of the search warrant.

Unfortunately, we found little additional information, on the computer or otherwise, that helped our investigation. Tate had done his spring cleaning after the first search. And then, the day after the second search, he struck back.

LA sent me a text just before noon on Tuesday with the latest. **WVRC doing an exclusive interview with Tate 2nite. 6:30 news. 10 minutes.**

I called LA to make sure I had it right. "They're going to interview him about the case?"

"Not just that," LA told me. "He's taking a polygraph on the air."

"What?"

"The man's got a flair for the dramatic."

◁▷

We gathered in the conference room to watch the big show—me, Regina, LA, and a half-dozen other staff members and attorneys from our office. Masterson was on the campaign trail. I had invited Dr. O'Leary, the medical examiner, but she had other pressing work.

The program started with an earnest young reporter named Lori Conrad asking Tate questions about his wife's death. Conrad was one of the most popular television reporters in the Atlanta market. She sat face to face with Tate, the way the big-name reporters did on *60 Minutes*. After a few softball questions, Conrad got to the point.

"Despite everything you've said, there are still some who believe that you poisoned your wife. What would you say to them?"

Caleb looked smug and seemed torn between looking at Lori and staring directly into the camera. "I've been mostly silent since my wife's death because I knew that defending myself would mean talking about some very private things in our lives—things that might tarnish Rikki's memory. But I've finally come to realize that she would not want this to be a double tragedy. We loved each other. And as tragic as her death was, she would not want that tragedy compounded by having me blamed for it."

Caleb swallowed hard and continued. "As you probably know, Lori, you can tell how long someone has been ingesting drugs by testing their hair. Drugs bond to the roots of the hair and become part of the hair shaft as the hair grows out. I'm assuming that the investigators have tested Rikki's hair. If they have, they should release those results."

"What do you think those results would prove?" Lori Conrad asked.

"That my wife had been abusing narcotics for a very long time."

When Tate said it, with that cocksure attitude of his, I glanced quickly around the room. It was the first time in the case that I wondered whether Tate had a source inside our investigation. If we indicted, we would have to reveal the hair-testing results. But right now, there was no way he should know about them. Unfortunately, his assessment was right on the money. The hair results had confirmed six months of drug ingestion.

Others in the room seemed transfixed by the interview, unperturbed by the hair-testing comments.

"But some of our viewers might think you had been slowly poisoning her," Conrad said. "How would you respond to that?"

Tate smirked as if it was ludicrous that he had to put up with such far-fetched allegations. "I would respond the same way I responded to the investigators and the DA's office. I told ADA Jamie Brock, who is spearheading this investigation, that I would cooperate fully. I said I would come in and answer questions, produce documents they needed, let them search my house as often as they needed, or take a polygraph test. I have nothing to hide."

Lori Conrad scrunched her face into a confused look, one that seemed rehearsed. I felt my stomach clench. I knew what was coming next.

"Did it surprise you that Ms. Brock was handling this case?"

"I'll say this: I was surprised that out of twenty-six attorneys in the DA's office, they chose the one person whom I have a history with. You may recall that I defended the man accused of killing Ms. Brock's mother."

When Conrad let the answer linger for a second, it felt to me as if the other attorneys in our conference room were stealing sideways glances at me. I braced myself.

"What did Ms. Brock tell you when you offered to cooperate?"

Caleb couldn't resist a little shake of the head. "She basically went off on me. She told me I had better watch myself. She told me if I gave her even the slightest bit of rope, she would use it to lynch me from the nearest tree."

Conrad acted startled. "She said that—'lynch you from the nearest tree'?"

"Those were her exact words."

A few of the ADAs in the room registered their disapproval at the dramatic tone of the interview. Those hadn't been my exact words, but still I felt my face turn red as I realized that Tate had set me up.

"That's why I came to you," Caleb Tate said to his host. He appeared sincere. Hurt.

I wanted to throw something.

"The DA's office wouldn't accept my offer to take a polygraph, so I asked if you'd be interested in doing one on the air."

I scowled at the audacity of it. I hoped the public would see through this.

Lori Conrad turned sideways to the camera, proud of herself for landing such an impressive stunt. "We brought in Dr. Stanley Feldman, one of the top polygraph analysts in the country. Earlier today, he sat down with Caleb Tate and administered an exhaustive test." She paused for effect, then turned back to Caleb. "We're going to show the viewers some footage from that test and then, after the break, we'll have Dr. Feldman on live to give us the results."

Once more she turned to the camera. The cheese factor was off the charts. "Even Mr. Tate does not know what Dr. Feldman concluded."

As the advertisements rolled, my friends in the DA's office jumped to my defense. Tate was a grandstander. Polygraphs were notoriously unreliable. Experienced liars like Tate could fool them every time. This was just a publicity stunt from a desperate defendant. The whole city would see it that way.

But Regina Granger was silent. So, too, was LA. I could tell he wasn't used to being outflanked in the media.

Dr. Feldman made quite a show of it after the break. He talked about the mechanics of the polygraph test and how it could detect even the slightest increases in heart rate, blood pressure, breathing, and perspiration. Yes, there were some hardened liars who were able to game the exam, but he had ways of telling whether somebody was trying to fake it. That was most definitely not the case here. Feldman was 100 percent convinced that these results were accurate; he would stake his formidable national reputation on it.

"How many polygraphs have you administered?" Lori Conrad asked.

"I don't know. Probably a couple thousand. Maybe more. Frankly, I don't even try to keep track."

Satisfied, Conrad asked the question everyone was waiting for: "So what's your conclusion? Did Caleb Tate poison his wife?"

"Absolutely not."

"Did Caleb Tate provide any of the drugs that caused Rikki Tate's death?"

"Absolutely not."

"In a court of law, you are required to express scientific opinions to a reasonable degree of scientific certainty. Do you have that kind of certainty with regard to this test?"

"I am familiar with the standard," Dr. Feldman said. "And my level of certainty here is well beyond the standard required for admissibility in a court of law."

The camera zeroed in on Caleb Tate, tight enough so you could see the pores, and his expression showed genuine relief. He didn't seem to know that this result was coming. Maybe he was just a really good actor, or maybe he didn't kill his wife. For a moment, even I had a flicker of doubt.

But only for a moment. "It's junk science," I said. "He'll never get that test admitted in this case, and he knows it."

"He just did," LA said.

23

TEN MINUTES AFTER Caleb Tate's media coup, I was called into Regina Granger's office. Masterson, who was campaigning in one of the far reaches of the state, was on speakerphone. Regina looked glum, and it was clear to me that she and Masterson had already been going at it.

"Jamie is here now," Regina announced.

"Regina says you watched the Tate interview with her," Masterson said.

"I did."

"We've got to put out a statement right away denying those lynching comments. I've already had a dozen reporters call. That whole episode taints the integrity of our investigation."

Masterson paused for a moment, and I decided not to answer.

"We could also put in the same release some verbiage about the unreliability of polygraph tests and urge everyone to withhold judgment until the police have completed their investigation. We need to have a measured but quick response."

In a prosecutor's office, there are things said and things left unsaid. That's especially true when it comes to legal ethics, where everyone tiptoes and talks in ambiguities.

Masterson was a wily veteran and one of the most straightforward and ethical men I knew. But you don't become DA without an extra portion of street smarts. I noticed he had never asked me if I made the statements. And that was no oversight. As long as he didn't know one way or the other, he could authorize the DA's spokesperson to issue a denial. It would be our word against Tate's.

But these were not the kinds of games I played. It was the same reason I could never bring myself to plea bargain. I had this idealistic view of justice where there were good guys and bad guys. And when you start blurring the lines—a white lie here, a little deal there—it becomes impossible to distinguish them again.

"What does Regina think?" I asked. It was playing Mom against Dad, but I needed some help.

Regina gave me a sideways look as if she didn't appreciate being put on the spot. "Regina thinks that no prosecutor in her right mind would threaten a defendant that way." Her voice was cold, and she clipped her words. "I would hope people in our office would appreciate how repulsive that imagery is to African Americans."

Regina glared at me, and I cast my gaze toward the floor.

"But I also told Bill I see no need to respond with any kind of public statement. It just dignifies what this clown did and deflects the focus from whether he killed his wife to whether someone in our office threatened him."

I nodded, though I didn't look her in the eye. I'd seen Masterson upset before, blustering about the office, chewing people out. But Regina was normally bubbly and cheerful, the grandmother who only saw the good in her grandkids. Seeing her this upset was unsettling.

"Let's cut the BS," Masterson said, his voice booming over the speaker. "Did you threaten to lynch him?"

I hesitated as my brain sifted through a hundred calculations. I had worked so hard the past four years, possibly harder than anyone. My integrity and judgment had never been questioned before. I was a rising star in the office, smart enough to know that a comment like this could be fatal to my career. I couldn't see myself in private practice. And I knew that nobody would ever be able to prove whether I said it or not.

But I also knew that I had to live with myself. Good guys make mistakes. But they don't lie to cover them up.

"Well?"

"I don't think I used the word *lynched*. But I did say something about stringing him up."

"A distinction without a difference," Masterson said. His voice was more resigned now, the tone of disappointment. Regina gave me a sympathetic glance.

"It's been a tough couple of weeks for her," Regina reminded the boss. "And it's not like Tate is a black suspect. We need to cut her some slack."

"It was stupid," I admitted. "I lost my temper. I've got no excuses."

Masterson made us both wait a full five or ten seconds that seemed even longer. I was mad at myself, embarrassed for the office, ashamed. Basically, I just wanted to melt into the floor.

"I need time to think about this," Masterson eventually said. "We'll need to sort through it and see if we can survive the blowback. But in the short term, we've got to do two things. First, Jamie issues an apology. Second, I take her off the case pending a full investigation. Although it may be a moot point if we can't get enough to indict."

I opened my mouth to protest, but Regina held up a hand. "I think that's a mistake," she said. "I'm okay with making Jamie apologize, but we can't let this publicity stunt dictate who handles the case. Put Jamie in front of the cameras, and let her do a complete mea culpa. She can talk about her mom and Tate's role in defending Antoine Marshall. She can mention losing her dad. The public will come around."

"We can't take that chance, Regina. It was a risk putting Jamie on this case to start with. We can't jeopardize the investigation."

"Bill, I think—"

"I'm not open for debate on this. Jamie, this is in your best interest. And frankly, none of this would be happening if you hadn't let this guy bait you into making some stupid comments."

"Yes, sir."

One thing I appreciated about my boss was that he didn't pull any punches, even when it hurt. You always knew exactly where you stood.

Yet this one was hard to swallow. If I ever needed somebody to cover my back, it was now. I felt like I'd given the last four years of my life to this office, and now the DA was leaving me flailing in the wind the first time I messed up. I wanted to ask him how much of this was covering his own rear in the political campaign. But my big mouth had already gotten me in trouble once, so I decided to swallow the words this time.

"Regina, why don't you help Jamie craft an appropriate apology, and I'll work with you on a statement about the investigation."

"I think Jamie's capable of doing her own apology," Regina said.

"Fair enough. Jamie, shoot me an e-mail within thirty minutes."

After the call, Regina asked if I needed to talk. I told her I thought things were pretty clear. I stalked down to my office, pounded out an e-mail apologizing for my insensitivity, and fired it off to Regina and Masterson.

When that was done, I headed home. I was tired of working late hours and getting no support in return.

24

I SPENT HOURS THAT NIGHT in my father's study, Justice lying next to the front window, while I obsessed over the blogs. I knew better than to surf the Internet and read all the vitriol from the hatemongers, but I couldn't help myself. The paper already had an article online about Tate's polygraph test and my "lynching" comment. My apology—short, sweet, and unconditional—was contained in the final paragraph. The comments following the story were brutal. One person called me the Mark Fuhrman of the DA's office. More than half the negative comments were aimed at Bill Masterson—another alleged Republican racist who tolerated folks like me in his organization.

I had a few defenders. One said this entire thing was overblown and that Tate had no business playing the race card. Another guy, who didn't attach his name, said my comments sounded presidential, citing an Andrew Jackson quote when the South threatened to secede from the Union: "If any man has been found to be plotting secession, I will find the nearest rope and hang him from the nearest tree."

But many of my defenders were explicitly racist. And seeing the online fury my statement had elicited, I felt more ashamed than ever.

Earlier that day, I had been angry at Masterson for not standing up for me. But as I spent time online, I realized that he had no choice. I was lucky I hadn't been suspended from the department altogether.

It was astonishing how one stupid comment and a clever media ploy by Caleb Tate could turn the momentum so quickly. I felt like I had betrayed not only the DA's office but also my family's quest for justice.

I was still in my dad's study at nine thirty when I saw a small sports car come flying around the corner into the cul-de-sac. There were only seven houses on our cozy little court, and from watching out the window in my dad's study, I knew by heart the types of cars that came and went. Once in a while, someone would come in and hang a U-turn, but this car came straight into my driveway and parked behind my dad's car. It was a red convertible, a car I had never seen before, and I wondered if the press was going to start stalking me over this story. I quickly left the study before I could be seen and peeked through a window in the dining room. Justice, on the other hand, stayed at the picture window in the study, his tail straight up and wagging, barking to welcome the new visitor to the Brock estate.

To my surprise, LA got out of the car and walked up the hill toward the house. He was wearing jeans with holes in the knees, a white T-shirt, and sandals. Definitely off duty.

What was he doing here?

The doorbell was Justice's cue to go bonkers, which was exactly what he did. I commanded him to sit, and he crouched into a near-sitting position, his butt a few inches from the floor, ready to pounce. His tail was wagging fiercely, he was already hyperventilating, and his wild eyes were focused on the handle of the door.

I cracked the door open, and Justice rammed through, jumped on LA, and began licking the poor man and rubbing against his legs.

"Hey, big fella," LA said. I could tell by the way he started scratching Justice's back that LA had a dog.

"Think your mom will let me in?" he asked Justice.

"You got a search warrant?" I asked.

He patted his pockets. "Uh . . . left it at the office."

I showed him in and Justice calmed down. A little. He fetched a rope toy, hoping LA would play tug-of-war.

"You want anything to drink?" I asked. "Or something to eat? I've probably got some two-week-old funeral food."

He smiled and showed off the dimples. According to my sources, that smile was nearly legendary for putting female witnesses at ease, even to the point of telling LA their deepest secrets. And now I realized I had *already* been acting a little stupid, trying a joke that was moronic at best.

I decided to keep my guard up.

LA and Justice had taken center stage in the family room, flexing their muscles. Justice hunched down, one end of the rope between his teeth, jerking as hard as he could. LA smiled and laughed while he egged Justice on with some trash-talking. I couldn't help but notice the muscles in LA's right arm, the one pulling the opposite end of the rope. I made an effort not to stare.

"I actually didn't have supper yet," LA said. "And funeral food wasn't exactly what I had in mind." He dropped his end of the rope— *darn*—and rubbed Justice's head. "You win, buddy. You're too tough for me."

He stood and showed me the dimples again. "Great dog."

"Yeah."

"Listen, I've got some theories about the Tate case that I want to bounce off you. Wanna go grab a bite?"

"I'm not on the Tate case anymore." *Where have you been?*

"I know," LA said. He knelt down and started petting Justice again. "But I thought as a completely disinterested observer with total objectivity, you might be a good person for me to talk to. And I hear there's an outside possibility that if you behave yourself and kiss all the right rings, they might ultimately allow you the honor of working 24-7 on the case again so you can make Masterson look good at trial."

Despite my cynical man-shield, I was starting to like this guy. As for Justice, he was on his back, allowing LA to rub his stomach. "Well . . . I actually haven't eaten either."

"I'll take that as a yes. But we'll have to take your car," he added.

"What's wrong with yours?"

LA gave me a hurt look as if he were shocked that anybody could suggest something was wrong with his car. "It's a Mazda MX-5 Miata with heated leather seats, a turbo-charged engine, and a six-speed manual transmission. Best car on the road. But it does have one glaring weakness."

I'm not much of a car person, so I gave him a bored, unimpressed look.

"It's only got room for two," he said. "When I take my dog, I drive the Element."

Okay, this guy was good. The way to a woman's heart is straight through her dog. But I wasn't going down without a fight. And I made a mental note—two vehicles on a detective's salary.

"I don't like to leave him in the car that long, especially at night."

"Who said anything about leaving him in the car? I say we get the food to go and eat in the car with him. We can stop by the grocery store and get him a rawhide."

"You've got a dog, huh?"

"An English bulldog," he said proudly. "Greatest breed going. . . . Well, maybe second greatest." He gave Justice a pat.

"What's his name?"

"It's a her. And her name is J-Lo."

"Figures," I said. Then I went to get my shoes.

25

WE DROVE to a nearby Steak 'n Shake and ate burgers and fries in the parking lot. For dessert, LA added a vanilla milk shake. He was sitting in the passenger seat sneaking fries into the backseat floor area, where Justice anxiously awaited the next installment.

"He's not allowed to have people food."

LA quickly showed me both open palms, his bottom lip sticking out. "I have no idea what you're talking about."

But Justice didn't know he'd been busted. He pawed at the outside of LA's seat as if he couldn't understand why the conveyor belt had slowed down.

"Bad dog," LA said.

I punched him playfully. "See what you've done?"

I then scolded Justice and made him climb up on the backseat, and the conversation with LA returned to the case.

We had two different theories about the polygraph. LA assumed that Dr. Feldman had been bought off. I thought it more likely that Tate was such an accomplished liar, he could beat the exam. I had talked to several prosecutors who said Caleb Tate could make the most outrageous arguments in his cases and act like he believed them 100 percent. I knew people who could self-delude to the point that they believed their own lies. I figured Caleb Tate was one of them.

But what really intrigued me was LA's theory about the hair evidence. "You remember that case out in Los Angeles where Kendra Van Wyck was accused of poisoning her backup singer after she found out that her husband and the backup singer had an affair?"

"Yeah. I've thought about the similarities." I'd done my research on the Van Wyck case as soon as I learned about the hair results in ours. Kendra Van Wyck was acquitted because hair testing proved her backup singer had been taking the drugs in question for a long time. But in a subsequent civil suit against Van Wyck, a hotshot young attorney named Jason Noble had proven that the hair results probably represented false positives from surface contamination—the result of improper washing techniques in the lab. The verdict on behalf of the backup singer's family had been nearly twenty million dollars. But I also knew that National Toxicology Testing, the lab used by Dr. O'Leary, had addressed any problems with the wash procedures.

"I asked our computer guys and the special master the judge appointed to check Tate's computer to see if he had ever accessed details of the Van Wyck case," LA said. "Even though they found cocaine in the backup singer's body—not a drug we found in Rikki's bloodstream—I just thought there were too many similarities for it to be coincidental."

LA, probably sensing that he had my undivided attention, stopped to take a bite of his cheeseburger. I could see where he was going. What if the Van Wyck case had somehow triggered Tate's plan for Rikki? What if Caleb Tate had secretly drugged his wife for six months so that her hair would be full of drugs from the roots to the outer ends? He could use the Van Wyck defense. Juries loved CSI-type evidence, and maybe Tate had created some of his own.

"About seven months ago, Tate pulled down several documents from the Van Wyck case on Westlaw. Not just the court's opinion but the briefs of the lawyers discussing the hair-testing issues in great detail."

LA was definitely proud of himself, and he took another bite to extend the drama. But I was already seeing holes in his theory. According to Gillespie's notes, Rikki Tate had problems with drugs off and on well before Caleb Tate accessed those legal documents.

"I also talked to some of Rikki Tate's friends about the change in her hairstyle," LA continued. He turned on the lights and showed me two pictures of Rikki. The first one was from a year earlier, when Rikki had long dark hair. The more recent one showed the short and layered look I recognized from the autopsy pictures.

"According to her friends, guess who pushed Rikki to get her hair cut?"

"Caleb Tate?" I asked hopefully.

"Told her he liked it short. Told her it made her look younger and hotter. She changed hairstyles about six months ago, and according to her friends, he heaped on the praise. A month before her death, she got another trim. Conveniently short."

And it was also convenient, I knew, that Tate had already disposed of his wife's old hairbrushes and other toiletries. "But what about Gillespie's notes? She had addiction issues for years."

"I thought about that. But to me the notes seemed to suggest that she would go through periods of recovery and then slide back into addiction. Off and on. She tried to quit again after her religious conversion. Plus, we don't know how many pills she was taking or how often. We do know that Caleb Tate is a control freak. Maybe he read the Van Wyck case and started slowly pumping these narcotics into her. A pill here and there in her food, whatever. He increases the dosage over time to make her look like a typical addict. He convinces her to get a haircut so we can only see the pattern for the last six months, a dramatically higher level of drugs in her system, and then . . . boom. He gives her a megadose, and he's free to go marry that cute little legal assistant of his."

"You've got more on the legal assistant?"

"I made a graph of Tate's phone calls." LA pulled out another set of documents. "He spent a lot of time on the cell phone with her. I can't prove it yet, but Caleb definitely had something going on the side."

LA had been working a lot harder than I'd thought. But we still couldn't put the drugs in Tate's hands. And phone calls were a far cry from an affair. Still, even this small bit of progress made me wish I hadn't been suspended from the case.

"I don't know," I said. "If anybody checked our phones, they'd find a lot of calls to each other."

"And . . . ?"

"And we're not having an affair. We work together. We've got a big case. . . ."

"Not yet."

"Not yet *what*? What does that mean?"

LA smiled his best sly, shy, melt-the-girl's-heart grin. "Not yet we don't have a big case. But I'm working on it."

I snorted. We both knew what he was really working on.

He wiped his hands on his pants and then handed me another photo. It was a shot of Rikki Tate's hands.

"What do you see?" he asked.

"Manicured hands. Bright-red fingernail polish. Surface veins."

"And long fingernails," LA added. "You know what you can do with fingernails?"

I thought for a second, and it hit me. "Please tell me you can grind them up, autoassay them, and test them for chemicals."

He smiled, nodding. "Yep. And from the lengths of those babies from the cuticles to the tips, I'd say two years' worth. Fortunately, the Van Wyck case didn't involve fingernail testing."

I finished my meal and put my trash in the bag, wadding it up. "Why are you telling me about this stuff now? I don't even know when or if I'll be back on this case."

He took a long slug of his milkshake, slurping as his straw caught air at the bottom. "I don't suppose you'd be willing to go on the air and give a tearful apology," he said. "Tell everybody about your dad dying. Tell them how this man who called your dad a liar got in your face and scoffed at you. Tell them how sorry you are for allowing your passion for justice to cause you to lose all sensitivity. You could melt a few hearts with those big brown eyes, especially if you could get them to brim with tears."

"Fake crying's not really my thing."

"Didn't think so. That's why I've got a plan B. Make sure you check the eleven o'clock news tonight on WATL."

"For what?"

"You'll see." And that was all he would say about the matter. Despite my cajoling, begging, and even pouting, I couldn't squeeze another word out of him about the upcoming newscast.

When we returned home, LA got out of my 4Runner, let Justice out the back, and gave him some love. Then he stood to face me.

"We're going to get you back on this case," he said. "You're the best lawyer in the DA's office, and I'm not willing to go to war with anyone else."

This man hardly knew me. Still, I appreciated his vote of confidence, especially on a night like tonight.

"Thanks."

He told me to take care of myself, jumped into his sports car, and backed out of the driveway.

I had clearly underestimated the man, once again proving that Justice was a better judge of character than I was.

◁▷

That night, a WATL reporter interviewed Isaiah Haywood, my law school buddy. Isaiah was the perfect choice for the interview, and I assumed that LA had met him at my father's funeral. Isaiah was not just a close friend; he was African American and a former football star at the University of Georgia. Most people in Atlanta knew of him. He now worked for a prominent sports agency.

"Jamie Brock is one of my best friends," he told the reporter. "I can guarantee you one thing—that woman does not have a racist bone in her body. I first met her in law school. And racist girls don't usually go out with dudes like me. In case you haven't noticed, I'm not exactly the redneck type."

Isaiah and I *had* been close friends. In truth, we had hung out together a lot, but I had refused every offer of a date. Yet I wasn't about to call the station to clarify.

"And I find it insulting that one of the other television networks would let this white criminal-defense attorney from an all-white law firm hide behind racism as if his people had somehow been the victims of lynchings." Isaiah was getting fired up now, his neck muscles tight. The camera zoomed in so viewers could better see the fire in his eyes.

"I've done some checking on Mr. Tate, and I found that his firm only employs two African Americans. One is a personal driver for Mr. Tate and some of his high-paid partners. The other is a courier."

Isaiah took a breath, and the reporter interjected: "Why is that relevant?"

"Because a guy who grew up in Buckhead with rich white parents and now runs with the country-club crowd shouldn't be allowed to trot out the race card against a young attorney whom I know to be one of the most tolerant and open-minded people I've ever met."

The reporter wrapped up the interview with a cutaway line to the anchor while Isaiah posed for the camera. I wanted to kiss the TV. Instead, I called Isaiah immediately.

"You didn't have to do that," I said.

"I got your back, Jamie. Just make sure you get a conviction."

◁ ▷

At midnight, I got my second unannounced visitor of the night. I had fallen asleep on the couch, and Justice went crazy when he heard the doorbell. I jerked awake, and my heart banged against my chest. I tried to collect my thoughts, separating the nightmare I had been experiencing from the reality I had just rejoined. I shuffled to the front door and turned on the porch light.

It was Chris.

I opened the front door, and Justice mauled him.

I had to blink twice to make sure I wasn't still dreaming. Chris lived several hours away in the mountains.

"Thought you could use a little company tonight," he said. "Got any extra rooms?"

He came into the hallway, and I gave him a big hug. But before I could say anything, before I could even thank him for coming, I started crying. I put my head on his shoulder and let the tears flow. To be honest, I wasn't sure whether I was missing my father or thankful for my brother or mad at everything that had happened at work. I just knew I had to let it out.

"Okay," I said when I finally pulled myself together. "I needed that. You can go back home now."

26

CHRIS DIDN'T GO HOME. Having him in the house overnight allowed me to get a good night's sleep. Knowing how much he hated being away from Amanda and the girls made it even more moving that he had made the trip. The next morning, I took Justice out for a run and struggled to complete my short three-mile course. The emotional trauma of the last few weeks had caught up with me.

After the run, Chris and I ate breakfast together, and he told me about his trip to the Georgia Diagnostic and Classification Prison in Jackson. Although I wished he had filled me in before going, I was proud of my brother for standing up to Mace James and Antoine Marshall.

After breakfast, I put on my black pin-striped skirt and jacket that I'd always considered my best power suit and went a little heavier than normal on the makeup. I used some concealer to get rid of the dark circles under both eyes and strapped on a stylish new watch I had bought last Christmas. On the way out the door, I hugged Chris and thanked him for coming.

"Do you need anything?" he asked. I knew he needed to get back to Rabun.

"I'll be all right."

At work, I went about my normal business of handling the morning docket, which consisted mostly of motions to suppress and bond revocations. Though nobody said anything about the prior night's news report, I could tell that most of the defense attorneys were happy I was getting my turn in the hot seat. By eleven thirty I was back in my office, working on a memorandum to Bill Masterson on the issue of

Caleb Tate's polygraph test. I knew that Masterson wouldn't be worried about the admissibility of the test into evidence—the law was clear on that. But I was concerned that he might give it too much weight in his evaluation of the case.

Because most law enforcement agencies rely on polygraph tests as one of their investigative techniques, the reliability of the test tends to be greatly overestimated by cops and prosecutors. I knew better, based in part on my experience with Antoine Marshall's appeal, where the admissibility and reliability of the test had been major issues.

In my memo to Masterson, I cited a National Academy of Sciences report showing that fifty-seven of the eighty research studies supporting the reliability of polygraphs came to their conclusions using flawed data. The NAS study concluded that the level of a polygraph's reliability was "greater than chance, yet short of perfection." There was a high percentage of false positives, and at the same time some famous criminals had beaten polygraph tests on more than one occasion. Aldrich Ames, for example, a notorious Soviet spy working for the CIA, passed with flying colors—not once but twice.

I also explained how people could defeat the test by manufacturing a crisis during the control questions. Some suspects would force themselves to think about their most painful real-life experience while others would bite the insides of their cheeks so the pain would increase their breathing and heart rate. These same persons would calm themselves when facing the relevant questions and make sure they kept their breathing under control. I thought Tate had probably taken the test a few times off air, mastered these techniques, and then subjected himself to the televised test we had watched.

I proofread the memo a couple of times and added a final paragraph stating that I knew I was no longer on the case but hoped this might help whoever took over.

That afternoon, I took the memo to court so I could personally deliver it to Masterson. I had to give the guy credit—while other DAs delegated all of the cases to their top assistants, Masterson insisted on trying some of the more-serious felonies. On this day, he was handling a murder charge against a man accused of killing a prostitute. Granted, he was probably getting some political mileage out of the case, but at least he wasn't afraid to get his hands dirty. In fact, Masterson looked like he was rather enjoying himself.

The defense attorney used a lot of electronic exhibits and relied heavily on PowerPoint during his closing argument. But Masterson just paced around the courtroom and thundered against the defendant—old school and very effective. It was the kind of dominating performance that I hoped to be able to replicate one day. I found myself studying his style as I had done so many times before. *When and why does he pause? How does he use voice inflections? How does he incorporate the testimony and exhibits into what he's saying?* I knew I had to maintain my own style in the courtroom, but I was humble enough to realize that I could learn a lot from an old pro like Bill Masterson.

When the jury retired to deliberate, Masterson came back to where I was seated and greeted me warmly. I was always a bundle of nerves while the jury was out deliberating, but Masterson appeared ready to move on to the next thing as if the verdict was a foregone conclusion.

"I did a little memo on the reliability of polygraph tests," I said, handing him the paper.

He glanced at it and gave it back to me. "Can you e-mail me an electronic copy?"

"Sure," I said, a bit disappointed. I'd been hoping we could at least discuss it.

"You got a minute?" Masterson asked.

"Yeah."

He led me out of the courtroom and down the hallway to a small conference room. We talked for a few minutes about his closing argument. I was sitting up straight in my chair while Masterson slouched back, draped over his chair, legs crossed at the ankles. He loved it when other attorneys came to watch him in court, and he was eager to get my evaluation. "What did you think of my closing? Anything you would have done differently? What's your take on the jury?"

I answered his questions, and then he abruptly changed direction. "What did Caleb Tate say to you before you told him you wanted to lynch him?"

"Well . . . again, I don't think I used that particular word. But he basically told me that if we tried to indict him for the murder of his wife, it would get ugly for him and for us. I took it as a threat."

Masterson grunted and I got his message—prosecutors need to have thick skin. "You sure he didn't call you some kind of name?"

"I'm sure."

"It would help if he cussed you out."

"But he didn't."

"Okay, have you ever used the N-word or made any racial slurs against anybody?"

"You know me better than that."

"Just answer the question."

"No. Never."

"This guy Isaiah Haywood did a nice job for you last night."

"I saw."

Masterson stretched a little. "You think they'll find him guilty?"

"Caleb Tate?"

Masterson laughed. "No, the defendant in the case I just tried."

I shrugged. "I've never seen you lose one yet. Some would say you cherry-pick 'em."

This made Masterson smile. "You get to be DA, you can cherry-pick 'em too."

"No thanks. I hate politics."

Masterson checked his watch and apparently decided he needed to get back to the courtroom. "I guess that wraps it up," he said.

I furrowed my brow. I was having a hard time keeping up with him today. "Wraps what up?"

"My investigation. I'll probably wait a few days before I issue an official report."

"That's it?" I wasn't sure I had heard him correctly. "That's your whole investigation?"

He gave me a sly look. "Are you saying I shouldn't trust you?"

"No, it's just—"

"Seems to me that you're still the best prosecutor for the job. If I let defense attorneys disqualify every prosecutor who stood up to them, it'd be impossible to run this office."

It felt like somebody had lifted a hundred pounds from my shoulders. "Are you saying—?"

"You'll get my report in a few days," he interrupted. "I'm just giving you fair warning that you shouldn't close your file out."

I wanted to give the guy a hug, but I decided to play it professional. Though I stayed calm on the outside, the party had started inside. "You won't be sorry."

He shrugged it off. "Next time, Jamie, keep your mouth shut."

"Yes, sir."

◁ ▷

Later that week, LA called with results from the fingernail tests. The levels of oxycodone and codeine in the fingernail segments that represented the last six months of Rikki's life were high, matching the hair results. But the levels from the fingernail segments that represented the year before that were barely detectable. Taken as a whole, the results indicated that she had probably started taking the drugs in earnest about six months or so prior to her death. "It might have been seven months," LA said, "which would explain the trace amounts in the older segments of her fingernails. Or she might have taken a few pills off and on during those earlier months. But nothing serious until the last six months of her life."

"That's good," I said.

"Baby, that's way past good."

I smiled. It was our first major break.

"And one more thing. The older fingernail extracts also contained trace amounts of morphine."

"Morphine?" I asked.

"Could be a result of heroin use," LA said. "But O'Leary doubts it. When heroin breaks down in the body, it turns into morphine and some other metabolite. The lab didn't find that other metabolite. Makes O'Leary think that somebody slipped her morphine."

"But not recently? More than six months ago?"

"That's the way it looks."

27

THAT WEEKEND, I went to the gym with Dr. Gillespie for what we both knew was a therapy session. During my college years, I competed at a national level in kayaking and became a workout fanatic. During law school, I worked part-time as a trainer at a downtown gym. So it came as no shock that the big and somewhat-awkward psychiatrist had a hard time keeping pace with me.

I pushed him pretty hard because he needed it. But that didn't keep him, while catching his breath between exercises, from asking a lot of questions about how I was doing. I pretty much blew him off while we worked out, but afterward we grabbed bottles of water and sat down in an aerobics room that was not being used. Leaning against the wall, sweat pouring from his body, Gillespie told me to put the ambulance on speed dial.

He asked me again how I was coping with my father's death, and I told him the truth—not very well. Nightmares about the shooting from twelve years ago were coming back with a vengeance and I had been sleeping very little. In fact, I hated going to bed at night because I knew the nightmares would start. Gillespie said this didn't surprise him, given the fact that I was still living in the same house where my mother died.

He suggested some sleeping pills, and I politely listened but had no intention of following through. I had always been careful about what I put into my body, and even now, fighting with nearly debilitating sorrow, I was determined not to become dependent on chemicals just to survive.

I eventually managed to shift the conversation away from me and to my theory about Rikki Tate's death. "I know you can't discuss your sessions with her, but we do have your notes," I told Gillespie. "And we've learned a few other things."

I told Gillespie about the recent developments in the case, everything except the fingernail-testing evidence. We discussed the polygraph test, and I told him how I thought Tate passed.

He wasn't buying it.

"Caleb Tate is a control freak. Even if he practiced beating the machine and had done it four times in a row, he would have known that there was a substantial chance of getting a bad result on live TV, particularly with stakes that high and the adrenaline pumping. He doesn't strike me as the kind of person who would take that chance."

I stood and started stretching. First one arm, then the other. I suggested that Gillespie might benefit from a little postworkout stretching too.

He was now seated on the floor and made no effort to move.

"So what's your explanation for the test?" I asked.

"I'd check out Dr. Feldman," he said. "I've spent a lot of time in my professional career studying the polygraph and even testified about it a few times. If the test is administered right, it's not as easy to beat as you think. I see three possibilities. Either Feldman did a poor job, Caleb Tate took an uncharacteristic risk, or maybe Feldman is not as much on the up-and-up as his reputation suggests."

I sat down, spread my legs, and leaned toward my right leg, stretching the hamstring. I liked the way Gillespie was thinking. Like me, he was committed to the victim and therefore wouldn't even consider the reason some people thought the polygraph test came back negative—because Rikki Tate had died of an accidental overdose.

28

TUESDAY EVENING I received a text message from LA. **Can u come to the jail? ASAP?**

What's up? I texted back.

An interesting development in Tate. Let's talk when u get here.

I changed from shorts to jeans. Black short-sleeved T-shirt. A pair of cute black patent-leather flats. I fussed with my hair a little and told myself I wasn't doing it for LA. I was out the door in five minutes.

By eight thirty I was sitting in a small interview booth. LA stood behind me, and a surly-looking Rafael Rivera sat in front of me on the other side of the glass. We could have met with Rivera in an interrogation room, but LA didn't want to make Rivera feel too important.

The gangster sat there, insolent as ever. His facial hair had grown, his dreadlocks were fraying, and his eyes were red with hate. I hadn't noticed it on the day Caleb Tate handled his bond hearing, but Rivera's eyebrows seemed to come together in a permanent sneer. I was certain that he blamed me for the judge's denying him bond.

"I understand that you wanted to meet with me without your attorney present," I said, trying to sound as calm and authoritative as possible. There was nothing this man could do to me now.

"That's right."

"Then I need to record our conversation and ask you a few preliminary questions." I took out a digital recorder and placed it next to the small round metal grate at the bottom of the glass that allowed us to hear each other.

Rivera glanced at it, then returned his stare to me. "Okay."

I turned the recorder on and confirmed that he understood his right to legal counsel and that he had waived that right for purposes of this meeting. When I finished with the preliminaries, I gave him the floor. "You called me all the way down here. This better be good."

Rivera glanced at LA, who probably nodded or gave him some other signal. Then Rivera turned back to me, like he was sizing me up, and leaned closer to the metal slits.

"Don't worry, baby. It's good. I've got what you need to convict Caleb Tate." He said it slowly, confidently, biting off each word. "But I need to know what's in it for me."

I kept a poker face. "You've been around long enough, Mr. Rivera, to know that's *not* how it works. First of all, you came to the wrong person if you want to cut a deal. And second, even if I *did* cut deals, which I don't, I'd make you tell me everything you have first—it's called making a proffer—before I decide whether it's something I can use."

We sat quietly for a moment, staring at each other. I already knew the gist of what he wanted to tell me, but I had to hear it from him, not LA.

"I need immunity for this," he said. "Complete immunity. Not that other crap."

He was referring to something called "use immunity," which only guaranteed that we wouldn't use what he told us to prosecute a crime against him. We could still prosecute if we could prove the crime independently.

"I'm not promising anything or making any deals until I know what you're selling."

Rafael leaned even closer to the glass, glanced up at LA, and then lowered his voice and called me a name that brought LA flying in over my shoulder.

"Listen to me, you little punk," he said. "You've got about two seconds to spill your guts, or we're leaving, and you're going back to jail to rot for the next fifteen years."

I held up a hand and nudged LA back. Rafael shot a taunting grin at LA.

"We're done here," I said. I turned off the tape recorder and picked up the phone to have the deputy come get Rafael. "He's got nothing," I told LA.

Rafael leaned back in his chair and ran his eyes over me from my head to my waist. He rested his elbows on the arms of his chair. "What if I was the one who provided Mr. Tate with the drugs?"

The door behind Rafael opened, and a deputy stepped into the booth.

This time I smirked. "That's it?" I asked. "You wasted my time to tell me that? Why would anybody believe *you*?"

The deputy moved in and took his place behind Rivera, but the inmate made no effort to rise. "I'm speaking hypothetically here. But what if I could testify about how much oxycodone and codeine and promethazine—" he rolled the words off his tongue, proud that he knew the types of drugs that had been found in Rikki Tate's system, facts that the entire public knew as well—"I provided to Mr. Tate?"

"Anybody can read a newspaper and figure out those were the drugs found in Rikki Tate's blood. Your testimony would be destroyed on cross-examination."

"Let's go," the deputy said. "Get up."

Rivera still didn't budge. "What if I knew that he only started getting those drugs six months ago? What if I could provide two other witnesses who knew I was getting drugs for Mr. Tate? Hypothetically speaking, again, what would that be worth?"

This time, he had my interest. Nobody knew about our working theory that Caleb Tate had started pumping his wife full of the drugs just six months ago. The corroborating witnesses, on the other hand, were probably useless if they hadn't seen Rivera give Tate the drugs. Their testimony would be struck as hearsay.

"I sold him more drugs every month," Rafael said. "I even gave him some morphine one time. Maybe you should test the hair for that."

The deputy grabbed the shoulder of Rivera's jumpsuit and started pulling him up. "Move!"

"Wait," I said, raising a hand. LA huddled closer to my shoulder.

I turned the recorder back on. "Say that again," I demanded.

"The part about the morphine?"

"All of it."

He repeated his assertions for the recorder, and my mind raced through the possibilities. You learn early as a prosecutor that you don't get to prove your case with Boy Scouts and nuns. Yes, convicted felons will say anything to get out of jail, but they also know a lot of things. And right now, Rafael Rivera was providing details he couldn't possibly have known if they weren't true.

When he finished, I shut off the recorder and stared into his bloodshot eyes. I gave him the hardest look I knew how to give and waited a few seconds before speaking. "If one word of this gets back to Caleb Tate, it destroys any possibility of a deal. Got that?"

"I get that," he said confidently, as if he had just locked down a deal.

"These witnesses—did they see you give the drugs to Tate, or did they speak to Tate themselves?"

"Nah. But I told them about Tate when I bought the drugs."

"I want their names. And I'm going to check out every piece of information you tell me. If you're playing games with me, you'll regret the day you ever saw my face."

"Pretty face like that?" Rivera said arrogantly. "I doubt it."

I motioned to the deputy, and he took the scum out of my sight.

Rivera gave me the creeps, but LA and I both tended to believe him. If Caleb Tate wanted to poison his wife, it would make sense to get the drugs from somebody like Rivera—somebody Tate could easily discredit in court. Nothing had been said in the press about our theory of Tate and the six-month drug window or about the slight trace of morphine in the fingernail samples. How would Rafael Rivera know about any of that?

Yet the thought of putting Rivera on the stand as one of my witnesses made me sick. Even worse was the thought of rewarding him with a plea bargain for it.

When I crawled into bed that night, I kept seeing the sneering face of Rivera leaning toward me, his vulgar comments running through my mind. I thought about the witnesses, themselves gang members, who had been slated to testify against him in a prior murder case. They had disappeared, and their bodies had never been found.

How could I turn a man like that loose just to fulfill my personal vendetta against Caleb Tate?

29

GETTING A MEETING with Bill Masterson the next day was like trying to schedule an audience with the pope. He had some radio interviews and meetings with campaign advisers in the morning, then was heading south to Macon to speak at a luncheon for a local bar association. That evening he had to be in Savannah for a fund-raiser at the home of a wealthy socialite. "Can't this be done by phone?" he had asked.

"I really need to talk to you in person," I replied.

He gave me eighty-three miles—the distance from Atlanta to Macon on I-75. We were riding in the back of his RV, sitting at a small kitchen table, while a young intern from his campaign drove. The kid had country music playing in the cab, and that, along with the drone of the engine, gave me and the boss plenty of privacy.

I had an outline I was following and got about five minutes into it when Masterson's phone rang. He handled some campaign business and apologized. I picked up where I left off and a few minutes later was interrupted by another call. This time, when he finished, he put his BlackBerry on vibrate and holstered it.

"I'm all yours. But I don't need to hear about every piece of evidence. Just give me the punch line."

I launched into a quick summary of my conversation with Rafael Rivera, which finally seemed to grab his attention. When I explained that Rivera claimed he had started providing Tate with oxycodone and codeine just six months ago and also had provided him with morphine once, Masterson really perked up.

After I finished, Masterson chewed on it for a minute, blew his nose, and wolfed down a few fish crackers straight from the cardboard box. "What's your gut telling you?" he asked.

"That Rivera is the kind of scum who would rat out his own lawyer."

Masterson nodded. Carrie Underwood was playing in the background. This was not the way I had pictured it in law school. Making strategic decisions about murder cases in the back of an RV heading south for a Macon barbecue.

"You want to cut Rivera a deal?" Masterson asked.

"Not really. I think he's more dangerous than Tate."

Masterson grunted. "Maybe. But Rivera will screw up again. If we let him loose tomorrow, we'll nail him again in six months. Plus, the media is not howling about Rivera."

I wasn't so sure the boss was right about nailing Rivera. I thought about the undercover narcotics officer who had risked his life to put this man behind bars. And I also didn't think the press should be a factor in determining which of these two men—Rivera or Caleb Tate—should go free. In fact, this whole conversation made me uncomfortable.

"I've never cut a deal with someone like Rivera, and I'm not sure I could live with myself if I did."

Masterson lowered his eyebrows. More fish crackers, this time chased by a swig of Red Bull. "And you could live with yourself if you don't get enough to indict Caleb Tate?"

I shrugged. "I don't know."

Masterson rubbed his face and scratched the back of his head. He was used to these kinds of decisions, but that didn't make them any easier.

"Think you could get Rivera to serve two years and still testify?"

"I doubt it. He thinks he's got us. He'll want to walk on this one."

"Sure would be nice to nail Tate, wouldn't it?"

"The thought has crossed my mind."

"Want some fish crackers?"

"No thanks. I'm good."

Masterson stood and stretched, bracing himself as the RV sped down the road. He sat back down. "This is why I get paid the big bucks."

He took out a Dictaphone and dictated a memo to his executive assistant while I listened. The memo reassigned the Rafael Rivera case from me to him. He copied Regina Granger, who oversaw the allocation of case files. He put down his Dictaphone.

"You're working too hard anyway. Decided you might have one case too many."

I wasn't sure where he was headed, so I didn't know whether to thank him or protest. But I could tell from the look on his face that he'd made up his mind. I had always admired that about my boss. I would agonize over things, analyzing first one side, then the other. Masterson would hear two or three minutes of explanation, cut to the chase, and make a call.

"Just so you know, I'm gonna deal with Rivera. I need you to get a videotaped statement of his proffered testimony and double-check to make sure there hasn't been a leak about the morphine. Our next grand jury starts Monday. I've got a campaign to run and an office in controlled chaos. Think you could get the grand jury to indict Tate?"

I sat up straighter in my seat. We both knew that you could get a Milton County grand jury to indict Santa Claus for trespassing. Defense attorneys weren't even allowed in the grand jury room. In fact, we probably could have indicted Tate even without Rivera's testimony. But you don't go to the grand jury unless you're ready to go all the way.

Despite my enthusiasm for indicting Tate, a small voice was telling me to protest. If I put up a big-enough fuss, Masterson would probably rethink dealing with Rivera. What if Rivera killed somebody when he should have been behind bars?

But I kept my mouth shut. I wanted Caleb Tate so bad I could taste it. And I told myself that I wasn't the one who would be cutting the deal with Rivera. My boss had taken it out of my hands.

"Thought you'd never ask," I said.

"Good. We'll hold a press conference once we get the indictment and bench warrant. Get your friend LA to stage a perp walk. Make sure every station in Atlanta covers it."

I could tell Masterson was having fun. He would make a good attorney general. There was nothing he liked better than a big fight with someone he considered truly evil.

"I wish your dad could have seen this," he said.

He must have been reading my thoughts. And that's the other thing I appreciated about Masterson. He came across as big and gruff and uncaring. But comments like that one displayed his true nature. And in that way, he reminded me of my dad.

"Me too," I said.

30

I HAD FIVE DAYS to get ready for the grand jury. I needed to push aside the emotions from my father's death and pour myself into the Tate prosecution. During the day, I prepared my witnesses. I spent evenings in my war room at home, where the documents and exhibits mushroomed, overflowing to the kitchen and eventually the family room. Justice would beg to go out and play Frisbee, but I just turned him loose in the fenced-in backyard without me. I skipped my morning workouts. I stayed awake until two or three in the morning, drinking caffeine and preparing my case.

At the most inopportune moments, I would break down and cry, loneliness ripping at my heart. I couldn't plan for those moments, and they would always sneak up on me, unexpected, triggered by something small that reminded me of my dad.

On Friday night, a thunderstorm swept through. The wind howled, bending the big pine trees in the backyard, causing them to sway back and forth. As a little girl, I was always afraid that the trees would snap and fall on our house, but my father had used it as a teaching point. "Those trees know how to bend with the wind, Jamie. You don't have to worry about them. It's the oak trees that don't know how to bend— they're the ones to worry about."

Now the pines were dancing in the storm, casting long shadows into the family room through the large picture window. I could almost hear my dad's voice in the howl of the wind.

On the day of the grand jury hearing, I drove my father's 300M to court. Nobody had driven it since my dad passed away, but it seemed like a good way to honor him. I also carried his worn-out brown leather briefcase. He had carried the thing around for at least fifteen years, and the leather was dark on the handles from the residue of sweaty hands. There was stuff in the bottom—curled-up yellow stickies, some dead batteries, an old highlighter, pills that had escaped from a bottle. Who knew how long that junk had been in there?

I took the briefcase into the grand jury room with me and vowed that it would stay with me every step of Caleb Tate's trial.

31

AT SOUTHEASTERN LAW SCHOOL, Professor Mace James paced back and forth at the front of the large lecture hall, waxing eloquent about the cruel-and-unusual-punishment element of the death-penalty debate. One of Southeastern's other law professors gave James this forum a few times every spring in a second-year constitutional law class. Mace usually taught only clinics and didn't typically get a chance to impose his views on such a big class of students, so he always jumped at the opportunity. His friend on the faculty liked having the morning off.

Mace was being his provocative self, telling stories about innocent death-row inmates who had been exonerated by DNA tests and arguing that the death penalty disproportionately impacted low-income black males.

"We use the same method of execution that we use on the family dog when Fido gets old or bites one too many neighbors," Mace said. "How many of you have actually witnessed an execution?"

Nobody raised a hand.

"Then let me describe it to you."

As he did, the back door to the lecture room opened, and Caleb Tate slipped into one of the seats. Mace gave him a surprised look but continued speaking. When he had finished speaking, Mace debated a few of the conservative students for five or ten minutes before calling it quits. A line of students came down front for a little post-class discussion, but Mace shut them down and excused himself.

He walked up the steps to the back of the room and greeted Caleb. The two men couldn't have been more different. Tate was wearing one of his finer charcoal-gray suits and a white monogrammed shirt. Not a hair on his head was out of place.

Mace wore his favorite pair of jeans, with a hole in one knee that grew each time they were washed. Since it was April, he had on the flip-flops he would wear through the entire summer. He told people he had grown accustomed to them in prison and could never kick the habit. A backward baseball cap covered his bald pate.

Tate surveyed the classroom, probably taking in the sight of the female law students. "How do I get a job like this?"

"Get convicted of a felony and become a poster boy for rehab. Then the liberals will love you."

As soon as the words were out, Mace thought about Rikki Tate's death. Caleb probably didn't appreciate the felony wisecrack.

"Actually, that's why I'm here," Tate said. "Can we go someplace and talk?"

They made their way upstairs to Mace's office, and Mace moved a pile of papers from one of the guest chairs. He sat behind his desk, moving to the side so his view of Caleb Tate wasn't blocked by his large monitor.

Caleb glanced at the dry-erase board on the wall with a series of numbers crossed out, announcing that only 106 days were left until Antoine's execution. Appellate briefs and cases littered the floor.

The two men had established a decent rapport, considering the circumstances. Antoine Marshall had spent what little money he had on Caleb Tate's services as trial counsel. Tate's real motivation for taking the case was probably the enormous amount of publicity the case had generated. Then, once the verdict was in, the money was gone, and the case was old news, Tate had passed Antoine off to Mace's free legal clinic and the pro bono program at Knight and Joyner.

Often, appellate lawyers like Mace would base an appeal on the allegation that the defendant had received ineffective assistance of counsel at trial. Mace hadn't made such a claim; Caleb Tate had been anything but ineffective. And Tate had seemed to appreciate the way Mace handled his former client.

"You cut it a little close last time," Tate said.

"We aren't out of the woods yet."

"He's lucky to have you." Tate crossed his legs and tried to get comfortable. "But that's not why I'm here. It's about Rikki."

Mace nodded. "I'm sorry about your loss," he said.

Caleb blew out a deep breath, but it didn't seem to Mace like there was any sorrow attached to it. "You know they're after me," Caleb said. "I've had a running feud with Bill Masterson and Jamie Brock, and they think they can nail me on this. They're presenting the case to the grand jury right now. They'll have their indictment by tomorrow at the latest."

"I'm sorry to hear that," Mace said, though he wasn't sure what this had to do with him.

"Yeah, not as sorry as me." Caleb inhaled another deep breath and then said the last words Mace had expected. "I'd like to hire you as my lawyer."

"What?"

"I want you to represent me. I like the way you've been bird-dogging Antoine's case."

Mace had never lacked self-confidence, but he was realistic enough to know there had to be more to the story. Mace was an appellate lawyer who filed long-shot motions on behalf of death-row inmates. There were a hundred lawyers in Atlanta who could do a better job at the trial-court level than he could.

"I don't try cases; you know that. I taught trial ad for a couple of years, and I've done a few felonies, but I've never tried a capital case in my life. The closest I come to trials is when I file incompetent-assistance motions on appeal and complain about the job guys like you do in court."

Caleb didn't smile. He was all business, and Mace couldn't blame him. "That's one of the reasons I want to hire you. All the hotshot criminal-defense lawyers will want me to just sit there and shut up. I'm going to be actively involved in my defense, and I think your ego can handle that."

He said it as if Mace had already agreed to represent him. But Mace was compiling a mental list of excuses.

"I've got my hands full with Antoine's case," he said. "And honestly, I don't think it's in your best interest."

"You're wrong about that. I need a lawyer who's not afraid to research. The court's evidentiary rulings will be critical. And you're as good at motion practice as anybody I know."

Though he knew better, Mace couldn't help but be a little flattered. Plus, the case *would* generate a lot of publicity. But still . . . "What about Bobby Conway or that guy with the ponytail who gets all those high-profile cases? I'm sure one of those guys would let you have an active role in the case."

Caleb sat for a moment and apparently decided to come clean. "I can't afford them. My firm's hit some hard times, and those guys are ridiculously expensive. And I'm not going to pick up any new cases until I get my name cleared."

Mace thought it ironic that Caleb Tate was complaining about rates charged by other lawyers. Last time he checked, Caleb's rate was somewhere north of five hundred an hour.

"I thought there was life insurance money," Mace said.

"They won't pay until I'm declared innocent. And, Mace, I *am* innocent. You know I passed a lie detector."

Caleb reached into his suit coat pocket and placed a check on the desk. "Here's a ten-thousand-dollar retainer. Charge me whatever your rate is, and I'll pay the rest as soon as I get my hands on the insurance money."

Caleb stood, apparently unable to resist adding some drama to the encounter. "This is my life, Mace. I need somebody to stand with me who's been in prison before. Somebody who's not going to treat this like just another case. Somebody who won't try to talk me into a plea bargain and fold the tents at the first sign of trouble. Basically, I need somebody who's willing to fight like hell."

Mace studied the man before him for a long moment. Even though he'd been acquainted with Caleb for the last eleven years while working on Antoine's case, he didn't really know the man. He doubted anyone did.

Was he capable of killing his wife in cold blood? And was he enough of a professional liar to pass a polygraph test?

"I need to think about it. Actually . . . I need to pray about it."

If Caleb was surprised by the comment, he didn't show it. But then again, Caleb Tate was a trial lawyer, well trained to never act surprised. "I can live with that," Caleb said. He made no effort to retrieve the check. "But I can tell you this—I'm not going to contact anyone else. And if the shoe were on the other foot and it were your life on the line, I'd take your case."

But I probably wouldn't ask you, Mace thought. "I'll let you know by the end of the day."

32

IN THE GRAND JURY ROOM, I spent Monday morning building a relationship with the good folks on the jury, obtaining indictments on more than half a dozen no-brainer cases. After lunch, I gave them an overview of the Tate case and called LA as my first witness. About ten minutes into his testimony, I realized I could have saved myself hours of preparation time.

LA was a charmer, and he didn't mind giving me a hard time to draw a few chuckles from the jurors. I took him through the investigation step by step. By the time he had finished, we were already in good shape. Next, Dr. O'Leary testified about the cause of death and seemed determined to make a few jurors puke before she left the stand. A toxicologist followed her and testified about the blood and hair testing.

Tuesday morning, the jury heard from Dr. Gillespie. Most of them seemed to like the man, though one or two drifted in and out during his testimony. I took the psychiatrist through each of Rikki's important counseling sessions. Yes, she had been involved in a few affairs. And yes, Caleb Tate had found out about them.

Next came a parade of church friends to talk about how Rikki's newfound faith had created a strain on the marriage and how Caleb Tate had been a control freak. I called Rikki Tate's civil attorney to testify about Caleb's opposition to the lawsuits Rikki had filed attempting to get her topless pictures removed from various websites. A few of the female jurors made noticeable faces during that testimony—*What kind of scum is this guy?*

I held my breath and put Rafael Rivera on the stand. The deputies

145

had dressed him up and brought him over from the county jail. He raised his hand, swore to tell the truth, and gave me a condescending sneer. He testified about providing Caleb Tate with oxycodone and codeine for the past six months. I did not ask him about the morphine. Though Tate and his defense attorneys were not allowed in the grand jury room, they would eventually be entitled to a transcript of the proceedings. I didn't want to tip our hand about the morphine any earlier than necessary.

Despite his repulsive attitude, Rivera stuck to the script, and I had him off the stand in fifteen minutes. For the first time in two days, I relaxed. The grand jury was going to indict. In truth, it was pretty hard to lose a case when the other side didn't get to show up.

I recalled LA to the stand after I finished with Rivera so LA could testify about Caleb Tate's financial status. Tate's law firm, despite its appearance of great success, was actually struggling with mounting debt. In his personal life, Tate was swimming in an ocean of credit, and the various banks that had loaned him money during his heyday were starting to tighten their grip. LA also testified about the million-dollar life insurance policy Caleb Tate had taken out on his wife shortly after he discovered her affair two years ago.

"Two years seems like a long time for someone like Mr. Tate to wait," I said.

"Poisoning is not a crime of passion," LA lectured. "It's a crime of deceit. It requires careful and patient planning. I've made some charts of Mr. Tate's cash flow and debt obligations. He probably knew he could afford to wait two years, but not much more."

I ended my case with a short and straightforward closing argument. I could tell the jurors' only question was how quickly they could sign the indictment.

After they voted unanimously to indict, I reminded them of the absolute confidentiality of the grand jury proceedings. I thanked them for their service, stuffed some papers into my dad's briefcase, and called Bill Masterson as soon as I got into the hallway.

"Get your bench warrant and take the rest of the day off," he said. It was a few minutes after three.

"Maybe I will."

Based on the grand jury indictment, I obtained a bench warrant from a Superior Court judge and met LA in the hallway. "Have fun," I said, handing him the warrant. I left the courthouse alone and walked down the large concrete steps. The sun was bright, and I could smell the freshly cut grass on the courthouse lawn. For the first time in months, I felt like I could fully breathe, like my chest wasn't constricted by pressure. I knew my dad would be proud.

I should have followed Bill Masterson's advice and taken the rest of the day off. Instead, I got in my car and headed back to the office.

33

MACE JAMES WAS A SUCKER for helping the underdog. It was what landed him in prison and what got him out. It was what he had been doing at the clinic since becoming a lawyer. Most of his clients were guilty, but somebody had to be an advocate for mercy. And when there was the possibility of innocence, the stakes were even higher.

Caleb Tate had passed a lie detector test. That had to count for something. From what Mace knew about the facts, he couldn't rule out Caleb's being just an innocent victim of a rush to judgment by prosecutors. He called Tate at 5 p.m. on Monday. "I'm in," Mace said.

He spent Tuesday morning regretting those two words, but he couldn't make himself pick up the phone and call Caleb again to retract. The guy needed help. He wasn't the most sympathetic client, but that didn't mean he was a killer. And Mace was brash enough to believe that Caleb was right in assuming that Mace would work the case harder and smarter than just about any other lawyer out there. Still, he wasn't quite feeling it. He had prayed about it but had no clear answer.

By three o'clock Tuesday afternoon, it no longer mattered. Caleb Tate's sources had confirmed a grand jury indictment. Expect the cops in thirty or forty minutes. Mace hustled over to Caleb's office, where he found his client dressed in an expensive dark-blue Armani suit as if he were ready to argue a case before the US Supreme Court. Mace had on jeans, a white T-shirt, a John Deere hat, and flip-flops.

The two men watched out the front conference room windows, thirty-five floors above street level, as squad cars and TV vans lined the curb. A young detective with unruly blond hair led the charge into the building.

"Game on," Tate said.

When the cops stepped off the elevators, Tate was there waiting. He held out his hands for the cuffs. "You can skip Miranda," he said.

Undeterred, the detective started reading loudly from his Miranda card while the cops jerked Tate's arms behind his back and slapped on the cuffs.

"Do you understand those rights?" the detective asked.

"Not really," Tate said calmly. "I'm a little confused by Justice Kennedy's opinion in *Berghuis v. Thompkins*, where he talks about whether the mere act of remaining silent is sufficient to invoke the privilege and render inadmissible subsequent voluntary statements, absent an explicit invocation of the right. Could you explain that to me?"

The detective grabbed Tate's arm and pushed him toward the elevator. "Get in," he said.

Mace tried to follow, but the same man held out his palm toward Mace's chest.

"I'm his attorney," Mace said.

"Fine. You can talk to him at the jail in a few hours."

Standing in the elevator, Tate looked at Mace and tilted his head to the side—*What can you do?* The elevator doors closed, and Mace pushed a button for the next car down.

He made it to the front plaza a few seconds behind the Tate perp walk entourage. Most perps hung their heads and tried to shield their faces, but Tate looked right at the cameras and provided a running commentary. "I told the police I would come down to the station anytime—day or night. I told them I would take a lie detector test. I told them they could look through anything in my house or office. But this is how they want to spend the taxpayers' money."

When they reached the squad car, the detective pushed Tate into the back and closed the door so the suspect would stop talking to the cameras. That was Mace's cue.

"Hey! I'm Caleb Tate's attorney. Any of you guys want an interview?" he yelled. Three camera crews scurried over to the steps where Mace had positioned himself.

"Are you ready?" he asked one of the cameramen.

The guy nodded.

Mace introduced himself and reminded the world that Caleb Tate had passed a polygraph and had gone to extraordinary lengths to cooperate with the authorities.

"We will not waive our right to a speedy trial," Mace said. He and Caleb had already agreed on this strategy. A Georgia defendant was not entitled to a preliminary hearing on a case initiated through a grand jury indictment. The first chance to prove Tate's innocence would be at trial. "We want the first available trial date. In fact, if the DA is ready to go next month, my client and I will be there. And I'm assuming the DA wouldn't have indicted Mr. Tate if they weren't ready."

The media ate it up. They were used to suspects cowering into police vehicles, their lawyers proclaiming that they would do their talking in court. But here was a defendant anxious to fight back! And a lawyer wearing a John Deere hat!

Inspired, Mace decided to weave in a subtle reference to Jamie Brock's remarks about lynching. "The DA's office has it in for Caleb Tate because he's had the audacity to represent criminal defendants the way the framers of our Constitution envisioned it. He had the guts to fight hard for his clients, and now he's paying the price. But fortunately for Mr. Tate, lynch mobs have been replaced by juries. And the quicker we can get his case in front of one, the quicker we can restore my client's reputation and allow him to grieve in peace."

It seemed like a good place to end, so Mace thanked everyone, did a one-eighty, and headed back into the building. It wasn't exactly riding off into the sunset, but it was the best alternative available.

How did I get myself into this mess? he wondered.

◁▷

At 6 p.m., I walked out the front door of the DA's office to find LA waiting at the curb next to his sports car. It was either a big coincidence or he had paid off the receptionist to tell him when I left. He opened the passenger door.

"Get in," he said. He had a serious look on his face, and I sensed that something was wrong. My elation from Tate's indictment became a sinking feeling.

"What's up?"

"Just get in." He glanced nervously around. "I don't want to talk about it out here."

I tossed my father's briefcase behind the seat and climbed in the passenger side. I closed the door and watched LA as he climbed into the driver's seat and pulled away from the curb.

"What's going on?"

"Can you call the neighbors and have them take Justice outside?" LA asked. "We've got a problem, and I need your help for a couple of hours."

I gave him a curious look. He was going through the gears like a madman, more serious than I had ever seen him. "What kind of problem?"

"Just call the neighbors."

I did and then demanded an explanation from LA. We were on the ramp for Interstate 400, heading south toward Atlanta.

"You're losing way too much weight," LA said. "I'm afraid you won't make it to trial at this rate. We're going to Ruth's Chris, and I'm going to force you to eat some steak."

I was not happy. "Are you kidding me? After what I've already been through today, you make me think we've got some kind of crisis just to get me into your car so we can go out and eat? What if I had plans?"

"Did you?"

"That's beside the point. I don't like being misled. And kidnapped."

"So noted." LA smiled, and I could tell he wasn't taking my protests seriously. Which was okay because dinner at Ruth's Chris was starting to sound pretty good. And it was hard to stay mad at a guy who claimed I was losing weight when in fact I was putting it on.

Thirty minutes earlier, I had been looking forward to a night at home without the pressure of the grand jury hanging over my head. But home was a lonely place, and there was no telling when the ghost of my father would cause me to break down. I was hungry, and I could think of worse men to look at than this quirky detective with the shaggy hair. Plus, he had done well on the stand. He deserved a reward.

"I'll go on one condition," I said.

"I don't think you're in any position to be negotiating."

"I'm paying for my own meal."

This brought out a broad white grin. "I never said you weren't." He glanced at me, the blue eyes playful. "You didn't think this was a date, did you?"

"Just drive."

34

I WOKE UP WEDNESDAY MORNING feeling rested for the first time in weeks. Late Tuesday night, against my better judgment, I had taken an Ambien that Dr. Gillespie had prescribed. He was concerned that I had never properly grieved my father's death before jumping so quickly into the Tate prosecution. "You've got to take care of yourself," he'd said. "It starts with rest, exercise, and nutrition."

"You're lecturing me about exercise?" I responded.

He chuckled. "Fair enough. But I do know a thing or two about rest. And your sleep habits are atrocious."

Maybe he was right, because on Wednesday morning, I felt like a new Jamie. I took my time showering and ironed a pair of black dress slacks that had not been to the dry cleaner's since the last time I wore them. I put on one of my favorite blouses along with a gray blazer and my favorite silver necklace. I even broke out heels for the occasion. I'm not usually much of a clotheshorse, but today the media would be out in force. Caleb Tate would be arraigned, bail would be set, and I would be squaring off against the two men who had defended my mother's killer for the last eleven years. How nice of them to team up so I could take them down together.

I could taste the revenge.

I told Justice good-bye and said a quick prayer before leaving the house. I stopped at a QT for coffee and sat in my car in the parking lot of Milton County Superior Court, rehearsing my argument one last time. I would have an ally in Judge Sharon Logan, a former prosecutor. Tate personified the two groups of people she hated most—defendants and defense lawyers. I would ask for bond to be set at five million and hope for two. If I got lucky, Mace James would claim that his client had recently experienced some financial setbacks—thus helping us establish motive later on.

I checked my makeup in the visor mirror and put on more lip gloss. I ran my fingers through my short hair and pushed a few loose strands behind my ear. I declared myself ready, grabbed my father's briefcase, and headed for the chaos of Superior Courtroom 2.

◁▷

Mace James hated wearing a suit. On a law professor's salary, he couldn't afford the custom-tailored ones, and the ones he bought off the rack never fit right. The shoulders and arms would be too tight and bind him up when he tried to move. If he got the shoulders broad enough, the sleeves would be too long, and the tailor would have to take in the pants several inches. There were athletic fits on the rack. But there were none for guys like Mace, fanatics who lifted weights for ninety minutes five times a week and did everything short of steroids to sculpt the perfect body.

For the arraignment, he'd donned an ill-fitting suit and arrived at court early. He took a seat in the middle of the first wooden bench and watched as the spectator section began to fill.

Jamie Brock showed up at five to nine, looking like she had just arrived from a Hollywood casting call. She had the strong facial features of a big-screen prosecutor—prominent cheekbones, dark-brown eyes, straight white teeth, and a determined jaw. She kept her chin up and her back straight as she walked briskly to the front of the courtroom and greeted the judge's clerks. Because this was a murder charge, it was only bondable here in Superior Court. And Mace had the bad luck to draw a judge who had worked in the Milton County prosecutor's office ten years ago. There was no question that this was Jamie's home turf.

◁▷

Mace James squeezed out of his row and met me at the front of the courtroom. We shook hands; his seemed to swallow mine whole.

"I'm sorry to hear about your dad," he said.

"Somehow I doubt that," I replied.

His expression darkened. "I guess you know I'm representing Caleb Tate."

"You manage to get all the good ones."

"Good luck to you, too."

Mace James returned to his seat, clearly offended. I might have made a mistake by picking the first fight, but I didn't like lawyers who would battle me in court and then try to buy me a drink afterward. Defense lawyers liked to claim they were just doing their job. I didn't buy it. Nobody was holding a gun to their heads. It might just be a job, but it was a job they had *chosen*. There were plenty of other ways a lawyer could make money.

There were five arraignments ahead of Tate's case, and all went according to script. When the clerk called Caleb Tate's name, everyone in the courtroom seemed to sit up a little straighter. Mace James took his place at the defense counsel table. A pair of sheriff's deputies led Tate into the courtroom, his wrists and ankles shackled as if he might make a run for it at any moment. He was wearing a suit but had a butterfly bandage over his left eyebrow. He smiled at Mace, and the two shook hands, causing the handcuffs to jangle. Tate never glanced in my direction.

After Tate took his seat, Judge Logan read the charges, and Mace pleaded "absolutely not guilty" for his client. He had also requested a bond hearing, and Logan said she would hear from the state first.

I rose and began describing in detail the crime Caleb Tate had been accused of committing. I watched him out of the corner of my eye. He sat pompously at the defense table, studying me as if I were some kind of lab specimen, never taking a note.

"Poisoning is a crime of planning and preparation," I emphasized. "And this is a defendant with means to flee the state *and* the country. He has a valid passport, and he once owned property in the British Virgin Islands. His law firm generated almost six million dollars in revenues last year, and his house is appraised at three million. Oh . . . I almost forgot to mention he once leased part of a private jet and probably knows pilots who can fly him anywhere in the world.

"We think the horrendous nature of this crime and the fact that the defendant could lose everything makes Mr. Tate a substantial flight risk. The last thing the state wants is for him to take his resources and flee to another country, where he could live the rest of his life fighting extradition. Accordingly, we are requesting bond of no less than five million dollars."

I sat down, and the judge nodded to Professor James. "Your response, Mr.—" she looked down and checked the paper in front of her—"Mr. James. And please keep it short; don't try to argue the merits of the case."

"My client is a flight risk," Mace repeated sarcastically as he rose. "Let's see—he volunteers to take a polygraph, he volunteers to come to the police station whenever they want to question him, he makes it clear that he will turn himself in if they want to arrest him, and he has substantial ties in the community. Not only is he the managing partner of a prestigious law firm, but he's also invested heavily in this community. He's given twenty thousand dollars to the children's hospital, he contributes ten thousand dollars a year to United Way, he is on the board of patrons for the aquarium—"

"I don't need a list of his charitable activities," Judge Logan said. "I know we've got lots of reporters in the courtroom today, but this is not the place to grandstand. I'm setting bond at three million and requiring that Mr. Tate surrender his passport and not leave the state of Georgia without prior court permission. Are those conditions clear?"

"They're clear," Mace said, looking stunned. "But I wouldn't call them fair. Caleb Tate is more anxious to get this case to trial than anyone. He's not going anywhere. In fact, he's ready to grab the first trial date—"

Logan banged her gavel and gave Mace a look of fire. "That's enough," she said. "I've ruled. Ms. Brock is absolutely right about the nature of this crime. If he did it—and I'm not saying that he did—but *if* he did, it means he's been planning this crime for at least six months. A man like that, who could kill his own wife in cold blood, wouldn't hesitate to take off for another country. So, Mr. James, you're lucky your client's getting bonded out at all."

From the look on Mace James's face, he wasn't feeling lucky. And neither was Caleb Tate.

35

MACE JAMES SPENT the next three days fielding collect calls from his new client. Milton County gave prisoners liberal phone privileges, and Caleb Tate took advantage of the freedom.

Mace's cell phone would ring, showing the jail's number. He would answer to an automated operator that explained this was a collect call, what the rate would be, and that the call might be recorded. Mace would accept the call and inform anyone who was listening that this was an attorney-client conversation and that all monitoring devices must be turned off immediately.

Even with those precautions, Caleb seemed reluctant to share much information. The attorneys at his firm were pulling together the collateral to secure the three-million-dollar bond, Caleb said. He spent much of his time complaining about banks who had been all too eager to take his money when times were good but were not willing to lend money now. There was no equity in Caleb's mansion. His firm's equity lines were all tapped out. Some of his friends were putting together a "Caleb Tate Defense Fund." Mace started wondering whether his ten-thousand-dollar retainer had been way too low.

"I may be in here through the weekend before we can get together the bond money," Tate said. "And I'm going nuts."

On Saturday, four days after Tate's incarceration, Mace went to visit his client.

The jail was a large brick building located on the outskirts of Alpharetta, a few blocks from the courthouse. It had a small concrete yard in the back, surrounded by shiny barbed wire. The place was always overcrowded. The inmates stayed together in pods based loosely on the types of crimes they had been charged with and their perceived level of danger to the guards and each other.

The facility, completed in 2002, was state-of-the-art. The guards sat behind bulletproof glass in a control room of sorts overlooking the pods. The inmates' cells opened into a small common area with bolted-down tables and televisions mounted high on the walls. Each pod was separated from the others by thick steel doors. In the event of a riot, individual pods could be isolated and the fights easily contained. The guards could activate tear gas or sprinklers in the pods by remote control.

The inmates spent an hour together during an afternoon recess, which was when gang alliances were cemented and new fish and outcasts were bloodied up. Mace had never served time in Milton County, but he knew the typical jailhouse routine and had the scars to prove it. Even in an environment like Milton County, which was a far cry from the state pen where hard-core felons served real time, a white-collar guy like Caleb Tate could be easy prey for other prisoners.

But Caleb Tate had a secret weapon every inmate desired—the know-how to exploit loopholes in the legal system.

Any worries about whether Tate would survive his time without being victimized were alleviated when Mace met with him in the private attorney conference room on Saturday morning.

"There are basically three gangs running this place," Tate explained. He looked pale and haggard, his body swallowed by the orange jumpsuit. "My firm is now representing two of the gang leaders. I've promised to personally handle their cases when I get out. I talked one of my buddies at another firm into representing the third one."

"How's your roommate?" Mace asked.

Caleb made a face. "Burned out. Brains fried on meth. Snores like a freight train."

The two men discussed what Caleb had learned about the evidence presented to the grand jury. Mace didn't yet have a transcript, but Caleb had his sources.

"It all comes down to Rafael Rivera," Tate explained. Mace could read the hatred in Caleb's eyes. "Former client. Told the prosecutors that he provided me with drugs."

"Is he serving time here?"

Caleb lowered his voice though it was just the two of them in the conference room. "Nope. They transferred him to Gwinnett County—at his request. With good reason. The boys here don't like snitches."

Mace wasn't too worried about Rivera's testimony. A three-time felon—how much credibility could he possibly have?

"When do you think you'll get the bond money together?" Mace asked.

Caleb waved the question off with a flick of his wrist. "Early next week. I've settled down, and I'm making good use of my time." He placed his forearms on the table and hunched forward, closer to Mace. "You ever hear of the prisoner's dilemma? You ever teach that in law school?"

"The prisoner's dilemma?"

"Yeah. It's what greases the system. The idea is that you take two co-conspirators, and the police interrogate them in separate rooms. The cops tell each suspect that if he confesses and testifies against the other, they'll cut him a deal. One year in prison. But if he doesn't deal quickly and the other suspect beats him to the punch, the other guy gets the one-year deal. The noncooperating suspect could be looking at trial and ten years if convicted.

"Now, both suspects know that if neither one of them squeals, neither one of them goes to jail. But if you don't squeal and the other guy does, you're looking at ten long years. What do you think happens?"

"They both try to cut the deal. There's no honor among thieves."

"Exactly. And that's how most of the crimes in our country get solved. You know what percentage of cases plead out in Milton County?"

Mace hadn't given the idea a moment's thought, but he knew Milton wasn't much different from other jurisdictions. "Probably 90 percent or so."

"Ninety-four percent." Caleb's voice took on a conspiratorial whisper. "What do you think would happen if the defendants all got together and decided none of them would plea-bargain anymore? What do you think *that* would do to the system?"

Mace didn't like where this was headed. "It would overwhelm the system. Chaos."

"Exactly," Caleb said, tapping his finger on the table. "The prosecutors would be swamped. Public defenders would drown. The state's already cut everybody's budget. Every defendant could ask for a speedy trial and then scream on appeal because they got ineffective assistance. The system would be backlogged for years. If every single prisoner in this jail right now insisted on full trial rights, the prosecutors would have to let half of them out because they couldn't try everyone fast enough to fulfill their constitutional right to a speedy trial. The other half would have great issues to bring up on appeal. Heck, government workers and teachers have unionized. Why not felons?"

Caleb leaned back in his chair, pride beaming from his thin face. Mace knew jail had a way of playing with your mind. Confinement created paranoia and conspiracy buffs. But Mace couldn't tell if this was just typical jailhouse bluster or something Caleb could actually orchestrate.

"Now, of course, this could only work if all the prisoners played along. And the prosecutors would probably start offering up some sweet deals to break the logjam. So you'd have to have all the gang leaders on the same page and ready to punish anyone who cut a deal. And that would require—hypothetically speaking, here—somebody to quarterback the whole thing. Somebody the gang leaders trusted. Of course, since these rival gang leaders hate each other so much, it could never happen. But if it did, just think how much it would help us. Because I'm taking my case to trial no matter what. And it wouldn't hurt if the prosecutors were busier than one-armed paperhangers with all the other prisoners who suddenly decided to quit plea-bargaining."

Caleb Tate sat there for a moment with a look on his face that really worried Mace. Either the man was losing it or the plan was already in place.

"Don't do anything stupid," Mace said, his uneasiness about the case expanding. "Any plan like that would require some pretty serious enforcement. You don't need to be tied in with any of that."

"You're right. That's why I'm just speaking hypothetically. But it sure would be fun to watch."

36

ON TUESDAY, I felt like I was reliving my first day in the DA's office, doing something I had never done before.

I found myself in court with twelve case files, each one a guilty plea of some type or another. None of the cases were mine. But I was there because Rafael Rivera would be sentenced that day, a bargain that had been worked out by Masterson himself. I was also covering for one of my friends who had handled my cases while I was grieving for my dad.

I knew I didn't exactly have to bring my A game to court for plea bargains. My job was to simply explain the charges to the court, inform the judge that the defendant had pleaded guilty, and recommend a sentence. Theoretically, the court could either accept or reject the sentence, but in reality, the court almost always went along with a recommendation jointly proposed by the prosecutor and the defense attorney.

Because Rafael Rivera was being held in another jurisdiction to keep him away from Milton County's inmates, his case was up first.

I thought Masterson had been too easy on Rivera, and I assumed that was why Masterson didn't appear in court himself—he didn't want to get stigmatized with this deal during his campaign. Nevertheless, I was grateful that the boss had taken Rivera off my plate. Masterson had struck a deal I would never have agreed to, but at least now we could move forward with the Tate prosecution.

Judge Harold Brown was a tall, thin man who had been sitting on the Superior Court bench for as long as I could remember. He'd been a distance runner in college and still prided himself on being in shape at sixty. He was prompt and efficient except when he hauled you back into his chambers and got started with his stories. Brown was the type of judge who made the judicial system click—he didn't favor either the prosecutors or the defendants, and he made sure every rule and procedure was followed punctiliously.

He took the bench, welcomed the public defender and me, and asked the deputies to bring in the defendant. While Rivera shuffled to his seat, shackled at his wrists and ankles, Judge Brown took off his watch and large college ring and placed them in front of him. It was one of his little idiosyncrasies that meant he was ready to get down to business.

When I explained that we were dropping the charge of possession with intent to distribute and that Rivera would plead guilty to the lesser offense of possession of cocaine, Brown raised an eyebrow. He had been around long enough to recognize a sweet deal when he saw one. I looked down and read the rest of my notes so I didn't have to look the judge in the eye when I explained the recommended sentence. Brown, like everyone else on the Superior Court bench, knew my policy on plea bargains.

"The state recommends that Mr. Rivera be sentenced to five years in prison, with all but sixty days suspended, including time served, conditioned on Mr. Rivera's continued cooperation in other cases where he is providing valuable information and testimony. We also recommend that Mr. Rivera be placed on supervised probation for ten years."

After I detailed the recommended terms for probation, Judge Brown had Rivera stand and took him through a litany of questions to ensure that the plea was voluntary. Rivera mumbled all of the correct answers, and Brown decided to end the festivities with a well-deserved lecture.

"You're getting a good deal, Mr. Rivera, and you ought to consider yourself lucky. But I will tell you this, son . . ."

I couldn't resist sneaking a glance at Rivera, who was bristling at being called "son."

". . . you'd better keep your nose clean and do everything the prosecutors ask you to do. Because if you come back in this courtroom having violated your probation or having failed to fully cooperate with every single thing they ask—" Brown let the words hang there for a moment, though Rivera didn't seem cowed by the court's threat— "I'll give you every day of the five years that will be hanging over your head. And I won't show you one drop of mercy on any new charges. Is that clear?"

Rivera mumbled something I couldn't hear.

"Speak up, son," Judge Brown said. "The court can't hear you when you mumble."

Rivera stared at the judge for a moment, contempt dripping from his sneer. "Yeah, *Your Honor*, I get it."

"Very good. Then the court accepts the recommendation of counsel and sentences the defendant to five years with all but sixty days suspended on the conditions cited earlier by Ms. Brock. The court also sentences the defendant to ten years of supervised probation on the terms recited by Ms. Brock."

A few minutes later, Rivera shuffled out of the courtroom. On the way, he gave me a menacing look over his shoulder. I hadn't expected him to be grateful, but I wondered again if we were doing the right thing.

I had no time to dwell on it, because the assembly line continued. A new public defender stepped to the defense table, and a defendant named Lucious Hazlett was brought in by the deputies. Hazlett had been charged with aggravated assault and battery for cutting his girl-friend's face during a domestic dispute.

Hazlett had agreed to plead guilty and save the state the trouble of trying him in exchange for a reduced sentence recommendation. There were some notes in the file, explaining that we were accepting the plea because the girlfriend was living with Hazlett again and there were "proof problems." I knew the implications of this euphemism. We could always compel the girlfriend to testify, but we couldn't keep her from shading the testimony to make the whole event look more accidental than intentional.

I explained the proposed plea agreement, and Judge Brown kept his raised eyebrows to himself this time. He had seen hundreds of cases where a boyfriend or girlfriend or husband or wife went to the police and swore out charges but later tried to back out. My colleagues would usually plead the cases out.

"Do you understand the nature of the charges against you and that you have a right to plead not guilty?" Brown asked.

"Yeah," Hazlett said.

"By pleading guilty, you understand that you waive the right to a trial by jury and to be confronted by the witnesses against you?"

"Yeah."

"Are you satisfied with your counsel's representation in this matter?"

"Not really."

"Do you understand—?" Brown stopped in the middle of the next sentence. It had taken a moment for Hazlett's response to register. "Did you just say 'not really'?"

"Yeah."

Brown frowned at the answer. Sometimes guilty pleas blew up because the defendants were too stupid to give the right answers. Maybe this was one of them. Brown decided to give Hazlett some help.

"You do understand that I can't accept your guilty plea unless you're satisfied with the services provided by your lawyer," Brown said. He sounded like he was coaching a five-year-old. "Otherwise, you could claim ineffective assistance of counsel and argue on appeal that the deal isn't valid."

Hazlett shrugged his shoulders. The issue of his own freedom was apparently not that interesting to him.

"So let me ask you again. Are you satisfied with the assistance of your counsel?"

This time, Hazlett turned to his lawyer and snorted. "This dude doesn't even know my name. See that pile of paper in front of him, Judge? All he wants to do is get to the bottom of those files so he can go have a beer with his buddies and get home to his woman. If the DA's office wanted to give me the needle, he'd cut a deal for that, too! When I told him I wanted to fight the charges, I thought he might pee his pants. So no, I ain't happy with my counsel. I think the state of Georgia got screwed if they're paying this guy more than twenty bucks for handling my case."

Judge Brown's face reddened. "Are you through?"

"Pretty much."

"Good. Then we're going to do two things. First, I'm going to allow your lawyer to withdraw, and we'll find you a new lawyer. And second, I'm going to reject this plea, and the DA is going to pursue this case against you and ask for the full sentence allowed by law. Is that clear, Ms. Brock?"

I stood. "Crystal clear."

The court talked logistics with the public defender for a few minutes. Hazlett smirked as he was escorted out of the courtroom.

When the next two defendants sabotaged their plea agreements too, I knew something was up. It was rare to have even one guilty plea fall apart. But three in a row defied any random explanation. For some reason, the defendants had all decided to take their chances at trial. I had never seen or heard of this happening before. The public defenders started whispering to each other, and the court clerk sat up straighter and took note. Since all twelve of the defendants had been in the same holding cell waiting for court, I assumed one of them was dissatisfied with his plea and was strong-willed enough to talk the others into rejecting their pleas too. Hazlett was the most likely candidate.

When the fifth straight defendant rejected his plea, Judge Brown ran out of patience. He dispensed with all the preliminaries on the next guy.

"Is it your intention to accept or reject this plea that has been worked out?" he asked the defendant even before I could explain the basics of the deal.

The startled defendant stood. "I'm having second thoughts, Judge." The man stared at the floor as if he was ashamed to be doing this.

"Next!" Brown said.

The surprises were not yet finished. The ninth defendant of the morning, a young man named Ricky Powell, had agreed to plead guilty to first-degree vehicular homicide. He had two prior DUIs, and this time his drunk driving had resulted in a buddy's death. Powell was appropriately repentant and had agreed to plead guilty for only a slight reduction in sentence.

"Are you going to take this guilty plea that's been negotiated by your counsel, or is it your intention to squirm your way out of the deal too?" Judge Brown asked.

Powell trembled as he stood. "No, Judge. I did what they charged me with, and I'll never forgive myself. I still want to take the deal."

The clerk stopped typing, and even the court reporter seemed surprised by this. A guilty plea that might actually go through! I never thought I'd be so excited to see a criminal defendant get a deal.

Judge Brown asked the usual questions and threw in a couple more for good measure. Powell, to his credit, looked the judge in the eye and answered all of them correctly. I felt so sorry for the kid that I thought about knocking another year off his sentence out of sympathy.

Brown sentenced Powell to ten years in jail, suspending all but five, and the kid actually thanked the court. "I've learned my lesson, Your Honor. I can promise you that."

"I certainly hope so," Brown said.

I noticed the victim's family had shown up in court to hear Powell's sentence. My notes in the file indicated that they thought Powell was remorseful and were in full support of this deal.

But Powell was the only success story that day. After the other defendants had rejected their pleas, Judge Brown called the public defenders and me up for a bench conference.

"What's going on here?" he asked.

"I don't have the slightest idea," I replied. "But I intend to find out."

◁▷

By the end of the day, the office was buzzing about what had happened in court that morning. It became a running joke. They told me I gave off anti-plea-bargaining vibes. They assured me they would never send me to court again on such a simple task. Even Bill Masterson got in on the action. He called me and said he would have to put in an emergency budget request for two new prosecutors if I ever handled plea bargains again.

The joking stopped on Wednesday afternoon. Ricky Powell was found dead in his pod at the Milton County jail. The inmates had somehow managed to shield him from the view of the security cameras while they sliced out his tongue. He bled to death before the guards knew what had happened.

Caleb Tate was not around to witness it. He had posted bond on Wednesday morning and was once again enjoying life on the outside looking in.

37

THE NEWSPAPER RAN a short article about the killing at the Milton
County Correctional Facility. It was buried on page three of the local
section and was short on details. The deputies managed to keep a lid
on the fact that the prisoners had cut out Ricky Powell's tongue and
that Powell was the only defendant who had followed through with
his guilty plea on Tuesday.

My colleagues had lots of theories about the plea rejections. Most
favored the idea that the gang leaders in jail had found out that I would
be the one accepting the pleas. In retaliation for my past refusal to
cut deals, maybe they had instructed every defendant to sabotage the
deals we had offered. When Powell didn't come through, they cut out
his tongue.

It was a symbolic killing, meant to send a message—there was no
doubt about that. But what was the message?

On Wednesday night, I slept with a loaded single-action .45 Kimber
Pro Carry II next to my bed. I had bought it during my third year of
law school at a gun shop in Gainesville after I got tangled up with
some members of the federal witness protection program. I also made
a point to stay away from the large window in my father's study at the
front of the house. I didn't take a sleeping pill because I was worried
that I wouldn't wake up if somebody tried to break in. I knew Justice
would bark like crazy, but if somebody actually made it inside, my
black Lab would just try to lick him to death. For protection, I pre-
ferred the Kimber.

It was a long night. Between missing my father, thinking about
Rafael Rivera, trying to work on Tate's case, and knowing that gang

leaders might now be targeting me, I was so wired I could barely sleep. I struggled to get through the next day, and by Thursday night, I was in dire need of sleep. Shortly after midnight, I finally succumbed and popped two Ambien. I was late for work Friday morning.

By noon on Friday, we knew my courtroom experience earlier in the week was not an isolated event. There had been no plea hearings on Wednesday, but every defendant scheduled to cop a plea on Thursday had backed out even though a different ADA had handled them. The public defenders had grown as jittery as the prosecutors and spent Thursday afternoon meeting with each defendant who was scheduled to plead guilty on Friday morning. All but one backed out on the spot.

On Friday, the only holdout, Rontavius Eastbrook, pleaded guilty to a lesser included crime in exchange for a reduced sentence based on his past cooperation with police on a major sting operation. After the court accepted his deal, Rontavius was escorted directly from the courtroom to the district attorney's office for processing. He was being released on time served and, in a deviation from prior procedures, was not sent back to the jail for processing. He was asked if he wanted police protection but scoffed at the idea.

◁▷

I got the text message on Saturday night, right after I finished my workout at the gym. Rontavius Eastbrook had been found dead in an alley in the projects. He died from a bullet wound to the back of the head.

38

ON MONDAY MORNING, there were no plea bargains on the docket. Instead, Bill Masterson called a meeting for all prosecutors. Unless we had to be in court, we were expected to be in the main conference room at 10 a.m. sharp.

In my three years at the prosecutor's office, I'd never seen an in-house meeting start precisely on time. But when I arrived a few minutes before ten, every seat was taken, and I had to stand along a side wall with several of my colleagues. There was a buzz of excitement and a good deal of nervous energy. Most of us had become prosecutors because we were crusaders; we wanted to right wrongs. We saw recent developments as a frontal attack on the integrity of the criminal justice system, and we weren't about to let the inmates run the asylum.

Admittedly, a few prosecutors took the opposite approach. They believed the only way to break this logjam was to divide and conquer. They wanted to target a Latino gang and offer some sweet deals to get the wheels of justice grinding again. Once the African Americans learned that the Latinos were getting preferential treatment, they would want in on the action. It was the law of supply and demand; we just had to price the deals right. I thought it was the dumbest idea I had ever heard.

Masterson walked into the meeting five minutes late, and the chatter quickly died down. He took a seat at the end of the table. Regina Granger stood behind him.

The boss surveyed the room and gave a slight nod to most of us. These were the troops he had hand-selected, and you could read the look on his face—*If I'm going to war, I want you men and women to go with me.* He took a deep breath before he began.

"I guess you've heard by now that the inmates have decided to play an interesting little game of chicken," he said. "I always knew this job would be a little harder if they ever unionized."

The remark drew a few smiles, but Masterson remained serious. "We're still trying to get to the bottom of who's behind all this, and we have our suspicions. But that's not why I called this meeting. Regardless of how or why this started, it's the new reality, and we've got to deal with it."

There were a number of theories flying around the office about how the inmates had gotten organized. Some focused on the gang leaders, and the deputies had now put them all in isolation. Many of us suspected that Caleb Tate was involved. The pleas had started falling apart soon after he was locked up, and his firm had suddenly begun representing two of the gang leaders. But nobody was talking.

"We're squeezing the gang leaders and threatening them with new charges," Masterson continued. "But until somebody blinks, we've basically got three choices. Some say we should single out the weakest inmates and give them blue-light specials—deals they can't refuse. Part of the problem with that approach is that we'd have to use precious law enforcement assets to protect them once they get out. A plea bargain looks decidedly less appealing if you know you only get to live twenty-four hours after your release.

"A second approach is to nol-pros all the nonviolent offenders. We've got limited resources. The public defender's office has limited resources. Under this plan, we'd set the druggies free and just prosecute the rapists and murderers. That feels to me like we're conceding defeat, and I'm not a big fan of playing dead before the first shot is fired."

Not to mention the fact that it might be a little hard to explain on the campaign trail, I thought.

"There is a third alternative. We let them know that two can play this game. We bust our butts and prosecute every one of 'em to the full extent of the law. We cut no deals until further notice with anybody in Milton County. If they want to plead guilty with no promise of leniency and save themselves a trial, well . . . maybe they could talk us into that. But otherwise, we do the job the taxpayers pay us to do."

There were determined looks on most of the faces in the room, but there were also some skeptics. Even if we worked around the clock, there was no way we could get *all* the cases to trial on a timely basis. And even if *we* could, the public defender's office would have no incentive to play along. Public defenders loved to complain about how overworked they were and how little budget they had. They would claim they couldn't adequately prepare all of these cases, and if we got convictions, the appeals would clog up the courts for years.

"Have you run the numbers on this, Bill?" one of the senior ADAs asked. "I mean, I'm willing to do whatever it takes, but we frankly don't have the staff to pull this off."

"I know that," Masterson replied. "And I know the PD's office faces an even greater challenge. But I've given that some thought. I could ask our state legislators for emergency legislation that would allow us to hire lawyers from private firms as part-time prosecutors. They can already volunteer to help the public defenders. We could put a lot of pressure on all the big Atlanta firms and give them some positive publicity when they send us their young guns for one day a week. If we publicize the names of the firms, we could have fifty new prosecutors by the end of the month."

"I don't know," ADA Larry Hinson said. He had a reputation for being the last guy in each morning and one of the first to leave at night. "It'd take too long to train them. They won't know what they're doing. Most of the big-firm lawyers have never seen the inside of a courtroom."

Masterson stared him down. "You got a better idea, Larry? Because I've got lots of people who can help me identify the problems. I'm interested in solutions."

Larry shrugged. "I like the first option. Divide and conquer."

"Not me," I said. Heads swiveled in my direction. "This is why I came to work here. I saw Mr. Masterson try the man who murdered my mother, and I knew that this was more than just a job for him. And that was not an easy case. To be honest, I don't know if I would have survived if somebody hadn't stood up for our family and put Antoine Marshall behind bars."

The room was still. Everybody in the office knew about my history, but I had never played the victim card once in the last four years. I was playing it now.

"If we back down from this, it's just a matter of time before they do it again. And I'm not willing to look a rape victim or the family members of a murder victim in the eyes and tell them that the man who committed that crime is getting a deal because we've offered some blue-light specials. All because we're not willing to work around the clock and train a few private-firm lawyers. So . . . I don't know. I've probably already said too much, but I think we ought to do the job we're getting paid to do."

The room became uncomfortably quiet while Masterson glanced around. "Anybody else want to say anything?" he asked. "I'm not putting this up for a vote, but I want your input."

I had mentored two first-year prosecutors who were sitting on the opposite side of the room. One at a time, they spoke up and echoed my concerns. The rookies were all in.

A soft-spoken man named Al, a guy who had dedicated his professional life to the Milton County DA's office, spoke next. He said he didn't think we could ethically do anything other than prosecute these men and women to the full extent of the law. In the old days, he used to handle three times as many cases as he was handling now. And he was ready to step up.

One by one, my fellow prosecutors spoke in support of Masterson's third proposal. A few of my more dramatic colleagues even got a little choked up when they reminisced about the reasons they had come to this office in the first place. By the time the last person spoke, we were ready to storm the beaches. At least most of us were. A few lawyers stayed conspicuously silent, and Larry stared at a spot on the floor. No more two-hour lunches.

"I guess that settles it," Masterson said. "There's never been a good time to commit a crime in Milton County. But God help anyone who breaks the law right now."

39

OUR ENTHUSIASM FOR LOCKING UP the bad guys and throwing away the keys lasted less than a week.

The deputization of private-firm attorneys proved problematic for a number of reasons. The state legislature took its time debating the idea, and it became clear that the Democrats didn't want to make a Republican attorney general nominee look like a hero.

In the meantime, Masterson had encouraged us to begin the training process with two or three private-firm associates each while we awaited legislative approval. That made my job twice as hard. Much of a prosecutor's work is done in her office or in the hallways of the courthouse. Having another lawyer tag along only complicated things and, because the defense attorneys wanted to look tough for the new kids, made working with the defense bar even tougher.

But the plan's true Achilles' heel became apparent when private-firm attorneys showed up to be appointed as lawyers for the defendants. The prisoners had been well coached by somebody. They would all ask their new lawyers how many years of experience they had trying criminal cases. The prisoners would then object to the judge's appointing the rookie lawyers to their cases. Everybody knew what was really going on—the felons were setting up an ineffective assistance of counsel claim for appeal.

At the end of a long and frustrating week spent trying to unclog the system, Masterson called another meeting and announced that he was withdrawing his legislative initiative. "We're just going to have to handle this in-house."

My colleagues and I grumbled, but we were secretly happy. It would be easier to do it ourselves than to train first-year lawyers who hadn't been outside their big-firm offices.

But by the second week, things started slipping through the cracks. I lost a motion to suppress because a witness hadn't been subpoenaed. My legal assistant blamed the avalanche of cases she was handling and cried when I told her we couldn't let it happen again. The judges started getting frustrated and abrupt in court. Reporters showed up at the arraignments to watch one defendant after another plead not guilty and demand a jury trial.

Every day I promised myself that I would work on Caleb Tate's case in the evening, but I would get home too late, drained from fourteen hours of chaos. I would feed Justice, veg out in front of the computer or TV, and fall asleep. Five or six hours later, I would wake up and start the whole routine again.

For his part, Masterson became something of a cult hero. His tough-on-crime stance generated interviews on Fox News, CNN, and all the local stations. Even the stories about defendants who slipped through the cracks only enhanced Masterson's status. What could he do? He had asked for the ability to deputize private-firm lawyers and been stone-walled. His minions were now working virtually around the clock.

The worse things got, the more folksy and comfortable Masterson became, staring into the camera, promising he would get to the bottom of how this started, warning the thugs they would regret this gamble with every fiber of their being. The public was now seeing the Bill Masterson I knew. "You can't hold justice hostage," he said. "We don't take kindly to extortion."

Always an opportunist, Masterson also announced that he was suspending campaign fund-raising and would instead ask his donors to give directly to the Milton County DA's office. He would use the funds to pay a small bonus to overworked lawyers, legal assistants, staff members, and investigators.

Bill Masterson soon became a household name with skyrocketing approval ratings. He shot from a distant third place in the polls to a five-point lead over Andrew Thornton, the assistant AG who had led the race since day one.

It was in the middle of this hypercharged environment, on May 21, that I took the morning off to attend oral arguments in the state Supreme Court for the case of *Marshall v. Georgia*.

40

THE JUDICIAL BUILDING that housed the Georgia Supreme Court on Capitol Square in downtown Atlanta was built to impress. The Superior Courts of Georgia—the trial courts—were messy and chaotic, their dockets jammed with criminal defendants cutting deals and spouses arguing over the kids—real-life courtroom dramas where arguments erupted and raw emotions played out. But the Supreme Court was above all that—magisterial, precise, and focused on the law. This was the last stage of the state's legal process, a place of finality, a place where hopes were dashed forever, a place where sudden reversals could wipe out everything that had occurred before.

Three-story pillars flanked the entranceway to the sturdy granite building. The lawn was manicured to perfection, a pristine mix of mature trees, trimmed shrubs, and freshly planted spring flowers. The grass itself was a deep green.

The May morning scheduled for oral argument could have been featured in a Georgia tourism brochure—sunny with temperatures in the high seventies, a slight wind out of the northeast. Weather like this normally made me upbeat and energetic. It would have been a great day to go for a run or to paddle my kayak on the Chattahoochee. But it was never a good day to hear Professor Mace James proclaim the innocence of my mother's killer.

I found out in advance that the state's side of the case would be argued by Andrew Thornton. Bill Masterson, who normally attended these appellate proceedings with me, could not be there. He claimed his services were needed in the Milton County Superior Court. I thought it had something to do with a reluctance to sit in the audience and be forced to watch—and cheer for—your political adversary as he handled a high-profile case. Either way, Masterson had told me to brace myself. He didn't like the amount of attention the Georgia Supreme Court was paying to Professor James's latest filing. Plus, he said, Thornton was more of a desk jockey than an appellate court lawyer.

When I arrived, the building was surrounded by scaffolding being used by construction workers to pressure-wash the courthouse and remove the old grout. Mist from their work floated in my direction, and I took it as a bad omen—finding a way to get rained on when there wasn't a cloud in the sky.

The building had seen its share of controversy, including some landmark death-penalty cases that had ended up at the US Supreme Court. In *Furman v. Georgia*, this court had upheld the death penalty arising from a murder conviction. But the US Supreme Court reversed, ruling that laws that gave juries wide discretion in the application of the death penalty constituted "cruel and unusual punishment." That 1972 ruling put a de facto moratorium on the death penalty in the United States that lasted for the next four years.

A second Georgia case lifted that moratorium. In *Gregg v. Georgia*, the courts considered a new statutory scheme that became known as "guided discretion," whereby trials would be divided into two phases. The first phase would determine the guilt or innocence of the defendant. The second phase, if necessary, would determine whether there were sufficient aggravating circumstances to impose the death penalty. The Supreme Court approved of that scheme, and the executions resumed.

In a third case, *McCleskey v. Kemp*, decided in 1987, the courts considered whether the death penalty should be ruled unconstitutional because of the allegedly discriminatory manner in which it was applied in Georgia. McCleskey's lawyers had examined over two thousand murder cases and statistically demonstrated that defendants charged with killing white victims in Georgia received the death penalty in 11 percent of the cases, but defendants charged with killing black victims received the death penalty in only one percent of the cases. The disparity was most pronounced in cases with black defendants and white victims, when the death penalty was given 22 percent of the time. If the roles were switched—white defendants and black victims—the rate dropped from 22 percent to one percent.

Both the Georgia Supreme Court and the US Supreme Court had considered the statistics and decided they weren't enough to nullify the death penalty. The executions continued.

As I passed through the metal detector at the judicial building, I thought about these cases and others like them that I had studied in law school. I had always defended the death penalty because I understood a victim's need to see ultimate justice. I wondered now if the Georgia Supreme Court, already famous for its death-penalty jurisprudence, would plow new ground on our case. Would future generations of law students read about *Marshall v. Georgia* and debate the merits of the death penalty while ignoring the personal toll a case like this takes on the victims?

I hoped not. I desperately wanted this whole saga to be over, for the court to declare that the Cooper affidavit was not a game changer, that Antoine Marshall's erratic march to the death chamber could continue. I wanted this case to be a footnote in the textbooks, not a section heading.

I arrived a full fifteen minutes early to the stately courtroom where the court heard arguments. There were seven high-backed leather chairs behind the oak dais at the front of the courtroom. The oak-paneled walls were lined with portraits of former chiefs. The carpet was a plush dark green, and the large wall behind the bench, in contrast to the oak walls on the sides of the courtroom, was covered in granite. That wall had a single Latin inscription highlighted in bold-relief letters: *Fiat justitia, ruat caelum*. I had looked it up after the first time our case had been argued here, more than eight years ago. It meant "May justice prevail though the heavens fall." I prayed that would be the case today.

Mace James and a few other lawyers were seated in front of the bar on the left. Mace always looked out of place in a suit with his hulking frame, bald head, and tattooed neck. As a teenager, I had been enraged by Caleb Tate's showmanship when he defended Antoine Marshall at trial. As an adult, listening to the arguments of Professor James made me equally livid.

Caleb Tate came across as a slick actor—I knew he didn't really believe in Antoine Marshall's innocence, but he had a job to do and knew how to put on a show. But for Mace James, it was more than a job; he was a true believer in Marshall's innocence. Though I admired his crusading spirit, his blind allegiance to his client and his refusal to acknowledge the truth of what his client had done infuriated me.

At the hearing, I was surprised to see Caleb Tate seated just behind counsel table for the appellant. Tate had not played a role in the appeals for Antoine Marshall to date but apparently couldn't resist a hearing if the press would be there.

I took my seat on the first bench on the right, hoping the Supreme Court justices would notice a member of the victim's family at the proceedings. Three appellate lawyers from the AG's office were in a huddle at counsel table. One of the younger ones noticed me and said hello. I stood, and all three reached over the rail to shake my hand and thank me for coming. Even Andrew Thornton, the oldest member of the team.

The handshake with Thornton was awkward, and he appeared even stiffer than normal. And this was the man who would be seeking justice for me and my family.

41

THE JUSTICES FILED IN right on time, and the clerk called the court to order. It was an imposing forum, and I wondered if I would ever gain the poise and ability to argue a case here. The setting didn't seem to bother Mace James in the least.

He settled in behind the podium without a single note and stared straight at the seven justices sitting a mere twenty feet away. A red digital clock at the right of the bench displayed the time left on his twenty-minute argument. From my perspective, I could see only a partial profile of his face—his jaw firmly set—the tattoo on his neck, the back of his head, and his broad shoulders flexing as he grabbed both sides of the podium.

"May it please the court, I represent the appellant, Antoine Marshall, in this capital murder case. Sixty days ago, the state of Georgia came within three hours of executing an innocent man. Fortunately, this court intervened."

James let them chew on that thought for a second, and I repeated the Latin phrase under my breath: *"Fiat justitia, ruat caelum."*

After his brief pause, James resumed with confidence, hammering home points that in my mind had already been addressed by the courts. The alleged impropriety of Bill Masterson's striking three African Americans from the jury panel, the questions Judge Cynthia Snowden had asked to rehabilitate my dad's testimony, her refusal to admit the polygraph results, and her refusal to allow the testimony of two expert witnesses.

"I'm not trying to replow old ground here," James said. The comment made me scoff, and the justices looked like they shared my skepticism. "But I think we need to look at the Cooper affidavit in the total context of this case. This is not a situation where the testimony of a jailhouse snitch was just one more incriminating piece in a mountain of evidence proving guilt. If you take away the testimony of Cooper, the only thing left is the disputed cross-racial eyewitness testimony of a man who failed to pick the defendant out of a lineup presented to him on the witness stand in court."

"But, Counselor," the chief justice interrupted. She was a conservative whom I was counting on as one of the four votes we needed to rule against Marshall. "Mr. Tate cross-examined Freddie Cooper at trial and discredited him so much that the DA hardly even mentioned Cooper in his closing. How can you ignore that and claim Cooper's testimony was the linchpin of the prosecution's case?"

"I'm not saying it was the linchpin, Your Honor. But we really don't know how much the jury relied on him. And that's the point. How can we say the state proved its case beyond a reasonable doubt apart from Cooper's testimony? One discredited eyewitness? No DNA, no confession, no corroborating evidence? This case begs for a retrial."

"How convenient," shot back Justice Sherman, a junior member of the court who was a former prosecutor. "The only eyewitness, as I understand it, is now dead, and your client wants a retrial."

Yes, I thought. It was frustrating to sit there and listen to James make these high-sounding arguments about why a killer should go free. But it was heartening to see at least a few justices challenging him. Still, as the give-and-take played out over the next twenty minutes, I couldn't tell whether we had the four votes necessary to win.

The swing vote, Justice Skelton, was a Southern gentleman, an unassuming moderate who had been on the court longer than anyone except for the chief. And Skelton just sat there, chin in his hand, listening intently but saying nothing.

What was that man thinking?

42

WHEN ASSISTANT ATTORNEY GENERAL Andrew Thornton stood behind the podium, the courtroom seemed to expand. He was slender, with a head that appeared too big for his body. He peered over reading glasses as he spoke. Unlike Professor James, he carried a thick black notebook to the podium and even read his introductory remarks from it, setting forth the procedural background for the case. He started slowly; the justices appeared bored, and I wanted to stand up and deliver the argument myself.

"We've read your brief," the chief interrupted. "We know how the case got here. Let's get to the point."

I cringed. Why did my mother's case have to end up in the hands of this guy?

Undeterred, Thornton reached down and held up a three-page document. "I have here a second affidavit from Mr. Cooper," he said.

I glanced at Mace James, who had been calmly taking notes. His head jerked up.

"In this affidavit, he recants his prior recantation. I would have filed this with our briefs, but we just found Mr. Cooper yesterday. I would instead like to file this with the court and provide Mr. James with a copy."

James stood, his neck red. "At the very least, Mr. Thornton could have provided me a copy before the hearing started. This is the kind of prosecutorial misconduct that landed us here in the first place—"

The chief justice banged her gavel. "Mr. James, this is not a trial. Have a seat." She scowled and turned back to Thornton. "And, Mr. Thornton, defense counsel is right. You could have provided him a copy before court started."

Thornton mumbled an apology, his theatrics backfiring. "May I proceed?" he asked.

He was answered not by the chief but by the man seated to her right—sixty-seven-year-old Christopher Wright, the court's most liberal member. "This affidavit is not timely filed," Wright said, "and frankly, it can only hurt your case. This is not a trial court. If you believe this court needs to decide the veracity of Mr. Cooper's testimony in order to determine the outcome of the case, why shouldn't we send it back for a new trial?"

Thornton didn't flinch. "If I could submit the affidavit and have Your Honor read it, you will see that it's more than just a question of Mr. Cooper's credibility. He swears in the affidavit that he was bullied into recanting his testimony by Professor James. That Professor James forcibly kidnapped him from a bar in Nashville, Tennessee, and threatened to falsely turn him in for drug possession if he didn't recant."

Mace James was on his feet, arms spread wide.

"Sit down, Mr. James," the chief justice said.

Thornton took it as a cue to continue. "In light of this information, which the state could not have discovered by due diligence before this hearing, I'm asking for leave to file a supplemental brief."

"Let Mr. James see a copy of the affidavit, and provide the clerk with copies for the court," the chief justice said.

Thornton did as he was told, and the clerk passed out copies to each of the justices. I could see the tops of all seven heads as they quickly read through the affidavit. Mace James showed his disgust while he flipped from page one to page two. I wished someone would have given me a copy.

"Continue," the chief justice said after she had finished reading.

"Your Honors have seen the video of Mr. Cooper that was filed with the defendant's original petition," Thornton continued. He no longer seemed so small and frail. "That video shows that Mr. Cooper had recently been in a fight. Now we know the rest of the story. The swollen left eye came from Mr. James. The video was recorded in a hotel room where Mr. Cooper was being held captive by Mr. James and his investigator. The recantation was coerced. At the end of the affidavit we just provided, Mr. Cooper reaffirms his original testimony."

Reporters in the courtroom were tapping on their laptops, fingers flying. Now this was a story! Because Supreme Court arguments were generally dull affairs, only a few diehards had even shown up for today. Just two Atlanta stations had sent camera crews, as permitted by the court rules, to film from the alcove of the courtroom. But their glee was nearly palpable. And I could envision the headline in the *Atlanta Times*: *Law School Professor Accused of Beating Up Witness!*

The motto of the Georgia Supreme Court was coming to life. Justice *was* prevailing.

When Thornton finished his argument, the chief justice granted Mace James five minutes for rebuttal. James took his place behind the podium, grabbed the sides, and stared at Thornton for a moment before addressing the court.

"That affidavit is patently false," he said, his words seething with anger. "I'd like to know what the state promised Mr. Cooper to get it."

"Counsel," the chief justice said sharply, "leave the personal attacks out of it."

"But, Your Honor, that's what this entire affidavit is. The state's using a three-time convicted felon to personally attack *me*. He lied in his trial testimony and now he's lying again."

"Did you pull him out of a Nashville bar and threaten him?" Justice Sherman asked. The former prosecutor had probably seen his share of defense-lawyer shenanigans.

"Before the bar incident, one of my investigators recorded an admission by Mr. Cooper that he had lied at trial. Because the quality of that recording was not good, we did pull him out of a Nashville bar on the night before my client's scheduled execution to get him sober enough to do another recording and sign an affidavit."

"Did you threaten to turn him in on drug charges if he didn't cooperate?" Sherman asked, the exasperation evident in his voice.

James hesitated, and I knew the justices had him.

"He had drugs in his possession, Your Honor. I told him that if he didn't come clean, I would turn him in. But he had already admitted that his trial testimony was false before this."

"Did you tell the authorities that Mr. Cooper was in possession of drugs?"

There was more hesitation, crimson crawling up Mace James's neck, swallowing his tattoo and coloring his bald head. "No. I didn't believe I had an obligation to do so."

"But you would have if he had not signed your affidavit?"

"I don't know."

Sherman leaned forward. "Did you tell him that you would turn him in for possession of drugs if he didn't give you an affidavit recanting his prior testimony—yes or no?"

"Yes. But that doesn't mean the affidavit is untrue."

"We'll be the judges of that."

43

THERE WAS A HUM of excitement as the justices called the next case. James stormed out of the courtroom without shaking hands with the prosecutors. Caleb Tate followed on his heels. I waited for both of them to leave and then followed at a distance, barely able to contain my excitement. I lingered in the hallway and thanked Andrew Thornton.

"That didn't exactly go down the way I anticipated," he admitted. "But I think we'll get the right result."

"There's no chance they'll order a new trial," I said. "And I appreciate you taking a bullet in there to make sure justice was done."

Thornton shrugged. He came across as self-effacing and likable, but I would still rather have Bill Masterson as Georgia's next attorney general. Masterson inspired confidence; Thornton inspired sympathy.

"Does this mean I can count on your vote?" he asked with a sly smile.

I smiled back. "Only if you win the Republican primary without me."

Following the court media rules, the reporters asked Thornton and me if they could interview us outside the judicial building. I told them I wouldn't be answering any questions and slipped away to the elevators. I rode to the first floor and was walking across the lobby when I saw Caleb Tate out of the corner of my eye. He veered toward me and I continued walking, eyes straight ahead.

"Jamie, you got a second?"

I didn't slow down. "Why? So you can bait me again and misquote me in the press?"

He fell in next to me. "I need to talk about my case. There's something you need to know for your own good. You don't have to say a word—just listen."

I had almost reached the door before I stopped to face him. "Forgive me, but when someone who lies about what I said before wants to have another conversation, I'm a little skeptical. And I also have a lot of work to do thanks to your influence on the other inmates when you were in the Milton County jail." I turned and pushed open the door.

"It's about your father," Tate said, stopping me in my tracks. He pulled a microcassette recorder from his suit pocket and held it out to me. "Here. You can record every word of the conversation and keep the tape. That way you don't have to worry about me *allegedly* misconstruing what was said."

I considered this for a moment. There was an old saying that any lawyer who represented himself had a fool for a client. The reason was simple—lawyers thought they were too smart for their own good. They believed the rules didn't apply to them. And one of the main rules is that no criminal defendant should *ever* talk to a prosecutor without a lawyer present.

"You're represented by Mace James," I said, standing in the doorway. "I shouldn't even be talking to you."

A couple walked through the door I was now holding open, and Tate took a step closer, turning on the recorder. He gave his name as well as the date and location of our conversation. "I waive my right to have counsel present, and I have specifically requested that Ms. Brock listen to what I have to say. She has informed me that I have the right to have my lawyer present, but I have emphatically told her that I want to speak to her without my lawyer."

He turned the tape off and rewound it so I could hear his voice. "Good enough?" he asked. He handed the recorder to me, and this time I took it.

"Let's go over there in the corner," I said.

We walked silently to the far side of the lobby. I did a couple of dry runs to make sure the machine was recording properly. "Go ahead," I said.

Tate cleared his throat and looked at me, watching my expression as he talked. "This is Caleb Tate, and I'm innocent. I loved Rikki, and I would never have done anything to hurt her."

I shifted my weight onto my right leg, left hand on hip, right hand holding the tape recorder between us. I knew Tate could read my impatience. *I'm not impressed.*

"Jamie, we both know you can't make the case against me without Rafael Rivera. And he's got more credibility problems than you realize. Because I served as his attorney, I can't tell you what those problems are right now. But if Rivera takes the stand and testifies against me, he waives the attorney-client privilege, and I'll be able to testify about every conversation we've ever had."

"So what's your point?"

Tate looked past my shoulder and then turned back to me. "Let me speak hypothetically for a moment—just so you'll understand the import of what I'm trying to say. Let's say that hypothetically my client came to me and told me he wanted me to bribe a certain judge so he could get acquitted. Let's say he explicitly mentioned Cynthia Snowden, a judge who has a reputation for being on the take. Let's say I refused, and my client threatened me, saying I would regret it. Let's say that same client later came to you and offered to provide false testimony against me."

Tate looked at me as if lightbulbs should be going off in my head. But none of this seemed to torpedo our case. It was still Rivera's word against Tate's.

"That's it? You did all this cloak-and-dagger stuff to tell me that?"

"We're still speaking hypothetically, right?"

"Sure," I said, playing his game. He had already revealed part of his strategy for the cross-examination of Rivera. Maybe he'd tell me more.

"What if I could prove that Judge Snowden *was* on the take? That would help corroborate my version of events, would it not? What if I gave you the names of three defense lawyers who had achieved uncommonly good results in front of Judge Snowden? Would you still put Rivera on the stand?"

I sensed that Tate was leaving a lot of things unsaid. And I knew better than to answer questions coming from a sleazeball like him. "Maybe you just heard rumors that Judge Snowden was dirty and concocted a story that would allow you to use those rumors to bolster your own credibility. As to whether I would still call Rafael Rivera as a witness—I guess you'll have to show up the first day of trial and find out."

"Clever . . . but maybe this will change your mind." He reached into his suit coat pocket and pulled out a folded sheet of paper, handing it to me. "These are the names of three criminal-defense attorneys who have had results in front of Judge Snowden that are inexplicable. Check them out for yourself. I think you'll see that the judge is definitely playing favorites."

I put the piece of paper in my pocket without looking at it. "Is that it?"

"You can keep the recorder," Tate said. "Have a good day."

I smirked at him. "In case you've forgotten, I already did."

◁ ▷

I waited until I got to my 4Runner in the parking garage before I unfolded the paper. The first two names were defense lawyers who had been around Atlanta for a long time and were known to get stellar results. They were Tate's competitors, and seeing their names on the list did not surprise me. But the third name sent my head spinning. The roller-coaster ride that was my life had just taken a breathtaking drop. I stared at the paper in disbelief. I knew it couldn't be true, but I was shocked at Caleb Tate's audacity for even suggesting it.

The man I despised more than any other man in the world had written in neat block letters the name of my own father: *Robert James Brock.*

44

MACE JAMES LEFT THE JUDICIAL BUILDING and kept his head down as two reporters chased after him, peppering him with questions. They soon gave up, and Mace marched straight to his car. His first call after leaving the parking garage was to the dean of Southeastern Law School. Sylvia Ellison answered on the second ring.

"There's something I need you to hear from me," Mace said. "It has to do with a hearing on the Marshall case at the Georgia Supreme Court."

For ten minutes Mace told the Freddie Cooper story, his narrative interrupted by occasional expressions of surprise and concern by Dean Ellison. She had hired Mace six years ago, had stuck her neck out for him, and had been one of his biggest supporters. But today he couldn't tell how she was taking this. When he concluded, she asked a number of terse questions and then fell silent for a moment. Mace waited her out.

"We've got a serious problem," she said. "When you represent these clients, you're not acting on your own behalf. You're representing our school through the clinic. I'm definitely going to be hearing about this from the other professors and alumni."

"I know, Sylvia. I'm sorry."

"I need some time to process this. I want you in my office at 8 a.m. tomorrow. I might have Elias and John here as well."

Elias was the dean of academic affairs. John was chairman of the law school's board of trustees and the managing partner of a large Atlanta firm. It was like being called into the principal's office and knowing that both parents would be there.

"Okay," Mace said. "I'll bring my Kevlar boxers."

"See you tomorrow," Sylvia said. It seemed the dean had lost her sense of humor.

◁▷

On the way to Jackson, Mace called a few law school colleagues to tell them his side of the story, such as it was. He also called a few buddies he didn't want hearing the story for the first time on the news. They were on his side before he could get halfway through the facts. His last call before he arrived at the prison in Jackson was to his pastor. The man listened patiently and promised to pray for Mace.

The conversation Mace had been dreading the most took place ten minutes later. Separated by glass from his client, phone to his ear, Mace gave Antoine a blow-by-blow description of the hearing.

Antoine's eyes were as big as saucers, and tears started forming as Mace continued. Antoine held the phone tight, struggling to keep his composure.

"You don't know how much I've been praying," Antoine said when Mace was finished. "I haven't eaten nothin' for three days because the Bible says we should fast. Why does God hate me like this?"

Mace knew he didn't have any satisfactory answers for a man who had already spent eleven years behind bars for something he didn't do. "I don't know what's going on," Mace admitted. "But I know you were three hours away from dying once, and God spared your life. This is no time to give up."

Antoine shrugged, his rounded shoulders signaling total defeat. "You're a good lawyer, Mace. But you can't beat the system. Maybe it's time to stop trying. Spend your time on somebody who's got a chance."

"I'm not going anywhere," Mace promised. He tried to sound more confident than he felt. "In fact, I'm just warming up."

"Right," Antoine mumbled, his pity party in full swing. "Maybe I should just help the state out a little. Make everyone happy. End it once and for all."

Mace leaned forward. If he could have reached through the glass, he would have shaken some sense into his client. "Don't ever say that again," Mace said firmly. "We're going to get you out of here."

45

BY THE TIME I ARRIVED BACK at the office, I had just enough time to grab my files and make it to court for the afternoon docket. I had been too nervous to eat much breakfast before the Supreme Court hearing, and now I'd skipped lunch. My mind was a million miles away from Milton County Superior Court. I needed to prove Caleb Tate wrong about my father.

The claim that my father had been bribing or extorting Judge Snowden was laughable. It cut against everything I knew about his character. But Caleb Tate had asserted his claim with such confidence, challenging me to check the records myself, that he had managed to germinate the tiniest seed of doubt. And that seed had now sprouted into a hundred what-if questions.

What if my father's record in front of Snowden *was* inexplicably good, even if he hadn't done anything illegal? What if Tate was telling the truth about his former client Rafael Rivera? What if—and I couldn't believe I was even asking this—my father had something on Judge Snowden? What if all of that became public? Would Antoine Marshall get a new trial? And if so, how could we possibly get a conviction now that my father, the only eyewitness to the crime, was dead?

These questions ate at me as Judge Pipes, a substitute judge who had been pulled out of retirement to help due to the plea-bargaining crisis, gaveled the afternoon session to order. I had about fifteen files stacked on the prosecutor's table. They were all probation violations and bond revocations—the types of things the court normally processed with utmost efficiency.

Defendants who had violated probation would come in and plead with the court for one more chance. I would express the state's frustration with a convict who had been given a second chance and thumbed his nose at the court. The judges would typically hand out whatever sentence I asked for and throw in a harsh lecture for free.

But that afternoon, Judge Pipes, who had been one of the tougher judges on the bench when he was active, was giving out light sentences and setting low bonds. My recommendations for tough love were ignored.

Halfway through the afternoon, I started arguing more forcefully and cross-examined the defendants at length to show their blatant disregard for the law. But none of this seemed to affect Pipes. By the time the day was over, I realized that a new kind of normal had been established in Milton County. Instead of judges listening to prosecutors, they were going light on nonviolent offenders, freeing up jail space for the hard-core felons.

I returned to the office at five and compared notes with other prosecutors. They had experienced the same thing. It was like the judges had gotten together and decided to change the sentencing guidelines. If word got out, Milton County would become *the* place for drug gangs.

We had lost round one.

I called both Bill Masterson and Regina Granger but got their voice mails. I shut myself in my office, checked my e-mail messages, and played around on the Internet. I was trying to get up the nerve to check our database to test Caleb Tate's claims.

After procrastinating for half an hour, I entered my father's name in the defense attorney field and searched the criminal cases in the Milton County DA's data bank. I started ten years before my mother's death and looked at every case my father had handled in front of Snowden and every other judge in the county. I took notes and categorized the results. After two hours of skimming through more than three hundred files, I calculated the results and stared at the paper in disbelief. My stomach ached as the reality began to sink in. The results jumped out at me, mocking my hope that Caleb Tate had exaggerated my dad's success.

As prosecutors, we normally win about 90 percent of our cases. In general, my dad did better than most defense attorneys, winning not just 10 percent of the time but nearly 30 percent of the time. But of the forty cases in Judge Snowden's courtroom, he had won twenty-nine—better than 70 percent. Worse, about half of those were decided on motions to suppress or other hearings where the judge played a critical role. It was exactly the way Caleb Tate suggested it would be.

I felt sick as I tried to formulate scenarios that could explain the results. Perhaps my father just understood the way Judge Snowden thought, the same way I had achieved better grades with some teachers than with others. Perhaps Snowden had a great deal of respect for my father and subconsciously gave him the benefit of the doubt.

Okay, so maybe the judge played favorites. Did that make her corrupt? Or maybe she just liked the defense lawyers who were better prepared than the others. None of these reasons would mean that my father or Judge Snowden had done anything wrong.

But as a thorough lawyer, I couldn't ignore the cold, hard facts. My father had won 72 percent of his cases in front of Judge Snowden and only 30 percent in front of other judges. In no other single judge's courtroom had he won even half of his cases. If he was just better prepared than other defense attorneys or quicker on his feet or got the breaks because of his reputation, then why didn't it apply with judges other than Snowden? Not only that, but my father seemed to have more cases go to trial in front of Snowden than with any other judge.

I also looked up the results for the other lawyers on Caleb Tate's list. They too won roughly 70 percent of their cases in front of Snowden. I ran a search for cases presided over by Snowden in general. Her overall conviction rate was about 90 percent. What could account for the fact that the three lawyers on Tate's list won 70 percent of the time in front of Snowden while other defense attorneys won only 10 percent?

By the time I finished, it was nearly midnight. I hadn't gotten up from my computer for at least three hours. Poor Justice was probably prancing around the house, his bladder ready to burst. But I was almost paralyzed, too crestfallen to move from in front of my screen as the stark reality of this data sank in. Whether or not my father and Snowden had done anything illegal was almost beside the point. This data alone would give Mace James something new to scream about. Snowden had ruled against Antoine Marshall on almost every major evidentiary motion and had even asked some questions to rehabilitate my father's testimony after Tate's cross-examination. People would jump to conclusions. Where there's smoke, they would claim, there must also be fire. My father's reputation would be trashed. And if Mace James got lucky, my mother's killer would walk out of jail a free man.

My only alternative—one that seemed equally abhorrent—was to dismiss the case against Caleb Tate. That way this data would never come to light. Tate would be compelled by the rules of ethics not to repeat anything Rafael Rivera had told him unless Rivera took the stand to testify against him. But how could I turn a killer like Tate free just to protect my father's reputation?

I had become a prosecutor because I believed in the justice system. Prosecutors were on the side of the angels. Yet suddenly everything was murky and unclear. Through no fault of my own, fate had conspired against me.

I shut down my computer and forced myself to leave the office at 12:08. Some nights I hated being a prosecutor.

46

I SLEPT FITFULLY THAT NIGHT, waking up several times, praying the whole thing was just a nightmare. At three in the morning, I thought about taking an Ambien but realized that I wouldn't be able to wake up in time for work. At four thirty, after lying awake for thirty minutes staring at the ceiling, I conceded defeat and got out of bed. I threw on my sweats, and Justice rolled over and looked at me like I was nuts. I padded down to my dad's study, sat in his chair, and started going through the desk drawers as if I might discover the key to the man's character there. Could I possibly be this wrong about somebody I knew so well?

In the top left drawer there were some old family photographs. Chris, Mom, Dad, and me, smiling on vacation. I was fifteen, and my hair looked like a rat's nest. Photographs of me from my college days racing kayaks and some from the Olympic trials when I came up one place short. There was one of Chris in his cap and gown, graduating from seminary, Dad on one side, me on the other. There was another family photo from my middle school years; Mom had cut herself out of the picture. Before her death, we made fun of her—my mom, the psychiatrist, who swore she didn't take good pictures. We said she needed to work on her self-image.

At Antoine Marshall's murder trial, Masterson had introduced the photograph into evidence and used it during his closing argument. "This is what Antoine Marshall did to this family."

Toward the bottom of the drawer were some yellowed pages from my earlier childhood, the wide-lined paper you use when you first begin writing. On the bottom right corner of one I had taped a picture of myself in my white cap and gown at kindergarten graduation. On that same page I had also taped two Atomic Fireballs, which had now gone from red to white with age. In large block letters I had written, *I love you, Dad. Jamie.*

Underneath that memento was a book I had put together when I was in second grade. Our teachers had asked us to write about our hero. I had a hard time choosing but had eventually landed on my dad. I could still remember feeling guilty about choosing him over my mom. I'd even talked to my mom about it. She was so excited that we spent hours working on the little book together. My mom's dad had left her family when she was in elementary school, and she said she had always prayed that her kids would have a special relationship with their father.

I read through the book now with tears rolling down my cheeks, and I was somehow certain that my dad would never have cheated in order to set his clients free. It was up to me to save his reputation. Antoine Marshall had killed my mother. I couldn't let my dad be destroyed by his lawyer.

◁▷

Mace James made a point not to read any newspaper coverage or watch television reports before he met with Dean Ellison on Tuesday morning. He wore his best blue pin-striped suit and white oxford shirt. A man ought to be dressed up when he faced the firing squad.

The dean welcomed Mace into her office, and he exchanged terse greetings with Elias Gonzales and John Shaw.

Ellison had a spacious office with an ornate desk and a round conference table that could have easily accommodated the four of them. But Mace had never seen Ellison meet with anyone at the table. Instead, as was her custom, she and the others took seats on the opposite side of the office, where two wingback chairs, a coffee table, and a small couch gave visitors a homey feel. Gonzales and Shaw hunkered down on the couch. Mace sat in one of the chairs, and the dean sat across the coffee table from him in the other.

"Anything to drink?" she asked.

"I'm fine."

"Have you read the papers this morning?" Shaw asked. As the managing partner of one of Atlanta's biggest firms, Shaw was proud of his reputation and also the school's. He guarded both like a rottweiler.

"No."

Shaw placed the paper on the coffee table. It was a long article, page one, local section. "Congratulations," Shaw said.

Mace didn't respond.

"Mace, before we talk about what to do, I think it might be helpful for us to hear from you exactly what happened," Dean Ellison interjected. "Why don't you just start from the beginning, and we can chime in with any questions?"

Mace cleared his throat, surprised at how nervous he felt. His voice was hoarse as he started, but he eventually relaxed a bit. When he got to the part about the bar fight, John Shaw grimaced in disbelief. "The papers haven't even figured that angle out," he said. "You staged a bar fight in order to kidnap this guy—wait until *that* comes out."

"Let 'im finish," Gonzales said.

From that point, Mace gave them a truncated and slightly sanitized version, ending with the hearing in front of the Georgia Supreme Court.

When he was done, heads turned toward Dean Ellison. Mace knew that Shaw wanted him gone. Gonzales had always liked Mace, primarily because Mace didn't complain about being overworked like the other professors. But the buck stopped at Dean Ellison's desk.

She hesitated too long for John Shaw's liking. "I counted five separate ethical violations, if anybody needs a scorecard," he said.

"And the execution of an innocent man postponed," Mace added sarcastically. "But maybe that doesn't make the scorecard in your world."

"In my world, the ends don't justify the means," Shaw retorted.

"*Gentlemen,*" the dean said. Hearing her tone, Mace swallowed his verbal counterpunch. He felt like a schoolboy caught in a fight.

The dean softened her voice. "Mace, what do *you* suggest we do?"

"I'm assuming that Teacher of the Year is out of the question?"

Ellison gave him a don't-toy-with-me look.

"Sorry," Mace said. "Look—you hired me to run a clinic and provide zealous representation for our clients. And that's not as clean as the civil cases handled by Mr. Shaw in his silk-stocking law firm. I regret that I stepped over the line. And I'm especially sorry that it has put Southeastern in a bad light and will cause you all sorts of grief. It's no excuse, but I just kept asking myself: How could I go to Antoine Marshall's funeral knowing that I hadn't done everything possible to save him?"

Mace glanced at his feet and back up at Dean Ellison. "Well, if I were you, I'd make me apologize, and then I would probably suspend me pending an investigation by the state bar. I'm sure Andrew Thornton has already reported me."

The dean turned to her colleague. "Elias?"

"That sounds about right. I would have the law school do its own independent investigation as well so we can issue a report that would help answer some questions the public might have. I'm not excusing what Mace did, but if I were Antoine Marshall, I'd be glad to have him on my side."

"John?"

"You know how I feel. I've been practicing law for forty years. There are ways to get things done that don't violate the ethical rules. We've all worked too long and too hard gaining national prominence for our school to flush it down the toilet with this kind of behavior."

John shot an accusatory eye toward Mace. "Frankly, if you were an associate in my firm, you would already be fired."

Frankly, if I were an associate in your firm, I would have committed suicide by now. But Mace didn't say it. He wasn't going to win Ellison's swing vote by arguing with the chairman of the board.

The room grew quiet, and the dean sighed. "You've put me in quite a dilemma, Mace. I like you a lot. The students love you. And your whole story has been good for the school. But how can we exhort our students to follow the highest possible ethical standards and condone conduct like this?"

It was a rhetorical question, and Mace didn't try to answer. He stared at the dean, unblinking, as she prepared to pronounce her sentence. He liked this woman and respected her integrity. He couldn't blame her if she fired him on the spot. She had the entire law school to worry about. But Mace's job was to take care of his clients.

"When I hired you, I told you that you would be under stricter scrutiny than the other professors. With your background, there were a lot of folks who warned me not to take a chance on you at all. So far, you've been fabulous for the school, so I'm taking that into account. But last night, I received eighty-six e-mails and phone messages calling for your head.

"What's especially troubling is that this recent conduct is somewhat similar to what landed you in jail in the first place. I thought you were a changed man, and I put my neck out there for you, Mace. And you've let me down."

"I'm sorry, Sylvia. I really mean that."

"I believe you. But that doesn't change what's happened." Another big sigh. For the dean, it was the same thing as banging a gavel. "I'm going to suspend you immediately through the end of the school year. By that time, the state ethics investigation should be complete. I'm going to hold your position open, and you can reapply this summer along with other candidates. We'll wait to make a decision until after August 7."

The implications weren't lost on Mace. August 7 was the new date for Antoine's execution. By then, the courts would have ruled on the substance of Mace's motion, and the state ethics investigation would be complete. Dean Ellison was giving him every chance to clear his name.

"Thank you," Mace said.

"Most people never get a chance at redemption," Dean Ellison said. "You've now been given two. Make the most of it this time."

"I think you're making a mistake, Sylvia," John Shaw piped in. "This thing won't die down unless we take decisive action."

"I'm not interested in making this *thing* die down. I'm interested in doing the *right* thing."

Shaw shook his head and frowned. Mace hoped the man would one day be in the hot seat himself. To a lawyer like Shaw, who had lived a charmed life, mercy was just a concept, one that constantly interfered with the true administration of justice. But for men like Mace, who had been forgiven much, mercy was like air. You couldn't survive without it.

47

JIMMY BRANDYWINE WAS A LOSER in every sense of the word. He was soft and pasty with a chipped tooth and curly brown hair. Even at thirty-one years old, he couldn't grow a proper beard—just a few strands of chin hair. He had been diagnosed as a paranoid schizophrenic and had lashed out at his previous two lawyers when his medication hadn't been right. Prior to his arrest, he had lived with his mother and collected unemployment intermittently for fourteen months. The police busted him as part of a pornography sting and found hundreds of pictures of child porn on his computer.

Jimmy had been in jail for six months when, one month before trial, his new lawyer claimed Jimmy wasn't competent to assist in his own defense. Rowena Guilford, one of the hardest-working public defenders I knew, argued that Jimmy had been repeatedly abused by other prisoners. That abuse had aggravated his preexisting psychiatric issues, pushing him over the edge. According to her motion, Jimmy now thought the entire world had conspired against him—including his own lawyer. "The defendant can no longer separate his own psychotic ideations from reality and therefore is not competent to stand trial," she wrote.

Shortly afterward, Dr. Aaron Gillespie evaluated Jimmy and declared that the defendant was fit to stand trial after all. The court agreed. And so, on Tuesday morning, the case began.

Judge Whitaker was a massive African American judge who was known to be deliberate and evenhanded. Following Rowena Guilford's advice, Jimmy had waived his right to a jury trial; judges generally went easier on pornography cases. But before Whitaker took the bench and called the court to order, Rowena approached me at counsel table. "I want to talk about a plea," she said.

At any other time, this would have been expected. We had a can't-lose case—the police had conducted a lawful search of Brandywine's computer and found the pornographic pictures of underage girls. But in the past two weeks, not one defendant had attempted to cut a deal.

I tried to play it coy. "What's the use? We've got him dead to rights."

Rowena frowned. "Cut the crap, Jamie. We all know things are out of control around here. My client's willing to step up, plead guilty, and put his life on the line when he walks outside those prison walls. He's asking you to recommend that the judge sentence him to three years and suspend all but the six months he's already served."

I scoffed. "You want him to plead guilty and walk without serving another day?"

Rowena lowered her voice. "He's willing to play ball. I haven't had one client willing to play ball in almost three weeks. This could break the logjam, Jamie." She hesitated and frowned, as if trying to talk herself into something. "Look, if you want him to serve a few more months, and you can make sure he's in isolation with a twenty-four-hour watch, I can probably work that, too."

I looked around the courtroom. There were a few folks in the gallery, but nobody could hear us. The defendant had not yet been ushered in by the deputies. "You know I don't do pleas, Rowena. Especially not on pornography cases."

"He didn't hurt anybody. He's a nonviolent offender."

That made me bristle. *Didn't hurt anybody?* "There are photos of hundreds of naked girls on his computer, and some of them are eleven and twelve years old. Don't tell me he didn't hurt anybody."

"That's not what I meant, Jamie. At least talk it over with your boss. This guy is getting abused so much in jail that he'll do anything to get out, even if people will be gunning for him once he does. We aren't going to have a perfect case to break this deadlock."

"I'll see what I can do."

I stepped out in the hallway and called Bill Masterson. I quickly filled him in on the details, expecting him to demand that I take the deal. Instead, he had the same concerns that I did.

"We can't make our first deal with a guy downloading child porn," Masterson said. "We've been busting our butts for two weeks trying to keep up with this new caseload. We can't cave in now and start dishing out deals that we wouldn't have made before the defendants started this nonsense."

"I agree," I said quickly. "I just wanted to make sure you were on board."

I relayed the message to Rowena, who said I was making a big mistake.

A few minutes later, when the trial started, Jimmy Brandywine pleaded guilty to the child pornography charges and took his chances with Judge Whitaker.

Both sides stipulated to the facts; then Rowena had Jimmy testify about how sorry he was for what he had done. Jimmy's mother took the stand and gave a sob story about the impact on her son's self-image from being laid off three times in the twelve months before his arrest. She had sacrificed on a fixed income so he could have a place to live. She slipped in testimony about how Jimmy had been abused in prison. I had seen it all a hundred times before—a mother's love for her son was willing to forgive all sins.

When it came time for our closing arguments, I urged Judge Whitaker to show no mercy. If it wasn't for men like Jimmy Brandywine, sex traffickers and Internet pornographers could not exist. Everybody in the chain was equally reprehensible, leading to the abuse of eleven- and twelve-year-old girls. Lots of men had been laid off from multiple jobs—that wasn't a license to prey on kids. "Some of these girls should be in the fifth grade, Your Honor." *The fifth grade!* What kind of animal sits at his computer all day and stares at pictures of naked fifth graders?

"The state is suggesting an eight-year prison sentence without the possibility of parole," I concluded. "We are also asking for an additional ten years of supervised release and that Mr. Brandywine be required to register as a sex offender when he's released from custody."

I could hear Brandywine's mother gasp at my suggested sentence. Brandywine would be nearly forty years old by the time he got out. I would have asked for more if I thought Judge Whitaker would go for it.

When Rowena rose to argue, she reminded the court that Brandywine had no priors. He had taken full responsibility for his crimes and apologized to the court. "If it were left to Ms. Brock, every convicted felon would die in prison." It was a cheap shot, but I didn't give her the satisfaction of a response.

"Let me address the elephant in the room," Rowena continued. "No defendant has had the guts to come into a court in Milton County in the past two weeks and plead guilty to anything. None of my clients have done it. Everybody in this county knows that plea bargains and guilty pleas have become a thing of the past. Why? Because men like Mr. Brandywine, who are willing to take responsibility for their crimes, end up being killed within thirty-six hours of their release. As the court considers its sentence, I think the court should take into account the fact that Mr. Brandywine pleaded guilty today because it was the right thing to do, even though he is risking his life to do it."

Judge Whitaker gave me a chance for rebuttal, and I went off. "Judge, I cannot believe what I just heard. This defendant—Jimmy Brandywine—just pleaded guilty to leering over hundreds of images of young girls on his computer, and now his attorney wants the court to treat him like some kind of hero? Ms. Guilford can't be serious! Just because the defendants in this county have entered a conspiracy to backlog the system doesn't mean we should reward somebody involved in child pornography."

I calmed down. Took a breath. "Each one of these pictures is a separate crime. Ms. Guilford is right; I *do* want Your Honor to keep this man in jail for the rest of his life. Because this man is evil. And there's no guarantee that a man as selfish and exploitative as him will not prey on young girls again the day he gets out. But I know a life sentence isn't possible. Eight years is a bargain, Your Honor. Anything less is an insult to the lives of these young victims."

When I sat down, Judge Whitaker made a face as if he didn't get paid enough to make these kinds of decisions. "Ms. Brock makes some very good points," he said. "And as the DA's office knows, this court has been very tough on sex offenders in the past. But Ms. Guilford is also right. This defendant had a clean record before his arrest. And there are no allegations that he distributed child pornography or produced child pornography. As Ms. Guilford also suggests, this court must take into account the overcrowding of our county correction center and give this defendant some credit for coming forward and admitting his guilt. No other defendant has been brave enough to do that in any Milton County courtroom for the past two weeks."

Whitaker stopped and made some notes on his yellow legal pad. I felt the hair on the back of my neck bristle. I knew I wasn't going to like the sentence.

"As Ms. Brock suggests, the court will require the defendant to register as a sex offender. In addition, the court will impose the eight-year sentence suggested by Ms. Brock but will suspend all but the six months that the defendant has already served. The court will require supervised probation for an additional two years and order payment of five thousand dollars into the Victim Restitution Fund."

"Praise God," I heard Brandywine's mother say behind me. I considered her comment blasphemous.

Judge Whitaker banged his gavel, and Guilford thanked the court for its ruling. I shook hands with Rowena, glared at Brandywine, and stalked out of the courtroom.

Things were out of control in Milton County. I couldn't remember another child pornography case where the defendant had gotten off so easy. The inmates were now officially running the asylum.

◁▷

When I told Masterson about the verdict, he suggested we call the Milton County police and park a vehicle in front of Brandywine's house for the next few days. I reminded Masterson that Brandywine was a porn addict, not a city dignitary. But I knew Masterson was right. If anything happened to Brandywine, there wouldn't be another guilty plea in Milton County for months.

It was two o'clock on Wednesday morning when a phone call woke me out of my Ambien-induced sleep.

"You don't have to worry about Brandywine getting off easy," LA said. "He and his mother just died in a house fire. They say the explosion was set off by a remote-controlled device."

I sat up straight in bed and tried to clear the cobwebs out of my head. "I thought they put Brandywine under surveillance."

"They did. But the explosive device was apparently planted in the house a couple of days ago."

48

ON THURSDAY NIGHT, I went into my dad's study and riffled through a corner filing cabinet. In the third drawer down, I found the VHS tapes my father's law partner had used to record the trial of *State v. Marshall*, which had been broadcast by Court TV. During law school, I had promised myself many times that I would watch the entire thing from gavel to gavel but had never mustered the emotional energy to do so.

I hooked up an old VCR in the family room, and it took me about twenty minutes to find the section I wanted. Judge Snowden's rulings had been dissected on appeal and criticized endlessly by Mace James but always upheld by the appellate judges. However, there had been some strong dissents about whether Caleb Tate should have been allowed to call an expert witness to testify about how the cops had supposedly manipulated my father into a faulty identification of Marshall.

From the beginning, the police had suspected Antoine Marshall. He had been previously arrested for breaking and entering to feed his meth habit. According to Caleb Tate, the cops had planted characteristics of Antoine Marshall in my father's mind with their suggestive questions: Did the suspect have dreadlocks? Was he African American? Did he appear to be thin and athletic?

When they showed a lineup to my dad, Marshall was the one person who displayed all of the characteristics seeded in my dad's brain.

As she did with the expert on cross-racial identification, Judge Snowden ruled that this testimony about the so-called faulty lineup was inadmissible. However, she did let Tate proffer the testimony outside the presence of the jury to establish a record for appeal. I found the start of the proffered testimony and watched it with an uneasy feeling in the pit of my stomach.

The expert's name was Dr. Natalie Rutherford, a diminutive and energetic professor of psychology at the University of Michigan who had published extensively on the issue of creating false memories. She had qualified as an expert in numerous other cases. In one notable trial, she had testified about a psychiatrist who had planted false memories in a patient under hypnosis. That patient came to believe that her priest had repeatedly raped her when she was a young child. But during the investigation for the criminal case, it was discovered that the patient was a virgin. The priest sued the psychiatrist, and Dr. Rutherford testified on behalf of the priest. The jury returned a verdict of $2.5 million.

Together with her students, Dr. Rutherford had conducted more than one hundred experiments involving over five thousand individuals in an attempt to document how misinformation creates memory distortion. One of her favorite tricks was to superimpose a picture of someone as a child, together with a parent, onto a photo of a place the person had never been. After viewing the image, that person would be asked to describe the experience pictured. Most subjects provided vivid details, remembering nuances about events that had never occurred.

Rutherford testified that the same phenomenon occurred when individuals tried to recall more-recent events. Our memories, she said, are constructed by combining actual memories with the content of suggestions received from others. Inaccurate memories, formed in part based on inaccurate suggestions from others, would be as compelling and real to a person as accurate memories.

Rutherford also testified about how we synthesize our memories by recalling certain details accurately and then filling in the blanks with details obtained from others. Once these new details become part of the event, they are seared into our memories just as certainly as the details we recalled independently.

On a theoretical level, even I had to admit that her testimony made sense. I thought about the case of the DC sniper attacks, when a media report had stated that the suspects might have been driving a white van. Immediately afterward, several witnesses at the scenes of several different shootings reported seeing a white van fleeing right after the shootings. When the suspects were eventually apprehended, they were driving a blue sedan.

Dr. Rutherford's example was even more memorable. People who had visited Disney World were shown a fake picture with text that described how they shook hands with Bugs Bunny. When they were asked what they remembered about that encounter, most of the subjects remembered hugging Bugs Bunny, and a few remembered touching his ears or tail. Others specifically recalled that Bugs Bunny was holding a carrot at the time.

Dr. Rutherford smiled, trying hard to win over a skeptical Judge Snowden. "Bugs Bunny is a Warner Brothers cartoon character," she said. "He would never be allowed to set foot in Disney World."

Moving to the case at hand, Rutherford testified that she had carefully reviewed the original lineup shown to my father and the questions that had been asked during the preceding police interview. It was her opinion, based on twenty-six years of studying the phenomenon of creating false memories, that the police had done so with my father. Antoine Marshall was no more likely to have committed the crime than any other person within driving distance of our house that night.

Judge Snowden listened carefully and then affirmed her earlier ruling that the testimony was inadmissible. "It seems to me that you simply want to use Dr. Rutherford to take the place of the trier of fact and tell the jury why they should or should not put weight on Mr. Brock's eyewitness account," Judge Snowden said. "It's a clever attempt, Mr. Tate, but the court is not going to allow it. It's no different than your proffered testimony on cross-racial identification."

The jury never heard Dr. Rutherford, and at the time I was glad. But now, with the new information about the success my father had enjoyed in Judge Snowden's courtroom, the Rutherford testimony bothered me. Could she be right? Had my father been unwittingly set up by the cops? And if so, could that mean my mother's killer was still at large?

The last twelve years of my life had been defined by an absolute certainty that Antoine Marshall had killed my mom and deserved to die for it. So much of my energy and time had been spent trying to make him pay for what he had done. I couldn't allow myself to doubt that now.

My father *had* to be right. Even if he did have uncanny success in front of Judge Snowden. Even if, God forbid, he was blackmailing her somehow, there was no motive for him to try to put an innocent man to death. My father couldn't be wrong about this.

Could he?

49

I HAD NEVER UNDERSTOOD how my father could continue to be a defense lawyer even after my mother's death. On Friday morning, sitting in traffic on my way to work, I considered that question again in a different light. Things that appeared innocent and even noble before now seemed more foreboding if Caleb Tate was telling the truth.

In the first few days after talking with Tate, I had refused to even consider the possibility that my father might have been corrupt. Even after I checked the results of his cases, I still chose to believe that there must be some innocent explanation. But as the week progressed, I found myself reliving past events, looking at them through the prism of this new information. And I began to wonder if my dad might have been keeping some very dark secrets.

I remembered, for example, a particularly poignant conversation at a P. F. Chang's during my junior year of college. I had just ordered the chicken dumplings. My father was eating beef fried rice. My brother was there as well. I was home for winter break, and I had decided to go to law school to become a prosecutor.

"How can you still be a defense lawyer after what happened to Mom?" I asked my dad.

Chris grimaced. My dad and I always spoke bluntly with each other, but Chris didn't like confrontation in the family.

My dad put his fork down and wiped his mouth. "Good question. And I'm not sure anything I say will convince you that it's been the right thing to do, but you should at least know that I've given it a lot of thought . . ." He hesitated, then added, ". . . and a lot of prayer."

"Your mother fell in love with me when I was a defense attorney.

Even after we were married, she would testify as an expert on both sides of cases. Her biggest thrill was working with me to defend someone who was innocent. So, Jamie, I know you want to honor your mom by being a prosecutor, and I think that's noble. But I hope you can see that there's some nobility on the other side as well."

"In theory, I see that," I had said, taking a bite of my food. "But when's the last time you defended a person who was truly innocent?"

"Here we go," Chris said.

My dad took a bite and started talking, as he always did, before he swallowed. And it was his answer that was tumbling through my mind now. "There's no such thing as a truly innocent person, Jamie. Evil is part of our nature. Some learn to control the evil impulses. Others don't. I represent the ones who don't. But they're really not that much different from us."

"So Antoine Marshall and Chris are basically the same?" I asked. I played it safe and used my brother as the example of innocence, given my own somewhat-checkered adolescent history.

"Actually," Chris said, turning into the preacher boy, "if you read the Sermon on the Mount, we are. Anyone who's angry with his brother is the same as someone who murders. If I lust after a woman, I've committed adultery. Dad is right from a theological perspective. We're all guilty if you look at our hearts."

I loved my brother. But at the time, one year into his theological education, he was hopelessly preachy. "With all due respect," I said, "I'm more of an Old Testament girl when it comes to justice. Let their children become fatherless and all that."

"Funny," my dad said, "you seemed to be a lot more enamored with mercy during your teenage years."

In high school, I had been grounded a few times. Okay, quite a few. But that was different.

"In my logic class, Dad, we call that an attack ad hominem."

My father's words hadn't convinced me that night, but I gave them some serious thought during my time in law school. I watched his law practice from a distance and admired the way he represented his clients. And I came to accept, at least at the time, that it was his own way of honoring my mom.

But now I had to ask the question. Could it possibly be that my father had been part of a corrupt system? Even thinking it, I felt like a traitor. How could I doubt my own father? But how else could that data be interpreted?

When my father died, I felt like someone had ripped out my heart. A part of me had died with him. But as Chris had reminded me, at least I had the memories.

Now I wasn't so sure. It felt like a cancer was eating at the memories, turning every happy moment into something sinister. It was hard enough to lose a father's love. It was harder still to lose a family's legacy.

50

ON MEMORIAL DAY, the *Atlanta Times* ran a front-page story on the mess in the Milton County judicial system. For the first time, the story connected the deaths of Ricky Powell, Rontavius Eastbrook, and Jimmy Brandywine to the no-plea-bargaining pact among the felons. The story quoted heavily from "a source with ties to the Milton County prosecutor's office and police department," and I knew it had to be LA.

The source noted that plea bargains had stopped right after Caleb Tate had spent a few days in jail. Tate's firm now represented leaders from two of the most powerful gangs. The writer stated that Tate had not been charged with any crimes other than the murder of his wife, but anybody with half a brain could have read the article and connected the dots. They were the same dots LA and I had connected shortly after the inmates launched their rebellion.

I called LA. "Nice article," I said.

"There's an article? In today's paper?"

"Right."

He laughed. "Are you implying I'm the unnamed inside source? Do you really think I'd give Caleb Tate that much free publicity? His phone's probably ringing off the hook with clients."

There were rumors that LA was having a fling with one of the female reporters at the paper. But then again, there were rumors about LA having flings pretty much everywhere.

"Have you come up with anything concrete tying him to the three killings mentioned in the article?" I asked.

"Not yet. But when I do, you'll be the first to know."

◁▷

The next day, everyone in our office received a memo from Bill Masterson. The subject: our new response to the plea bargain crisis.

I'll be holding a press conference later today to announce a change in strategy for dealing with the crisis in the Milton County judicial system. I wanted you to hear it from me first.

As you know, enabling legislation authorizing me to deputize private-firm lawyers has gone nowhere. Accordingly, we're taking a different approach.

First, we need to increase personnel. Ten large firms in the Atlanta area have each volunteered to send one of their associates to me for the next six months. This means the firm will pay the salary of the associate, but he or she will be an employee of the Milton County DA's office and accountable to us. A similar arrangement has been made with ten other firms that will help the public defender's office. We don't need enabling legislation to do this, because they will be treated as employees, not volunteers.

In two weeks, once these attorneys are trained, they will be responsible for handling a large chunk of our misdemeanors. But still, this increases our workforce by only 25 percent, whereas our caseload has gone up 900 percent. And these new attorneys won't be ready to handle felonies for several weeks. Which leads me to part two of the plan.

From now on, each of you should triage your cases. We can't continue to prosecute all the cases that come across our desks. Prioritize. Devote your attention to violent repeat offenders and reputed gang leaders. Let the small operators and nondangerous felons go.

Which ties in with part three. A big challenge for us

right now is the overcrowding of our prison system. In the last few days, three federal lawsuits have been filed alleging that the jail is overcrowded to the point that it constitutes cruel and unusual punishment. This situation will only worsen as we warehouse criminals awaiting trial.

Accordingly, starting this week, we will release all nonviolent offenders on a personal recognizance bond. In addition, we will no longer seek jail time for nonviolent offenders.

Our first responsibility is to protect the citizens of Milton County from those who would inflict physical harm or death. In the present crisis, we need to make some difficult choices. Either we can continue down the current path and allow many violent offenders to slip through the cracks, or we can crack down on them and allow others a second or even third chance.

Please see the attached guidelines that divide the crimes into violent/nonviolent categories and specify the types of bond requests and sentences we will now be seeking.

Bill Masterson held his news conference at eleven. I wasn't able to watch because, like the other prosecutors, I was busy in court. But over my lunch break, I heard that Masterson had explained the new guidelines and handled a myriad of questions in his normal blunt and straightforward manner. The story was now a national news feed, and commentators were applauding Masterson's leadership in a time of crisis. They liked the emphasis on prioritizing violent crimes and believed this could be a template for other jurisdictions facing similar challenges.

I had mixed emotions about it. I understood the practical need to prioritize, but I hated the thought of drug offenders getting off without any jail time. Addicts would eventually turn to violence, if that's what it took to feed their addictions. When they did, innocent people would die, and families would be shattered. Families like mine.

But I didn't have a better plan, so I didn't criticize Masterson's. Somehow we had to break the back of this criminal cartel.

◁▷

When I returned to Milton County Superior Court that afternoon, LA was waiting for me on the other side of the metal detectors with a blonde-haired woman who looked to be a few years younger and three or four inches shorter than me.

"Jamie, this is Megan Armstrong, Rafael Rivera's probation officer."

I shook hands with Megan. "Nice to meet you." I turned to LA. "I'm running late for court; can you walk with me?"

"Sure."

We headed down the hallway and up the escalator, LA at my side and Megan trailing half a step behind.

"Somebody tried to kill Rafael Rivera last night," LA said.

I muttered a curse but didn't slow down. It seemed like the bad news just kept piling on.

"Drive-by shooting. Rivera's got the shattered windows and bullet holes in his car to prove it. Fortunately—or unfortunately, depending on your point of view—he managed to get away."

"Without him there's no case against Caleb Tate. So I guess I'd reluctantly fall into the 'fortunately' camp," I said. We were now going up the escalator steps as fast as I could, and Megan was falling farther behind.

LA lowered his voice. "I talked to him this morning. He's actually running scared."

"Good."

"We can't lose him. And we don't have the resources to give him any kind of protection."

We arrived at the top of the escalator, and I checked my watch. Already three minutes late. And it was Judge Westbrook, who liked to start on time.

I nodded toward a corner. "This has got to be quick," I said as Megan finally caught up.

"It will be."

The three of us huddled together, and LA explained his idea. He suggested that we get a private hearing with one of the judges and ask for modification of Rafael's probation terms. We could send him to California, where he would be supervised by one of LA's friends who worked as a probation officer. We could also make Rivera call Megan daily and update his status. "We need to get him out of Atlanta," LA said. "At least for the next few months, until the trial starts."

I didn't like it. I was afraid Rafael was just playing the system and would disappear once he got outside the jurisdiction of Georgia's courts. "Can't we send him down to Savannah or someplace like that?"

LA shook his head. "I checked out his car, Jamie. These guys are playing for keeps. We've already lost three convicts who copped a plea. We can't afford to lose Rafael."

LA was right. But I didn't have to like it.

"I'm supposed to be in Judge Westbrook's courtroom," I said. "After I finish, let's find Judge Brown and see if he'll modify the terms of Rivera's probation order."

At nine o'clock the next night, Rafael Rivera boarded a plane to California. LA promised me that I would see Rivera again on August 20, the first day of Caleb Tate's trial.

◁▷

Mace James was fired by text message. Caleb Tate didn't have the guts to call or even the class to send a letter or at least an e-mail. No, he shot off a text message. Actually, two text messages, back to back, because it wouldn't all fit into one.

> Mace, I'm grateful for your help on my case, and you've done good work. But I'll no longer need your services, b/c I've decided 2 represent myself.
>
> I know, a fool for a client and all that, but I think it's the way 2 go for now. Thanks for understanding. Caleb.

There was no mention of the trouble swirling around Mace from the Antoine Marshall mess. But Mace wasn't stupid. And in a way, he couldn't blame Caleb. Caleb Tate had enough problems of his own right now. He didn't need a lawyer who was being investigated by the state bar and who had just been suspended from his job at Southeastern Law School.

And frankly, it was good riddance. Though Mace believed in Caleb's innocence, he was pretty sure Caleb was behind the no-plea-bargaining strategy that had already cost three men their lives. Mace didn't want that kind of blood on his hands.

By the time he read through the text messages a second time, Mace actually felt like he could breathe a little easier. In addition to his concerns about Caleb Tate, Mace had only two months and a few days before the scheduled execution of Antoine Marshall, and he wanted to devote all of his time and energy to saving his client's life. Caleb Tate's case was scheduled to start just thirteen days after Marshall's scheduled execution. And now Mace had been granted a reprieve on Tate's case.

He felt like a bit of a new man.

51

EVERYBODY HAS LIMITS. I reached mine on Wednesday, June 13, at 3 p.m. Ironically, the meltdown took place in front of Judge Brown, a judge for whom I had the utmost respect. In fact, we were kindred spirits. I was straightforward and methodical in presenting my cases, and he was equally straightforward in his rulings.

But unfortunately, we also had equally strong wills.

I had obtained a guilty verdict on a breaking and entering. The defendant had two prior drug convictions. For me, he was Antoine Marshall all over again, except that fortunately the homeowners hadn't been there this time. Ignoring the guidelines in Bill Masterson's memo, I asked for a seven-year prison sentence with two years suspended.

Judge Brown seemed taken aback by my recommendation. All the judges knew about Masterson's guidelines—no jail for nonviolent offenders. And B and Es didn't qualify as violent crimes if nobody was home.

Brown listened politely as the public defender went through the usual spiel about how her client had gone through an addiction recovery program and was no longer a threat to society. She suggested that seven years was extreme even under normal circumstances—and these were not normal times in Milton County. She asked Brown to give her client two years, suspending the entire sentence except for time served.

I stood. "May I respond?"

"That won't be necessary."

"But, Judge, this is ridiculous. Just because the defendants all refuse to plea-bargain doesn't mean they get to dictate what the sentence should be."

"Nobody said they did," Brown said, his voice growing edgy. "Now sit down."

He put on his glasses and reviewed the file. All the judges in Milton County knew my family's history, and it was certainly a subtext in today's sentencing. I would have some explaining to do later with Bill Masterson, but I just couldn't bring myself to let this man walk out of the courtroom on time served.

"In pronouncing its sentence, the court must consider a variety of factors," Judge Brown announced. I played with my pen, watching him intently.

"Included among those is whether the defendant is a further risk to society, making sure the punishment fits the crime, and advancing the twin goals of retribution and rehabilitation.

"The court finds that the defendant poses some risk for recidivism but that such risk will only be increased by additional time spent in jail. Moreover, the court is mindful this was a nonviolent crime and that, pursuant to directives from DA Masterson, most prosecutors have been recommending such defendants be released on time served. Given the overcrowding in our county's prison system and the fact that this man served thirty days before posting bond, I'm going to release him on time served. I will impose a seven-year prison sentence as the prosecution suggests, but I will suspend all but thirty days."

"That's ridiculous," I mumbled.

"Ms. Brock," Judge Brown snapped, "do you have something to say?"

I stood again, bristling from the court's ruling. In four years as a prosecutor, I had been nothing but unflinchingly respectful of the judges. I would always mumble, "Thank you, Your Honor," even when rulings went against me. But on this day, fatigued from an endless case-load and weighed down by the concerns about my father and his reputation, my patience had worn thin.

"With all due respect, Your Honor, I think it's a sad day in Milton County when a repeat offender like this man, caught red-handed, gets to walk without one additional day in jail."

"Maybe you should take that up with your boss," Judge Brown said.

"Last time I checked, my boss was not the one handing down the sentences."

Judge Brown's face reddened, and his lips pursed. He stared at me for a moment. "Ms. Brock, I realize you're under a lot of pressure right now; otherwise that comment would have earned you contempt. But I suggest you think twice before addressing the court in such a flippant manner again."

I bit my tongue, but my smirk apparently telegraphed my disdain.

"Is there something funny about my remarks?" Judge Brown pressed.

"I just find it ironic that the jails are too crowded for defendants but not too crowded for prosecutors."

I had always been too much of a smart aleck for my own good and usually regretted my words later. But this time, saying them felt right. I was tired of defendants calling all the shots in Milton County. It was about time somebody stood up for the victims.

"That remark *will* cost you a five-thousand-dollar fine for contempt," Judge Brown ruled. "Is there anything else you'd like to tell the court?"

"No, Your Honor. That's about all I can afford."

◁▷

Word of my meltdown made it back to the office faster than I did. Bill Masterson was on the road, so I was called into Regina Granger's office for a chewing out via speakerphone. I apologized to both Masterson and Regina and didn't have much to say in my own defense. I agreed to apologize to Judge Brown the next day, but I balked when Masterson also suggested some counseling.

"I'll be okay," I said. "It's just that what this guy did was so close to what Antoine Marshall did. The only difference was that nobody was home."

"Jamie, I understand that," Masterson said. "But I've got a responsibility to the public as well as to everyone in our office to make sure my ADAs are taking care of themselves. And I really would like to see you get some counseling. I know you're friends with Gillespie. Even if it's just one or two sessions with him, I think you should at least talk to him."

Regina looked at me and nodded. "It's a good idea, Jamie. I think you're under a lot more pressure than you realize."

I slouched a little lower in my chair and mumbled, "Okay."

"Jamie, your work ethic is an inspiration to everyone in the office," Masterson said, apparently trying to change the tone of the call. "But you're not Superwoman. I want you prosecuting cases for a long time, and that means you've got to take some time to work through some of these issues you're up against."

I could hear somebody in the background on Masterson's end of the call. "Sorry," he said. "I've got to run."

Masterson ended the call, leaving me stewing. If anybody thought he was superhuman, prosecuting cases by day while running a campaign by night, it was Bill Masterson.

Regina thanked me for agreeing to the counseling.

"One session," I said.

◁▷

Bill Masterson usually had an acute sense for all things political, but it turned out he was dead wrong on this one.

That night, I read the newspaper article online that quoted verbatim from a transcript of the hearing. It was titled "Prosecutor Held in Contempt." The comments following the article ran four to one in my favor. The citizens believed the judges were letting defendants off too easy. They liked the fact that at least one prosecutor thought a guy with two prior drug convictions and now a B and E ought to spend some time in jail.

My in-box was flooded with supportive e-mails, and the local TV shows had no problem finding lawyers who would speak out in my defense. For some reason that escaped me, I was becoming a folk hero.

By the next afternoon, even before I could attend my first appointment with Dr. Gillespie, Bill Masterson had become one of my loudest defenders. "Jamie Brock has apologized to Judge Brown for her lack of respect, and I think her apology was very appropriate. But I must say, I would take another dozen prosecutors just like her tomorrow."

Only in the land of fun-house mirrors known as Milton County Superior Court could a prosecutor's emotional meltdown turn her into a legend. *Maybe I should do it more often,* I thought.

52

AS MUCH AS I HATED the thought of professional counseling, I found it impossible not to be charmed by Aaron Gillespie. He sat in his office on a brown leather couch, white shirt rolled up at the sleeves, a paisley tie hanging down over his soft stomach. I took my place in a wingback chair and crossed my legs. He knew I was there under protest, but within minutes we had picked up where we left off at the gym a few weeks before.

He had a way of asking gentle questions and waiting patiently for the responses. Are you getting any sleep? Are you planning to attend Antoine Marshall's execution? How do you feel about that? How are you dealing with your dad's death? The rhythm of the conversation relaxed me.

The questions were straightforward, and he didn't take notes or make any of those soft, guttural noises that signaled deep insight about some psychological flaw in me. We talked for about forty-five minutes before he even mentioned the incident in court.

"Do you think Bill Masterson overreacted when he required that you get counseling?"

"Yes."

"Do you think you need to be here?"

"Not really."

"Do you think he did it just to save political face?"

That one made me stop. The Republican primary was next month, and Masterson was certainly a political creature. But I had always believed that he had my best interests at heart.

"Not really. I've seen him make some pretty unpopular decisions

233

even though he's in the middle of a campaign. I think he was just reminding me who's boss."

Gillespie stuck out a bottom lip and nodded. He pulled his arm down from the back of the couch and leaned forward slightly. "Jamie, if you want me to, I'm perfectly happy to sign off that you've been through counseling and that you're good to go. Frankly, I was glad to see you blow off a little steam in court the other day. I think your biggest problem is that you tend to hold too much inside and don't have anybody to talk with."

He was right about that. Partly right, anyway. I did hold a lot inside. But my biggest problem was that the one thing bothering me most was the one thing I couldn't talk to *anybody* about. At least not until I figured it out. I certainly couldn't talk to Gillespie—someone who had known my mom and dad. But the days for Antoine Marshall's scheduled execution and Caleb Tate's trial were ticking closer. And I was sitting on a piece of dynamite that could blow my father's reputation into tiny pieces of shrapnel.

"Jamie?" Gillespie said, bringing me back around.

"Oh . . . sorry."

He tilted his head. "Is there something you want to discuss?"

"No. I'm fine."

He paused. "Okay, but let me ask you a question that's unrelated to what happened in court. Like everything else, this stays between you and me."

Gillespie waited until I nodded my assent. He had made a subtle shift from friend to professional counselor, and there was a new tone of seriousness in his voice.

"Do you blame yourself, even a little, for your mother's death?"

The question landed like a sledgehammer, and I jerked my head back, furrowing my brow. "No. Why do you ask?"

"Are you sure?"

He must have been able to read the guilt on my face. When my mother died, I was sixteen. I had been in some trouble that week and had a midnight curfew. But that night, when I still wasn't home and didn't answer my cell phone at one in the morning, my parents sent Chris to my friend's house to pick me up. He left the garage door open.

Fifteen minutes after he left, Antoine Marshall slipped into our house and tried to steal enough stuff to feed his meth habit. My mother heard him and came downstairs, thinking Chris and I were home. She screamed. Shots were fired. My dad came running to see what had happened. Marshall shot him, too. Chris and I discovered the bodies. My dad was unconscious, my mom dead.

"No. . . . I'm not sure."

It was the truth. But it was also the first time I had admitted it out loud.

"Jamie, you can't put that on yourself. There's nothing you did to cause it, and there's nothing you could have done differently to prevent it. That man was high, and he had a gun. If you and Chris had been home, there might have been two more deaths."

I had heard it all before. And I couldn't argue with the logic. But none of that made the guilt go away.

"I still ask the questions, Doc. What if the garage door hadn't been open? What if Chris or I had heard somebody and called out—would Marshall have left?" I felt myself getting emotional, which I was determined not to do. "Plus . . . the hardest thing . . . is that the last time I saw my mom, we had a fight." I felt my bottom lip begin to tremble and decided not to dig any deeper. I bit my lip and looked down at the floor.

"You want to talk about that—your relationship with your mom?"

I shook my head. Not right now.

"Okay," Gillespie said. "But if I can be honest with you, I think you've got some survivor's guilt, and it wouldn't hurt for us to talk some more about this."

"I'll be fine," I assured him.

I left without scheduling another appointment.

But later that evening, I couldn't let it go. I kept reliving that night twelve years ago and wishing I had been at home. The what-ifs kept churning through my mind—and in every scenario, if I had just stayed home or at least kept my curfew, things would have turned out differently. Antoine Marshall would have moved on to another house, and my family would have been saved.

A few minutes before midnight, I sent an e-mail to Aaron Gillespie requesting available dates for my next session.

53

ON THE LAST SATURDAY OF JUNE, I woke up early and took Justice for a walk. It was already in the eighties, and the temperature was predicted to hit the high nineties by afternoon. Sprinkler systems were running throughout the neighborhood, and there were a few early-morning joggers trying to beat the heat.

When I returned to the house, I mowed the lawn for the first time in two weeks. My yard was not large, but the house sat on a hill, and by the time I finished, I was sweaty, tired, and out of breath. Part of my fatigue was due to lack of sleep and the emotional strain of everything I was facing, but I had also exercised less in the past few months than at any other point in my adult life.

In a few days, I would join thousands of crazy Atlanta residents and run the Peachtree Road Race on July 4. I had done it for eight straight years and wasn't about to skip a year, even though this would be one of my slowest times yet.

I sat on the deck, thinking about the race and sipping some sweet tea while Justice begged me to throw his tennis ball. On top of everything else, I was now feeling guilty for ignoring Justice over the past month and for being so out of shape. Jamie Brock, once an Olympic hopeful in kayaking, now winded from mowing the lawn.

Even Justice seemed to have put on a few extra pounds. It was not quite nine o'clock, and I was usually at the office by this time on Saturday morning, but I knew I couldn't keep living like that.

"Want to go for a swim?" I asked Justice.

His ears perked up as if the words were too good to be true. His tail began wagging, thumping against the railing on the deck. Then he started jumping a little, prancing around the deck, excitement and adrenaline coursing through his body.

He hopped over to the back door and pawed at it. His enthusiasm made me smile. I changed into some workout clothes and barely kept Justice under control as I loaded my kayak onto the 4Runner.

We're going to the river! Justice could sense it, and just the thought of it made him crazy.

Last summer, we had gone to the Chattahoochee almost every weekend. But this spring, with everything else happening in my life, I hadn't had my boat in the water once. It had sat in the garage, covered in dust. Today that would all change.

Thirty minutes later, Justice thought he had died and gone to doggy heaven. I stood on the bank of the Chattahoochee and threw his big rubber toy into the middle of the current. He performed a flying belly flop into the water and swam out to his toy, grabbed it in his mouth, and chugged back to shore. He exited the water, shook himself off, dropped the toy at my feet, and waited at attention for my next throw.

Throw, retrieve, drop. *Let's do it again!* Throw, retrieve, drop. Over and over until his tongue was hanging so far out of his mouth I thought he might trip on it.

"Time for Mommy to get some exercise," I said finally. And he knew the drill from there. I carried my boat to the river and paddled to the middle of the current while Justice stayed on the shore. I sprinted hard against the current for about five minutes and turned around at a concrete abutment under the bridge at Medlock Bridge Road. Justice followed along the banks of the river, fighting his way through the underbrush and slipping occasionally down a muddy slope into the water. I cruised back down the river to where we started and then turned and sprinted again.

All the while, Justice shadowed me. Back and forth, back and forth.

Last year, I would do this for a solid hour, but today my arms were burning after thirty minutes. On the last sprint, my lungs felt like they might explode, and I leaned forward in exhaustion when I cleared the bridge abutment. It felt great to be out on the water with Justice getting enough exercise to last him a week. It was the first time in months that my mind wasn't preoccupied with thoughts of Antoine Marshall's appeal or Caleb Tate's prosecution or how much I missed my dad. I floated back down to the small park where I had launched my boat and carried it to the 4Runner.

The last part of our routine was undoubtedly Justice's favorite. I took the Frisbee out of the backseat and got ready to give it a good toss. But before I did, I noticed that the red light on my BlackBerry was blinking.

"Hang on a minute, buddy." The missed call was from LA. Justice was panting at my feet, pawing at the Frisbee, but something about that blinking red light was addictive. I returned the call.

"Where are you?" he asked.

"None of your business. It's Saturday."

He laughed. "Nice to see your foul moods aren't limited to working days."

"Last I knew, Saturday was a working day."

"Good point."

I threw the Frisbee and watched Justice take off after it.

"I stopped by the office to see if you were in," LA said. He sounded more tentative than usual. "Had something I wanted to talk to you about, but it's better person to person."

Justice came racing back, dropped the Frisbee at my feet, and sat at attention. "Can you give me a hint?"

"Not over the phone. I want to be there to see you smile."

Now he had me. "You better not be toying with me. I've had a long week."

"There's only one way to find out. Tell me where you are."

He sounded a little flirtatious, and I surprised myself with a grin. "Chattahoochee River Park on Medlock Bridge Road. Hard at work on next week's cases."

"Sounds like you need some help. Maybe I should bring J-Lo."

"Justice would like that very much."

◁ ▷

LA showed up twenty minutes later driving a pale-green Element that looked like a box on wheels, his brown-and-white English bulldog riding shotgun. J-Lo was about sixteen inches high with short, stocky legs, a wide muzzle with a short pug, and a broad, black nose. Her dark eyes were deep set, and her skin hung from her face—XL skin on a size-M face.

"She's a bit of a prima donna," LA said. "She doesn't do well in the heat."

LA kept her on a leash. He wore jeans, flip-flops, and a T-shirt. I assumed he had come straight from work. I still had on my bathing-suit top and shorts. LA started asking questions about the kayak, like he might want to try it out.

I knew he was a good athlete, but I also knew that my racing kayak was extremely tippy. I had never met anybody who could stay upright the first time he tried it.

"You want to give it a shot?" I asked.

"I didn't bring any shorts."

"You can always roll up your jeans. But, I mean, if you can't handle it . . ."

After some hemming and hawing, he agreed to give it a whirl. He carried it to the water for me, as if somehow a woman couldn't handle the thirty-pound boat, even though I had already done so earlier. I gave him a quick demonstration and made it look easy. I showed him how to brace on one side and how to sit up straight and pump with your legs at the same time you rotate your body to get maximum power in each stroke. I went a few yards up the river before doing a sharp turn and came flying back past him. I eventually pulled next to the launching pad where LA was standing in water almost up to his knees.

He took off his shirt, and I tried not to notice the six-pack abs. I steadied the boat as he climbed in and grabbed the paddle.

"You ready?"

"Not really." He was already a little shaky, and he hadn't even started.

"It's like riding a bike. Once you get going, it's actually easier to keep your balance."

I gave him a gentle shove, and he took off into the current. The boat was shaking, but he was smart enough to use the force of his stroke to brace himself. He looked like he was starting to get the hang of it. He had broad, muscled shoulders and stayed focused on the water, staring at a spot a few feet in front of the boat, just like I had told him. Before long, he started feeling comfortable and picked up the pace a little.

That's when he got into trouble.

The current caught the front of the boat and started turning it downstream. "What do I do now?" he shouted.

"Paddle on your left."

LA tried to comply, but it's hard to paddle on just one side with a kayak paddle. He took a couple of strokes on the left and almost tipped. He braced with the paddle on the right, but then the current pushed the boat around farther. He tried to take another stroke on the left. His paddle caught the water on the recovery, and before he could blink, LA was in the water, swimming next to the kayak, hanging on to his paddle.

Justice stood on the shore and barked. I held J-Lo's leash. "You okay?"

He looked over at me as he tried to scramble into the kayak. His jeans were waterlogged and weighing him down. "Other than my pride, I'm great."

He looked clumsy during his first two attempts to get back in the boat. On his third try, he finally managed to clamber aboard, almost losing his pants in the process. He took a few more strokes heading downstream. He flipped a second time when he tried to turn around.

All told, LA flipped five times in the next twenty minutes, but he still impressed me with his tenacity. Before quitting, he managed to paddle nonstop to the same bridge where I'd made my turns and sprinted back to me without going in the drink. His strokes were still lunging and rough, but he had figured out how to balance the boat.

"You're a born kayaker," I said, holding on to the boat as he got out.

"That's harder than it looks," he said. "You've definitely got to know what you're doing."

Together, we carried the kayak back to my car. As we were tying it on, I asked LA for the third time what was so important that we had to talk about it face to face. He walked over to me, water dripping off his body.

"I've got friends with some inside information at the Georgia Supreme Court," he said. "They're issuing an opinion on Monday."

He paused, and I braced myself for the news.

"Your boy Antoine Marshall is not going to like it."

I blew out a breath in relief. I almost gave LA a hug but caught myself. I'm not a hugger by nature, and there was no real joy in any of this. I certainly didn't want Antoine Marshall to win the appeal, but knowing he was going to lose would not bring my mom back. It would not make things right. At the most, it would bring closure to this chapter.

"That's good news, I guess."

"That's it? I came all the way out here and made a fool of myself for *that* reaction?" He pretended to be hurt, but I could tell he was kidding.

"I don't know, LA. It just feels like there're never any real winners in this. I guess I just want it to be over."

"Yeah. I have no idea how you've been able to handle it this far. And I know it doesn't bring your mom back, but at least the court didn't buy this garbage about Cooper's change of heart."

LA put his shirt on, then knelt down to play with Justice. I was really starting to like this guy. He had a softer side than I had previously thought. Plus, he'd handled the humiliation of kayaking much better than most guys I knew would.

There were some other folks who were taking advantage of the park. A few boaters had launched from the same spot we had just used. Other dog owners were here; a few guys were throwing a football and drinking.

"I need to talk to you about something else," I told LA. "I don't live that far from here, and my dad's probably got some dry clothes you could wear. Though they might be a little big in the gut." I smiled.

LA grinned. "J-Lo and I would be honored." He put the dimples on overdrive. "Come on, boy," he said to Justice. "You're riding with me."

◁▷

LA was a good sport, wearing a pair of my dad's jeans that were three inches too big around the waist and a few inches too short. I gave him one of my dad's belts, which he tightened down, bunching up the waist. He rolled the legs up so they came to the middle of his calves.

We talked at the kitchen table with both dogs lying at our feet.

Haltingly, I told him about Caleb Tate's threat and what my research had uncovered.

LA shook his head and furrowed his brow. "You really think your dad had something on the judge?" he asked.

"I don't know. But I do know that these numbers make it *look* like he did, and they give Caleb Tate something to talk about."

"Not to mention what it does to your dad's reputation," LA said softly.

I nodded, and we both sat there for a moment, thinking it through.

"Antoine Marshall's execution is scheduled to take place two weeks before Tate's trial starts," I eventually said.

I could tell by the look on LA's face that he understood immediately what was at stake. If we sat back and let Antoine Marshall's execution proceed, Tate would destroy us at trial. He would tell the jury about Judge Snowden and the information he had given me. He would explain that I had sat on the information and let Marshall be executed. And then he would use the information to corroborate his own story about why his client, Rafael Rivera, would turn on him.

LA stood and stared out the window. Justice glanced at him but then put his head back down on his paws and closed his eyes.

LA thought for a moment and turned back toward me. "Jamie, you're the lawyer. If this information about Snowden and your dad comes out before Marshall's execution and the judges grant Marshall a new trial, can somebody read into evidence your dad's testimony from eleven years ago?"

I shook my head. "That's the problem. The defense lawyers will object on the grounds that they don't have a chance to cross-examine him on this new information."

"Then there's no evidence left to convict Antoine Marshall."

"Right."

This troubled LA, the knit brow deepening. "As a prosecutor, do you *have* to hand this over?"

"It's not clear," I said. "I've researched it, but there's no definitive answer. A prosecutor has to turn over all exculpatory evidence to a defense lawyer. But our office isn't handling the appeal, and I would argue that this isn't really exculpatory."

"What do you mean?"

"Well, it doesn't really tend to prove Marshall's innocence. It just casts doubt on my father's and Judge Snowden's reputations."

LA made a face—even he was having a hard time swallowing that one. "Either way, we can't say anything," LA said. "Unless we put Rafael Rivera on the stand, Caleb Tate can never mention this information; it's protected by the attorney-client privilege. But if his former client testifies against him, the privilege is waived. Frankly, I'd rather have us dismiss the charges against Tate than allow Antoine Marshall to go free." He waited and then mumbled, "Not to mention your dad's reputation."

"I don't know if I agree," I said. "I've dedicated my whole life to justice. How can I start making exceptions now? Shouldn't I just put this information out there and let the chips fall where they may?"

LA sat back down at the other end of the table and looked me straight in the eye. "You've got a good heart, and you're a straight shooter. But, Jamie, sometimes the system isn't fair. And sometimes it needs a little help."

"Like what?"

"I'm not even sure myself," LA said. He was drilling into my eyes with an intensity that I hadn't seen before. "But Antoine Marshall is not going to kill your mother, shoot your father, and walk out of jail after eleven years because of this. I can tell you that much."

We analyzed the situation for over an hour, tearing apart every option, thinking through all the possibilities. We didn't come to any conclusions, but it felt good to talk about it. He told me again that he had no idea how I had held up so well under the pressure. Before leaving, he reached out to give me a hug, and I let him, lingering longer than mere friends do. It felt right to have his arms wrapped around me for those few seconds.

"Act surprised when you see the opinion on Monday," he reminded me as he pulled away. "And don't worry about this other thing. We'll figure it out."

It would have been the perfect way for us to part, but real life doesn't work like that.

"J-Lo!" he yelled. He had left her off leash in the house and now noticed a yellow spot under the corner of the dining room table, right where Justice typically lay at my feet.

"Bad dog," LA scolded.

He insisted on cleaning it up, and I let him. Justice kept looking at me as if to make sure he wasn't in trouble too. "Good boy," I told him as I rubbed his head.

LA scrubbed the carpet until the stain disappeared.

"She gets a little jealous," he said.

54

AT 9:30 A.M. ON MONDAY, July 2, Mace James received an e-mail from the Georgia Supreme Court with the opinion in Antoine's case attached. Mace said a quick prayer and clicked his mouse with a sweaty hand.

The court had denied his petition and reaffirmed the August 7 execution date. And they had some harsh language for Mace as well.

> Defense counsel has a duty to zealously represent his client. But that duty has bounds. In this case, counsel transgressed those bounds and came dangerously close to committing fraud on the Court. While the Court understands that defense counsel was driven by the perceived exigencies of the circumstances, his role as an officer of the Court prohibits the type of trickery and violence he apparently used to obtain the affidavit of Mr. Cooper. His actions reflect poorly on the legal profession and show a lack of judgment that is troubling to this Court.

Mace felt his emotions collide as he read the opinion. Frustration because the justices did not appreciate the truth of what had happened. Embarrassment at the stinging criticism. Helplessness because he was representing an innocent man on death row and everything he tried seemed to make matters worse. But mostly he just felt drained. He had spent years butting his head against one brick wall after another. And now he only had a few weeks left.

Mace got in his car and drove to Jackson to personally deliver the news to his client. By the time he got there and picked up the telephone, staring at Antoine Marshall on the other side of the glass, he had become despondent.

"The Georgia Supreme Court denied our petition," Mace said. He slid a printout of the opinion through the slot under the glass. Antoine picked it up without speaking and turned sideways in his seat so he could hold it at arm's length. "I left my reading glasses in the cell," he said.

Mace watched Antoine squint as he read the opinion slowly, grunting and shaking his head while he turned the pages. He read for an agonizingly long time, slowly devouring every word. Mace could see the hope leave Antoine's face, replaced by a grim certainty that his years on this earth were now numbered at thirty-six.

When he finished the opinion, Antoine placed it on the shelf in front of him and turned back to Mace. There were tears welling in his eyes.

"I'm sorry," Mace said.

"These other dudes on death row—their lawyers don't care," Antoine said. His voice was raspy and close to breaking. "But me, my lawyer drives all the way down from Atlanta just to look me in the eye and tell me he's sorry. My lawyer beats up some dude in a bar and risks his law license just to give me a chance. You ain't got nothing to be sorry for, Mr. James."

Antoine sat up straighter in his chair and looked directly at Mace. Mace had come to console his client, but it was working the other way around.

"I'm proud that I've got the best lawyer of anybody here on death row."

"I appreciate that," Mace said. And he did. More than Antoine would ever know. "But maybe I'm not so hot if I can't get you out of here."

Antoine shook his head. "Some things were meant to be. You did everything you could. Don't blame yourself."

Antoine passed the opinion back under the glass, and Mace put it in his briefcase. He had actually intended it to be Antoine's copy, but it was clear his client didn't want it hanging around his cell.

"After I pass, I want you to make me a promise," Antoine said.

Mace looked him in the eye. Despite the redness and tears, Antoine seemed determined.

"Don't just put my file in a cabinet and move on to the next case. I know I got no family who care about this, but I need to have my name cleared. It's the only way to make sure that this doesn't happen to the next dude. Maybe that's why God's got me here in the first place."

"I hear you, Antoine," Mace said. They had been through this before. "But now you listen to me. Because I'm not done fighting to keep you alive."

Antoine gave Mace a sarcastic chuckle. "August 7 is coming, Mr. James. Whether you're ready for it or not. I just want to make sure that after it comes and goes and I'm no longer here, you're going to keep working to clear my name."

"You have my word on that," Mace said.

Antoine nodded, and Mace noticed a slight twitch. The pressure was taking its toll.

"I've got one last strategy, but it's a long shot," Mace warned. "I'll need the court's permission to even give it a try."

Antoine shrugged. "Right now, a long shot sounds pretty good."

55

THE PEACHTREE ROAD RACE is held each year on the Fourth of July in the city of Atlanta. It is the world's largest 10K race—and in my opinion, also the wackiest. Sixty thousand runners are released from twenty different starting corrals. Among them this year would be about half the ADAs from Milton County. We had divided into two groups—serious runners and those who planned to walk. We all had T-shirts that said *Masterson for Attorney General* on the front and on the back had a copy of the Miranda warning. The shirts would be some of the tamer outfits worn by runners.

I got up at 5 a.m., took care of Justice, and drove to the MARTA line, where I squeezed onto the train with runners of all shapes and sizes. My competitive instincts always kicked in for events like this, and I would look around, pick out the fastest-looking runners, and compare myself to them. I could probably beat them if only I had trained more. If only I had longer legs. If only I didn't have a job that required seventy or eighty hours a week.

I met the other prosecutors at our designated spot. Masterson was there, patting everyone on the back and thanking us for coming. He wouldn't be running today, but he would set up an outpost about half-way through the course with big signs and banners and pass out Shot Bloks to the runners to give them a boost of energy.

My colleagues and I ended up standing around for more than an hour waiting for our corral to start. Even when it was our turn, it took a few minutes before I could take my first step. Eventually, like a giant amoeba, the runners all started to move, walking at first, then slowly jogging, and eventually running.

The Peachtree was not the place to go for a personal record, but it was great for the scenery. A lot of people wore costumes that should have earned them jail time. There were always a few folks dressed like the Statue of Liberty and men wearing kilts and women in bikinis. I always cringed at the guys wearing Speedos.

Eventually, our little pack of prosecutors spread out, and I left many of my colleagues behind. I picked up my pace so I was doing sub-eight-minute miles, dodging people like a running back on the football field. I was passed at mile three by a squadron of Marines, all running in formation, as if this were just another morning PT exercise.

By mile five I was paying for my earlier enthusiasm, and my pace had slowed to eight-and-a-half-minute miles. Ten kilometers had never seemed so long. Some of the runners passing me were laughing and having a good time, but I was sucking wind so badly that I could hardly breathe. It was just before mile marker six that a man running in prisoner's stripes with a black mask came up beside me.

"Almost there," he said.

"Yeah." I hated it when people tried to talk to me while I ran. One-word answers usually ended the conversation.

"You guys are doing a good job in the Milton County prosecutor's office," he said. "Keep it up."

"Thanks."

"Here's something that might help you. You can read it after the race."

He handed me a folded piece of paper, and I instinctively took it. The whole exchange was strange, but I was tired and not thinking clearly at the time.

"Have a great finish," the man said. He took off at a pace I couldn't possibly match. I kept on running, unfolding the paper as I ran.

I slowed down and pulled over to the side even as the spectators urged us on. I read the paper and started running again. But now I was in a different zone, running slower, not even thinking about the finish anymore. The note was typed, and it wasn't signed.

> Be careful who you trust. Not everyone paid by the
> government is working for the government. How else
> do you think Rivera knew about the morphine?

◁▷

In the Atlanta area there are dueling fireworks on the Fourth of July. The most spectacular ones take place at Centennial Olympic Park in downtown Atlanta. But they are rivaled by the fireworks that cap off the country music festival ten miles away in Buckhead. The problem with both places is that you sit in traffic for an hour just trying to get home.

LA had the solution.

We were sitting on the shoulder of the interstate, halfway between downtown Atlanta and Buckhead, with the portable blue strobe light doing its dance on the roof of LA's unmarked police car. He had tuned the radio to the AM station that played music synced to the exploding fireworks over Centennial Park. That display had started first, but now, halfway through, it was joined by fireworks from Buckhead exploding behind us. Fireworks in stereo, and we would be gone before the traffic jams started.

I stole a glance at LA's handsome profile, the reflections from the fireworks sparkling in his eyes. It should have been the perfect romantic night.

But I found myself wondering, *How much do I really know about this guy?*

There were, of course, rumors about LA and the ladies. And though he had always treated me with respect, he seemed to have two or three different schemes working at any given time. I had watched him work the system with little regard for ethics. I was pretty sure LA had leaked Rikki Tate's psychiatric records to the press, for example. How far would he really go to get a conviction? Far enough to leak the information about morphine to Rivera so the felon's testimony would be more believable? It bothered me that LA could read other people so well but was impossible to read himself.

"What's wrong?" he asked.

"Nothing."

"Okay. So what's really wrong?"

"Don't use that Truth Wizard stuff on me," I said.

A bright spiderweb of fireworks burst in the window before us.

Behind us, visible in our side mirrors, staggered rockets shot up from the ground and exploded into a mushroom cloud of red and blue.

"It doesn't take a Truth Wizard to know that when a woman says, 'Nothing,' she really means, 'Keep asking until you figure it out.'"

I pushed some hair behind my ear. "Let's see . . . my father died, I'm stressed out at work, my mother's killer is scheduled to be executed in one month, and our case against Caleb Tate is hanging on by a thread. Other than that, it's just another great Independence Day."

LA turned to me. "But that's not all, is it?"

He was right. I felt like I was sitting in the car with a mind reader. Even so, I wasn't about to tell him about the paper I had been handed in the race that day. About my suspicions. About the tension between a growing emotional attachment to him and the seeds of distrust that had taken root in my mind.

"I'm fine." I glanced toward him. I could tell from the look on his face that he didn't believe me, but he got the picture. I didn't want to talk about it.

The radio was playing "Only in America." Fireworks were exploding overhead. A guy with movie-star good looks was sitting next to me.

He extended his hand across the middle console, and I hesitated before I put mine in his.

"Your hands are cold," he said.

"Cold hands, warm heart."

"That was going to be my line."

56

FOR MACE JAMES, half the battle had been getting court approval to even conduct this test. He had filed his motion under seal because the test results would remain confidential unless they tended to exonerate Antoine Marshall. The attorney general's office had responded under seal, citing all the reasons the test itself would be inadmissible.

But Mace had done his homework. The Brain Electrical Oscillation Signature test, or BEOS, had already been used by a court in India to affirm two murder convictions. The technology had been tested and peer-reviewed by eminent neuropsychologists around the globe. Mace had attached affidavits from several of them to his motion.

The test involved the unique use of an electroencephalogram to distinguish experiential knowledge from conceptual knowledge. A suspect would be hooked up to thirty-two electrodes, two of which would be placed on his earlobe and the rest on various areas of his scalp. The suspect would sit quietly with his eyes closed as the administrator read a series of statements. Computer software would map the electrical signals the suspect's brain generated in response to the statements. Because experiential knowledge of an event is accrued only through participation in it, electrical activity would map differently than if the suspect had only learned about the event through others. In other words, the test could distinguish between memories created by experience and memories created by being told about an event.

Mace had lined up one of the top neuropsychologists in the country to conduct the test. Perhaps out of a reluctance to give Mace James another issue to complain about on appeal, the court had finally consented. But the court made it clear that it reserved judgment as to whether or not it would ultimately consider the test results as evidence. That decision would wait for another day.

Now, nineteen days before Antoine Marshall's scheduled execution, Mace James sat in an enclosed conference room at the Diagnostic and Classification Prison in Jackson, watching a scene straight out of a George Orwell book.

Antoine Marshall wore a cap with the thirty-two electrodes that measured his brain waves. He had his eyes closed, listening intently to the statements suggested by Dr. Rukmani Chandar. They began with baseline statements—"The sky is blue"—and Chandar studied the responses on the computer. Next, Chandar moved to events that he knew would elicit an experiential response, such as "In the early part of 2000, I was high on meth" or "I ate eggs this morning for breakfast." He also interspersed statements that would only elicit a conceptual response, such as "I've argued a case before the Georgia Supreme Court."

Once the baselines were established, Chandar carefully went through a short series of factual statements about the crime in question. "I broke into the Brocks' house at 130 English Oak Court. . . . I was carrying a gun that night. . . . I saw the open garage door. . . . I shot Dr. Brock when she interrupted me. . . . I shot Robert Brock in the stomach."

Mace watched his client's expression as these questions were asked. Antoine showed no external reaction, his demeanor the same during the description of the crime as it was during the baseline questions. Chandar was focused only on his computer and the electrical patterns he was seeing in front of him. Mace knew it would take a few days to fully interpret all the results, but Chandar was plainly seeing something interesting even now.

Mace couldn't tell whether it was good news or bad.

The test lasted no more than an hour. After it concluded, Chandar was tight lipped about the results. "I cannot say definitively until I've had more time to analyze each pattern."

"How long will it take?"

"Two days. Maybe three."

Mace had waited this long. He could begin drafting the briefs now, assuming that the test results would be good news. After all, Antoine had already passed two polygraphs. How could he not pass this test? The real issue would be whether the courts would regard the results as reliable evidence. On that point, Mace knew he faced an uphill battle. But at least the battle would bring a new wave of publicity to the case, one that would center around a cutting-edge scientific test that once again confirmed his client had been nowhere near the Brock house on the night in question.

If Mace won, defense lawyers everywhere would have a powerful new weapon in their arsenal. The Fifth Amendment guarantee against self-incrimination would prevent prosecutors from using this test in America unless the defendant acquiesced. It would be like DNA evidence, but the defense would have a veto over whether or not the evidence could be used. This test alone could radically turn the tables in favor of defense lawyers everywhere.

But Mace couldn't concern himself with the broader societal implications of what he was doing. Right now he had a laser focus. He was trying to save Antoine Marshall's life.

57

THE REPUBLICAN PRIMARY TOOK PLACE on the last Tuesday in July, a date I had been dreading for more than a week. On the good side, the ubiquitous commercials featuring me and other "Women for Masterson" would finally stop running or, if Masterson won, would at least run less frequently. But on the bad side, I had volunteered to man one of the polling stations for my boss.

At the time, it had seemed like a good idea. All the other ADAs were signing up. But when I woke up at five o'clock so I could be at the polling station by six, I simply wanted to know one thing: *What was I thinking?*

It wasn't just that the forecast called for temperatures around ninety degrees and morning rain showers; it was the very thought of going to a strange place and greeting people I didn't know—who probably didn't want to talk to me—so I could urge them to vote for Bill Masterson. I believed he was the best candidate. But I always hated those bothersome poll workers when I went to vote. Today, I would be one of them.

I arrived on time and sat down at the *Masterson for AG* table with another volunteer. She had already placed a few Masterson signs at the curb and around the parking lot, but the area was dominated by Andrew Thornton's signs. When the Thornton volunteers finished setting up their large tent with free bottled water, right next to our much smaller Masterson table, my competitive juices kicked in. The other Masterson volunteer was content to sit behind the table and answer questions, but I joined the Thornton volunteers on the sidewalk, jockeying for position so we could be the first to greet the voters.

A steady rain moved into the area by eight o'clock, and the Thornton volunteers started jogging toward the cars of any voters who didn't have umbrellas, sharing a big golf umbrella and walking next to them until they reached the bubble zone around the polling place where campaigning was prohibited.

My coworker headed to her car to wait out the storm. Not me. I got out my own small umbrella and tried to escort voters too, though I got soaking wet in the process.

By noon the rain had stopped, but the parking lot felt like a sauna. I was tired of being outnumbered and outhustled by the Thornton folks, so I decided to bring in some reinforcements. I left my coworker at the polls for thirty minutes while I drove home and picked up the wonder dog. When we returned, Justice greeted everyone with the tongue-hanging, tail-wagging enthusiasm of a black Lab. People would stop and talk. And for the rest of the afternoon, I had a constant huddle of people around me as I explained how Bill Masterson was working hard to make sure criminal defendants didn't succeed with their no-plea-bargaining strategy.

At three in the afternoon, Masterson himself came by, and our little crowd of well-wishers grew. He stayed for about two hours and gave me a fist bump before he left. "You're a natural politician," he said.

"You owe me," I replied.

That night, Masterson's supporters gathered in a Marriott ballroom. There were unconfirmed rumors that Bill had run away with the nomination. I sipped a Diet Coke and made small talk with my officemates, wishing I could be home working on Caleb Tate's case. At nine fifteen, local television stations began calling the race in Bill's favor. He took the stage at nine thirty, and the room erupted.

I was genuinely happy for the man. He thanked a long list of people, including me and most of the other prosecutors in our office. I didn't like the political process, but I was pleased to see a good man have a chance at statewide office. And selfishly, it wouldn't hurt my career to be on a first-name basis with the attorney general.

I didn't get home until eleven o'clock, and I absentmindedly grabbed the mail at the end of the driveway. My first order of business was to let Justice out. While he was outside, I shuffled through the bills and magazines I had picked up. Among them was a letter with a handwritten envelope and the return address for Antoine Marshall. I stared at it for a moment before finally summoning the emotional energy to open it.

The letter was two pages of small block printing. It had been years since he had sent me a few letters, and I couldn't believe what I was now reading.

I was so shocked that I had to read the letter twice just to convince myself it was real. Marshall had been fighting this case for twelve years, and now, just seven days before his second scheduled execution date, I finally had what I always craved: an admission of guilt.

Dear Ms. Brock:

I am writing to tell you how sorry I am and to ask your forgiveness. My lawyer does not know I am sending this letter and would probably tell me not to, but I had to anyway.

For twelve years, I believed I was innocent of the charges against me for the murder of your mother. I passed a lie detector test—actually two—and I do not remember ever being in your house. But I just went through a test that scanned my brain when they asked me questions about the shooting of your mother. The doctor who gave me the test said my brain activity showed I had been there that night.

I must have been high on meth or something because I honestly don't remember.

I know you probably can't forgive me but I've prayed to God and know that he has forgiven me. After I gave my life to him, I told him I would do the right thing from that day forward and this now seems like the right thing. I am sorry I have put you through twelve years of hell and eleven years of appeals, but soon you won't have to worry about that no more.

I pray that you will find it in your heart to forgive me. I am having a hard time forgiving myself.

Sincerely yours,
Antoine Marshall

I finished the letter, folded it neatly, and placed it back in the envelope. I couldn't begin to make sense of my feelings. I was numb with the shock of it. Could this really be happening? After all these years?

I had to tell somebody, so I picked up the phone and called LA. I started reading him the letter, but halfway through I had to stop, my voice choking on the emotion.

"Are you okay?" he asked. I loved hearing the concern in his voice, but I honestly didn't know how to answer.

He gave me a moment to gather myself and then asked softly, "Do you want me to come over?"

"I'm okay," I said. "I really am okay."

◁▷

Mace James was not okay. His novel concept for proving Antoine's innocence had backfired. Since receiving the results, Mace had tried to downplay the reliability of the BEOS test, but Antoine wasn't buying it. And Mace himself was left to wonder whether he was truly defending an innocent man or just one who had been so high he hadn't remembered the night of the murder when he took the polygraph.

But what did it really matter? Mace had a job to do; he had seven days to save Antoine's life. The debate over the reliability of the BEOS test and Antoine's innocence could be fully resolved later. Mace's job was to make sure his client was still around when it was.

58

I WOKE UP ON WEDNESDAY, August 1, the day after receiving the letter from Antoine Marshall, and opened it again. I reread it while I drank my morning coffee. The euphoria of finally having an admission from my mother's killer had worn off. Melancholy took its place, a strange sense of despondency that I could not shake.

I had always been honest with myself, even hard on myself—something Dr. Gillespie had been trying to beat out of me in my counseling sessions. It wasn't working. And this morning, I had second thoughts about the way I was handling the information about Judge Snowden.

Antoine Marshall was a thrice-convicted felon who had the integrity to send me a letter revealing evidence that might just seal his fate. And here I was, an attorney sworn to uphold the law, sitting on evidence that might have provided him with a way off death row. Sure, I had lots of rationalizations and justifications. And in terms of true justice, I now felt more vindicated than ever. Antoine Marshall had certainly killed my mother. But did that justify burying evidence that might give him a new trial?

The system sometimes required us to set guilty people free in order to protect the integrity of the process and everyone's constitutional rights. When I took my oath as a prosecutor, I was reminded by Bill Masterson that our job was to pursue justice and not just win cases. But now, on the most important case of my life, I was playing fast and loose with the rules.

I had no appetite for breakfast. The information about my dad haunted me; I couldn't do anything to take my mind off it. I watched Justice in the backyard, but I didn't really see him. Instead, I zoned out, wondering whether I had compromised my integrity and ethics to such an extent that my soul would never recover.

Antoine Marshall's execution was six days away. What would happen if I provided this information to Mace James now? Was it too late to matter? Even if it wasn't, would the attorney general be able to use this new letter from Antoine to offset the impact of the information about Judge Snowden and my father? Should I even be asking these types of questions? Phrased differently, could I really sit on this exculpatory evidence and watch the state put Antoine Marshall to death?

I needed to talk to Dr. Gillespie. I called him before I left for work, and he promised to squeeze me in as soon as I got out of court.

◁▷

I talked to Chris later that afternoon. He had left four messages earlier in the day about a similar letter he had received. I had procrastinated calling him, knowing it would be emotionally draining to discuss it.

He answered on the first ring. "Did you get a letter?" Chris asked.

"Yes. I had to read it three times before it sank in."

"Me too. I've been calling since last night."

"I know. You might have heard we're a little busy down here."

Chris was slow to respond. Knowing my brother, I realized he was getting up the courage to tell me something. "Jamie, I think this letter is genuine. I know how you feel about this, but I really believe Antoine Marshall has experienced a sincere religious conversion and that this brain test helped him come to grips with what he did. I'm not saying he's innocent, but I am saying he's not the same man today who he was back then."

Chris stopped and waited for a response.

I thought it over, choosing my words carefully. "I deal with guys like Antoine Marshall all the time. They all claim to have come to Jesus in prison. Helps them get a better sentence. I think it's highly suspicious that he finally admits guilt just one week before his execution but only after he's tried everything else to get his case reversed."

"His lawyer called today." Chris kept his voice soft. I knew he didn't want an argument, and in truth I didn't either. "Wants to know if I'll give an affidavit urging that Marshall's death sentence be commuted to life without the possibility of parole." He hesitated, probably expecting an explosion from me. When none came, he dropped his own bomb.

"I'm thinking about giving him one, Jamie. I've never been in favor of the death penalty, and I don't think I could live with myself if I didn't ask for mercy here. I keep coming back to the Sermon on the Mount, where Christ tells us to forgive others if we want to be forgiven."

"We've both got to do what we think is right," I said. I knew Chris expected more of a fight, but I was too weary and frazzled to talk about it. Even though I faced my own ethical dilemma surrounding Marshall's execution, I now felt abandoned by my older brother. Antoine Marshall had killed our mother, and my brother was going to voluntarily sign an affidavit suggesting that the man's life be spared? It felt like treason to me.

"Will you still go to the execution with me?" I asked.

"Yes. And I'm praying that you can find it in your heart to forgive this man even if you believe the state should put him to death."

"Then keep praying. Because right now, I'm not feeling it."

◁▷

Clarity came halfway through my session with Dr. Gillespie. For the first time, I told him everything about the predicament I found myself in. True to form, he listened patiently and asked insightful questions. When he spoke, his words were measured and illuminating. He helped me look at my dilemma in a whole new light.

"At the core of your being," he said, "you're committed to fairness and justice. Withholding evidence from Mace James and watching Antoine Marshall die would be like raping your soul."

I said nothing.

"On the other hand, you also have a need to protect your father and preserve the ideal of this perfect family that was torn apart by Antoine Marshall."

"So what should I do?" I asked.

"You should hold fast to the good memories of your dad and remember that he loved you very much. Nothing can take that away. But you've also got to embrace your father's shortcomings.

"Nobody's perfect, Jamie. We learn from our parents' mistakes and

266 || THE LAST PLEA BARGAIN

create a better world for ourselves and our kids. We only compound their errors by trying to cover them up."

I left Gillespie's office saddened by the prospect of what I had to do. I would tell my boss about the evidence linking my father and Judge Snowden. He would feel duty-bound to share that data with Mace James. In a worst-case scenario, Antoine Marshall would walk out of jail a free man.

And so I prayed. Not that I would find it within me to forgive Antoine Marshall. My prayers had more of an Old Testament flavor—that one way or another, Antoine Marshall would get the type of justice he undoubtedly deserved.

59

BILL MASTERSON WAS NOT in the office on Thursday. According to
his assistant, he had decided to take Thursday and Friday off after his
big primary win and decompress at a friend's cabin on Lake Oconee.
It was, she said, his first time off in months. He was trying to read
through some policy papers and get ready for the fall campaign. He
had left Regina Granger in charge of the office, and he wasn't answering his cell phone.

I left the office at noon, went home to change, and picked up my
file with the information about Judge Snowden and my dad. With any
luck, I would be at Lake Oconee by four.

I thought about calling LA, but I knew he would try to talk me out
of it. If he truly cared about me, he would understand.

◁ ▷

The "cabin" where Bill Masterson was staying turned out to be a beautiful two-story house on a private wooded lot shaded by two-hundred-
year-old pine trees. It had a long, sloping backyard that led down to the
lake. Masterson's car, a Ford Taurus, was in the driveway. I knocked on
the door of the house a couple of times, each time louder than the last,
and even rang the doorbell. When there was no answer, I wandered
around to the back.

I spotted my boss at the end of an enormous pier that stretched
out onto Lake Oconee and served as a dock for two Jet Skis, a motor-
boat, and a small white yacht. I started walking down the hill, file in
hand, and called out to him. Masterson pulled his sunglasses down
and squinted at me over the top of them. Once he recognized me and

the shock wore off, he put the sunglasses back on and waved for me to come on down.

He was wearing only a pair of baggy shorts; I felt a little awkward seeing my boss with his shirt off, especially since nobody had ever accused Bill Masterson of staying in shape. If the voters could see him now, I thought, his poll numbers would drop by 20 percent. He was a hairy man, and he had either layered on gobs of sunscreen or he was sweating like crazy in the ninety-degree heat. Under the hair that covered his arms, chest, stomach, and back, his skin was white except for the farmer's tan he had from the biceps down. He had broad shoulders and a thick chest, but his gut hung over his shorts. He didn't seem the least bit self-conscious about it—I noticed a T-shirt on the deck, but Masterson made no effort to put it on.

"Jamie! What a great surprise! I didn't know you and I shared the same fishing hole."

It wasn't until he said it that I noticed a pole propped up with its line in the water. But the boss didn't seem to be paying much attention to it. A pile of briefing books surrounded his chair, and he had been lost in his studies when I first approached.

"Sorry to interrupt. I know you only have a few days to wind down, and I wouldn't be out here unless it was an emergency."

He waved it off. "Don't worry about it. I was already getting lonely. Had half a mind to start going door to door around the lake, passing out political flyers just to get my daily quota of handshakes. Here, have a seat."

He moved some books, and I pulled up a lounger a few feet away. I was wearing shorts and a tank top, and I kicked off my flip-flops. It felt good to be out in the sun.

"It's beautiful out here," I said.

Masterson talked for a few minutes about the friend who was letting him use his lake house and how hunting and fishing helped him keep a sense of perspective. He warned me to be careful—my life would be consumed by the law if I never took time to smell the roses.

"You think you're indispensable," he said. I sensed that he was talking more about a younger Bill Masterson than about me. "You think you're Superman. But as you get older, you get burned a few times, and you get pretty cynical. One of two things can happen. Either you get obsessed with putting the bad guys away and start to cut corners to make it happen, or you just throw your hands up and say, 'What's the use?' You feel like you're trying to drain the ocean with a teaspoon. I've seen a lot of good prosecutors either blur the lines or get burned out."

The boss looked out over the water and spoke with his relaxed Southern drawl. For the first time, I noticed the beer on the other side of his chair. "I don't want that to happen to you, Jamie."

It should have been easy to assure him that it would never happen, but I wasn't so sure anymore. Lines that once seemed clear had already started to fade.

"Actually, that's why I'm here. I need to talk to you about Caleb Tate's case, and I needed to do it now because it may have some bearing on Antoine Marshall's execution."

The boss put down a briefing book and took a swig of his beer. "Okay. Shoot."

It turned out to be a good setting for me to walk him through everything that had happened in the past several weeks. There were no interruptions. No smartphones buzzing to distract the boss's attention. No computer screens to glance at. I took him back to the Georgia Supreme Court hearing and Caleb Tate's threat. I told him about my search of the computer records and my discovery that my father and two other criminal-defense attorneys had enjoyed improbable success in front of Snowden. I left out my conversations with LA and Gillespie, but I told the boss that I had been wrestling with whether to say anything for weeks. I told him that, with Antoine Marshall's execution just a few days away, I couldn't keep this information to myself any longer.

With every sentence, I felt the weight of this secret, which had been beating me down for two months, slowly lifting. Part of it might have been the day or the setting, but it felt undeniably right to talk to my boss about this. I knew this step was irrevocable and that once Masterson had this information, he would have to do something with it. And I knew in my honest moments that it would mean the end of my father's reputation. But Dr. Gillespie was right—if I didn't share this information, it would mean the end of who *I* was and what *I* stood for.

Masterson showed no emotion, even when I detailed the statistics implicating my own dad. He had a few questions—the same ones I had already answered to my own satisfaction—about my father's success rate in front of other judges and whether this might just be an aberration. Then he took off his sunglasses and rubbed his face for a minute, deep in thought. He noticed what he thought was a nibble on his line and quickly jumped up, jerked the fishing rod, and reeled in the line.

"Nothing," he said. He cast it out again before he sat back down.

"I wish you had said something earlier," he said. "But you did the right thing coming to me before the execution."

He leaned forward and looked out over the lake again. "It's in my hands now, Jamie. I can make some decisions that you can't make without being accused of protecting your father and trying to make sure your mother's killer doesn't get another reprieve or even a new trial."

"I appreciate that, but it's not why I told you—"

"I know that," Masterson interrupted. "But you're not the first person to make these kinds of allegations about Judge Snowden." He let that thought seep in before he continued. "I've already started a below-the-radar investigation on her. I'll add this to the file."

Add this to the file? It wasn't the reaction I had expected. Prosecutors had a duty to share exculpatory information with defense attorneys.

"Don't we need to tell Mace James?"

Masterson shook his head. "Not until we confirm some kind of link between these defense attorneys and Snowden that's based on more than just statistics and conjecture. Case results are public information. James could have figured this out on his own. Maybe he already has. Besides, I can't let our investigation of Snowden hit the press just yet. And don't worry; your dad's cases haven't come up in that investigation."

His approach made me uncomfortable, but I reminded myself that I had come to Masterson for precisely this reason—because he saw the big picture.

"She'll find out about it anyway in a few weeks," I reminded him. "If we put Rafael Rivera on the stand, Tate will use it on cross-examination."

Bill Masterson took a deep breath and looked straight at me. "With what you've just told me, we can't go to trial against Tate. He'd destroy us. Not only would his cross-examination of Rivera be devastating, he'd be able to put into evidence the fact that he told you about these matters two months before the execution of Antoine Marshall and that you just sat on them until after he died."

"It's not too late," I said. "We could still give this stuff to Mace James and take away that argument."

"I'm sorry, Jamie, but not after you've been sitting on it this long. The courts would have a field day with that. Plus, it would compromise my investigation of Snowden." He shook his head. "Caleb Tate is a big fish, but there are bigger fish out there. I know you don't like this part of what we do, but we're always making choices. And this one's pretty clear. We preserve our investigation against Snowden, protect your father's reputation, and make sure Antoine Marshall gets exactly what's coming to him."

"But what about Caleb Tate? He's the reason every defendant in Milton County has quit plea-bargaining. Not to mention the deaths of the ones who did."

Masterson didn't respond immediately. When he did, his tone was low and reassuring. He didn't want a debate. And he wasn't the one who had been withholding the information for two months.

"We don't know that for sure. But if he *is* behind these recent killings, we'll eventually catch him. Somebody will talk; somebody will slip up. They always do."

"And if they don't?"

Masterson looked at his line. "Jamie, you ever go fishing?"

"No. I don't like taking the hook out of the fish's mouth."

"Well then, let me tell you the first rule about fishing. Even the best fishermen don't catch 'em all."

I understood exactly what he meant. But in typical Bill Masterson style, he left nothing to chance.

"And neither do we," he said.

60

THANKS TO ATLANTA TRAFFIC, I had a four-hour drive home to think about what Bill Masterson had said. Before I left, he agreed to leave the overall investigation of Caleb Tate open but said we had to nol-pros the pending case since we were only three weeks from trial. If we obtained new corroborating evidence linking Tate to the drugs, we could reindict.

I called LA as I approached Alpharetta, and he agreed to meet me at a local Starbucks. I thought I owed him a face-to-face explanation.

He sipped on a latte and listened without expression as I described my meeting with Masterson. There was a long and awkward silence when I finished.

He ringed the top of his glass with his finger and said softly, "I thought we agreed to keep that information to ourselves. At the very least, I didn't think you'd go to Masterson without letting me know."

I shifted in my seat. I was tired of apologizing to everybody for doing the right thing. And I was still thinking about the letter I had been handed in the Peachtree Road Race. Was LA really disappointed, or was he just acting the part?

"The letter from Marshall changed things. It made me realize that I couldn't just sit on this information and let him get the needle. That's not the way I do things."

"But that's what's going to happen anyway. Except now your boss is going to sit on it, and the price of him doing that is that Caleb Tate walks free."

"It's out of my hands," I said.

"Is it? I don't know much about the politics of the DA's office, but I do know one thing: you're the biggest story in that office right now. If the press had its way, they'd just declare you a saint and get it over with. Even judges who hold you in contempt get skewered. If you insisted on something, Masterson wouldn't cross you."

I thought LA was overestimating my popularity, but I could see his point. I also knew he had worked so hard on nailing Caleb Tate that he couldn't let it go. And frankly, neither could I.

LA had interviewed more than forty witnesses. We had put together a compelling case of financial motive, marital disputes, and eerie similarities with the Kendra Van Wyck case. Trial was only three weeks away. But it still all hinged on the testimony of Rafael Rivera.

"We can still make the case if we can get some corroborating evidence on Tate's access to the drugs," I said.

LA frowned. "That's just a bone Masterson threw to you. Doing that is impossible, and he knows it."

I spent nearly an hour with LA at the Starbucks before I excused myself. I had to go home and take care of Justice. I left feeling unsettled, and I could tell that LA felt the same. The chemistry from our prior times together was gone. It had been replaced by a battle of wills between two professionals who no longer seemed to entirely trust each other.

◁▷

I couldn't shut my brain down that night even after taking an Ambien. I was tormented by the thought of Caleb Tate winning this legal battle without ever going to trial and even more by the possibility that my father had been walking on the dark side of the law. But those concerns, grave as they were, took a backseat to the one vision that literally made me sick. In five days, I would be standing in a small room at the Diagnostic and Classification Prison in Jackson, watching medical technicians inject a deadly mixture of sodium thiopental, pancuronium, and potassium chloride into Antoine Marshall's veins. How could I stand there in silence, knowing that there was evidence that might provide a legal defense? But how could I turn over that evidence when I had been ordered by the DA not to and when I knew that doing so might free my mother's killer?

I had nightmares about the execution on both Thursday and Friday nights and woke up in a cold sweat Friday and Saturday mornings. Even during the day, I couldn't get my mind off the impending execution of Marshall. It wasn't just my dad's reputation or my obligation to the system that kept my stomach in a knot; it was my belief in a God who rewarded those who honored him and punished those who didn't. Even if we never tried Caleb Tate and the allegations about my father never came out, God would know that I had this information and had stood idly by while Antoine Marshall was put to death.

Late Saturday afternoon, I called Masterson and shared my concerns. "Whether or not we try Caleb Tate, I think we've got a duty to share this information with Mace James," I said.

"You're too close to the case to make that call," Masterson said evenly. "You did the right thing by bringing it to me. I'm having some people double-check your results. If the data holds up, I'll share it with the AG's office first thing Monday because they're the ones handling the appeal. I'll let them know I'm concerned about jeopardizing the investigation of Judge Snowden, but if they decide it's exculpatory and material evidence, they should disclose it. In my view, the appellate courts have already ruled that Snowden acted appropriately in this case. I don't view this as exculpatory evidence. I think it would be just another red herring for Mace James to carry on about."

"Shouldn't we at least ask the AG's office to agree to a stay pending the results of the Snowden investigation?" I asked.

"Jamie, you're the last person I thought I'd be saying this to, but this man's had plenty of stays over the last eleven years. There's always going to be some new piece of information or a different angle the courts haven't considered. At some point, we've got to let the authorities finish the job."

When I hung up, I still had a bad feeling in the pit of my stomach. Masterson was playing this like the ultimate politician—taking his time and then passing the buck to the AG's office. By the time they got the information on Monday morning, it would be too late to verify much of anything, and they would probably decide the information wasn't material.

On Saturday night, I called my brother and asked him to explain again why he had signed an affidavit trying to get Antoine Marshall's death penalty commuted to a life sentence. This time, I was ready to listen.

He said a lot of things, but my mind was racing so fast that I couldn't really concentrate on most of it. It was the usual stuff about our duty to forgive and the state's inconsistent application of the death penalty and the fact that he believed Antoine Marshall was a changed man. All of that I had heard before. But he quoted a Bible verse I never knew existed, and it was the one thing that stayed with me long after our conversation: "Judgment without mercy will be shown to anyone who has not been merciful. Mercy triumphs over judgment."

At eleven o'clock on Saturday evening, I picked up the phone and did the unthinkable. I called Mace James and asked him for a meeting first thing Sunday morning.

61

MACE JAMES HIT END CALL and stared at his phone. He had slept a total of six hours in the last two nights, and he felt like he was close to delirium. But there was no doubt he had just heard exactly what he thought he had heard. Out of the blue, Jamie Brock had called and wanted to meet first thing Sunday morning.

It was a miracle of biblical proportions. He hadn't felt this jazzed since he was allowed to walk out of prison a free man years ago.

Jamie wouldn't say what she wanted, but he knew she wouldn't request a meeting just to reiterate her desire to see Antoine Marshall die. Chris Brock had already signed an affidavit asking the Georgia Board of Pardons and Paroles to commute Antoine's sentence. At the very least, Mace was hoping Jamie would join that request.

Antoine had sent his letters of apology to Jamie and Chris Brock without first checking with Mace. When Mace confronted him, Antoine said he'd sent them without asking because he knew Mace would oppose the letters. For the last several days, as his Tuesday execution deadline grew closer, Antoine had taken on an air of grim resolution. This time, he said, there would be no stay.

Until now, Mace couldn't argue otherwise. He had run out of tricks. Even with the fertile and creative minds at Knight and Joyner helping out, Mace couldn't come up with a single legal issue that might get the court's attention.

And so it had come down to seeking mercy from the Georgia Board of Pardons and Paroles. They had already denied him four months ago. But if Mace could get affidavits from the only two surviving family members . . .

He had arranged for Jamie to meet him at the Southeastern Law School library at 7 a.m. He could no longer use his office at the school and so, like a first-year law student, he had his books, papers, and computer spread over a carrel in the far recesses of the book stacks. He was not looking forward to another night of coffee and Red Bull, drafting motions and briefs that might never be read.

◁▷

When I arrived at Professor James's study carrel on Sunday morning, he was slouched over the desk with his head on his arms, sound asleep. The study lamp was shining on his bald head, and he was snoring loud enough to echo against the bookshelves.

I placed a hand on his shoulder and nudged him. Nothing. I shook a little harder, and his head popped up. He rubbed his hands down his face and shook his head like a dog drying off.

"Thanks for coming," he said, his voice scratchy. He checked his watch and looked up at me with bloodshot eyes. "You want to go get some coffee at the student center?"

"Sure."

The student center snack shop was closed, but the vending machines dispensed coffee as thick as oil, and Professor James brewed a big cup. I went for an orange juice from another machine. We sat down at a table, and James slurped his coffee. Steam rose from the cup.

He looked like death. He had dark circles under his bloodshot eyes, and he probably hadn't shaved in three days. He had on a black T-shirt and board shorts, and he smelled like the men's locker room.

"I really appreciate you coming," he said. "I honestly never thought I would get a chance to talk to you one on one."

He took another slurp of coffee, and I sensed that he was just getting warmed up. "I've never had a chance to tell you how sorry I am that you lost your mother and now your father," he continued. His eyes were still only half-open, but they radiated sympathy. "I'm sorry I have to be the one representing the man accused of killing your mother, and I can understand why you would despise me for doing that. But somebody's got to. And I've watched you work the other side of cases.

I know you appreciate the fact that when you do something, you have to do it with everything you've got."

"You're doing your job," I said. "I don't have to like it."

"I don't expect you to. But I also know you didn't come here just to give me a lecture."

I didn't care for this man, and his apology did little to change my mind. Yes, he had a job to do. But that job did not include threatening a witness and beating him up just to get him to lie for Antoine Marshall. Yet he was right—I wasn't here out of respect or even revulsion for Mace James. I was here because I wanted to be able to live with myself.

"I'm willing to sign an affidavit requesting that your client's punishment be commuted from the death penalty to life in prison. I'm not as gullible as Chris, and I don't believe for a second that your client is a changed man. But I appreciate the fact that he's taking responsibility for this crime. That ought to count for something."

Professor James stared at me for a moment, his droopy eyes registering his disbelief. After all, I was the cold-blooded prosecutor who was rumored to have ice in her veins. James probably thought Chris had guilt-tripped me into this. In truth, it seemed like the only way out.

I couldn't tell Mace James about the evidence implicating Judge Snowden without risking my job for insubordination. Plus, I didn't want Antoine Marshall to get a new trial. At the same time, I couldn't just sit back and do nothing. This approach seemed to be a reasonable compromise, the best I could do under the circumstances.

"It takes a big person to step up and change direction like that—"

"Spare me," I said. "If you have someone bring the affidavit to my house today, I'll sign it. I'm not saying your client shouldn't be punished. But I'm willing to help you save his life."

Mace James looked down at his coffee and seemed to be thinking hard about what he should say next. He gave me a tentative look and chose his words carefully. "I know you said to spare you the accolades, but it does take a lot of guts to do this. My client will be very grateful. And, Jamie, he and I are both very sorry."

"I appreciate that," I said. "And I hope this will at least prevent any more surprise affidavits from jailhouse snitches."

"I think I've learned my lesson."

62

REGINA GRANGER MET ME at the office on Monday morning and asked for a few minutes of my time. She closed the door and said she had cleared my schedule for the week. I had already planned on taking Tuesday off, which was the date for Marshall's execution, as well as the day after. But she had reassigned all of my cases that week to other ADAs.

"You're under a lot of pressure right now, and you need some time away," she said. I wondered how much Bill Masterson had told her.

I started to protest, but the matter was not open for debate. When I realized I couldn't change her mind, I thanked her for taking care of things. She gave me a big Regina Granger hug and then held the outsides of my arms.

"Jamie, there's already been a lot of talk around the office about the affidavit you signed. You're probably aware that Mace James is making the media rounds. For what it's worth, I think you did the right thing."

I nodded and told her how much I appreciated her support. But it bothered me that my colleagues were talking.

"The press will try to interview you today," Regina said. "You can do whatever you want—this is a personal matter—but I don't think you need to throw any more fuel on the fire."

"They'll have to find me first," I said. "And that's just to get a 'no comment.'"

"Attagirl." Regina gave me a pat on the shoulder, told me to call her cell phone if I needed anything, and turned to leave. "I want you out of here in fifteen minutes," she said over her shoulder.

I didn't know what to do with myself the rest of the day. I went to the gym but after a few listless exercises realized that I didn't have much energy. So I went home and started obsessing over the online articles and television snippets covering Marshall's scheduled execution.

Predictably, James was making lots of noise about the fact that even the victim's family now wanted the execution halted. He continued to talk about the polygraph and the unreliability of cross-racial eyewitness testimony. Not a word was spoken about the test Antoine had taken. It was frustrating to see the speculation about why Jamie Brock, notorious hard-nosed prosecutor, had now flipped and gone soft on the death penalty.

I ignored the calls from reporters that flooded my cell phone. But I had to do something to clear up the confusion.

I called LA and asked him if he could leak some information to his sources at the newspaper and TV stations. "My specialty," he said.

By early afternoon, the story was more complete. There were unconfirmed reports that Antoine Marshall had taken a new type of lie detector called a BEOS test and failed. His brain waves supposedly proved that he had killed Dr. Laura Brock. Unnamed sources also revealed that Antoine Marshall had written a letter after receiving the test results, apologizing to the victim's family. The reporters now speculated that this admission of guilt had struck a chord with me and caused my about-face on the issue of whether Marshall should be executed or given life without the possibility of parole.

I was prepared to be castigated by my colleagues, but instead I started receiving accolades from other prosecutors who defended my right to show mercy in my personal life even though I advocated for the death penalty when I represented other victims. Their praise was echoed by death-penalty opponents who welcomed me with open arms to the side of the angels. All the while, my own emotions swung desperately back and forth. Regina had been right to send me home.

My ability to think logically and unemotionally about this matter was gone. So much so that at 5 p.m. on Monday, when the Georgia Board of Pardons and Paroles announced its decision to deny the petition for commutation, I went into a downward spiral. Though Mace James still had twenty-six hours to pull out a miracle, I knew that this time it wouldn't happen.

I felt a tsunami of guilt wash over me. Not only had I withheld information about my father's success rate in front of Judge Snowden, but I had leaked information about Antoine Marshall's confession. I had done so on the assumption that the Georgia Board of Pardons and Paroles would grant the commutation to a life sentence. I wanted everyone to know that even if they did, there was no doubt about Antoine Marshall's guilt. But now that his execution was a certainty, I was having a hard time coming to grips with my own role in the process.

But why was this different from four months ago?

The answer to that question was the one reality I tried desperately to ignore. Four months ago, I had no doubt about Antoine Marshall's guilt. But now, even with this new BEOS test, I couldn't erase a nagging question from my mind.

What if my father was mistaken? There was no DNA evidence. No murder weapon. No corroboration for the eyewitness testimony of a man whom I was no longer sure I really knew. If he was willing to bribe or blackmail a state court judge, would he also be willing to fudge his testimony in order to make his eyewitness identification appear more certain?

Not my father. He had always been fair and merciful. There was no way my dad would have shaded the truth when it would put a man on death row.

But there was no way my dad would have exercised undue influence with a judge, either. And what about those expert witnesses Snowden had kept from testifying? Dr. Rutherford had seemed pretty persuasive to me.

And so I would be forced to watch the execution of Antoine Marshall with these doubts swirling in my head. Had my father put an innocent man on death row? And if he did, had I just taken away the last chance that man had of escape?

63

THE NEWS ABOUT ANTOINE MARSHALL'S execution was eclipsed on Tuesday morning by news that a plea bargain had been struck in Milton County Superior Court. A man accused of armed robbery had copped a plea in exchange for a reduced prison sentence. He had been sent to an undisclosed location in another part of the state to serve his time, and Bill Masterson held a press conference to announce that the logjam had been broken. The prisoner, whose name was Latrell Hampton, still had eighteen months left to serve on his reduced sentence, and the question on everyone's mind was whether he would survive long enough to experience the daylight of freedom.

Masterson sounded certain that he would: "I can assure you that he is safe in solitary confinement. He will not be a part of the general inmate population at any time during the remainder of his prison term. While we cannot do this for every inmate who pleads guilty, we are making special arrangements for those who are brave enough to be the first ones to break ranks."

I was intrigued by Hampton's guilty plea, but my mind was elsewhere. I checked the court filings throughout the morning, actually hoping Mace James and his Knight and Joyner counterparts might somehow pull it off. But by the time Chris picked me up at the house at 1 p.m., three different courts had already issued opinions denying new requests from Antoine Marshall's lawyers. There was one chance left—the US Supreme Court—but there wasn't anything new to make the justices there take notice.

A session with Dr. Gillespie on Monday had helped me work

through some of my guilt. He had also changed my sleep medication to Lunexor, which he said would provide a sense of deep relaxation leading to better REM sleep and also create an improved feeling of well-being. Whether or not the medication was helping, I was less jittery on Tuesday than I had been the day before. But I still couldn't get any peace about what I was going to witness.

On the way to Jackson, Chris tried to assure me that we had done everything we could to avoid this moment and that God would provide a reprieve if Antoine Marshall was not supposed to die. I admired my brother's blind faith in God's intervention, but he didn't know the things I knew. The manipulations behind the scenes were ugly and made a mockery of the naive notion of justice I had embraced when I first came to the DA's office.

This time, there were no traffic jams, and Chris and I arrived in Jackson two and a half hours early. We sat in a McDonald's and nursed Diet Cokes for an hour, each deep in our own thoughts.

"You ready?" Chris finally said to me.

"I guess so."

We made it to the prison parking lot a few minutes later, and the protesters stopped to stare. Television cameras swung our way. Chris left the car running so we could enjoy our last few seconds in the air-conditioning. He took my hand and suggested we pray.

"Good idea," I said.

I bowed my head as Chris prayed for Antoine Marshall with the same earnestness I remembered from when Dad first went into the hospital. He ended with a request that God would have mercy on Antoine Marshall's soul. I murmured an amen and opened my eyes.

I touched my mother's necklace and felt my eyes brim with tears. "I never thought this day would come," I said. "And now that it's here, I wish it hadn't."

"It's out of our hands now," Chris said. "It always has been."

We got out of the car, and I kept my eyes straight ahead, ignoring the small crowd of protesters as I walked next to Chris. To my surprise, the protesters started clapping. First just a few, and then they all joined in—a respectful applause as they lined up to face us and show their appreciation for the fact that two innocent victims had advocated to save a man's life. Even the television crews, though they followed us with their cameras, refrained from shouting questions at us.

Chris nodded at the protesters and thanked them, but I didn't say a word. I just wanted to get into the relative obscurity of the building and get this over with.

We went through five levels of security—the guard at the barbed-wired gate, the metal detector and second set of guards, two sets of hydraulically controlled doors, and a final pat-down—before we were ushered into the waiting room. Bill Masterson arrived a few minutes later, followed by the sheriff who had led the investigation into my mom's murder. I gave them both a hug and thanked them for coming.

In a few minutes, we would be taken by van to the small white building at the edge of the property that housed the execution chamber. We would be joined in the observation room by Mace James, the prison chaplain, and five reporters. Caleb Tate would not be there. He was too much of a coward to attend.

◁▷

At 6:19 p.m., sitting next to his client in a small cell, Mace James received the text message from an attorney at Knight and Joyner. The Supreme Court had denied their final plea for a stay of execution. This time, there would be no last-minute drama.

Antoine looked at Mace with expectant eyes, a last glimmer of hope, and Mace simply shook his head. Antoine nodded and looked down, and the tears began to flow. After a few minutes, he wiped his eyes and raised his head. He put his hand on Mace's shoulder. "You've done one heckuva job. I don't deserve a lawyer like you."

Mace felt a lump in his throat, and he had a hard time speaking. "What you deserve is a lawyer who could put a stop to this."

"Nah." Antoine shook his head. "What I deserve is exactly what I'm going to get."

Mace cursed himself for the umpteenth time for setting up that BEOS test. He had been shocked when he saw the results. Afterward, Mace began doubting the reliability of the technique. He'd talked to experts who questioned the test's trustworthiness, experts he had ignored in his earlier crusade to get the test authorized. But even when he explained all this to Antoine, his client wouldn't believe him. Antoine became convinced that he had been fooling himself all along and that he must have killed Laura Brock in a drug-induced state. And now, rather than freeing his client, Mace had only managed to send him to the grave with an overwhelming burden of guilt.

The men sat there in silence for another five minutes until the chaplain showed up for a final prayer. The prison pastor was big and soft-spoken and had taken a particular liking to Antoine. The two men hugged and then knelt together on the floor. Mace joined them on his knees. He felt like his heart would rip out of his chest when Antoine began to pray for Chris and Jamie Brock but couldn't finish his thoughts. The chaplain stepped in and prayed while Antoine cried unashamedly.

Mace wondered whether his client would be able to compose himself in the thirty minutes he had left before the scheduled execution.

◁ ▷

When they pulled the curtains back at precisely 7 p.m., Antoine Marshall was already strapped to the gurney located just a few feet away on the other side of the window. The room was clean and clinical with white walls, a tile floor, and the single gurney in the middle. Four deputies stood next to the prisoner, and I knew that one of the deputies was a trained medical technician. I'd been told that doctors would not participate in the procedure because of their pledge to do no harm to their patients.

Chris and I were sitting in the front row, along with Masterson and the sheriff. Mace James and the prison chaplain sat behind us, and five reporters occupied the last row. A few prison guards kept an eye on everyone.

The warden who pulled the curtain back moved to Antoine's side and read the execution order. He then asked the prisoner if he had any final words. Chris reached out and took my hand.

I was shocked at how helpless and frail Antoine Marshall looked. I remembered him from the trial and expected a man more surly, with more swagger. But the man in front of me had bleary red eyes that darted back and forth from one observer to the next. in abject fear. He appeared smaller and thinner than I remembered. In fact, he seemed nearly anorexic, dwarfed by his orange jumpsuit. Only later would I learn that he had been fasting for forty days.

"I just . . . want to say," he stammered, "that I am so very sorry. Jamie and Chris Brock—" his lip began to quiver, and I could see tears rolling down his cheeks as he looked at Chris and me—"thank you for trying to save my life even though I took your mother's. I have been praying for you every day, and if you can find it in your heart to somehow forgive me, please pray that God will have mercy on my soul. My only hope now is in Jesus."

He closed his eyes, and I wanted to look away. The medical technician swabbed his arm with alcohol, found a vein, and punctured it with a needle. The man then hooked up an IV, which ran through a hole in the wall to an adjacent room. He did the same thing with Antoine's other arm—a backup IV in case the primary line failed.

The warden took out his cell phone to check one last time, just to make sure no miracle had occurred in any of the appellate courts or at the Georgia Board of Pardons and Paroles. He announced that there had been no stay granted and signaled that the execution should continue.

I had done my homework and knew that in the room behind the prisoner, two staff members would take three syringes and empty them sequentially into the IVs. The first would contain the drug sodium thiopental, a quick-acting barbiturate, which would induce a coma within thirty seconds of injection. The second drug, pancuronium bromide, was a muscle relaxant that would cause paralysis of the respiratory muscles. The third drug, potassium chloride, would stop the heart.

Antoine was hooked up to a heart monitor, and I watched his chest rise and fall. I knew death could occur anywhere between five and twenty minutes after the drugs were injected.

He closed his eyes, and his lips started moving as if in prayer.

My mother's killer never opened his eyes again. His chest rose and fell, rose and fell, rose and fell. Chris squeezed my hand harder. Antoine's lips stopped moving, his heart rate began to slow, and within a few minutes, almost imperceptibly, the chest stopped expanding. The heart monitor flatlined. And just like that, it was over.

I closed my own eyes and said a silent prayer.

God, have mercy on this man. And, Lord, forgive me for allowing this to happen.

When I opened my eyes, I saw two doctors enter the room wearing long white coats. One at a time they checked the prisoner's pulse and put a stethoscope on his chest. They looked at each other and nodded.

The warden pronounced Antoine Marshall dead at 7:07 p.m. I felt myself getting dizzy, my knees starting to buckle, but I somehow held it together long enough to walk out of that room under my own power.

I left the facility in a daze. After we cleared the prison walls, Bill Masterson talked to the press while I walked somberly to the car. Chris drove home; I stared out the side window, trying to come to terms with what I had just witnessed.

64

CHRIS ASKED ME if I wanted him to stay with me Tuesday night, but I lied and said I would be fine. I had always thought that once Antoine Marshall was executed, I would experience a sense of closure and be ready to move on to the next phase of my life. But on the way back from Jackson, I realized how much this struggle had defined me. Now that he was dead, now that the fight was over, I felt like a big part of me had died as well. What made it worse was the convoluted way it had all ended. Antoine Marshall had stepped up and done the right thing, taking responsibility for his actions. But I had dodged my responsibility to the justice system, finding ways to keep harmful information secret—an approach that had sealed Antoine Marshall's fate.

It was over so abruptly. And the image of Antoine Marshall strapped to the gurney, eyes closed and the IVs in both arms, was seared into my memory. That night I took the Lunexor that Gillespie had prescribed but didn't experience the same type of high I had experienced before. It did help me sleep, but the next day I couldn't force myself out of bed before eleven. I just wanted to stay in a fetal position under the blankets until the pain went away, until my mother and father came back and the ache in my heart disappeared.

For two days I stayed in my sleep clothes until the afternoon hours and seldom ventured outside my house. I had a session with Gillespie on Thursday night, and he tried to walk me through some relaxation techniques, but nothing worked. With the death of Antoine Marshall, and especially the circumstances surrounding his death, I had lost my zeal for being a prosecutor. Without that, I wasn't even sure who Jamie Brock was anymore.

I spent most of Friday going through old scrapbooks and

memorabilia that reminded me of my mom. When I was a teenager, I hadn't been that interested in her work as a forensic psychiatrist. But now, as I read some of the newspaper clippings she and my dad had saved, I gained a new appreciation for what a powerful witness she must have been. She testified all over the country against defendants who claimed insanity through irresistible impulse. She had apparently developed a subspecialty in what it took for somebody to be brainwashed and was the psychiatrist of choice for many high-profile cases when prosecutors were debunking that defense.

Out of all the articles I read, it seemed that she lost only once. The defense lawyer was a young showboat from Las Vegas named Quinn Newberg.

But my mom testified for the defense side as well. On that side, she specialized in cases involving alleged sexual abuse when the victims claimed to recall the abuse under hypnosis. My mom was apparently a national leader in showing how persons who were susceptible to hypnosis were equally susceptible to the power of suggestion from the person who had hypnotized them. Oftentimes the counselor or psychiatrist would help the "victim" create a detailed account of sexual abuses that never actually occurred.

It was such a tragic waste that my mom had been cut down in the prime of her professional career, not to mention at a time when her daughter needed her most.

I called Chris a few times, and he seemed to be moving on better than me. But then again, he didn't have to live with the secrets I did. I had decided that I would never tell him. I felt I was already paying a high price to protect my father's reputation. There was no sense destroying Chris's memories as well.

Late Friday afternoon, I finally got sick of feeling sorry for myself and called Bill Masterson. He asked how I was doing, and I told him I had been better. His solution didn't surprise me.

"I think it's time that you get back in the saddle. That's what both your mom and your dad would have wanted."

I agreed with him because I didn't have the energy to tell him the truth—that I was wondering whether I even wanted to be a prosecutor anymore.

"We need to get the Caleb Tate case nol-prossed next week," Masterson said. "And we need to get ready for the press onslaught when we do."

I knew what that meant. I would be the one to face the reporters and tell them we didn't have enough evidence to go to trial. Everybody knew how much I wanted to nail Caleb Tate. The fact that we were backing off, at least for the time being, would go down easier coming from me.

When I went to bed Friday night, the last image in my mind was the same one I had seen every other night before the medication kicked in—the face of Antoine Marshall, a man who was haunting me in death as much as he did in life.

65

THE PHONE WOKE ME out of a sound sleep early Saturday morning. Too early. I checked the caller ID—LA—and rolled over to go back to sleep. Next he sent a text message saying we needed to talk and followed this with another phone call. He left a voice mail, but I was too tired to check it and before long had dozed back to sleep, the medication doing its job.

But LA knew how to be persistent. The next time I woke up, it was because Justice was barking like mad at somebody knocking on the front door. I decided to ignore this too, but whoever it was couldn't take a hint. I squinted at the clock. It registered 7:05. I tried to shake off the effects of the medication, and it finally dawned on me that nobody would come to the house this early unless it was an emergency.

I looked at my bed hair in the mirror and matted it down a little before I padded to the front door. I squinted at the sunlight and saw LA standing there, hands in his pockets, patiently waiting. I opened the door, and Justice jumped on LA, licking as usual. I tried to think of something clever to say, but my mind wasn't really functioning yet.

"Can I come in?" he asked. "We've got to talk."

I could tell by the grave look on his face that something was desperately wrong. Perhaps Caleb Tate had gone public with the information about my father and Judge Snowden. Maybe the press was getting ready to do an exposé about something someone had dug up on Masterson. It was still hard for me to concentrate and formulate my thoughts, like my mind was wading through a swamp.

"Sure. I'll make some coffee."

LA came in and sat down at my kitchen table. He absentmindedly rubbed Justice's head while I got the coffeemaker started.

"Remember the kid who pleaded guilty on Monday?" LA asked. He wasn't going to wait for the coffee. He just needed to unburden himself.

"Yeah. But I don't remember his name."

"Latrell Hampton," LA said.

I was standing next to the coffeemaker with my arms crossed. This whole conversation wasn't making sense. "Okay," I said.

"We put him in solitary," LA said, his face ashen. "We did everything we could to protect him. We knew the gangs would try to take him out."

As I waited for the coffee to brew, the cobwebs started clearing. Something had happened to Hampton.

"That was my case. I put 24-7 surveillance on both his mother and his former girlfriend for two days. But resources are scarce, so we reduced it to drive-bys. Late last night, they attacked his girlfriend and her three-year-old son. Slit the girlfriend's throat. Stabbed her thirty-two times. Killed the kid, too. Stabbed him multiple times."

The thought of it made me sick. And I knew the newspapers would be all over this. The cops would get crucified.

"I spent the night over there working the crime scene. Jamie, we just didn't have enough officers available to stand watch at that house and at his mom's house 24-7. And now . . ." His voice trailed off.

"I'm sorry," I said.

"I've worked a lot of crime scenes," LA continued, looking at me with those sad, steel-blue eyes, "but I don't think I've ever seen so much blood."

The coffee finished brewing, and I poured our cups. I sat at the opposite end of the kitchen table from LA and spent thirty minutes trying to tell him it wasn't his fault.

He asked if he could hang out at the house for a while, and I went upstairs to take a shower and change clothes. When I came back down, he was sleeping on the couch.

We spent the day together and avoided talking about Latrell Hampton except for a few phone calls LA had to field about the investigation. We went out to dinner that night at a local Macaroni Grill. It was the first time I had felt like a human being in a week.

When he dropped me off at the house, I stayed in his car and talked for another thirty minutes. Just before I got out, he steered the conversation back around to the case that brought him there in the first place.

"We both know who's behind this, Jamie. You can't let him off the hook on that murder case. Until we take him out, we'll never break the back of this conspiracy."

"It's out of my control," I said. "Masterson made the call."

LA turned in his seat and looked at me. "You know what I love about you? You have no idea how popular you are. If you threatened to quit over this, there's no way Masterson would let you."

"You don't know Masterson."

"I know he's a politician. And I know the surest way to lose votes right now is to tell the public that he forced Jamie Brock to nol-pros the Tate case and she quit. Think about how that would play out."

LA had a point, but I knew it wasn't that easy. "If we go to trial, all this stuff about my dad comes out. Tate will annihilate Rivera on cross, and the press will crucify Masterson and me. It's too late now."

"That's where you're wrong," LA said, his voice animated. "First, I don't think you had any obligation to divulge that information to Mace James. Nobody can prove anything except that your father did well in front of Judge Snowden. And even if you did have a duty to divulge it—you told Masterson, and he told the AG. What more could *you* do?"

"I don't know," I said. "It sounds logical sitting here tonight, but Caleb Tate would play it—"

"Jamie," he interrupted, "they made the little boy watch while they slashed his mother's throat. The CSI guys could tell because of the blood-spatter evidence. What kind of animals do that? What kind of warped man incites them?"

It seemed to me that LA was piling assumption on top of assumption. But I shared his burning desire to take down Caleb Tate. Maybe I was doomed to live life as a fighter, my self-image defined by my enemies more than by the people I loved.

"I'll think about it," I said.

"That's all I can ask." And then, as if to seal the deal, LA reached over and gently placed his hand behind my head. He leaned in and gave me a kiss, and I didn't fight him. It had been a long day, and my emotions were raw, but this felt right.

We pulled back and lingered there for a moment, a few inches apart.

"I need to get going," I said.

I got out of the car because I didn't trust myself to stay there. I closed the car door but leaned back down. He rolled down the passenger window. "Thanks for the kiss," I said.

"There's more where that came from."

I smiled. Probably for the first time in more than a week. "I never doubted that," I said.

66

I SET MY ALARM FOR 6 A.M. on Sunday, and Justice forced me out of bed. He wagged his tail and jumped around while I fixed him breakfast, as if to celebrate the fact that his master was coming back to life. I worked all day on a memo arguing that we should proceed with the Tate trial, now scheduled to start in just eight days. I knew we could get a brief continuance and push the case into September if we needed to. But we had subpoenaed the witnesses more than a month earlier, and I had developed outlines for each person's testimony. I wanted to start on schedule.

Sunday evening, LA came to the house and fixed dinner while we discussed everything we needed to get done in the next few days if Masterson allowed the case to go forward. We avoided talking about the alternative—what would happen if Masterson called my bluff and I had to resign.

◁▷

I got to work at eight o'clock Monday morning and left a copy of my memo on Bill Masterson's desk in an envelope marked *Personal and Confidential*. At nine, I checked with his assistant to make sure Masterson would see the memo that morning. He had gone straight to court, she said, but she would make sure he got it.

I checked back with Masterson's assistant twice and would have checked a third time, but she was clearly getting perturbed. At four thirty, just before I picked up the phone to call his cell, Bill Masterson walked into my office, shut the door behind him, and sat down across from my desk.

"I got your memo," he said. "You put a lot of work into it."

"We've got to take a shot at this guy. It's the right thing to do. As you can tell, I feel pretty strongly about it."

There was no need to say anything else; I'd put it all in the memo. I believed Caleb Tate was the man who had initiated the no-plea-bargaining chaos. I was sure he had killed his wife. I was willing to risk the reputations of my father and Judge Snowden just to get a chance to argue Tate's case to the jury. My last paragraph contained my ultimatum. I would resign rather than drop the case.

Masterson and I talked for a while about how we might handle Rivera's testimony. Masterson confirmed that he had provided the information about Snowden to the AG's office. They had decided last Monday not to pass it along to Mace James.

"You're willing to put your dad's reputation on the line?"

"Yes, sir. I am."

He rubbed his face and thought, staring at the floor. Then his eyes lit up as if he'd had an epiphany.

"Rivera's going to deny saying anything about bribing Snowden, right?" Masterson asked.

His excitement got my heart pumping faster. "Yeah. He denies that conversation ever took place."

"Right. So Tate will ask Rivera about it on cross-examination. Rivera will deny the conversation ever occurred. Your dad's record in front of Snowden isn't direct evidence—at best it's corroborating evidence. But before corroborating evidence like that can be considered, somebody's got to testify about the underlying threat by Rivera. And who's the only person who can do that?"

"Tate," I said. It suddenly seemed so obvious. *How could I have missed it?* "You're right," I continued, thinking out loud. "Even if we believe Tate's version of events, Rafael Rivera never mentioned my father. He only mentioned Judge Snowden. The only witness who can drag my father into it is Tate. And if Tate waives the Fifth Amendment and takes the stand, we'll nail him."

Masterson was standing now, watching it all play out in his mind. "So Tate can still gut Rafael Rivera's testimony, but the price he pays is that he's got to take the stand himself."

"I think that's right," I said. I was disappointed I hadn't realized this earlier. But at the same time, Masterson's excitement was contagious.

"And if he does that, this whole case will come down to our cross-examination of Tate," Masterson said. I could tell by the look in his eyes that he relished the thought.

"Here's what we're going to do," he said. "We go to trial next week. You take the opening and every witness except Rivera and Tate. I'll take those two and the closing."

"Yes, sir," I said.

We discussed the details of the case for another hour. Masterson wasn't worried that he hadn't fully prepared for the case; he'd get up to speed watching the first part of the trial. I wished that I had half the man's confidence.

After he left my office, I called LA.

"We're in," I said.

67

MACE JAMES SPENT THE DAYS after Antoine Marshall's execution trying to make good on his oath to vindicate his dead client's name. Mace was no psychiatrist, and he didn't know the DSM-IV criteria for an obsessive disorder, but he was pretty sure his focus on Antoine Marshall qualified. He had other clients, but he spent nearly every waking hour working on Antoine's case. Something wasn't right about this case, but after all these years, Mace still couldn't put his finger on it. Now Antoine was dead. Yet how could he just close out the file? What if he had allowed an innocent man to die?

He started by rereading the entire case file, looking at the matter from a different perspective. In the past few years, he had focused on errors in the trial court's rulings in order to get his client a new trial. But now he searched the file for clues about who the real killer might be, the way he had when he first got involved in the case. Once the police had zeroed in on Antoine, they had never really pursued the kinds of questions Mace was re-asking now.

What if this wasn't a random breaking and entering? Who might want Laura Brock dead? What if the real target was Robert Brock? Who were his enemies?

Mace started running down all the cases where Laura Brock had testified. Next, he looked at the high-profile cases that Robert Brock handled. And because he had always been suspicious of Snowden, he started studying her other decisions as well. Why had she bent over backward to protect Robert Brock? What did she have against Caleb Tate? What other cases had Caleb handled in front of Snowden?

He did some additional digging into the scientific research in order to understand how Marshall could have passed a lie detector test but failed the BEOS. He called some scientists in India who were on the forefront of the BEOS procedure and who swore to its reliability. Lie detector tests, on the other hand, had well-known credibility problems.

Mace had downplayed the reliability of the BEOS test to Antoine during his client's final days because it seemed like the right thing to do. But now, the more he researched, the more Mace became convinced that the BEOS test was reliable. Maybe Antoine had it right. Maybe he had been so drugged that he had no conscious memory of that night and could pass a polygraph. But Mace couldn't talk himself into closing the file just based on the BEOS test. Not yet. Maybe not ever. Mace had watched a client die. He couldn't just move on to the next case while he still had doubts.

One thing that intrigued Mace was the number of times Caleb Tate's clients had passed a polygraph. That fact, coupled with Tate's own on-air performance on the lie detector, caused Mace to investigate Dr. Stanley Feldman, the polygraph expert who had tested Tate.

Mace left no stone unturned. He spent hours combing through files in the Milton County clerk's office. He went to the jail and interviewed defendants who had been involved in the cases. He talked to lawyers and expert witnesses and made charts and spreadsheets about what he found. He went to bed thinking about his research and woke up with new ideas to pursue.

He felt close to a breakthrough, like he was onto something, something that eluded him, something just beyond his reach. But he couldn't quite figure it out. And sadly, even if he did, it would all come too late to save his client's life.

68

I FELT MYSELF SPINNING out of control the week before the biggest trial of my life. Like any young lawyer, I always got nervous before an important case. But this was different. I was so jittery I could hardly concentrate or get anything done.

Part of it was my certainty that Tate would figure out a way to inject the information about Judge Snowden and my father into the case. Even if he didn't take the stand and testify, he would leak it to the press. He would also let them know that he had shared the information with me nearly three months ago and I had been sitting on it even when Antoine Marshall was executed. Tate would figure out a way to turn the tables so he wouldn't be the only one on trial. I would join him. And so would my dad.

There were times during the week when I thought about the trial, imagined all the terrible things that could happen, and felt my heart start racing, my breathing becoming short and shallow. I checked my pulse and a few times found my heart beating over 150 times per minute. When it happened at work, I closed my office door and sat at my desk, eyes closed, forcing myself to calm down. At home, I would pace back and forth or lie down on the bed until I relaxed enough to think straight.

I took Lunexor at night and muscle relaxers during the day. I told myself that these anxieties were no different from the nervousness an athlete experiences before a big game. Once the trial started, I would be all right.

But I had been an athlete, and I had never experienced anything like this. At times I honestly thought I was losing my mind.

It got worse when LA and I prepared Rivera for his testimony via Skype. Not surprisingly, the man came across as surly and defensive. "He's lying," LA said as soon as we hung up.

I had my own suspicions, but I was hoping we were both wrong. "How could you tell?"

LA looked at me for a moment as if trying to weigh whether he should further destroy my confidence.

"Tell me," I insisted.

He shrugged. "You asked."

We had been using his computer for Skype, and I didn't realize he'd had a software program recording the video. For the next thirty minutes, he played back portions of Rivera's testimony. He pointed out microexpressions that had flashed across Rivera's face. He showed me a graph of pacing and voice pitch that his software program had computed. Rivera's word flow slowed and his pitch changed when he answered questions about providing drugs to Caleb Tate.

"The most reliable signals of deception come from the cognitive efforts and emotions that surround a lie. It takes more mental horsepower to construct a lie than to remember the truth," LA explained. "As a result, our pace and pitch change in ways that are usually imperceptible to the naked ear. But a computer program can pick it up."

The most fascinating clues were the nonverbal signals Rivera gave off. LA called it "duping delight"—the joy a sociopath takes in deception. "Look at that—did you see that sinister little smile flash across his face?"

He was right. It wasn't something I had noticed in real time, but I could see it when LA ran the tape in slow motion. "He's playing us," LA said. "Caleb Tate may be guilty. But this guy is lying through his teeth."

The whole experience created more anxiety for me. I couldn't prove Rivera was lying, but I knew in my gut that LA was right. And so Jamie Brock, the by-the-book prosecutor, the woman who valued integrity and justice above all else, the same woman who had recently withheld information from Mace James, was getting ready to put a lying witness on the stand in a high-profile murder case.

But how could we win the case without him?

69

OF ALL THE LUCK. There were nine judges in Milton County Superior Court, and we ended up with the one judge who had a personal stake in the matter. And the way she glared at me from the bench, she acted like the entire case was my fault.

One bizarre ruling followed another, and I seemed to be the only one in the courtroom who noticed. Tate would object, and the judge would sustain the objection automatically. If I tried to object, she told me to sit down. Masterson, sitting next to me, was too busy jotting notes for his cross-examination of Caleb Tate to pay it any mind.

And then it dawned on me. I had been so focused on my dad's results in front of Judge Snowden that I had never checked on Tate's. What if Tate had wised up after the Antoine Marshall trial? What if he had started paying off Snowden like the other defense lawyers? Or started blackmailing her, or whatever it was my dad had been doing?

It suddenly made sense—the rulings against me, Tate being allowed to strut around the courtroom and say whatever he wanted. I now knew how Tate must have felt all those years ago trying to defend Antoine Marshall and fighting the judge as well.

Things turned truly bizarre when Tate took the stand and Masterson said he had no questions. I stood and objected. I had questions myself! But Masterson was pulling on my elbow, and Snowden was yelling at me to sit down, over and over, her shrill voice drowning out my questions.

Tate started laughing, a truly heinous laugh, taunting me, mocking justice.

And then, when I had reached the breaking point, the alarm broke through. I sat straight up, my heart pounding. I reached over to the nightstand, found my BlackBerry, and turned it off. I struggled to get my bearings.

Relief and dread flooded me at once. Relief that it was all a dream. Dread because part of it could still become reality. We wouldn't know the judge for our case until Monday morning. And we had a one-in-nine chance of drawing Snowden.

Masterson and I had talked about it at length. If we drew Snowden, we would request a meeting with her and Tate in chambers to tell her about Tate's anticipated cross-examination of Rivera. Snowden would probably be furious, but we guessed that she would ultimately recuse herself. In the process, Masterson's investigation of the judge would have lost the element of surprise.

Sitting in my bed, I forced myself to calm down. Justice, lying on the floor, made a sleep noise, a dog grunt that told me to go back to sleep.

Not on your life. I was exhausted, but I got up anyway. Going through the day bone-tired was better than facing the nightmares.

◁▷

By Thursday night I realized that if I couldn't stop the anxiety attacks, I would be of no use at trial. As usual, Aaron Gillespie agreed to juggle his schedule so he could see me.

For nearly an hour, I unloaded all of my concerns. We hadn't been able to prove any affairs by Tate. Our only witness tying him to the drugs was probably lying. The issues about my dad and Judge Snowden. My own role in the execution of Antoine Marshall. The loneliness I felt. The guilt.

Gillespie listened patiently and reminded me that I was under a tremendous amount of pressure. He said I had never properly mourned my dad and that it was catching up with me. "But considering the circumstances, I actually think you're handling things quite well," he said.

It helped to hear his calm reassurance. And he had some thoughts about managing the trial pressures as well.

"Have you ever heard about Advanced Performance Imagery?" Gillespie asked.

"I've heard of it."

I had once been an elite kayaker, finishing fourth in the Olympic trials. I knew several of my competitors used API as a sort of "mental steroid" to enhance their performance.

"It's the company that's trained a lot of professional and Olympic athletes," Gillespie said. "I guess you never worked with them."

"No. I had enough self-confidence on my own."

I thought groups like API were for athletes with inferior willpower who freaked out during intense competition. The whole idea smacked of Eastern religion and hypnosis to me. I never needed any of that. Or at least I didn't think I did.

For the next few minutes, Gillespie talked to me about the idea behind what he called "neurolinguistic programming."

"What you practice in your mind, you perfect in reality." He explained how numerous athletes had trained their minds for success through visualization. Mary Lou Retton had employed a hypnotherapist named Gil Boyne prior to her 1984 gold-medal performance. Mark McGwire used visualization techniques—along with some less benign assistance—to set the home-run record in 1998. Gillespie ticked off a list of other famous athletes and coaches who used similar approaches to find "the zone." He had worked with several athletes himself.

"I know you're going to hate this," he said, "but I want you to try something."

He asked me to lie down on the couch and close my eyes. "You've been envisioning every bad thing that's going to happen next week," he explained. "I want to teach you a few relaxation techniques and then help you reprocess this trial in your mind."

The whole thing felt a little weird, but I was willing to give it a try. He had me concentrate on my breathing and took me through a protocol of relaxing each muscle in my body, one at a time. He had me picture various parts of the trial—my opening statement, the examination of witnesses, handling Caleb Tate's antics. I imagined the jury handing the verdict slip to the judge. Deep breaths. Slow. Keep the pulse under control. Purposefully focus on each muscle. Relax.

"Control, Jamie. It's all about control."

I envisioned a guilty verdict, and despite my skepticism, I had to admit that this was the most relaxed I had felt all week. I left Gillespie's office glad that I had taken the time to meet with him. I had almost talked myself out of it. But now, I at least had some tools for when the anxiety hit the hardest.

I used them on Friday at 3 p.m. when we found out who the trial judge was. It wasn't Snowden, but it was nearly as bad.

"Your old buddy Harold Brown," Regina Granger told me. The judge who had held me in contempt. One of the clerks had given Regina a heads-up. "Let's try to keep it civil," Regina said.

Deep breaths, I told myself. *And think positive.*

70

BILL MASTERSON KNEW how to pick a jury. I watched in awe on Monday and Tuesday as Masterson made friends with the potential jurors for the Caleb Tate murder trial. He was relaxed and self-effacing, even poking fun at himself about his weight.

He had a manner that allowed the jury to open up and share with him, and he had his own theories about the best potential jurors for our case. He wanted men. "They'll be a lot more forgiving of Rikki." He wanted Hispanics because Rafael Rivera was a key witness for us. And of course, he wanted bona fide evangelical Christians. Since he couldn't use his peremptory challenges solely on the basis of religion, he got at the issue in other ways.

"Now, the evidence will be that Rikki and Caleb Tate argued about a lot of things, and those things included Rikki's conversion to Christianity. Have any of you ever argued with your spouse about religious issues? If so, would that impact the way you looked at this case, or would you be able to put that aside and base your decisions solely on evidence?"

A few hands went up, and Bill chatted with them about the spats they'd had with their spouses. He discussed how Rikki's conversion caused her to change in a big way. I watched the body language carefully. There were two nodders, and I circled them on my list. They were keepers. Would anybody be unable to judge this case fairly because of these religious aspects? Of course not.

Then Bill explained how Rikki's conversion caused her to file a lawsuit against websites that contained her topless pictures. Caleb Tate opposed the lawsuits. This time I circled the frowners. Bill knew a lot of people struggled with pornography. Would anybody be unable to give Rikki a fair trial because she had once had topless pictures taken? Nope.

Caleb Tate had his turn in front of the jury as well. It frustrated me that he could talk to the jurors under the pretext of voir dire and then hide behind the Fifth Amendment and not take the stand. But there was nothing Judge Brown could do about it. On the plus side, Caleb seemed much stiffer and less at ease than Masterson. A couple of jurors crossed their arms when he asked them questions. When Masterson cracked a joke, everybody smiled. But for Caleb Tate, they were all business.

After two days of probing and haggling and trying to prejudge people based on limited information, both sides finalized their peremptory challenges, and we had a jury in the box. It was a diverse cross section of the citizens of Milton County, and it made me thankful for the jury system. Unlike a lot of trial lawyers, I trusted jurors. They didn't know the law as well as the judges, but they had an instinct for justice, and they usually got it right.

Judge Brown dismissed the jury with the usual instructions about not discussing the case with anyone. He told them we would start openings first thing in the morning. The thought of it made my palms sweat. Normally I settled down during jury selection, and my nerves would be well under control by the time I gave the opening. But in this case, because Bill Masterson had handled all of the chores of jury selection, I just sat at counsel table and made myself more nervous.

That night, I knew I couldn't sleep without the help of medication, and I didn't even try. When I closed my eyes, I thought about my sessions with Gillespie and visualized the jury enraptured by my opening, affirming me with their eyes, drinking in the evidence against Caleb Tate. *Deep breaths. Relax every muscle. Remember how they smiled at Bill Masterson.*

I fell asleep dreaming of guilty verdicts.

◁ ▷

For the most important day of my professional life, I wore a charcoal-gray suit, a white silk blouse, black pumps, and a gold chain around my neck. I had bought into the philosophy of my trial advocacy professor—don't turn off the jury by the way you dress. It was better to keep it conservative so the jury could focus on what you were saying rather than how you looked.

I arrived ridiculously early and was able to riffle through my notes several times before the courtroom began filling up. During jury selection, the courtroom had been half-full. But this morning there would be standing room only. Judge Brown had allowed one pool camera, which would send a live feed to all of the local television stations. A few of my friends from law school came, as did a good number of Milton County's prosecutors.

Bill Masterson had been coaching me and assured me that I was ready. Just before Judge Brown came out to gavel the court into session, Masterson leaned over and put his arm around my shoulders. "Your father was one of the best trial lawyers I've ever seen," he said quietly. And Masterson had seen his share of trial lawyers. "You're just as good, Jamie. Maybe better."

"Thanks. But I feel like I'm going to puke."

Masterson chuckled and patted my shoulder. Then he put his left hand on the table in front of me. "Notice anything about the fingernails?" he asked.

He had gnawed them down so far that they looked painful. I had never noticed that Masterson chewed his nails.

"They looked pretty good before I started jury selection," he said. "If you aren't nervous for a case like this, you're in the wrong business. We just learn to hide it."

The man was a genius. Who knows—maybe he had just chewed his fingernails that morning to put me at ease. But the trick certainly worked. Even the legendary DA of Milton County got nervous before a big murder trial. And look how well he performed.

By the time Judge Brown took the bench, called in the jury, and finished the preliminaries, I was ready.

"Does the prosecution wish to present an opening statement?" he asked.

"Yes, Your Honor. We would love to."

71

MY HEELS CLICKED as I approached the jury. I left my notes on the counsel table and walked in front of the podium—nothing between me and them except the jury rail.

"As the court has already told you, my name is Jamie Brock, and it is my privilege in this case to represent the State of Georgia. My job is to seek justice on behalf of Rikki Tate. She cannot speak for herself because she was murdered by the man she loved and trusted more than any other. But I am here to speak on her behalf, and I'm here to help you piece together the story of how and why she was killed."

I delivered this part of my opening with hardly any movement. I kept my chin up and tried to appear confident. The jury would never believe my case unless I first believed it myself. I paused, took a deep breath.

"Caleb Tate is a control freak," I said. "And what he cannot control, he kills."

I was hoping the line might draw an objection from Tate, emphasizing my point. I had a ready response—*See, he's even trying to control my opening.* But he was too smart to take the bait.

"I like my hair short," I said. I took a few steps and began to pace as I talked. "It only takes me a few minutes to get ready that way. I've always been an athlete, and I didn't always have time to fix my hair after I worked out. Once I got used to the convenience, I just liked this layered look. You women on the jury know, our hair is a big part of who we are."

They were looking at me like I was crazy. They expected something more dramatic—a confession, DNA, maybe the 911 tape. But hairstyles?

I had set up a video screen for the jurors. I pushed a button, and Rikki Tate appeared. Computer monitors at the defense table and on the judge's bench reflected the same PowerPoint slide.

"This is Rikki Tate a year ago." I flashed up another picture. "And one year prior to that." Another one. "This is from five years ago. . . . And this one is from when she and Caleb Tate first met."

Now all the pictures appeared, lined up on the screen. "You'll notice that Rikki Tate had a different philosophy about hairstyles than mine." The pictures all reflected Rikki's long, dark hair. In one picture it was pulled into a tight ponytail, but in the others it hung below her shoulders, full and meticulously brushed. She could have done shampoo commercials.

"Rikki Tate was a performer. And one of her greatest assets had always been her long hair."

A different shot of Rikki flashed on the screen. It was a close-up of her face from the night she died. You could see the vomit, and her skin looked pale and rough. There were circles under her eyes; she appeared to have aged ten years compared to the picture taken just a year before. The screen flashed again, bringing the two pictures side by side.

"Six months before her death, for the first time in her life, Rikki Tate cut off her long hair. Her friends from church will tell you why. Out of the blue, that man, Caleb Tate, started telling her how much he had always loved women with short hair. How sexy it looked. How she should try it. He became obsessed with it. He wanted—he *needed*—to control her hairstyle."

I looked at the jury and twisted my face as if I were trying to figure something out. "In any investigation, there are a hundred seemingly minor pieces of evidence like this. Things that don't seem quite right. And so I decided to do a little research and look at some of the women Caleb Tate has loved."

I took the jury through slides of Caleb Tate's first two wives and three of his girlfriends. They all had long, flowing hair. "Maybe the defendant did love short hair. Maybe he was just unlucky, and none of the short-haired women would go out with him. Or maybe . . ." I hesitated, and I could tell the jury was with me. "Maybe he began pumping his wife full of narcotics six months before he intended to give her an overdose and kill her. And maybe he needed to make sure that her hair was just the right length to appear she had been taking these drugs for a very long time. In other words, short enough so we could only test for six months of drug use and have to make assumptions about the time before that."

For a few minutes, I explained how hair testing worked. Then I went to an easel and listed the drugs found in Rikki Tate's blood. I stepped back and looked at my handiwork, repeating the names of the drugs as if to myself. I turned to the jury.

"It's like that game—which of these is not like the other. Codeine and oxycodone are narcotics and can be fatal if taken at the right levels. But promethazine—that's just an antinausea drug. It's known in medical circles for helping patients keep narcotics in their system so the narcotics can achieve maximum medical effect. Yet Caleb Tate is no doctor. How would he know something like that?"

I centered myself in front of the jury box so I was looking squarely into their eyes. "Some of you may remember the case of rock star Kendra Van Wyck, accused of poisoning a backup singer because she thought the singer was having an affair with Kendra's husband. It may interest you to know that this exact same cocktail of drugs, along with a few others, was used in that case. And it may also interest you to know that the Van Wyck opinion and several briefs filed with the court had been downloaded by Caleb Tate *seven months* before Rikki Tate died. *One month* before she got her hair cut at the urging of her husband.

"You expect attorneys to download cases on their computers. But the evidence will show that he wasn't working on anything remotely similar to the Van Wyck case.

"You know what else the evidence will show? That even control freaks miss things once in a while. As a result, in this case, even though we don't have fingerprints, we do have something just as incriminating—fingernails."

I explained to the jury how you could test fingernails for drug use, just like you could hair. When we had tested Rikki's fingernails we had learned that the drug ingestion had started in earnest just six months before her death. "They didn't test fingernails in the Van Wyck case, and apparently Caleb Tate didn't realize that could be done."

For the next half hour, I put together the pieces of the puzzle. Opportunity. Motive. I emphasized Rikki's conversion to Christianity and how that had threatened Caleb's control. Rikki was making up her own mind now, and her husband didn't like it. "He had married a Las Vegas showgirl," I said, "not Mother Teresa. And he grew tired of living with someone who constantly reminded him of his own sins and shortcomings."

I showed how Caleb Tate had become financially desperate. I mentioned the life insurance policy. And I ended by describing the night Rikki died. How her husband drugged her with a massive overdose. How he must have stood in the bedroom and watched her suffocate, maybe even kept her from calling 911. He'd waited until she was definitely gone before calling in the paramedics, and then he'd put on the greatest acting performance of his life, even staging the way his wife would be found—lying half-naked on the bedroom floor. "He had married a showgirl," I said again, "not a nun. And he staged her death to remind the world of that."

I paused and stared at Caleb Tate. He looked back, impassive, as if my accusations were about someone else. He was being the lawyer now, considering how he should respond during his own opening statement, but I could also see the seething hatred in the eyes. And as I turned back to the jurors, I realized that my own nerves had left a long time ago.

"Caleb Tate is too smart and too cunning to leave a smoking gun. But if you listen closely, Rikki Tate is whispering to you from the grave. She will speak through her psychiatrist, Dr. Aaron Gillespie. She will speak through her friends from church. She will speak through the medical examiner, Dr. O'Leary."

I waited and soaked in the silence of the courtroom. "And yes, she spoke through her hair. And through her fingernails. And through her blood—coursing with poisons that her husband had been pumping into her system for six months, even as he coddled her, even as he made love to her at night. Poisoning is the crime of cowards. And at the end of this case, we will ask you to put this coward, this murderer, in prison for life.

"Because there are some things that Caleb Tate can't control—and thankfully, one of those is your verdict."

72

CALEB TATE'S OPENING made me sick to my stomach. He started out by saying how much he loved his wife. I partially stood to object, but Bill Masterson put a hand on my arm and kept me in my seat. "Don't highlight it," he growled under his breath.

We both hated the fact that just because Tate was a big-enough fool to represent himself, he would have this opportunity to talk to the jury without being cross-examined. Because of the Fifth Amendment, we couldn't even comment on this little sleight of hand. The only concession Judge Brown had given us was to agree that Tate could not bring a lawyer on board after the opening statement. "If he wants to represent himself, I can't stop him," Brown had told us at a pretrial motion. But then he had turned to Caleb Tate. "But you better make your choice before we start the trial. If you decide to go it alone, I'm not letting you bring a lawyer into the case later, after you've had a little chat with the jury in your opening."

Caleb Tate had shrugged it off. This wasn't a game, he told the judge. His life was on the line, and he wanted to represent himself.

He told the jury how much he missed Rikki and how hard it was to live without the woman he had been married to for twelve years. I glanced at Masterson, and he gave me another subtle shake of the head. It seemed to me that Caleb Tate was just pushing the envelope to see how far he could go before drawing an objection.

"The prosecutors called me a 'murderer' and a 'control freak.' So ask yourself this: Would a control freak call Rikki's psychiatrist and beg him to help get her off the drugs? Because that's what the evidence will show. I called and told her psychiatrist that Rikki was struggling with addiction issues. I was begging for help.

"And about the hair—I wish I had brought pictures of myself in college," Tate said. He was dressed in one of his slick navy-blue windowpane suits with a pocket square that matched his tie. The suit seemed to shimmer as he moved and I had to admit that the jury was paying close attention.

"I had long hair too. Styles change. Rikki had such a beautiful face that I thought her short hair would frame it—"

"I object," I said. I had hopped up before Masterson could hold me down. "May we approach the bench?"

Judge Brown called us up and played some white noise over the loudspeakers so the jury couldn't hear us.

"Judge, he's testifying without taking the stand. An opening statement is supposed to be a preview of the evidence. If he doesn't plan on testifying, how is he going to prove that he asked Rikki to get her hair cut because he thought it would better frame her face?"

I could feel the blood pumping through my temples. I was so mad I wanted to just elbow Caleb Tate in the ribs as he stood there next to me.

He held up his palms as if he didn't understand what the fuss was all about. "I haven't decided yet whether I'll take the stand," Tate said with a straight face. "And we all know that what counsel says during opening statements is not evidence. If you think it will help, I don't have any objection to you reminding the jury of that."

Brown leaned forward and spoke under his breath. "I know what you're doing, Mr. Tate. And I don't want one more statement that sounds more like testimony than a preview of the evidence. From now on, stick to telling the jury about witnesses you *know* you'll put on the stand and exhibits you *know* you'll introduce. Is that clear?"

"Got it," Tate said.

Bill Masterson and I returned to our counsel table, and I leaned forward, ready to pounce if Tate crossed that line again. He appeared to be gathering his thoughts.

"I previously represented a man named Rafael Rivera," he said. He glanced over his shoulder at the judge. "I mean, the evidence will show that I previously represented a man named Rafael Rivera. In fact, the district attorney will put him on the stand to testify that he provided the drugs I allegedly used to poison my own wife."

Tate stood straighter and stuck out his jaw in indignation. "Rafael Rivera has been convicted of three drug offenses. By testifying against me, he cut a deal to avoid a lot of jail time. Watch him very closely when he takes the stand—because I'm going to ask him some questions that will get at the truth of what happened. I'm going to ask him if he told me to approach a certain judge in order to bribe that judge and get the charges dismissed. I'm going to ask him if he threatened me when I refused to do his bidding. And I want you to watch his face because it will be the face of an arrogant man who thinks he can get away with a lie. A man who cuts a deal with the state as if justice were a flea market."

Caleb had been pointing to the witness stand but now turned back to the jury. "And then I want you to watch his face when I catch him in his lie. It will be a moment you'll never forget. And I will tell you right now: if I don't destroy Rafael Rivera's credibility on cross-examination, you ought to convict me. But if I do, you must—and you should—acquit."

The words, and the confidence that oozed from Caleb Tate when he delivered them, sent chills down my spine. Despite all of my attempts to envision only positive outcomes, the cross-examination of Rafael Rivera had haunted me. I could see Tate asking him about Judge Snowden. I could see Rafael denying it and a big fight ensuing between the lawyers as to whether Tate could introduce collateral evidence about Snowden—evidence of my father's record in front of her. I could see Tate strutting and shouting and accusing Rivera of making it all up just to save his own hide. And I could see the doubt on the faces of the jurors as they pondered the question that I had been asking for months: *Where did Caleb Tate really get the drugs?*

"I miss her," Tate said. He appeared on the verge of tears. "But to be honest, I won't even begin to mourn her until this case is over. The only thing harder than losing someone you love is being accused of murdering that person."

I debated whether I should stand and object again, but I knew it would just mean another conference in front of the bench while those words echoed in the jurors' ears. I decided to sit tight and endure it.

"And if, after hearing all the evidence, you decide I'm not guilty, you won't see me pumping my fist like other defendants or high-fiving someone in the courtroom. I will walk out that door—" Tate pointed dramatically to the back door of the courtroom—"and go to my wife's grave and weep like a baby. I tried to get her off those drugs, but I didn't try hard enough. And whatever you decide, that failure will haunt me the rest of my life."

Caleb Tate hung his head and walked slowly back to his counsel table. I cursed him under my breath, and the boss shot me a look.

Perhaps I had spoken a little louder than I thought.

73

BILL MASTERSON AND I had spent a lot of time discussing our order of witnesses. Every trial lawyer knows that you start strong and finish strong and bury all of your weak people in the middle. Rafael Rivera would be the low point of our case, so we would bury him. We decided to start with Dr. Grace O'Leary, who was pretty much bulletproof, and end with Dr. Aaron Gillespie, who was equally unimpeachable. We would put LA on the stand right after Rivera so that LA could do immediate damage control.

O'Leary inspired confidence as she raised her right hand and swore to tell the truth. She had done this a time or two before.

She climbed into the witness box, and I placed my notes on the podium, catching a whiff of the cigarette smoke that trailed behind her. She settled in and lowered the mic. She told the jury good morning, and I started with my preliminary questions about her qualifications.

O'Leary was businesslike and disciplined in her choice of words, her style contrasting nicely with the unruly black hair that looked like it hadn't been brushed in a week. She exhibited great self-assurance, and she spoke rapidly as if she was anxious to get through the preliminaries so she could tell the jury how Rikki had died.

She testified that she had performed thousands of autopsies. Her résumé contained twenty pages of publications from trade journals and seminars. She had been interviewed extensively on shows like *20/20* and *60 Minutes*, so I had her talk about a few of her more interesting cases. She reminded me of a strict elementary school teacher—someone who knew a lot more than you did and didn't tolerate any nonsense. Spit out your gum. Sit up straight. Dr. O'Leary is talking to you.

I knew it was time to get to the heart of her opinions when I asked her about some consulting work on the Kendra Van Wyck case and she gave me a lecture in response.

"Counsel, I'm sure the jury knows all about the Kendra Van Wyck case. But I'll bet what they'd really like to hear about are my opinions in *this* case. And to be blunt, I'm anxious to tell them about this case as well."

My face reddened, but I didn't really mind the lecture. It only bolstered the credibility of my witness if she felt the freedom to chew out the prosecutors.

"Then let's get down to it—do you have an opinion as to what caused Rikki Tate's death?"

"If I didn't, we've probably wasted a lot of the jury's time."

That made a few of the jurors smile.

"Then why don't you tell me what that opinion is."

"Rikki Tate died from acute drug poisoning. Specifically, the combination of codeine and oxycodone in her blood caused pulmonary congestive edema, which basically means that her lungs were filled with fluid and she suffocated. The drugs I mentioned are narcotics, which have the effect—if taken in massive doses such as we see here—of repressing and shutting down the central circulatory and respiratory systems, beginning with the lungs."

"Do you have any doubt that Rikki Tate died from acute drug poisoning?"

"I would stake my professional reputation on it." Dr. O'Leary gave me a sly smile. "In fact, I guess I already have."

We spent about an hour discussing the details of the autopsy, including the absence of any trauma or signs of choking or any other cause of death. O'Leary talked about the hair-testing evidence and the finding of promethazine in the blood. She also testified about the specific levels of oxycodone and codeine that were found.

"How do these levels—.74 milligrams per liter for oxycodone and .27 milligrams per liter for codeine—how do these levels compare with other autopsies you've done?"

O'Leary made a face and turned to the jury. "These levels are very high. The codeine alone would have killed her. The oxycodone alone would have killed her. Combined, they have an additive effect and basically guaranteed that Rikki Tate would not survive.

"Have I seen higher levels? A few—but most of those are hospice patients who have been on these drugs for a long time and have built up an incredibly high tolerance. Just out of curiosity, I went back and made a chart of over two hundred cases in the past five years involving either oxycodone or codeine as a potential cause of death. Of those, this was the twelfth-highest case of oxycodone concentration and the fourteenth-highest case of codeine concentration."

So far, I knew O'Leary's testimony was unassailable. But I wanted to take her one step further because everyone agreed that Rikki Tate had died from a drug overdose. The question that really mattered was whether it was suicide or poison.

"How long had Rikki Tate been ingesting oxycodone and codeine?"

"It's hard to tell. From the hair testing I described earlier, it's clear she had been taking some level of oxycodone and codeine for six months. Of course, the distal segments of the hair—those furthest away from her head—showed much lower levels of oxycodone and codeine."

I moved now to a new piece of evidence—one that would form a central focus of our case. "Are there ways to determine drug use further back than six months?"

Dr. O'Leary shifted in her seat, and it seemed to me that she needed a smoke break. But I wanted to get this critical piece of evidence in first.

"Absolutely. Once you found the evidence on the defendant's computer that he had reviewed the Van Wyck case, and once Detective Finnegan talked to witnesses who said that Mr. Tate—"

"Objection!" Tate was on his feet. "That's hearsay."

"Sustained," Judge Brown ruled.

I knew that might happen, but I was hoping the jury understood the point I was trying to make. And I was hoping they would remember my opening statement—that it was Caleb Tate who had suggested that his wife cut her hair.

"What did you do, if anything, to determine whether Rikki Tate had been on these drugs for more than six months?"

Dr. O'Leary's eyes flashed a little smile. This was what she loved—the subtle cat-and-mouse games of the courtroom. "Well, on the off chance that somebody talked Rikki Tate into getting her hair cut so we wouldn't know whether she had been taking drugs more than six months prior to her death—"

Caleb Tate was on his feet again, looking disgusted. "Come on, Judge, that's just pure speculation."

Judge Brown looked slightly amused, but he turned to Dr. O'Leary. "Doctor, please just stick to the facts of what you did." Turning to the jury, he said, "The objection is sustained, and you should disregard Dr. O'Leary's prior answer."

"Sorry, Your Honor," Dr. O'Leary said. "Anyway, I suggested that we test the victim's fingernails. She had relatively long fingernails, and I thought we could reach back at least a year by testing them. You basically do the same thing that you do with the hair—grind them up and run them through some gas chromatographs."

"Did they test the fingernails in the Van Wyck case?" I asked.

"No. So someone reading that case wouldn't realize that we could go back more than six months by testing the fingernails."

Tate stood but apparently decided it was no use. He sat back down.

"And what did you find in testing the fingernails?"

"Well, it's important to understand that when we pulled the fingernails, we divided them into segments at varying distances from the cuticle. In other words, we divided them into segments that would represent growth in the last six months and in the six months just before that. The results showed very low levels—just trace levels—of oxycodone and codeine in the fingernails that represented the growth from six months prior to her death to one year prior. In other words, somewhere around that six-month time frame, the amount of oxycodone and codeine that she ingested increased dramatically."

"Did you find any promethazine in the fingernail segments that represented the period of time from between six months prior to her death to one year prior to her death?"

"None at all."

"Did you find any other drugs that you weren't expecting?"

"Yes. We found trace amounts of morphine."

"Morphine?"

"Yes. It surprised me too."

"Did you draw any conclusions based on those findings?"

Dr. O'Leary turned to the jury. Time for the punch line.

"It seemed clear to me that somebody started poisoning the victim with oxycodone and codeine in the last six months. To keep the drugs down, they also gave her promethazine. Perhaps this same person had experimented with morphine prior to that time but realized how unusual it would look for morphine to show up in an alleged drug addict's blood. Perhaps they waited a few months before changing over to oxycodone and codeine and thought that by having Rikki Tate cut her hair no one would be able to tell."

I was surprised that she got through the entire answer without an objection from Caleb Tate. Maybe he realized that the jury had already pieced it together, and he would just have to deal with it on cross-examination. *Good luck,* I said to myself.

"I have no further questions," I said. "Please answer any questions that Mr. Tate might have."

74

CALEB TATE STOOD QUICKLY and went to the well of the courtroom, ignoring the podium. "That's an awful lot of speculation, isn't it?"

O'Leary gave him a stern look. "I would call it reasonable inference from the medical data. Your wife, may she rest in peace, is telling me a story, and I'm doing my best to pass that along to the jury."

Tate took a step closer. "People addicted to narcotics tend to need more and more of the same drug to get the same effect; isn't that correct?"

"Of course."

"That's why some of the highest blood levels on your list came from hospice patients, isn't that right?"

"Yes. And as far as I know, your wife was not a hospice patient."

Tate froze for a moment, staring at the doctor. "Do you think this is funny?"

"No, I think this is a horrible tragedy. And I hope you do as well."

"I lost my wife. I haven't been able to sleep since the night I found her dead. I would trade places with her if I could—"

I jumped up. "Objection. He's testifying, not asking questions."

"She's right," Judge Brown snapped. "Stick to questions."

Tate chewed this over for a moment. I knew this was a show for the jury and that he already had his next line of attack prepared. "You can't rule out the possibility of an accidental drug overdose, can you?"

"Anything's possible."

"You're aware that the police found pill bottles with OxyContin and codeine in the bottom of my wife's dresser drawer?"

"I was aware of that."

"And that those bottles had her fingerprints on them and not mine?"

"I would presume that if you are smart enough to poison your wife, you would also be smart enough to use gloves when you handled the pill bottles. I would also presume that you'd be smart enough to make sure her hand touched those bottles one way or another."

O'Leary's answer made me relax. I was usually tense when my witnesses were cross-examined. I felt helpless watching the other attorney hammer away, knowing there was nothing I could do about it. But O'Leary could handle herself. And Caleb Tate's ego was way too big for him to do the smart thing—sit down and shut up.

"Fingernail testing is much less reliable than hair testing, is it not?"

"There are more possibilities for false positives, yes."

"That's why you didn't do the fingernail testing in the first place. Right?"

"That's correct."

"So let me ask you a few questions about the morphine."

Tate had recovered some, and his voice was picking up confidence. He had learned about the morphine when we turned over the fingernail tests as part of our Brady materials—any exculpatory or impeachment information favorable to the accused.

"The morphine didn't show up in the hair?" he asked.

"No."

"It only showed up in the fingernail testing, which, as we just established, tends to have more false positives."

"Because of the length of the fingernails, we were able to test for drug use over a longer period of time. The tests indicate the morphine was taken more than six months prior to her death."

"Are you aware that my wife had an affair about two years ago?"

"I was told that. I don't know it to be true."

"Well, let me assure you that it's true—"

I was up again. "He's testifying, Judge."

"Approach," Judge Brown demanded.

Caleb Tate and I went to the bench and stood side by side. "Mr. Tate, she's right. You need to quit testifying. Don't think I don't know exactly what you're trying to do." Judge Brown then turned to me. "And you can make your objections without pointing out the fact that he's testifying. Every time you say that, it comes dangerously close to highlighting the possibility that he might take the Fifth Amendment and refuse to testify. You know prosecutors can't comment on that."

I bit my tongue. I was determined not to pick a fight with Judge Brown in this trial, and I reminded myself of that. "Yes, Your Honor," I said.

I returned to my seat, and Caleb Tate returned to the well of the courtroom. "Do you know the name of the man my wife had her affair with?"

"No."

"And therefore you don't know whether he was a recreational drug user or not."

"I'm a medical examiner, not a detective."

"That's exactly my point," Tate fired back. "You don't know where my wife might have obtained these drugs."

"First of all, my understanding is that the affair occurred two years prior to her death. The fingernail tests only measure back just over a year. And second, I don't know many recreational drug users who get high on liquid morphine."

"But isn't it true that heroin metabolizes into certain compounds when it's processed by your body and that one of those compounds is morphine?"

"Yes, that's true."

"So even if the fingernail testing was right and my wife had morphine in her body, that could have been caused by using heroin; isn't that correct?"

Dr. O'Leary made a face. "Not really."

The response was classic O'Leary. She threw it out there as a challenge. She was hoping Tate would be foolish enough to ask why. And she knew that even if he wasn't, I would circle back around on redirect.

But Tate was no rookie. He smiled and put his right hand in his pocket. "Okay, I'll bite. Why did you say, 'Not really'?"

"Because when heroin metabolizes in your body, it produces not only morphine but also a substance called 6-acetylmorphine, which is found in the vitreous humor fluid. That's the eye fluid of the victim. In Rikki's case, we found no 6-acetylmorphine."

It was a "gotcha" moment for O'Leary, but Caleb Tate didn't seem fazed by it. He walked slowly back to his counsel table and leafed through some papers until he found what he was looking for. He asked his next question while holding the document.

"But 6-acetylmorphine has a relatively short half-life, doesn't it? It breaks down over time until it processes itself out of the body."

"I see you've done your homework," Dr. O'Leary said. "Of course it has a half-life, but I would still expect to see some amount of 6-acetylmorphine in Rikki's eye fluid—depending on the exact date that she injected heroin."

"But the half-life for the 6-acetylmorphine is shorter than the half-life for morphine—isn't that right?"

"That's correct."

"So it's possible, if Rikki experimented with heroin with one of her lovers well before her death, that the heroin might have broken down into 6-acetylmorphine, which processed itself out of the body, and morphine, which was still found in Rikki's fingernails."

"Mr. Tate, there are a lot of things that are possible. But I'm here to testify about the medical probabilities. And in my view, it is not probable that your wife just happened to experiment with heroin at the precise point in time that we would later find morphine in her system but not 6-acetylmorphine."

It was a good response, but Tate had also made his point. And he was smart enough to know when to quit. "That's all I have for this witness," he said.

The rest of the day was much less eventful. I called the toxicologist who had generated the results for both the hair testing and the fingernail testing. I paraded five other witnesses to the stand to show the chain of custody for the tests. Through one of the officers involved in executing the search warrant, I introduced a number of exhibits found in Caleb Tate's home. It wasn't necessarily riveting testimony, but brick by brick, I was methodically laying the foundation for my case.

That night I watched a little of the news coverage, which featured O'Leary's testimony. In the eyes of the press, we had scored some major points on the first day of trial.

But that was to be expected, and it gave me no solace. I knew the commentators would have a different perspective after Rafael Rivera took the stand on Friday. Besides, the commentators didn't matter.

And as for the twelve people who did, it had been impossible to read their expressions.

75

WE SPENT THURSDAY trying to nail down the elusive issue of motive. A financial expert named Nathaniel Barnes took the stand and testified about the financial status of Caleb Tate's law firm prior to his wife's death. The firm had lost nearly four hundred thousand dollars and had laid off three young associates. Tate's personal finances were in no better shape. He had borrowed heavily against his house and maxed out all of his credit cards. He'd sold two expensive automobiles. Rikki had a million-dollar life insurance policy payable to Caleb if she died. Caleb and Rikki had a prenuptial agreement, so he wasn't worried about alimony. But Rikki didn't work outside the home. To Caleb Tate, she was worth more dead than alive.

Tate wasted no time debunking Barnes's allegations. He established that the policy had been in place for two years and hadn't been increased during the last six months of Rikki's life. The life insurance company hadn't paid out yet and never would if Caleb were convicted of murder.

The cross-examination ended with an exchange that showed how quick Caleb Tate was on his feet.

"Are you really suggesting that I would kill my wife and risk a murder conviction just to get out of a financial jam? Haven't you ever heard of bankruptcy, Mr. Barnes?"

"I doubt that you would ever seriously consider bankruptcy," Barnes said. "It has a stigma."

"And murder doesn't?" Tate asked.

I objected, but the judge let him answer.

"Yes, of course it does," Barnes admitted.

In my heart of hearts, I didn't really believe that Caleb Tate had killed his wife for money. LA believed Tate was having a fling with his legal assistant, though we had never been able to develop the kind of proof needed for court. We hadn't been able to drum up one incriminating text message or e-mail. We hadn't found one eyewitness, just a lot of rumor and disgruntled former coworkers who said Caleb and his assistant "couldn't keep their hands off each other." According to the associates he had laid off, "everybody in the office knew they were having an affair." But judges have a few choice words for that kind of testimony—*hearsay*, *speculative*, and *inadmissible*.

I wasn't so sure Tate was even having an affair. For me, it was more a question of the glamour wearing off. Rikki was no longer the ex-Vegas showgirl. She was a Christian. Someone not willing to be Tate's suggestively dressed eye candy at the cocktail parties. Someone whom Tate could no longer control.

Barnes was followed by the emergency responders who took the stand and explained what they had seen and heard on the night Rikki Tate died. Caleb Tate's statements to police officers from that night were admitted into evidence. He'd told them that Rikki had been taking drugs for some time but that he didn't know the specifics of where she got them or what she was taking. The police had found promethazine in the medicine cabinet and the half-empty bottles of OxyContin and codeine in Rikki Tate's dresser drawer.

I ended the day with the testimony of Elizabeth Franks, Rikki's best friend from Alpharetta Community Church. Elizabeth had befriended Rikki and played a large role in Rikki's conversion. For the year and a half prior to Rikki's death, Elizabeth had attended a women's Bible study with Rikki, and the two became soul mates over coffee. She testified about Rikki's determination to get her embarrassing pictures removed from the Internet and Caleb Tate's lack of support. She testified about the problems Rikki had experienced in her marriage and how she had requested prayer for Caleb. But most importantly, Elizabeth testified about how Rikki had changed with her new faith and how much she was enjoying life. She loved the women at the church and had found something worth living for. Nobody could listen to Elizabeth's testimony and think Rikki was suicidal.

Caleb Tate came out swinging. Did you know that your good friend Rikki Tate was ingesting large amounts of oxycodone and codeine even after her conversion? No, Elizabeth didn't know that. Wouldn't that be something you would expect such a good friend to share? Yes. Did you notice any signs that she was addicted? No. She didn't act funny or lethargic or out of it? No, not really.

The subtlety of what Caleb Tate was doing might have been lost on Elizabeth Franks, but it wasn't lost on me. Addicts can tolerate higher and higher levels of the same drug without it having much effect. He was painting the picture of Rikki as a functioning addict, taking more and more of the narcotics until one night she just accidentally overdid it. I knew we would hear about this testimony again during Tate's closing.

"You read about my wife's lawsuits trying to get her topless pictures removed from various websites?"

"She told me about them."

"But you also saw reports about those lawsuits on TV, right?"

"Yes."

"What do you think that did to the traffic on those websites?"

Elizabeth hesitated before answering, but there was no way out. "It probably increased it."

"Would it surprise you to know that it increased the traffic by 9,000 percent?"

"I don't know. Not really."

"Did it ever dawn on you and the other women praying for my lost soul that maybe I was just trying to protect my wife by keeping her from filing those lawsuits? That maybe I didn't want to see her become a sex object for millions of perverts all over this country?"

Elizabeth appeared surprised by the assertion. "I guess I never looked at it that way."

Caleb Tate walked back to his counsel table, but I knew he wasn't done. I had seen him do this to several witnesses during Antoine Marshall's trial. It was like the Columbo routine—turning around as if he had just remembered one last question.

"Oh, one more thing. . . . You testified that I seemed controlling; do you remember that?"

"Yes."

"That Rikki would have to call me to get authorization even to use the credit card for a fifty-dollar purchase?"

"Yes. I saw that happen several times."

"Have you ever lived with a drug addict before, Ms. Franks?"

"No, sir. I haven't."

"Then you probably didn't realize that one of the things you do is try to cut off the source of the drugs. And this means controlling that person's spending very tightly. Did you realize that?"

Elizabeth shook her head. "No, sir, I didn't."

"I didn't think so," Caleb said. "Thank you for your honesty."

I had wanted to end the day on a high note, but Caleb Tate was no slouch. It seemed that for every witness I put on the stand he was able to raise enough questions to muddy the waters. And so far, I had only been questioning my best witnesses. This part of the case should have been my high-water mark. Instead, I felt like Tate was landing one body blow after another.

And I knew he would go for the knockout punch tomorrow.

76

ON THURSDAY AFTERNOON, Mace James sat face to face with Rashad Reed, inmate number 34721 in the Milton County Correctional Facility. Like most inmates, Rashad and two others shared a jail cell that was designed for two men, not three. The overcrowded conditions had spawned a rash of federal lawsuits. Rashad was sure he would be a rich man before he left jail. *If* he left jail.

Rashad was thin with a goatee and close-cropped hair and tattoos everywhere. He had a gold tooth and a left eye that didn't seem to open all the way. He reminded Mace of the little brother who constantly tried to hang with the big kids and would get beat up occasionally and sent home but would always come back. Rashad had a kind of nervous energy going, his eyes darting back and forth, leg constantly bouncing.

He'd been charged with multiple counts of carjacking, and he was looking at a sentence of up to eighty years behind bars if convicted. He had paid a big retainer to Caleb Tate nearly nine months ago, and his trial date was fast approaching. Like certain other Tate clients who had paid big retainers, Rashad had passed a polygraph test.

Mace had now spent nearly an hour with Rashad, urging him to fire Tate and hire him. He told Rashad the plain, hard truth—that a lie detector wouldn't be admissible in court. But if Rashad agreed to take this new brain-scan test and the results turned out the way Mace expected, Mace thought he could work Rashad a sweet deal. He might have to serve eighteen months or two years, but he could do it in solitary confinement in a different prison.

Rashad shook his head. "No way, man. I seen what they did to those other dudes. Man, they'll find me and slice out my tongue or something. Nobody in here deals anymore."

Mace could see the fear in the inmate's eyes, and it was hard to blame him. In the last few months, cutting a deal had been like signing a death warrant for yourself or your family. But eighty years in jail was a long time.

"What if I could get you into the witness protection program?" Mace asked. "The Feds never lose anybody. They'd move you to the other side of the country, give you a new ID, a new start on life." Mace didn't know if he could really make it happen, but right now, he would promise anything.

Rashad's leg bounced faster. He blinked a few times, and Mace could tell the man was interested.

"You're looking at eighty years, and you'll have to serve at least twenty," Mace reminded him. "You'll never get a chance like this again."

"I don't know, man."

"Just do the test," Mace persisted. "What can that hurt? It's all protected by the attorney-client privilege. At least then we'll know."

Rashad fidgeted and leaned back in his chair as if he could distance himself from the whole proposal. He snuck a glance over his shoulder and then leaned toward Mace again. "You sure no one will know?"

"They'll know you're taking the test. But nobody has to know we're talking plea bargain until you're out of here."

Rashad studied the floor.

"Look," Mace said, "I lost my job because of what I did for my last client, and I might lose my bar license before it's all over. Once you hire me, I'll do *anything* to get you out of this mess. Or you can stay with Caleb Tate, who's more concerned with saving his own butt than he is with yours. When's the last time he came to see you?"

Rashad looked up and shrugged. "I don't know."

"Which means never," Mace said. "If I walk out that door and you don't hire me, I'm never coming back. I'll get this deal for somebody else, and you can sit here and rot for eighty years. You like it in jail? Looks to me like you get knocked around pretty good."

Rashad stared at Mace and shook his head a little. It was torture for this kid to decide.

Mace stood up to leave.

"Where are you going?"

"To find somebody with guts," Mace said.

"Wait, wait, wait," Rashad said. He held out his hands, palms toward the floor, trying to slow things down. "Sit back down, Mr. James. Tell me again how this witness protection thing works."

◁▷

I spent the first part of Thursday evening meeting with Bill Masterson and Rafael Rivera in our conference room, trying to get our star witness ready to testify. When Rivera left, Masterson shook his head. "He's *our* witness, and even I don't believe him."

I rubbed my temple, a raging headache spreading across my scalp. "I know what you mean. But how did he find out about the morphine? How did he know about the six-month time frame?"

"He's either telling the truth or we've got bigger problems," Masterson said.

Bill and I had been through this line of reasoning before. There were only a few people who knew about the fingernail results when Rivera came to us. The state toxicologist, Dr. O'Leary, LA, and the two other detectives working the case. A few staff members in our own office. Neither Bill nor I wanted to believe any of them would have leaked the results.

But every time we discussed this issue, I thought about the Peachtree Road Race and the note somebody had slipped me. I had told no one about it at the time, and it seemed too late to bring it up now. It was another one of those Jamie Brock secrets, my failure to divulge something that might get in the way of the result I wanted on the case.

◁▷

I got home just before eight o'clock to prepare my second witness of the night. LA was waiting on my front steps and broke into a big smile when he saw me. "Justice has been going crazy in there," he said. "I almost decided to break into your house, but I didn't want you to worry about how insecure it was."

"Thanks. That makes me feel a lot better."

When we opened the door, Justice went straight for LA. They wrestled around a little bit, and I tried not to feel jealous.

Before I knew it, the two were in the family room playing tug-of-war and causing a big ruckus. I told LA I would be with him in a few minutes and went upstairs to change.

When I came back down, there were two plates of Chinese food on the kitchen table. I had skipped supper, and the broccoli and chicken smelled incredible.

"Where did this come from?"

"Been cooking all afternoon," LA said.

I was too antsy to relax during dinner, so I got out my list of questions and grilled LA as we ate. Afterward we moved into the war room and spent another three hours going over details of the case. By eleven thirty, I could see LA beginning to fade. The eyelids were getting heavy, despite his third cup of coffee.

"Do you ever take a break?" he asked.

"No. Now, what are you going to say when he asks about the fingerprint evidence on the pill bottles?"

LA shook his head. "We've been over this twice already. I'll probably say the same thing I told you last time."

Justice pawed at the back door, and I got up to let him out. LA followed and stood behind me as I waited for Justice to finish. My favorite detective put his hands on my shoulders and began rubbing my neck.

"Man, you are wound tight," he said. His strong fingers started kneading the muscles.

"Mmm, that feels great."

"You must have a wicked headache," he said. "These muscles are about to snap."

This time I didn't talk. I just put my head down and leaned back into it a little bit. This guy knew what he was doing. The fingers did their work up and down my neck and along the tops of my shoulders. I took a deep breath and tried to relax, focusing on the techniques I had learned from Gillespie. Neither one of us spoke, and in the stillness I could hear the soft, rhythmic breathing of my lead detective.

I wished Justice would have stayed out all night, but he eventually returned, and I had to break the trance to let him in. I gave him a treat and headed back toward the war room.

"I wasn't done," LA said.

I turned to face him and knew what my decision would be. He held out his hand and led me to the couch. I kicked off my shoes, and he sat behind me, massaging my shoulders and back as I felt the tension leaving my body. After several minutes, I leaned against him and pulled my knees up on the couch. He put his arm around me and I just burrowed in, listening to him breathe, feeling the beat of his heart.

Within minutes, I had dozed into that zone between consciousness and unconsciousness, disjointed thoughts floating through my mind in a last-ditch effort to worry about the day ahead. LA had succeeded where Gillespie had failed. I felt secure, relaxed, needed. I sat against him with my eyes closed, and the world seemed to be a safe place for the first time in months. I curled my knees toward my chest and snuggled in a little tighter. I fidgeted to get comfortable, leaning my head against his chest. It all felt so natural that I don't even remember falling asleep.

I woke up at 2 a.m. in the darkness with a blanket over me and a pillow under my head. It took me a minute to get oriented, but then I sat up and looked around. LA was gone. The house was dark. Justice was sleeping on the floor next to the couch. I got up and staggered to my bedroom, not even bothering with the sleeping pills. I was so relaxed that I felt like I had already taken them.

I brushed my teeth, changed into my sleepshirt, and climbed into bed. I set the alarm for six. And as I dozed off for the second time that night, I pretended I was in the arms of my favorite Milton County detective.

77

UNFORTUNATELY FOR US, Rafael Rivera decided to dress like he was up for an MTV award. He wore a dark-purple pin-striped suit with a pink shirt and a broad, striped tie. His shoes were light purple and pointed at the ends, making his feet look gigantic. I had told him to dress like he was going to church. I decided next time I would be more specific.

Bill Masterson walked to the middle of the courtroom and buttoned his old gray suit. It must have been a favorite, because it was nearly threadbare. He had on a white shirt that wouldn't quite button at the neck and was held together by his tie. Bill liked to project a man-of-the-people image.

Rivera smiled and preened while he testified about his relationship with his former attorney. The witness couldn't decide whether to look at the jury or at Masterson, so he sprinkled his eye contact around the courtroom as if he were a rock star everyone wanted to admire.

"Did there come a time when Mr. Tate asked whether you could provide access to certain narcotics?" Masterson asked.

Rivera chuckled. "He didn't have to ask. He knew."

"Did you provide him with any?"

Rafael tilted his head a little. "Do OxyContin and codeine qualify?"

"That's what I'm asking," Masterson said disgustedly.

"Oh yeah. We started back in September, and then I got a big shipment in November. Anyway . . . yeah, I gave him a few drugs."

"To the best of your memory, precisely when did you start providing drugs to Mr. Tate?"

Rivera looked at the ceiling and then over at the jury before turning back to Masterson. "Woulda been September of last year. Coupla weeks after Labor Day."

"Other than OxyContin and codeine, did you provide any additional drugs to Mr. Tate?"

"One time. Got him some morphine. He said his wife was in a lot of pain. That was back in the summer sometime."

"Why did the defendant say he needed the OxyContin and codeine?"

Rivera spread his palms. "He was a good customer. He was also my mouthpiece. I didn't ask a lot of questions."

"Did there come a time when you approached Ms. Brock with this information?"

Rafael smiled at me, and I wanted to slap him.

"Once I saw Mr. Tate get busted for offing his wife, I knew I had something you folks might want. When the po-leece picked me up on another drug charge, I approached Ms. Brock and told her I'd be willing to deal."

"Did Ms. Brock believe what you told her?"

Out of the corner of my eye, I could see Caleb Tate begin to rise, but then he brushed it off.

"No, the—" Rafael stopped, catching himself short. "The woman dissed me. Blew me off."

"Do you have any personal knowledge as to why she might have changed her mind?"

"I told her about the morphine. Apparently nobody was supposed to know about that. The reports on the fingernails and stuff weren't out there yet, and so that's when she knew I was straight up."

"Objection," Tate said. "He's not a mind reader. Move to strike."

"Sustained."

Masterson shrugged. "What were you given in exchange for your testimony today?"

"I got off on time served on the drug charge. Plus—" Rafael gave Caleb Tate a sly grin—"I got to fire my attorney."

"Do you have any text messages or phone calls that would verify these drug purchases?"

This made Rafael chuckle. "Sorry, Mr. Masterson. We don't keep very good records on our drug deals."

Masterson looked at the judge, contempt for the witness written on his face. "That's all the questions I have for this man," Masterson said. He walked back to counsel table and sat down next to me, slouching in his chair. I caught myself grinding my teeth.

I had been dreading this moment since the day I'd talked to Caleb Tate after the Georgia Supreme Court arguments. I knew Tate would tear into Rafael Rivera, trying to expose my father and Judge Snowden in the process. Masterson had said he was ready. He would object at the first hint that Tate was trying to bring my father into it and ask for a private conference with the judge. He was convinced we could keep my father's record in front of Judge Snowden out of the case.

I wasn't so sure. My hands were leaving sweat marks on the glass top of the counsel table. My heart felt like it was trying to escape my chest. And at that moment, if I had it to do all over again, I would have taken the advice of Masterson and dropped the case against Caleb Tate weeks earlier when we still had the chance.

78

TATE WALKED TO THE MIDDLE of the courtroom and stroked his chin, eyeing the witness. Rafael shifted in his seat and changed the position of his legs, right over left.

"Good morning, Mr. Rivera," Tate said. Sarcasm dripped from his voice.

"'Sup," Rivera shot back.

"You understand that because you're testifying against me today, the attorney-client privilege no longer covers our communications, don't you?"

Rivera shrugged. "Fine by me."

"And that I can ask you questions about things you asked me to do while I represented you?"

"If you say so."

"It's not me saying so; it's the rules of ethics."

"Whatever."

"Isn't it true, Mr. Rivera, that you asked me to approach Judge Cynthia Snowden and bribe her to dismiss this drug charge against you?"

I glanced at Masterson, who appeared too relaxed for my liking. I decided that, even though it would break every rule of courtroom etiquette, I needed to be ready to object myself if Tate mentioned my dad.

For his part, Rivera scoffed at the question as if it were the most ridiculous thing he had ever heard. "Maybe in your dreams. In reality, nothing like that happened."

"Do you deny telling me that some of your gang members had bribed Judge Snowden in the past?"

"Wait!" Judge Brown said. He glared at Tate, then shot an equally perturbed glance at Masterson. "Approach!"

I joined Tate and Masterson at Judge Brown's bench.

"What's this all about?" the judge hissed. "A three-time convicted felon trashing the integrity of a well-respected member of the bench?" Before Tate could answer, he turned to Masterson. "And why aren't you objecting?"

Caleb Tate quickly explained his reasons for asking the question. I could tell Judge Brown didn't like it, but there was no way he could prevent Tate from asking. It went straight to Rivera's bias. Once Brown figured it out, Masterson didn't need to explain why he wasn't objecting.

"You're on a very short leash here, Mr. Tate," Brown said. "I don't like unfounded accusations like this against another member of the judiciary."

"I understand that," Tate said. "But I'm not the one who put this guy on the stand."

"A very short leash, Mr. Tate."

After our conference, Tate returned to the well of the courtroom and asked the question again.

"I never said that," Rivera claimed.

"Do you deny threatening me when I told you that I wouldn't do such a thing and that you should never suggest it again?"

"Another ridiculous question. None of this happened."

"Isn't it true, Mr. Rivera, that you threatened to go to the prosecutors and testify against me in this case because I wouldn't approach Judge Snowden?" Caleb Tate was raising his voice now, the first showing of real emotion and anger in this case. He jabbed his finger in the air, and I couldn't understand why Masterson didn't object. "Isn't it true that you said you had something the prosecutors would *have to* believe? That you would watch them put a needle in my arm someday?"

"Mr. Tate!" Judge Brown interjected. "That's three questions. Let him answer the first one."

Masterson cast me a glance. *See, it's better if you let the judge intervene.*

"Those are three lies," Rivera said. "Not questions."

Caleb Tate just stood there for a moment, nodding. He went back to his conference table and grabbed a handheld digital recorder. He gave Bill Masterson a transcript and handed one to the clerk so the court could follow along.

I felt my stomach drop to my feet. *He had a tape?*

This time it was Caleb Tate who was smiling. "You called me back after that first threat to give me one more chance. Do you remember that?"

Rivera eyed him warily. In all our conversations, in all my endless questioning about these events, Rivera had never mentioned a telephone call. But I could tell that his mind was reeling now, trying to recall exactly what he had said.

"You do recall that, don't you?" Caleb Tate taunted. "Or do you need to be reminded?"

I could tell by Rivera's body language that he remembered the call. The only question left was how stupid he had been—how much he had said and how much he had left unsaid.

"Judge, it appears that the witness may need his recollection refreshed," Tate said.

Finally Masterson was on his feet. "We object, Your Honor. The defense hasn't authenticated this tape yet. We've never heard it. We don't even know if it's Mr. Rivera's voice."

Judge Brown was studying the transcript and looked at Masterson over the top of his glasses. "Let's take a short recess," he said.

A few minutes later, with the jury out of the box, Judge Brown asked Caleb Tate to play the tape. I followed along on Masterson's copy of the transcript, my heart sinking lower with each word.

Rivera: You've got twenty-four hours; then I'm talking.

Tate: Be my guest, Rafael. Then you can have a drug charge and a charge for lying to the prosecutors. They'll never believe a three-time convicted thug like you.

Rivera: People talk. I know things I'm not supposed to know. They'll believe me.

Tate: Like what?

Rivera: You've got twenty-four hours.

Tate: If you go to the DA, I'm no longer your lawyer. I'm free to tell them everything you've ever told me. Maybe they can add a charge for attempted bribery.

Rivera: [Laughter] What makes you think they'd believe a thug like you?

[End of call]

After the recording was played, Masterson rose slowly to his feet. Like me, he was trying to process this at warp speed. It seemed to confirm what Tate was saying. But there was nothing on the tape that could explicitly give us grounds to renege on Rafael's deal. The tape was too ambiguous to support a charge of lying to us.

"Judge, you can't let him introduce something like this without even authenticating the voices."

"I'm entitled to play the tape and ask the witness whether that's his voice," Tate shot back. "That's how you authenticate these things."

Judge Brown turned to Rivera. "Is that your voice?"

Rivera glanced at me, and I glared back. He looked to the judge. "Sounds like it."

Brown took off his glasses, rubbed his temple, and turned to Masterson. "I don't have any choice in the matter. The tape's coming in."

After the jury settled back in the box, Caleb Tate played the tape. I couldn't bear to watch the jurors' reactions. Tate then asked Rivera again whether it was his voice on the tape.

"Sounds like it," Rivera repeated.

"Does that refresh your memory about threatening me?" Tate asked.

Maybe Rivera would be smart enough to talk his way around this. Maybe he would make up something that would sound innocuous.

But the guy was obviously dumb enough to threaten his lawyer in a phone call, so I tried to keep my hopes in check.

"That had nothing to do with Judge Snowden," Rivera said. "I was talking about something else you were supposed to do. Filing some kind of pleading or something. I was just messin' with ya."

"So let me get this straight," Tate said, his voice mocking. "You were saying I had twenty-four hours to file some kind of pleading or you were going to go to the prosecutors to cut a deal based on some information that somebody told you about my case?"

"Somethin' like that."

Tate motioned to the jurors. "And you expect these people to believe that?"

Masterson was on his feet. "Objection."

"Sustained."

"In that tape, you said that you knew things you weren't supposed to know. That 'people talk.' Were you referring to knowledge about the trace amounts of morphine found in the fingernail testing?"

"All I know is that I had given you morphine just like you asked. That's who talked. You talked."

Tate smiled broadly, and I could tell it was making Rivera mad. "Let me make sure I understand. You're saying that in this telephone call with me, when you said that 'people talk,' you really meant that *I* talk?"

"I don't remember."

"I see. Well, let me ask you this—when you decided to talk to the DA, whom did you approach first?"

"The lead detective on the case."

"Would that have been Detective Tyler Finnegan?" Tate asked.

Rivera shrugged. "If you say so."

"And after you met with Detective Finnegan, then the two of you together met with Ms. Brock—isn't that right?"

"Yeah. I already said that when Mr. Masterson was asking me questions."

"Are you saying under oath, at the risk of your sterling reputation, that Detective Finnegan didn't feed you a little information about the case before that meeting with Ms. Brock?"

"I don't know what you're talking about."

"I'm talking about giving you information about the morphine and about a six-month time frame for supplying the drugs."

"That didn't happen."

"So when you said on that phone call that 'people talk,' you were not referring to Detective Finnegan?"

"No. I wasn't talking about him."

"You're sure about that?"

"One hundred percent."

79

RAFAEL RIVERA'S TESTIMONY had been an unmitigated disaster, but Bill Masterson insisted on eating lunch at the same place we had all week. "You don't change your routine," he whispered to me. "They'll think we panicked."

"They would be right," I whispered back.

I followed Masterson out of the courtroom, and the usual reporters were waiting on the courthouse steps. They flung questions at Masterson, but he shrugged them aside, the way he had every other day.

"What are you going to do now?" one of them asked.

"Eat lunch."

"No. I mean about the testimony of Rafael Rivera."

Masterson stopped for a moment and looked at the cameras. "This office will conduct an investigation of Rivera and see if his testimony should lead to any charges. However, the case against Caleb Tate does not hinge on Rivera's testimony. Where Tate got the drugs is not the issue. As Dr. O'Leary said, the drugs in Rikki Tate's blood and stomach were so great that it was clear she died from an intentional poisoning, not an accidental overdose."

"Then why did you put Rivera on the stand?"

"Don't you guys ever eat lunch?" Masterson asked. He started walking away, and I fell in behind. "As you can tell, I don't miss many lunches myself."

When we got to our secluded table in the back of a local Alpharetta diner, his mood darkened. He talked about whether we should nol-pros the case. He couldn't believe Caleb Tate had a tape.

"Maybe LA can pull our fat out of the fire," Masterson said. "He's pretty slick."

I didn't see how LA could undo Rivera's damage, but I kept my thoughts to myself. At least we would have the weekend to regroup.

"He didn't mention your dad," Masterson said between bites. "Didn't have to. He probably just wants to keep that hanging over our heads. Figures he'll give us one last chance to nol-pros before he drags your dad into it."

"Now that he's proven Rivera's threat by the tape, how is my dad's success rate in front of Snowden even relevant?"

"Probably isn't. But that doesn't mean he won't throw it out there anyway. Drop it like a nuclear bomb and let Judge Brown sustain our objection. Then let the press take the story from there."

I picked at my food as we discussed how to salvage the remnants of our case. I had seen witnesses tank before but never quite so spectacularly. Masterson didn't seem to be as distraught as me. "Eat something," he said as he wolfed down a sandwich. "You won't make it through this afternoon if you don't."

Just before paying, Masterson swung the conversation back around to my dad. "It's one thing to jeopardize your dad's reputation if we've got a chance to win the case," he said. "It's another thing to do so if our case is basically toast anyway."

"I don't think my dad's reputation should be the deciding factor," I protested.

"That's very noble of you," Masterson said. "But I liked your dad. And I'm the one who gets to decide whether we sacrifice his reputation for what's left of our case. Fortunately, now that Rivera is off the stand, Tate won't be able to raise the issue of Judge Snowden's susceptibility to bribes until he starts putting on his own witnesses. Let's get through the rest of the afternoon, and then we'll talk."

"Okay," I said, grateful that the case was hanging on, if only by a thread.

80

LA TOOK THE STAND looking dapper and decidedly Hollywood. He smiled widely for the ladies on the jury, and just the sight of him lifted my spirits. Witnesses aren't allowed to hear the other testimony in the case, and so as far as LA knew, everything was still on track.

I walked him through the investigation, and he testified with confidence and precision. I found myself ashamed that I had been doubting his loyalties throughout the case.

LA did a beautiful job putting the pieces of the puzzle together—the links to the Van Wyck case, the dramatically increased levels of drugs in Rikki's bloodstream starting shortly after Tate's research of that case, Tate's financial distress, the life insurance policy, the marital difficulties, Rikki's conversion to Christianity, and her determination to become something other than Caleb Tate's trophy wife.

I then asked him if he was aware that Caleb Tate had called Dr. Aaron Gillespie about four months prior to Rikki's death, informing Gillespie that his wife was addicted to painkillers and asking for Gillespie's help.

"Yes. We learned that during our investigation."

"Doesn't that show that Caleb Tate wasn't poisoning his wife?" I asked.

LA nodded as if to say, *Excellent question.* "On the contrary, it sets up the perfect alibi. Think it through," LA suggested. "If Caleb Tate was secretly slipping a few pills now and then into his wife's food, she would deny she had an addiction problem if Dr. Gillespie asked her. Or maybe Tate discovered a few painkillers and saw it as his opportunity to call Dr. Gillespie and establish an alibi. That way, when he gave her a massive overdose, he would be able to point to this phone call as proof of his innocence, proof that he tried to stop her from taking the pills."

I noticed that some of the younger female jurors were nodding along. I couldn't blame them. LA could be very persuasive.

"What about the absence of fingerprints on the pill bottles?"

"Well, Ms. Brock, the defendant is smart enough to know that there's going to be an autopsy. That means the authorities are going to find OxyContin and codeine in his wife's blood. He has to account for that somehow. So he slips the pills in her food, watches her die, then puts her hands on the pill bottles. He's probably wearing gloves the whole time. As soon as he does that, he calls 911, and the show is on."

Next, I walked LA through the timing of the fingernail testing. I established the fact that when Rivera first came to us and told us about the morphine, nobody other than LA, the DA's office, the medical examiner, and the toxicologists knew about the morphine. "What did that tell you about Rafael Rivera?" I asked.

I thought this would draw an objection, but Tate let it pass. That worried me.

"He was telling the truth about supplying the drugs to the defendant."

I took a deep breath to calm myself. I had been working on the phrasing of this next question since Rivera left the stand earlier that day. I was hoping that LA would pick up on my vibes.

"What if, during the course of your investigation, you had learned that Rafael Rivera had threatened the defendant? What if you found out that Rivera asked the defendant to bribe a judge and that, when the defendant refused, Rivera came to us with this evidence about supplying the defendant with drugs? What would that have done to your investigation?"

LA twisted his face into a *who cares* frown. "It wouldn't have done anything. We already knew Rivera was a convicted felon. Would he try to get his lawyer to bribe a judge before coming to us? Probably. Everybody knows that you're tough on plea bargains. There was no guarantee he could get a good deal from you. So if he could get out of jail by bribing a judge, he'd try that first.

"But that doesn't mean he lied to us. What Rivera told us was confirmed by the scientific evidence. The fact that he knew about the morphine before it was physically possible for him to know proves that he was telling the truth about supplying the drugs."

I wanted to kiss the man. Honestly, I had been wanting to kiss him for a long time. But the answer was so smooth, and so believable, that it almost felt like he had been listening to every word Rivera had said earlier that day. Had he been? I really didn't want to know.

But I knew that I would never forget that moment in the case. The tape, which had seemed so devastating before lunch, now seemed like an afterthought. In a few short sentences, LA had brought things back into perspective. Some couples find out that they have chemistry on the dance floor. For me, it was this exchange in the courtroom.

"No further questions for this witness. At least not right now," I said. *Maybe later. Maybe at my place.*

My heels clicked across the floor, and I sat down at counsel table. "Nice work," Masterson said under his breath.

Unlike with prior witnesses, Caleb Tate did not spring up to confront the witness. I assumed for a minute that he had been stunned by the turn of events. In the euphoria, I had forgotten a cardinal rule that I had been taught by my trial advocacy professor.

Never assume anything at trial.

And another rule, this one harped on by my brother, the preacher.

Pride cometh before a fall.

81

MACE JAMES WATCHED the readout from the machine that measured the brain activity of Rashad Reed. This was the third time he had seen this machine in operation, but he still couldn't figure out what the graphs meant. So he also kept an eye on Dr. Rukmani Chandar's expressions to see if he could pick up any clues about the test. But Chandar never flinched, his poker face giving nothing away.

The BEOS test lasted for nearly ninety minutes in the cramped cell as Chandar took Reed through every step of all three carjackings. When he was finished, he politely thanked Reed and removed the electrodes from the prisoner's scalp. Mace still couldn't figure out if the news was good or bad.

"Let's talk outside," Chandar suggested.

Mace said good-bye to Rashad and waited for the doctor to pack up. They left the secured area, saying nothing as they passed through one fireproof door after another. Only after they had reached the parking lot and found a place in the shade did Chandar give his preliminary opinions.

"He was there for every one of the carjackings. I don't know how he beat the polygraph; the young man does not strike me as very savvy. But that is why I prefer the BEOS—you cannot bluff your way through it."

"Is there any doubt about this?" Mace asked. He towered over Chandar, who was a full seven or eight inches shorter.

"As always, my preliminary opinions are subject to confirmation after I study the graphs," Chandar said. "But this one seems pretty clear."

Mace thanked the doctor and told him he would need an affidavit.

After discussing some logistics, Mace returned to the jail to meet with Rashad. He considered the irony of justice in Milton County. Because a new type of brain scan had just proved his client guilty, Rashad Reed might be able to get out of jail in a couple of years. But if the brain scan had suggested Rashad was innocent, the judge probably wouldn't allow it into evidence, and Reed would have to go to trial. Odds were, he would spend at least twenty years in prison.

The roulette wheel of criminal justice in Milton County was spinning, and Rashad Reed might have just landed on a lucky red seven.

◁▷

Caleb Tate shuffled some papers at his table and lined up the edges as if he had all the time in the world.

"Does defense counsel have any questions?" Judge Brown prompted.

"A few."

"Well, now would be a good time to ask them."

Without rising, Caleb Tate asked his first one. "Are you aware that I represented Antoine Marshall, the man accused of killing Jamie Brock's mother?"

The muscles in LA's neck tightened. "Of course."

"And because of that, she really wanted to nail me in this case," Caleb Tate said in a matter-of-fact style, as if everybody knew it.

I stood and looked at the judge. "Objection. Relevance."

"Goes to the witness's bias," Tate said.

"I'll sustain the objection," Judge Brown said.

"Are you aware that Ms. Brock promised to lynch me in this case?" Tate asked.

"Mr. Tate," Brown snapped, "leave Ms. Brock out of it."

Tate looked at me and then back at the witness. "Do you have a relationship with Ms. Brock?"

"What did I just say?" Brown asked.

Tate finally stood. "If Your Honor will just allow me a few questions. This goes directly to Detective Finnegan's bias."

Brown waited. Thought about it. Probably worried about how it might look on appeal. "Proceed," he said.

"Do you remember the question?" Tate asked.

"Yes. And the answer is that I have a professional relationship with Ms. Brock. It involves putting people like you in jail for life."

"Do you want to see me lynched as well?" Tate asked.

"Not really," LA said. "It would be a waste of perfectly good rope."

"You think this is a joke?" Tate shot back. "A man is on trial for his life, and you think it's time for humor?"

"I think it's extremely sad—the way you manipulate and abuse the system."

I knew that LA was baiting Tate, waiting for an opening to mention his assumption that Tate was behind the prisoners' no-plea-bargaining strategy.

But Tate proved once again that he had good courtroom instincts and changed the line of questioning. "In fact, you have more than a professional relationship with Ms. Brock, do you not?"

I stood but Judge Brown waved me off. "I'll allow it," he said. "Goes to bias."

"No. We work together on cases. That's all. I would like for it to be more."

Surprisingly, even in the heat of the courtroom battle, the comment gave me a surge of adrenaline. But I couldn't dwell on it.

"Did you go to her house last night?"

It hit me at the same time that it hit LA. We had been followed. He shifted in his seat. "I went to her house to work on the case."

"Did you stay until after 1:30 a.m.?"

LA hesitated, and I knew it wasn't lost on the jury. "I don't know exactly what time I left."

I thought about the big picture window that ran across the back of my house, the length of the family room. The backyard was fenced in, so I seldom pulled the blinds. I wondered if Tate's investigators had pictures.

"You weren't working the whole time. Were you?"

"I don't see what this has to do with the case."

"I take it that means no." Tate said it with a snide tone that made me furious. "I take it that means you weren't working the whole time?"

"We worked until she fell asleep. I continued to work until I left."

Alarms went off as soon as LA finished the answer. My best witness had just lied on the stand, and I was a sworn officer of the court. Not only that, but I was afraid that Tate would expose him the same way he had Rafael Rivera.

"Would it surprise you to know that your car left Ms. Brock's residence at approximately 1:45 a.m.?"

LA shrugged, but all of this was having an impact on the jury. "Not really."

"Isn't it true, Detective Finnegan, that you would do anything you could to help this woman nail me to the wall?" Before LA could answer, Tate amended his question. "Or perhaps I should say, lynch me from the nearest tree?"

"There was no bloody glove for me to plant at your house, Mr. Tate. The drugs were undeniably in your wife's bloodstream and stomach. There are lots of witnesses who can talk about the difficulties in your marriage. I didn't make up your financial problems. Nor did I download the Van Wyck case to your computer. All of that evidence has nothing to do with me."

"Ahh," Tate said, drawing it out with smug satisfaction, "but you didn't mention the morphine. Isn't it true that you told Rafael Rivera about the morphine and the fingernail tests even before he met with Ms. Brock?"

"That's ridiculous."

"And just so the jury is clear, I'm assuming that means you deny it?"

LA's face had turned crimson. His muscles were tight and his jaw was set. "That's right; I deny it."

Caleb Tate stood there for a moment as if trying to determine whether he should take the next step. Then he reached into his briefcase and pulled out a few photographs. I looked quickly at LA and hoped he picked up on the cue. He stared at the pictures, but Tate was holding them facedown.

"I want to make sure I've got this right. Are you denying that you and Ms. Brock spent intimate time together last night?"

"No. We were not intimate."

"Did you give her a back rub on the couch?"

LA swallowed hard and seemed to be weighing his options. *How did Tate know? Did he have pictures?* "I might have."

"Might have," Tate taunted. "Is that a yes or a no?"

"I gave her a back rub. She fell asleep next to me on the couch. After that, I went back to work." LA's voice had adopted a defeated tone. He stared at Tate while making the admissions, avoiding eye contact with me. "Then that's all I have for this witness," Tate said.

My mind raced, but I could think of no way to undo the damage. "No redirect," I said.

On the way by my counsel table, LA looked at me and whispered a "sorry." I pretended to be busy writing something on my legal pad. I hoped the jury hadn't seen the quick exchange.

I could practically feel the steam coming from Masterson's body. This was why, on my first day in the office, he had drilled into me cardinal rule number one—no relationships with victims or members of the force.

"It's nearly five o'clock," Judge Brown said. "This court stands in recess until Monday."

82

MASTERSON ASKED ME to follow him back to the office for what he called a brief meeting. I expected an angry tongue-lashing. But when we arrived, he spoke in measured tones, conveying a profound sense of disappointment rather than anger. I wished he would have just yelled at me.

He estimated our chances of pulling out a guilty verdict as "slim to none." Continuing with the case would just put my father's reputation at risk and make the DA's office look vindictive. And even if we won, Tate now had too many issues for appeal. Instead of fighting Tate on this case, we should work on tying him to the recent gang killings of Ricky Powell, Rontavius Eastbrook, and Jimmy Brandywine and the brutal murder of Latrell Hampton's girlfriend and her young son. "We're going to nol-pros this case first thing Monday morning," Masterson told me. "It's not open for discussion."

I didn't say anything. But I wondered how much of this was driven by politics. Dismissing the case would make Masterson look magnanimous, like he was committed to justice more than winning. Losing a jury verdict would make us both look incompetent.

"We'll turn Rivera loose, and he can get what's coming to him," Masterson continued. "I'm not sending him out to California, and I'm not wasting any police protection on him. He lied on the stand, though that tape is too ambiguous for us to prosecute him for perjury. But now that he's cut his deal, let's see how long he survives."

Even to me, the most hard-nosed of prosecutors, it seemed harsh. The man had perjured himself and played us for fools, but I didn't like the idea of just abandoning him on the streets to die. Yet I was so angry with so many people right now—including Rafael Rivera—that I wasn't about to stick up for him.

"And, Jamie, I hope you've learned a few things from today. You're one heckuva prosecutor, but you've got to keep your emotions out of it." Masterson paused and gave me a look that could melt steel. "And I mean that in every respect."

"Yes, sir," I said.

I sat there for another moment as Masterson got busy on some paperwork. He looked up. "That's all," he said.

◁▷

I checked my BlackBerry on the way home, and I had more than twenty messages. Most of them were from friends who tried to encourage me. There were two phone calls and one text message from Mace James, who wanted to meet with me as soon as possible. The text said it was a critical issue that could impact Caleb Tate's case. But Caleb Tate's case was over. I ignored the message.

I didn't ignore the text messages from LA asking if we could get together. I texted him back, telling him that getting together right now would be a bad idea. I wished with all my heart I could have taken back the night before. It wasn't necessarily LA's fault, but I knew Masterson was right. I'd let my emotions get out of control, and now I was paying for it in so many ways.

When I arrived home, there was a car in my driveway, and I recognized it immediately. My brother, Chris, to the rescue. He was sitting in the driver's seat and got out to give me a big hug. Somebody had apparently called him about our day in court.

Justice greeted us both like conquering heroes. He jumped all over Chris, who laughed and played with Justice because anybody who came to our house had to play with Justice. They wrestled in the family room for a few minutes with Justice hunkering down and making runs at Chris and rolling on the floor and doing his fake growl. The only way I could calm him down was to feed him dinner.

Chris and I sat opposite each other at the kitchen table, waiting for the burgers to cook on the grill. I know Chris expected me to cry, but I had done enough crying in the last few months. Tonight I was just confused, frustrated, and angry. I started talking and put it all out there—the guilt at being away from the house when Mom died, my resentment toward Dad for being a defense lawyer, the frustration of not knowing whether Antoine Marshall was truly Mom's killer, and even my disappointment in Chris for not being a more forceful advocate for justice. But most of all, my bitterness at everything that had happened in Caleb Tate's murder trial and Masterson's decision to nol-pros.

"I can't believe God's going to let him get away with killing his wife," I said.

Chris listened patiently and responded softly. He had his hands laced together on the table and looked down as he spoke. He told me that I couldn't blame myself for Mom's death. He assured me that Caleb Tate wasn't getting away with anything.

He paused and looked at me. Tonight, it was Chris who had tears in his eyes. "When you hurt, I hurt," he said. Then he turned philosophical. "We can't bring about perfect justice in this world, Jamie. It pleases God for us to try. But at the end of the day, this is a fallen world. Even the best systems put together by men—and I believe our justice system is pretty darned good—are going to be imperfect. But there's a verse in Genesis that I've always loved: 'Will not the Judge of all the earth do right?'

"That's what I hold on to. Even on days like today, when the world is so messed up. That jury doesn't have the last word. And Judge Brown doesn't have the last word. And neither does Bill Masterson."

Chris used the back of an index finger to wipe a tear from the bottom of his eye. "Sorry to preach," he said. "I'd better go check on the burgers."

83

MY SLEEPING PILLS DID THEIR TRICK, and I might have slept forever if Justice hadn't pawed at me until I took him out at about 10 a.m. Chris had gotten up early to get ready for his sermon the next day and had fixed chocolate-chip pancakes for breakfast.

"What did I do to deserve a brother like you?" I asked.

My saint of a brother left at noon. I was still in my sleepshirt and a pair of shorts and planned on staying that way all day. I had received a few more phone calls and text messages, including ones from Mace James and LA. I was tempted to call LA, but I suddenly had mixed emotions about that relationship. It wasn't just that our lack of discretion might have cost us the case. I was also getting bad feelings about the way LA could adjust the truth when it served his purposes. He came from a different place than me spiritually, and our values were very different.

Plus, there was the issue of trust. He had seemed as devastated as I was after his testimony, but what if that was all an act? My emotions were swinging wildly back and forth, which was precisely why everybody said you should never start a relationship in the middle of a pressure cooker like the Tate case.

When the doorbell rang at twelve thirty, Justice went flying from the family room toward the front door at full speed, barking all the way. I half expected to see LA standing there and maybe J-Lo on a leash. A big part of me wanted to see LA standing there. Instead, I opened the door and found myself looking into the eyes of a man I had never wanted to see again.

Justice squirmed through the crack in the door and jumped all over Professor Mace James.

"Justice!" I said. "Sit!"

But Justice, with his lousy lack of character judgment, ignored me. Mace laughed and rubbed Justice's head. "He's okay," Mace said.

Though I wanted to tell Mace James to get out of my life forever, I found myself apologizing. "Sorry about that," I said. "He thinks everybody comes to see him."

Mace got down on one knee and patted Justice a little. He looked up at me. "His name's Justice, huh?"

"Yeah."

"Fitting. You got a minute?"

Not for you. "I'm pretty busy."

Mace stood to his full height. He was wearing a pair of jeans, flip-flops, and a white T-shirt tight enough to remind everyone he could bench-press a small car. He had on a pair of mirrored sunglasses, and it looked like he hadn't shaved in a few days. "This really can't wait," he said.

I frowned.

"I know you don't trust me, Jamie. But just give me a few minutes."

It was late August and over ninety degrees outside, but I wasn't about to let this man in my house. There were two wooden rocking chairs on the front porch, and I decided they would have to do. "Hang on a second," I said.

I went into the house and got Justice's leash, my running watch, and my shades. If I couldn't see his eyes, I didn't want him seeing mine. I came back out and pointed to the rocking chairs. "Three minutes," I said. "Not a second more."

The last time somebody had asked for a few minutes of my time was when Caleb Tate dropped the bombshell on me about my father. My stomach had a similar feeling this time.

We probably looked like quite the pair on my front porch, gently rocking back and forth. A six-two bodybuilder with sweat beading on his bald head and a five-eight former kayaker in her sleepshirt and shorts, her hair sticking up, her face void of makeup, her mouth in a permanent scowl, trying to look hard. Justice took a spot between us, still on his leash, his head resting on his front paws.

I started my stopwatch and Mace said, "I guess that's my cue."

"Two fifty left," I said, looking at my watch.

Mace didn't waste any more time. "Before Antoine Marshall died, I promised him I would keep working to vindicate his name. Though I had some doubts after the brain-scan test, I've spent two weeks reevaluating every aspect of his case. I reread the entire case file, asking myself if there were any hints that someone else might have murdered your mom. I researched a number of your mom's and dad's cases to see if they had any enemies. I also researched the two things that bothered me most about Antoine's case. The first was the way Judge Snowden treated my client. The second was the fact that Antoine passed a polygraph, even though, to my surprise, he failed the brain-scan test."

Mace took a breath, and I said, "Two minutes." I realized where he was headed, and it made my heart start pounding. He must have discovered the connection between my dad and Judge Snowden. *Deep breaths. Slow pulse. Relax.*

"I figured that Caleb Tate must have done something to get on the bad side of Judge Snowden, so I looked at all his cases in front of her. I didn't find any reason for their apparent animosity, but I did find something else that intrigued me."

I was rocking faster, realized it, and forced myself to slow down.

"In three cases, Tate's clients had taken lie detector tests and passed. In each case, Snowden ruled the results inadmissible."

Some birds landed in the bushes in front of the house, and Justice's ears perked up. "It's all right," I said, petting his head. He lay back down as if he were just as intrigued about this story as I was.

"I thought that was unusual, so I changed my research strategy. I went through all of Tate's cases for the past ten years and found a total of nine defendants who had passed lie detector tests. Even though the tests were inadmissible, in seven of the cases, he worked out sweet deals for the defendants."

Mace had been looking out over the cul-de-sac as he spoke, but now he turned to me. I suddenly had no idea where any of this was going.

"Jamie, you've been prosecuting long enough to know that no defense lawyer gets that many innocent clients. So how did Tate's clients do so well on the polygraphs? I figured he must have had a polygraph expert on his payroll, so to speak."

Mace James's story had taken an interesting twist. I quit worrying about my father's reputation. And I quit looking at my watch.

Mace returned his gaze to the street. "Wrong again. Instead, I discovered that the tests were performed by a variety of polygraph examiners. Nine tests. Five different examiners. So it must have been something else."

He stopped and checked his own watch. "I'm sorry; I see my time is up." Mace smiled. I did not. "Will the court give me an extra two minutes?"

"Just say what you came to say, and say it as fast as you can."

"Anyway, as you know, the polygraph test doesn't really detect lies. It detects physiological changes that occur because we get nervous when we lie. Increased heart rate. Perspiration. Blood-pressure changes. That type of thing."

"I wasn't born yesterday," I said.

"Right. Sorry. So anyway, I assumed Tate had figured out a way to game the test. I talked to a few polygraph examiners and started researching countermeasures—"

"I'm aware of the countermeasures," I interrupted. "I researched them for Antoine's case."

"I figured you had. Well . . . I actually met with several of Tate's former clients who had taken the test, and they denied knowing anything about countermeasures. Plus, I think Antoine would have told me if he had used them. And another thing—these other clients didn't seem all that sophisticated, yet every single one of them had passed the test. To the best of my knowledge, Tate never had a client fail a polygraph."

"Where's all this heading?" I asked.

Mace James stopped rocking. He leaned forward, elbows on his knees. "There's another way to beat the lie detector—you make yourself honestly believe that you didn't commit the crime. The polygraph can't tell the difference between false memories and true memories; it can only test whether you *think* you're telling the truth.

"I started focusing on this when I tried to reconcile Antoine's polygraph results with his brain-scan results. Jamie, there's this whole branch of neurology focused on suggestive memory creation, a form of hypnosis that works on a large segment of the population. The effectiveness is even greater if the subject is taking certain drugs. This isn't carnival hypnosis with swinging watches and all that stuff; it's a very sophisticated form of top-down processing that can be tracked using neurological studies. The CIA experimented with it more than twenty years ago to develop agents who would carry out certain assignments with no remorse and no memory of the events afterward. Physicians in India have used it as anesthesia when they perform surgery—even the amputation of limbs. This stuff is real, and it works."

My mind was shooting in a hundred different directions. "It can re-create your memory?"

"For certain segments of the population—yes."

"And Tate's clients were nine for nine?"

"Nine for nine."

"And ten for ten if you count Tate."

"I think you've got the math pretty much figured out," Mace said.

"But how does all this help me with Caleb Tate?" I asked. "Your text message said you might have something I could use."

"I'm just getting started," Mace said.

I was no longer worried about how long he was taking.

84

BEADS OF SWEAT HAD FORMED on the back of my neck, but I wasn't about to move. "What's your agenda?" I asked.

"I couldn't let Antoine's case go—not with so many unanswered questions. And that's led me to some information you may want to have."

He paused, but I waited him out. I had decided it was hard to rush a law school professor—you just had to let him tell the story his way.

Sure enough, he started up again. "I met with two of Caleb Tate's former clients who had passed the polygraph. One of them has done his time and is out. He retained me because he thinks Tate screwed him over, and he wants to get some revenge. A second of Tate's former clients has a trial date in two months and is looking at a long stretch if he's convicted. He hired me to handle his case."

"God help us," I said. But Mace ignored it.

"Dr. Chandar gave them the same brain scan he used on Antoine. The guy on the outside got the same results as Antoine."

"He failed?"

"Yeah, he failed."

Mace got out of his seat and took off his sunglasses. He turned and faced me, leaning against the railing and crossing his bulging arms. His big body blocked out the sun.

"I want to tell you about the results for my guy awaiting trial, but I have to know it won't be used against him. I'm here to see if I can work out a deal."

I didn't respond immediately. I needed time to process everything. "Let's just speak hypothetically," I said.

"All right, let's assume the same result as the other two guys," Mace replied. "So now we've got three guys who passed a polygraph but failed the brain scan."

I nodded, conceding the point. "Some would call that a pattern."

"But think about this," Mace continued. "I know you've done enough work with the insanity defense to realize that people can access memories stored in their subconscious through hypnosis. So let's say, again hypothetically, that we put my two clients under hypnosis again and help them access information about their original hypnosis sessions. We get the name of the psychiatrist or the place where the session occurred or a description of the person who created the false memories. I'm sure Caleb Tate would have used that same hypnotist in order to help him pass his own polygraph. You get a phone tap. Then you execute a surprise search warrant at that person's house or office, and they'll call Caleb Tate in about two seconds. That's your path to Tate's conviction. You see what I'm saying? What would that information be worth?"

I thought about it, connecting the dots, and Mace was smart enough not to interrupt. "What's your client's name—the one looking at time?"

Mace hesitated before answering. We were both finding it difficult to trust. "Rashad Reed."

"What are the charges?"

"Carjackings. Three separate occurrences."

"Was anybody hurt?"

"No. Traumatized a little, but not hurt."

"Did you tell him I don't do plea bargains?"

"I did. But I also told him there might be an exception."

"What does he want?"

"Five years, all but two suspended. Move him to a prison system in a remote part of the state and give him a private cell. He also wants some recess privileges, but he doesn't want to be in the general inmate population."

"And I want a Ferrari," I said. "But we don't always get what we want."

Mace frowned and looked down at the porch. "Jamie, I know you find this hard to believe, but I care about justice too. I'm not really that excited about putting Rashad Reed back on the street in two years. But you've made no secret of your belief that Caleb Tate is the one behind the events that are terrorizing Milton County right now. And while the ethical rules don't allow me to breach any confidences from a former client, they also impose on me a duty not to let my clients defraud the court. This is the only way I know to get at the truth, fulfill my ethical duties, and get Milton County's criminal justice system back on track."

He waited as I chewed on it but then apparently ran out of patience. "Listen, Rashad Reed is willing to be the next guinea pig to cut a deal. But he's got to have solitary confinement and protection. I'm not sanctioning what he did, but he's my client, and I can't let him cut a deal if it means I'm signing his death warrant."

"I understand that," I said. "But this is a lot to work through." My thoughts were racing with everything I needed to do just to process this. "I'll get back to you as soon as I can."

"That's all I can ask." Mace knelt down and rubbed Justice's head, then stood. I stood as well, and we awkwardly shook hands.

"Thanks for coming," I said.

"Thanks for hearing me out."

I watched him walk to his truck and drive away. I sensed that the alliances were somehow shifting under my feet. Mace James and I still weren't friends. But I was no longer sure that we were sworn enemies.

85

BEFORE I CALLED BILL MASTERSON, I needed to get some things lined up. Energized, I went inside and changed into my running shorts and a sports bra. I put Justice on a leash and took off over the hills in the neighborhood, working my legs and lungs for the first time in nearly two weeks. The heat was almost unbearable, and I circled around after the first five minutes to let a panting Justice back into the air-conditioning. I told him that Mom would be back and headed out for round two.

I ran until I was completely exhausted and then walked for another two miles. I was in lawyer mode again, processing everything that Mace James had just told me. I played out several different scenarios in my mind, and by the time I returned to the house, I knew what I needed to do.

While I was waiting to cool off enough to take a shower, I called Dr. Gillespie and asked him some general questions about polygraphs, suggestive memory creation, and hypnosis. For the most part, he confirmed what Mace James had told me.

"Why are you asking?"

I took a deep breath and told him about my conversation with Mace. I tried to be careful, knowing that if I could talk Masterson into letting Caleb Tate's case go forward, Gillespie would be taking the stand next week. I couldn't tell him how our case had imploded on Friday. But I did explain, in general terms, that unless we came up with some convincing new evidence we would probably drop the case.

I was on the phone with Gillespie for nearly fifty minutes, discussing various scenarios. Eventually he had an idea. "Before you cut a plea bargain, don't you sometimes make the defendants proffer their evidence?"

"Sure. We usually get full disclosure before we confirm the deal."

"Then why don't you do that with Rashad Reed? Find out whether you can get into his subconscious and figure out what he knows *before* you agree to any deals."

The suggestion made me chuckle. "When we get a proffer, it's usually the attorney giving me a carefully worded explanation of what his client will say as a cooperating witness. I don't know of any lawyers—and especially not Mace James—who are just going to say, 'Sure, put my client under hypnosis, ask him whatever you want, and then we'll deal.'"

"You're right," Gillespie said. "I should probably stick to the expert-witness side of the law practice."

But then it hit me. "Wait a minute," I said. "Mace can't let us do that with Reed. But what about his other client? The guy who's already served his time. We could put him under hypnosis. We could make that a condition of even considering a plea for Reed. If the hypnosis doesn't work, we haven't lost anything."

"Wouldn't that put James in a conflict of interest?" Gillespie asked. "Having to get one client to do something so the other can get a deal?"

"Yeah, it would. Which makes me even more intent on doing it."

I was only half-serious, though it would serve Mace right to squirm a little. In reality, Mace said the client who had served his time wanted to help nail Caleb Tate. This would be one way to do it.

"Can you do the hypnosis?" I asked Gillespie. "Or do you know somebody who can?"

"All psychiatrists know the basic techniques. It's really just a question of getting the patient to lower his defenses enough to let me into the subconscious. I would need some time alone with this guy. And I can't guarantee that I can make it happen during the first meeting."

Things were coming together fast. We didn't have time for multiple meetings. "What if we tell Mace we want to meet with his guy right away? Could you do it tonight?"

There was a pause on the other end. "Let me get to my Outlook calendar." After a few seconds, he said, "I might have to move some things around, but I could probably make it happen. But we need to think through this a bit." He sounded tentative now. "If I'm going to testify next week, we've got to be careful about how we do this. First of all, who else knows about this?"

"Right now, it's just Mace James and me."

"Okay, let's keep it that way for now. Of course, you've probably got to clear it with Masterson. Why don't you call James and see if he can get the green light from his client. If we need to, we can have a follow-up session on Sunday."

After hanging up with Gillespie, I put in a call to Bill Masterson. Not surprisingly, I got his voice mail and left an urgent message.

Then I called Mace James and gave him my ultimatum. He didn't like my suggestion, but I was in no mood to negotiate.

"The guy's name is David Brewster," Mace eventually said. "Served five years for armed robbery of a convenience store."

"Have Mr. Brewster at Dr. Gillespie's office at 8 p.m., and let's hope this works," I said.

After I showered, I wrote a long e-mail to Bill Masterson, explaining everything. I also sent him a text message telling him to check his e-mail. Next, I started doing my own research about hypnosis and polygraphs.

I skimmed through a few articles listed on the first two Google pages and got more comfortable with what Mace James had been explaining. Just as Mace had suggested, I learned that the CIA had done experiments with agents whom they had put under hypnosis and given polygraph tests. The agency had been able to create false memories in their agents and cause amnesia for events that actually occurred. The scientific advances surprised me, but not nearly as much as what I found on the third page of my Google search.

There was a long article published in *Psychiatry Today* about the power of hypnosis to create and erase memories. Like the other articles, this one confirmed that hypnosis could cause people to forget things that happened and remember things that never occurred. But this article went further, analyzing the suggestive effects that took hold when someone was under hypnosis. Under the right conditions, subjects prone to hypnosis could not only have their memories changed but could also have their futures influenced by suggestions that the subjects embraced as their own thoughts and ideas. The author then illustrated these principles through various legal cases where hypnosis had been used to make subjects "recall" childhood abuse that had never happened. It was the suggestive nature of the questioning under hypnosis and the way these suggestions were embedded into the subconscious that made the subject think abuse had taken place.

The author showed how persons who experienced deep-trance hypnosis could also have their future likes and dislikes affected by the hypnotist. Sometimes the subjects could be instructed to do things totally contrary to their normal natures. As proof, the author detailed three instances where a hypnotist had lured three different women into sexual relationships while the women were in a hypnotic trance. The whole disgusting scheme might have never come to light except for the fact that the perverted hypnotist videotaped the encounters.

All of this was disturbing and shocking new information to me, and I started rethinking everything I knew about Caleb Tate and Antoine Marshall in light of it. But the most shocking revelation of all was the person who had authored the article. Her name was Dr. Laura Brock. And the article had been published just eight months prior to her death.

86

I LEFT A SECOND VOICE MAIL with Masterson, then called Dr. Gillespie back to tell him about my mother's article. He suggested that the two of us meet before getting together with Mace James. Maybe my mom's death wasn't just a random result of a breaking and entering gone bad. Gillespie believed it was all too coincidental. Caleb Tate used deep-trance hypnosis on his clients, my mother had been researching it, and then she just happened to be murdered by a man defended by Caleb Tate. Neither of us could put the pieces completely together, but we both knew that we were onto something.

Gillespie wanted to meet at my house so he could take me through the events from the night my mother died. For twelve years, I had tried to avoid thinking about that night. I had blocked out the images of my mother lying on the floor dead and my father covered in blood. But now, Gillespie wanted me to relive the trauma to see if there was something lodged in my subconscious that might help us unlock this puzzle.

He showed up at five thirty, and even Justice seemed to understand how somber the night had become. He didn't greet Gillespie with his usual tail-wagging, jumping-around, let's-play-tug-of-war approach. Instead, he stayed next to me as if sensing my dread at what we were about to do.

Dr. Gillespie greeted me with a warm hug and told me that he understood how difficult this would be. I thanked him for coming on a Saturday. He said that he had been in the clubhouse when I first called, sharing a few drinks with his trash-talking buddies after a miserable day on the links. "I needed an excuse to leave," he said graciously. "I owe you one."

He said he had been thinking about our call and was convinced that my mother's death was not an accident. He proposed that we look through her old files, focus on anything having to do with hypnosis, and see what we could find. We both believed that Caleb Tate was somehow behind all this.

"Do you still have those records?" he asked.

I told him I thought they were in the attic someplace. It might take an hour to find them and several more to go through them. We agreed it could wait until tomorrow. For tonight, the important thing was to see if there was anything lodged in my memory about the events of my mom's death, anything I had previously overlooked.

"Is this one of those focus-on-the-swinging-watch type things?" I asked.

Gillespie smiled. "You can do that with your local gypsies. I prefer to talk over a cup of coffee."

I fixed some coffee for Dr. Gillespie and a glass of water for me. We settled into the chairs in the family room, and he started with the questions. Where was I the night my mom died? How long had I been out? Did I have anything to drink? What was the weather like? Could I remember anything about the food I ate?

"The food I ate?" I asked.

"We need to engage all the senses from that night. Re-create as much as we can before I start asking questions about when you came home and found your mom and dad. You're going to have to work with me, Jamie. We've got to walk through this whole series of events and keep it uninterrupted, if possible."

I took a deep breath. "I'll do the best I can."

"Maybe we should put Justice out back," Gillespie suggested. "That way, when we re-create you walking into the house, he won't disturb your train of thought."

I did as Gillespie suggested, and we talked for several more minutes in the family room. He helped me remember the emotions from that time in my life, and I recalled as many details as I could about the party I went to that night. Then we went outside and got in his car. He backed out of the driveway and drove around the cul-de-sac before pulling back in.

"Let's go in the house exactly the way you did that night with Chris. I'm just going to follow along, and I want you to describe what you see and what you feel at every step. I may ask some short questions but only to prod you along."

We came in through the garage, and I had a sense of foreboding. "I think Chris was actually ahead of me," I said. "I think I was kind of sulking because he had come to get me."

Gillespie took a step ahead and opened the door that led from the garage into the laundry room. I followed him past the washer and dryer and into the family room. The family room opened to the kitchen eating area, where my mom was killed.

"I didn't really know anything was wrong until we got right here and I saw them," I said, pointing. "There." Chills ran up my spine, and I started shaking a little. "That's where they were. I think I stopped here. My hand over my mouth."

I closed my eyes again and wanted to scream just at the thought of it.

"How were they lying?" Gillespie asked. He had stepped off to the side of the kitchen area.

"My mom was on the floor in an awkward position. Not too far from the table. Her head was back and her mouth was open. She had been shot in the head. But what I really noticed was my dad. He was right over here."

I moved to where my dad had been and knelt down. "His shirt was covered in blood, darker here next to his rib cage where he had been shot. Chris started yelling things. I don't remember what. But it was like 'Call 911! Get a cold washcloth! Hurry up!'"

As I described the events, I felt my blood pumping faster, and I started to get a little dizzy. I walked over to the sink, where I had gone that night to grab the washcloth. "It was so stupid—Chris telling me to get a washcloth. My parents were both lying there dead."

The night was coming back now in all its gory detail. "Chris put his ear next to my mother's mouth and checked her pulse. I ran over and knelt down next to my dad."

As I talked, I acted it out again, kneeling on the carpet next to where my father had been.

"I tilted his head back and started CPR," I said. "His eyes were open a little, and it felt like he was breathing, but I didn't know for sure, and I was just crazy with adrenaline. Chris kind of pushed me aside and told me to press the washcloth against the wound. Chris started doing CPR. and I can't even remember. . . . I think the washcloth didn't seem big enough, so I ripped off my shirt and pressed that into my dad's side. My hands were covered with blood all the way up my wrists."

I sat down and stopped for a moment. I had to take a break. I saw Justice sitting at the back door and Gillespie standing next to the island in the middle of the kitchen. But the room had become a blur. I was losing focus. I tilted my head back and took a few deep breaths.

"Was the back door open or closed?" Gillespie asked.

I held up my hand. "No more questions for a second," I said. The words came out a little garbled. I couldn't think about this right now.

"Did Chris act surprised? Did he scream when he saw the bodies?"

I couldn't deal with Gillespie's questions anymore. The room was spinning and getting darker. I lay down on my side. Justice started barking on the porch, clawing at the door.

"Do you remember anybody looking in from the back porch? Do you remember any noises upstairs? Do you remember . . . ?"

The questions no longer concerned me, mere static that merged into the barks from the porch, my whole thought process spinning out of control. It felt like I was falling into a deep well and couldn't reach the end of the darkness. I tilted my head back and closed my eyes. Anything to make the room stop spinning. Anything to calm the noises in my head.

I sensed that perhaps Gillespie was kneeling over me now, his face inches away. So close that I could smell the alcohol on his breath. "Can you hear me?"

I tried to respond, but nothing came out.

"Good night, Jamie," Gillespie said.

The room stopped spinning, peace overwhelmed me, and the darkness took control.

87

MACE JAMES ARRIVED EARLY at the office of Dr. Aaron Gillespie. He waited alone in the shaded parking lot, secluded from Johns Creek Parkway, hoping David Brewster would keep his promise. At 8:00 he started getting nervous. At 8:05 he called Brewster and left a message. At 8:10 he texted Brewster and called Jamie. She didn't answer either.

Gillespie pulled up at 8:15 and greeted Mace. "Is your client here?"

Mace explained that Brewster had promised to show but now wasn't answering his phone. Gillespie suggested they wait inside. He unlocked the front door, and Mace followed through a lobby area and down a dark hallway.

"Don't move," a voice behind Mace said. "Hands behind your back." Mace felt something like a gun barrel on the nape of his neck. He tried to glance quickly over his shoulder, but the man pressed the gun harder. "I mean it. I'll blow you away in a second."

Gillespie turned and looked at Mace. "Do as he says," Gillespie warned.

Mace tried to size things up, but everything was happening too fast. *Gillespie's in on this?* Mace knew he needed to make a move—try to catch the guy behind him with an elbow. If he let the man handcuff him, he would lose his one opportunity. He felt the gun pull back a few inches, no longer touching his skin.

In the next second, without warning, Mace felt a debilitating pain shoot from the small of his back through his entire body. He tried to jerk away but collapsed to the floor. The electrical current from a Taser had set every nerve ending on fire.

Stunned, Mace felt two men pull his hands behind his back and slap handcuffs on. He looked up, blinked, and saw Caleb Tate and Rafael Rivera.

"That was stupid," Caleb snapped.

"It won't leave marks. It went through his clothing."

They yanked Mace up by his arms, and Caleb held a gun to the back of Mace's head. Rivera kept the Taser a few inches from Mace's side.

"My car's out back," Caleb said to Gillespie. "Have you got the girl?"

"She's in the other car."

Rivera and Caleb forced Mace out the back door and into the passenger seat of Caleb's car. Caleb drove, and Rivera sat behind Mace, the Taser touching Mace's right shoulder.

"Try something," Rivera said. "I'd like to see you squirm again."

Mace considered his options, none of which were appealing. "You won't get away with this," he said. "Too many people know."

Caleb scoffed. He was wearing a pair of jeans and a black T-shirt, and for the first time since Mace had known him, his hair wasn't perfectly in place. There were dark circles under his eyes, and he hadn't shaved that morning.

"This isn't TV," Caleb said. "You can save your clichés."

"Masterson knows. Finnegan knows. Plus, three or four of your former clients all know about this."

Caleb kept his eyes straight ahead.

"Shut up," Rivera said from the backseat.

"Masterson just got an e-mail thirty minutes ago from Jamie's computer," Caleb Tate said smugly. "It tells Masterson to ignore the prior messages. It says that your theories about me were all wrong. That you were just trying to get a deal for Rashad Reed. That Gillespie hypnotized this other client of yours—David Brewster—and found out there was no prior hypnosis. As for Detective Finnegan—nice try, but Jamie doesn't trust him. He's out of the loop."

"Where's Jamie?" Mace asked.

"You don't get to ask the questions," Caleb said. He switched on the radio and made a left turn. "Besides, you'll figure it all out when we get there."

◁▷

It was dark by the time Caleb pulled into the long driveway that looped around to the front of his mansion. Motion detectors flicked on streetlamps, illuminating the scene in a hazy glow. Mace James had spent some time here when Caleb had first retained him. Caleb had escorted Mace through the house, showing him the bedroom where Rikki died, explaining what had happened step by step. Now Caleb was staging yet another drama at the house that murder built, and Mace would have a starring role.

"Get out," Rivera said from the backseat.

Mace made no effort to move. Why cooperate? He realized that whatever plot these men had in mind depended on leaving no Taser marks or bruises from blunt blows. They were probably going to stage some kind of shoot-out.

When Caleb reached over to unbuckle Mace's seat belt, Mace decided to make his play. He lunged at Caleb and landed a vicious head butt just above Caleb's eyebrow. Caleb grunted in pain, but before Mace could land another blow, he felt the Taser dig into his shoulder and the current surge through his body. He convulsed in the front seat for five seconds, ten, while Caleb spouted obscenities and pressed his palm to his forehead to stanch the flow of blood.

"Get him up the steps! Now!" Caleb demanded.

Caleb half jogged to the front steps, trying to keep the blood from dripping on the sidewalk. Rivera pulled Mace from the car, but Mace had a hard time getting his muscles to cooperate. He fell once, stood up at Rivera's prodding, and staggered toward the front steps. Rivera held the Taser inches from Mace's body and pushed him along with his free hand.

"Make another move, big man," Rivera taunted. "You like being a hero?"

Mace felt like somebody had clawed his insides out. He tried to focus and come up with a plan while he walked. When he reached the front porch, he saw an SUV pull into the driveway. Aaron Gillespie got out, wearing gloves and brandishing a gun. He stopped about twenty yards from the front porch.

"What happened to you?" he asked Caleb.

"Our boy wants to be a hero," Caleb said, his face covered with blood. "We're going to have to change this up a little. He's going to have a contusion on his head, so we'll need to make sure that when he falls, he hits that part of his head on the steps. I'll twist out of the way and fall against the doorpost or something so I've got an explanation for this. Everything else stays the same."

Mace still didn't know the details of this script, but one thing was obvious—his character didn't make it to the final credits. He suspected that Jamie was already dead. He realized it was her 4Runner that Gillespie had driven. He decided to at least give the medical examiner and cops something to work with.

He was still on the porch, not far from Caleb Tate, which was apparently where they wanted him to die. Gillespie was facing them, gun in his right hand. Mace could feel his muscles starting to regroup and he said a quick prayer. A thought crossed his mind—Samson in the temple. He might have to die, but why die alone?

He bolted down the steps, straight for Gillespie, gambling that Caleb didn't want to shoot him in the back.

"Stop him!" Caleb yelled.

Gillespie pointed the gun but froze, his hand trembling. *A few more steps.* But just before Mace got to him, Gillespie lowered the gun and fired. Mace felt his left thigh explode with pain, driving him to the ground.

"Get Jamie!" Caleb yelled. "And finish him off right there!"

Mace's left leg felt like it had been ripped apart. The pain was shutting down his thoughts. He tried to stagger to his feet, but Rivera pushed him back down and stood over him with the Taser. Caleb had a gun pointed at Mace's head.

Gillespie jogged to the 4Runner and tucked the gun in his waistband. He opened the passenger door and pulled Jamie out. She appeared lifeless, a rag doll. Gillespie carried her down the sidewalk, his arms squeezed around her waist.

He stopped a few feet from Mace, close enough in the muted light that Mace could see the sweat on Gillespie's brow, his eyes wide with panic. Caleb came closer, his gun still trained on Mace's head. Rivera was there as well, finger on the trigger of the Taser. Gillespie propped Jamie up and positioned himself behind her, his arms wrapped around her. He pulled out the gun and wrapped her dead hands around it, pointing it at the front door. Using Jamie's finger on the trigger, Gillespie squeezed off four random shots.

That's when it clicked for Mace.

They were setting it up to look like Jamie had killed him. Like he had been at a meeting at Caleb's house while Jamie was lying in wait outside. She had opened fire, killing Mace, perhaps thinking she had killed Caleb too. They would probably stage Jamie's subsequent suicide, and Gillespie, as her counselor, would claim she had been suicidal for some time.

After Gillespie fired the shots at the front door, he turned the gun toward Mace. Three weapons—two guns—all pointed at Mace. It was time to pick one.

He took a deep breath, ignored the pain in his wounded leg, and lunged headfirst at Caleb Tate. But Tate sidestepped, managed to keep his balance, and threw Mace to the ground. Mace felt the pain bite at his leg as he hit the turf and rolled. He cringed, anticipating the impact of the bullet.

He heard a shot and looked up in time to see the bullet rip through Rivera. Gillespie had dropped Jamie and had the gun pointed squarely at Caleb Tate.

When he had lunged, Mace had knocked Caleb's gun to the ground, but it was still several feet away. With his hands cuffed behind his back, Mace had no chance of getting to it in time.

He did a quick reassessment. *Gillespie killed Rivera?*

Before Mace could process it all, Gillespie fired two more shots, one that hit Caleb Tate's left shoulder, the other exploding Caleb's face. "That was for Rikki," Gillespie said as Caleb crumpled to the ground.

Mace rolled twice, trying to get to Caleb's gun, but Gillespie beat him to it. He stepped on it and pointed Jamie's gun straight down at Mace.

"I saved Jamie," he said. His hands were shaking, his eyes wild with fear. "I can't save you."

Mace closed his eyes, thought about the things in life he had left undone, and heard the next shot echo through the night air.

88

FOR THE SECOND TIME, Mace felt no pain.

He opened his eyes in time to see Gillespie blown backward, blood spattering his shirt. There were sirens in the distance. And big Bill Masterson, gun in his right hand, appeared from behind Jamie's 4Runner. He raced over to Jamie and checked her breathing.

"You all right?" he asked Mace.

"Just a flesh wound," Mace gasped. His hands were still cuffed behind his back, so he couldn't put pressure on the wound in his left thigh. He was losing blood, but that wasn't his first concern. "Is she alive?"

Masterson had his hand on Jamie's neck. "Alive, but I don't like her pulse."

◁▷

Mace James asked as many questions as he could on the way to the hospital, but nobody seemed to know anything. The first ambulance had taken Jamie away. He was in the second. The paramedics told him to calm down and try to relax.

Easy for them to say. He had just seen three men killed with stupefying speed, all within arm's length. He had been Tasered and had a gun pointed at his head. He had a bullet lodged in his thigh, which still hurt like crazy. He was losing blood fast.

His mind was spinning trying to process all this.

When they hit the emergency entrance at Johns Creek Hospital, there was a flurry of activity, lots of serious faces and urgent orders and people hustling this way and that. He signed consent forms as the pain medication started to kick in. They hooked up IVs and pumped in some blood, preparing him for surgery.

Mace's questions were still being deflected, but he wasn't sure he was making sense anymore. The surgeon and anesthesiologist talked for a few minutes, and then the bright lights of the operating room went dark as Mace James drifted into a well-earned sleep.

89

I FINALLY CLAWED MY WAY to the surface of consciousness, fighting through the nightmares I had been slipping in and out of. I was still disoriented. My head felt like it might explode. I was lying in a hospital bed in a dark room with the television on. I had no idea what time of day or night it was. There were IVs hooked up to both arms, and my thoughts felt like they were wading through quicksand.

I tried to blink my eyes a few times so I could bring my memories into focus, but it wasn't happening. *How did I get here? How long have I been passed out?* There were fragments of memories—Aaron Gillespie at my house, images of my parents covered in blood, a visit from Mace James.

I turned my head slowly to the left, but the dizziness and pain came charging at me. I closed my eyes, blinked slowly, and opened them again. Bill Masterson was sprawled out in a chair, mouth open, snoring loudly. I had no idea why he was in my room.

I tried to talk, but my mouth was dry as cotton. I needed something to sip on but felt like my muscles were paralyzed and wouldn't respond to my brain's commands. I managed to murmur something and thought I saw Bill start in his chair. But then he settled back into a rhythmic snoring, and I realized there was no use fighting the sleep. I closed my eyes, relaxed, and let the nightmares take over again.

◁▷

Mace came out from under the anesthesia feeling groggy but ready to answer the nurse's questions. "What's your name? Where are you? What kind of surgery did you have?" His words sounded a lot like grunts, but he apparently got all the answers right, and she offered him water and some crackers.

"The doctor will be here in a few minutes," the nurse told him, "but he says you're a lucky man. The bullet tore into your quadriceps muscle, but it didn't hit any bone. It's a good thing you're a weight lifter."

As Mace gathered his bearings, the events of the last twenty-four hours settled back in his mind, creating a sense of sadness and apprehension. He needed some answers.

He asked for his BlackBerry, but the nurse said he didn't have one when he came in. He wanted to use the phone, but the nurse told him he needed to wait and talk to the doctor first. "After that, there's a Detective Finnegan who wants to talk to you."

"Is there a Jamie Brock in the hospital?" Mace asked.

"I'm sorry, but I can't give out that kind of information. Why don't you relax a little bit? If the leg starts to hurt, you can push this button right here, and it will release another shot of morphine."

Mace grunted in frustration, but there was nothing he could do. He waited patiently for his surgeon to make the rounds and then threatened to check himself out of the hospital if they didn't get him a cell phone. A few minutes after his display of belligerence, Detective Tyler Finnegan came into the room and gave Mace an update on Jamie Brock and David Brewster.

"We found Brewster in the trunk of Rivera's car," Finnegan said. "Tied up but basically unharmed. They were probably going to dispose of him later.

"Jamie's okay too. Gillespie gave her a drug called ketamine, a fast-acting narcotic sometimes used as a date rape drug. It's hard to detect in the system and can cause some short-term memory problems. Jamie's coming around, but she probably won't remember much."

Mace had a thousand questions, but Finnegan had a few of his own. He pulled up a chair, crossed his legs, took out a notepad, and began asking. Thirty minutes later, with Finnegan still probing about details, Mace drifted back to sleep.

◁▷

I opened my eyes again, encountered the lights in the room, and closed them. My head was still throbbing, and I felt like throwing up.

I felt numb, and I couldn't seem to get out of the haze. I started drifting away again.

"Jamie?" A familiar voice cut through the fog. I felt a touch on my arm, an insistent shaking, and then heard the same voice. "Jamie, can you hear me?"

I tried to reach out for him, squinting to bring into focus the silhouette standing over me.

"Thank God," Chris said.

He bent over and gave me a gentle hug, and I raised my arms to hug him back.

He offered me something to drink, and I sipped it gingerly through the straw. He propped my head up with the pillow. I looked to the other side of the bed and found LA sitting, watching me intently, a thin smile showing his relief.

I struggled to form some questions, but my tongue was thick and uncooperative. I couldn't remember how I had gotten here or what had happened, but I had this strange sense that whatever it was, it wouldn't go away. Images started creeping into my mind.

"How . . . how did I . . . get here?" I managed to stammer.

Chris pulled a chair up to the side of my bed and slowly, in a soft voice, started telling me everything that had happened. I tried to absorb the news as best I could, but I couldn't wrap my stumbling mind around the notion that Gillespie had been working with Caleb Tate the entire time. I shook my head as if I could change what had happened by a sheer act of will.

I wanted to understand, but my body needed to rest. I asked a few questions, but it all seemed like a terrible nightmare. When Chris finished updating me, he told me how thankful he was that I was still alive. He said that God was looking out for me, that God must have big plans for my future.

I closed my eyes with Chris holding my right hand and LA holding my left. I felt secure between these two men and safe here. And I knew, on some level, that Chris was right. The same God with whom I had been angry, for whom I'd had so little time, had now spared my life.

The pillow was soft. The bed was warm. And my body needed its rest.

90

SEVEN DAYS LATER, I found myself ready for a picnic, wondering why I had agreed to go in the first place. I had on a pair of shorts, a tank top, and flip-flops. It was eighty-five degrees, so I put on some sunscreen and grabbed a few towels. Justice seemed to sense that something was up, and he started getting antsy. At least one of us was excited.

The doorbell rang at a few minutes after one, and I took a deep breath before heading to the front hall. Justice, on the other hand, sprinted to the door, barking like a maniac, ready for the day's great adventure. I opened the door, and Justice attacked with an exuberant display of dancing, licking, and hyperactive motion that nearly knocked my guest off his crutches.

"Sorry about that," I said.

"We're buddies," Mace James said. "Besides, I grew up with dogs." He rubbed Justice's head. "Ready?" he asked me.

Not really. "Sure."

Mace crutched down the front steps and sidewalk. He beat me to the passenger door of his truck and held it open like a perfect gentleman. Justice, of course, jumped in first.

Mace hopped around to the driver's door, threw his crutches in the back, climbed into the driver's seat, and gingerly lifted his bad leg in with both hands. He scooted back in the seat at an angle so he could keep the left leg straight.

"You need me to drive?" I asked.

"Nah," Mace said. "Once I get in, I'm fine."

He drove to my favorite park on the Chattahoochee River. Before we ate lunch, Mace hobbled down to the river and started throwing a stick for Justice. Each throw went a little farther, and Justice seemed to be having the time of his life. Then Mace hobbled over to the woods next to the boat ramp and picked up a nice fat stick about three feet long. He stood on one leg and hurled it almost across the river. Justice did a flying belly flop into the water and swam like a bandit all the way to the stick, barely able to hold it out of the water as he swam back to Mace, proud of what he had done. Mace threw it again, and Justice took off. And the game was on. Mace seemed determined to eclipse his last throw every time, and Justice seemed equally determined to bring it back and beg for more. I eventually found a seat in the shade and caught myself smiling at the two alpha dogs trying to outdo each other.

When I finally thought Justice might drown if he went in one more time, I called off the dogs, so to speak, and suggested we start the picnic. Mace had gone all out. There was a cooler with a fruit salad, Gatorade to drink, a chef salad with sliced meat and eggs, and three kinds of dressing in little Tupperware containers. I wondered how he had carried the cooler to the truck in the first place. He'd also brought celery, carrots, and two PowerBars for dessert.

"What are you, some kind of health nut?" I asked.

"Basically."

We spent the first half of lunch talking about workout routines and the second half trying to piece together exactly what had happened with Caleb Tate, Aaron Gillespie, and Antoine Marshall. I found it hard to stay mad at a man who had tried to save my life. I also discovered that Mace James was a lot less arrogant and more fun to be around than I had ever imagined.

Some things had become clear in the last seven days. Gillespie was the one who had been hypnotizing Caleb Tate's clients and helping them pass the polygraphs. With a little digging, detectives had found two former patients of Gillespie's who claimed he had taken advantage of them sexually during their counseling sessions. The working hypothesis at the DA's office was that he had done the same thing with Rikki Tate and that Caleb had found out. We assumed Caleb Tate had threatened to report Gillespie unless Gillespie played ball.

The women who had been abused by Gillespie, including Rikki Tate, all fit a similar pattern. They had been abused as children. They were prescribed narcotics by Gillespie. They were apparently in that 20 percent of people who were easily subjected to hypnosis. When I learned these facts, I thought about my relationship with Gillespie and it creeped me out. He had tried to pump me full of narcotics and had tried his suggestive routine on me as well, but fortunately it had not worked.

The link between my mom and Gillespie had also been clarified. By checking some old hard drives in storage at my mom's psychiatric center, investigators learned that Mom had at one time counseled Rikki Tate. The notes from those counseling sessions had been stolen the night of my mother's murder. But the existence of the counseling relationship and the fact that my mom had been researching psychiatrists who used narcotics and deep-trance hypnosis to sexually exploit their clients made it clear that Mom's death was no accident.

Antoine Marshall had obviously been working for Gillespie and Caleb Tate. Perhaps he had not expected my father to be home that night. Perhaps Marshall had been instructed to kill both my mom and my dad. Either way, my mom must have been ready to blow the whistle on Gillespie, and somehow he and Tate had found out.

Mace assumed that Antoine Marshall had been hypnotized and had committed the murder under hypnosis.

"Isn't it far more likely that they paid him to murder my mom and then hypnotized him afterward so he could pass the polygraph?" I asked.

Neither of us could prove our theory, and we agreed to disagree. "This much I know," Mace said. "Antoine Marshall was a changed man in the end."

I took a bite of the fruit salad. We were sitting at a picnic table under a pavilion, but even with the breeze, it was stifling hot.

"You're probably right," I said.

Mace looked at me, his eyes registering surprise. "It takes a lot for you to say that."

"My brother's been preaching at me all week," I said. I didn't mention the fact that coming so close to death also had a way of forcing a person to reevaluate. "And I think he's right about something. Not being able to forgive someone is like a cancer. Even if you get revenge, it pretty much destroys your soul."

"Spoken like a true defense lawyer," Mace said.

"Let's not get carried away."

We talked for a while about the prior Saturday night. From what Mace had learned, Gillespie and Tate had planned to make it look like a murder/suicide. The gun used to kill Mace James would have my fingerprints on it. Tate would claim I was waiting at the end of the sidewalk when they came out of the house. Mace started walking toward me, and I opened fire. I fired at Tate, and he fell to the ground. Thinking I killed him, I left. My body would be discovered, full of drugs, in my 4Runner on some abandoned road.

Gillespie would testify about my psychotic break. A ranting e-mail sent to Bill Masterson from my own computer earlier that evening would confirm that I had snapped. An eyewitness. The word of a psychiatrist. Fingerprints on the gun. An incriminating e-mail. What more did they need?

That night, Gillespie apparently had a change of heart. Instead of giving me a fatal drug overdose, he knocked me out with ketamine. He obviously had some kind of plan to keep me alive and make the deaths of Caleb Tate, Mace James, and Rafael Rivera look like a gang killing. None of us could figure out the details of how that plan would work.

In a way, the events of last Saturday night had brought some closure, but in another way, they just raised a new set of questions. And there would be no trial to sort it out; all of the conspirators were dead, killed in a shoot-out that occurred while I was lying unconscious on the ground.

"I understand you were quite a hero," I said to Mace.

"If you call getting shot in the leg and crying like a baby heroic," Mace said. He decided to change the subject. "Tell me how you ended up with Justice."

I told Mace the story of my first dog, how Snowball had been poisoned when I was in law school. A few weeks later, some friends brought Justice by in a crate and left him outside my door. They had their own suggestions for names, but I decided to call him Justice.

On the way home, Mace James earned some more brownie points when he stopped at the local PetSmart.

"What are we doing here?" I asked.

"You're going to turn Justice into a girlie dog if we don't get him a real bone," Mace said. I put Justice on his leash, and Mace got out on his crutches. The three of us walked around the store and looked at the puppies that had been brought in by the SPCA.

"What kind of dog did you have as a kid?" I asked Mace.

"A mutt. A big mutt."

"Shocker."

Eventually, Mace found what he was looking for. It was the biggest bone in the store. First the biggest stick on the bank of the river and now this. "Here you go, boy," he said to Justice. He peeled back some of the plastic so Justice could sniff the bone, and the two boys cemented their friendship on the spot.

On the way home, Justice sat behind us in the second seat of the cab, chewing on his new bone and wondering if the day could possibly get any better.

Mace seemed to think this was the perfect moment to discuss a little business. "We've still got our deal with Rashad Reed, right? He gets out in two based on his help in Caleb Tate's case?"

"Is that what this was all about? A picnic in the park to soften me up on Rashad Reed?"

"Yeah. And I figured taking a bullet in the leg trying to save your life wouldn't hurt either."

"Okay. Point taken. I'll go for three."

"Three?"

"Rashad Reed really didn't do anything in Tate's case," I said. "But at least my dog likes his lawyer."

"If it wasn't for Rashad Reed and David Brewster, Gillespie and Tate might have gotten away with everything. I think you're getting a gift at two."

I didn't respond right away. I had every intention of honoring the original deal, but I wanted to make Mace sweat it out a little. After all, I didn't want the word spreading around that I was getting soft.

News of Rashad Reed's likely deal had spurred a few others in the past week. Masterson was pretty sure the logjam was broken now that Caleb Tate wasn't around to keep the gang leaders together.

"All right," I said, after waiting a sufficient amount of time. "But don't get used to it. I gave you my word, so I'll honor our deal. But, Mace James, that's your last plea bargain. At least with me."

"Man," Mace moaned, "no wonder Masterson had a hard time finding a pulse. It's hard for a body to pump blood without a heart."

I punched him in the arm, but I was pretty sure he didn't feel it.

He was seven years older than me and he worked on the dark side of the law. But he was a man of faith, and he knew that the way to a woman's heart was straight through her dog. I could get used to spending time with Mace James, I decided.

◁▷

The next morning, I woke up to somebody ringing the doorbell at 8 a.m. I had finally gotten back into a normal sleep pattern without drugs, and I didn't appreciate somebody coming by that early on a Sunday morning. Justice and I marched down to the door, opened it, and almost tripped over the cage sitting in front of us.

Oh no. Without even looking, I knew what was happening. I had been through this same routine with Justice. I didn't have time to train another puppy. I was perfectly happy with the dog I already had.

When I knelt down, the brown little furry thing in the cage was as cute as he could be. I opened the card on top of the cage. Apparently it wasn't a "he" after all.

> I thought maybe Justice could use a little sister. I'm not a purebred like him, but the SPCA says I'll be just as big. I've got a little brown Lab in me if that helps. And, oh, by the way, they also said they would have to put me down if I didn't find a home.
>
> I know you've got a big heart, and I felt like maybe you needed somebody who could keep Justice company. Maybe you could call me Grace.

"You are so cute," I said, sticking my finger in the cage. Justice was sniffing Grace as if welcoming this new little girl into our home already. But I knew we wouldn't have to. At the bottom of the note, there was a PS:

If you're too busy to puppy-train right now, maybe you could pawn me off on a defense lawyer I know. He says that he'll be at the river at noon and that you have to come if you want to give me back.

I carried the cage inside, smiling to myself. I sent a text message to Mace James confirming that his ransom note had paid off. He texted back, inviting me to church before our rendezvous at the river. I surprised myself by accepting.

I also replied to another text, this one from LA. He wanted to hang out that afternoon.

LA seemed perfect for me. He believed in law and order, just like I did. He was younger and had a full head of hair and could have stepped from police work straight into modeling. Plus, he was another dog lover.

I sent a message telling him that I would be busy. Grace started barking and wanted to get out and play. I shook my head, knowing what I was getting into. Justice and Grace, they would make for some intriguing companions.

EPILOGUE

ON TUESDAY, NOVEMBER 6, Bill Masterson won the election for attorney general by four percentage points, propelled in part by the dramatic turn of events that had ended Caleb Tate's case. Masterson had become the Wyatt Earp of Georgia, taking law and order to a whole new level.

After a rousing acceptance speech at the Atlanta Hilton and a little postcelebration drinking with some friends, Masterson told everyone he was heading home to get some well-earned rest. Instead, he went straight to the office.

It would be his last night as DA. He would resign immediately so he could start focusing on the transition to attorney general, a job that technically started in January. Regina Granger would be appointed as the interim DA until a special election could be held.

Masterson turned on the lights in his office, kicked off his shoes, and poured himself a bourbon. It wasn't often that he had a moment of quiet reflection to consider the events of the past several years.

Men didn't reach his elevated status, he told himself, without a fair amount of baggage. There was Ted Kennedy and Chappaquiddick. His brother John and Marilyn Monroe. And more recently, Eliot Spitzer, governor of New York, who had been sleeping with prostitutes while serving as New York's attorney general. And who knew how many others? Great men who accomplished great things but had skeletons in their closets that nobody knew about.

The difference between the John Kennedys of the world and the Eliot Spitzers wasn't that some had superior moral compasses; it was just that some of them were smart enough to never get caught.

And that's why, on the night of his greatest achievement, Bill Masterson was in his corner office tying up a few loose ends. Details were the difference between success and failure.

It had been thirteen years since his troubles first bubbled to the surface. Rikki Tate, who was then known as Rikki Pearlman, had an impressive list of johns. And her lawyer was no fool. When Caleb Tate first came to Bill Masterson to cut a deal for Rikki, he proposed a side agreement as well. Rikki would conveniently forget one of her clients, so long as that man agreed to recommend no jail time for the young escort and occasionally return a favor on selected future cases for her lawyer. When Masterson went along with the deal, he knew that the devil had just slapped a mortgage on his soul.

But Masterson and Caleb Tate were professionals, and everything was fine until Rikki's conversion to Christianity. When she started telling Caleb that she just couldn't live with herself unless she told the truth about Masterson, Caleb had come straight to Masterson. Caleb had grown disenchanted with his wife and her holier-than-thou ways. He had a brilliant plan for taking care of her that would land both Caleb and Masterson on the front page of the paper, coverage that both men desperately needed. They each knew Gillespie was their ace in the hole, the man who could rig the counseling records of Rikki Tate to say whatever the coconspirators needed. Masterson had agreed to eventually nol-pros the Caleb Tate case so they wouldn't have to risk a renegade jury.

When Tate spent three days in jail, he thought up the no-plea-bargaining idea, which took the plan to a whole new level. That serendipitous twist had propelled Masterson to the AG's office and made him a player on the national stage.

Jamie Brock had almost ruined everything. Her insistence on prosecuting Tate, even when Masterson decided to nol-pros, was problematic. The first plan was to rig the DA computer files so it appeared that Jamie's father would be implicated in a bribery scheme if the case proceeded. This required bringing Rivera into the conspiracy. But Jamie surprised everyone by still insisting on going forward. That's when

Masterson and Tate had implemented plan B—the tape recording of Rafael Rivera that imploded the state's case.

The casualties could have ended with Rikki Tate if Mace James had minded his own business. But once James started figuring things out, he had to go. Masterson never intended to let Jamie die. He knew Gillespie was supposed to give her an overdose of narcotics. But Masterson had always intended to show up at Caleb Tate's house like the cavalry, kill Tate, Gillespie, and Rivera before they could implicate him, and rush Jamie to the hospital in time to save her life.

He'd had to improvise a little, but things had turned out even better than he'd expected.

There was a saying that Masterson subscribed to completely—two men can keep a secret, as long as one of them is dead. A corollary, of course, was that four men could keep a secret as long as three of them were dead.

The investigation into the shoot-out at Caleb Tate's house was now complete. The hardest thing for Masterson had been explaining his sudden last-minute appearance. But he was a man of details. He had told Gillespie to keep Jamie's cell phone with them in her 4Runner at all times. That way, according to the plan, Gillespie could send a text from Jamie's phone while at Caleb Tate's house, helping to place her at the scene of the crime.

Knowing this, Masterson had called some colleagues with the state police after receiving Jamie's fake e-mail rant against Tate and Mace James. He had asked them to triangulate her cell phone. That gave him the excuse he needed to go to Tate's house, where he knew his coconspirators would be. Once there, he parked at the end of the driveway, snuck up behind Jamie's 4Runner, and called for backup. Before help could arrive, he took decisive action and shot Gillespie, saving Mace James in the process.

The timing had been tricky, and the story wasn't perfect, but it satisfied the investigators.

Now he needed to tie up the final details. He accessed the DA's computer database and pulled up Robert Brock's case files for Milton County. Six months ago, he had changed the names of the actual judges on many of Brock's successful cases to Judge Snowden's name.

He had even scanned in a few substitute orders with her name and forged her signature so the backup documents matched. He had done the same thing with two other defense lawyers.

And now, on his last night in the office, Masterson undid all those changes. The DA's electronic database was once again an exact copy of the actual court files. When he completed the task, he proofread the resignation letter that he had drafted earlier in the week, anticipating this moment. He stuck it in an envelope, put Regina's name on the outside, and placed it in his out-box.

He finished at about 4:30 a.m. and took a final swallow of bourbon. He turned out the lights and thought about how much he would miss this place.

The justice system wasn't perfect. Sometimes it needed a little help from men like him. He was determined to make up for his past mistakes by doing a good job as attorney general. Georgia needed an AG who would kick butt and take names, and Bill Masterson was just the man.

He left the office, backing out of his reserved parking spot one last time, and headed home to get some sleep. In two months, he would start his job as Georgia's top law enforcement official.

There would be a new sheriff in town. And the bad guys had better watch their backs.

◁▷

ONE MONTH LATER

Regina Granger's second press conference as the interim district attorney for Milton County did not garner much interest. I was there, sitting in the back row. Next to me sat Mace James. LA was leaning against a side wall.

The room had been set up for more than a dozen reporters, but only five had come. They assumed that Regina had called the press conference to announce her intention to run in the special election—a foregone conclusion. The reporters looked bored, checking their smartphones as Regina talked about the organizational changes she had made in her first thirty days. The plea-bargaining crisis was behind us, and things had returned to some semblance of normalcy.

As Regina talked, my mind drifted to the events of the last few months. I still found it hard to believe that I had been spending so much time with a defense lawyer, someone seven years older than me, and someone who had defended my mother's killer. But after that first picnic together, we found excuses to get together again. It turned out that we had a lot in common and, yes, some pretty stark differences, too. But I liked hanging out with a man who was challenging and unpredictable and not at all threatened by my strong opinions.

I knew we had something special after I told him about Judge Snowden and my dad. I had to say something. I felt like a fraud carrying around that secret, but it still took me three days to get up the nerve. I told him when it was just the two of us, sitting on the back porch, the dogs playing in the grass.

I told him everything—how I had struggled with whether to say anything before Antoine's execution, how I had eventually passed the information on to Masterson, how he had relayed it to the AG's office, and how it had led me to sign the affidavit trying to save Antoine's life. Mace took it stoically, staring at the back lawn as I spoke. He asked a few questions and got pretty quiet.

He left that night without a hug or a thanks or any other display of emotion. As I watched his truck pull out of the cul-de-sac, I was certain that he would never come see me again.

The next day, he came back. And this time, he was all business. "I checked the court records for all of Snowden's cases," he told me. "Your dad's as well. And Caleb Tate's. What you're saying doesn't make sense."

We compared notes, and later that day I checked our research against the DA's database. That's when I discovered that somebody had changed the names of the judges in the database. My father's cases all still had the same results, but somebody had made it look like Judge Snowden had presided over most of his winning cases.

I told Mace about the mysterious runner in the Peachtree Road Race, the one who handed me the note about being careful who I trusted, the note that mentioned morphine. I had assumed that Caleb

Tate paid someone to slip me the note—trying to keep me from trusting LA and talking to him about my dad's involvement with Judge Snowden. But how did Tate know about the morphine? I had concluded that either he had been working with Rivera all along, just setting us up, or he really did have a source on the inside.

Now I realized it was both.

We broadened the investigative circle to include LA and Regina Granger. On election night, when Bill Masterson changed the DA's files, we knew we had him. From there, LA did the legwork. He interviewed women who had been in the same escort service as Rikki Tate nearly thirteen years earlier. There were rumors that one of Rikki's clients was a powerful public official who had never been caught. On a hunch, LA enlisted one of Rikki's church friends to call Bill Masterson and tell him that she knew about Masterson and Rikki. After all, new believers like Rikki liked to confess their past sins. LA had the woman wired when Masterson paid her the hush money.

For me, working on the Masterson investigation caused some of the greatest heartache and confusion of my life. The only bright spot was that it felt like I had regained my father. The man I knew and loved was exactly who I thought he was—hardworking, principled, committed to his clients, and successful in front of a variety of judges. But the man who had taught me how to practice law was a fraud. And now, as Regina Granger prepared to make an announcement that would take down Georgia's attorney general–elect, I couldn't help but feel melancholy.

The Bill Masterson I knew had defended me when defense lawyers attacked. He had shown me tough love and taught me how to hold my own in the courtroom. I had seen him risk his life to convict gang leaders and refuse to prosecute cases when he believed the cops had it wrong. This was the man who had been beside me and given me strength as I watched the execution of Antoine Marshall.

But, of course, all that was nothing but an act from a man living a double life.

I looked at LA, and he gave me a wink. If he was upset about my relationship with Mace James, he never showed it. And who could blame him? He had undoubtedly moved on to women more beautiful and fun-loving than me. We had been thrown together by the pressures of the Tate case, but we were very different people.

"I also want to read a short statement about a recent indictment," Regina Granger said. "I won't be taking any questions, however."

Two of the reporters glanced up from their smartphones. The others shrugged it off.

"No matter how long I serve in law enforcement, I am sure that this day will be one of the saddest moments of my professional career," Granger continued.

She now had everybody's full attention.

She swallowed hard and stared straight ahead, gathering her composure. Bill Masterson was her friend too. More than that, he had been her mentor. He had appointed her as his chief assistant years ago and just recently offered her an endorsement for her campaign.

"Yesterday, a Milton County grand jury indicted Attorney General–Elect Bill Masterson on multiple counts of murder in the first degree. As I speak, Milton County deputies are placing him under arrest. I don't believe in perp walks, and I don't believe in trying my cases in the press. When you leave today, I will have copies of the indictment for each of you. In fact, you can take multiple copies since so many of your colleagues decided not to show up."

Regina paused for a long moment to keep her emotions under control. Her struggle brought my own emotions to the surface. Masterson had been like a second father to me, and I felt my eyes tearing up. I recalled the chest of my natural father, rising and falling as he took his last breaths. And I had that same feeling now, like I was losing a second father. I had watched Antoine Marshall's execution with this man, and now, if Regina Granger was successful, Bill Masterson would someday be on the other side of the glass.

I reached over, and Mace James took my hand. He had no sympathy for Masterson. He held Masterson responsible for Antoine Marshall's execution and for all the other deaths that had occurred in Milton County just to advance Masterson's political ambitions. "There's a special place in hell for men like that," Mace James had said.

But now he squeezed my hand to comfort me.

"Bill Masterson was a friend and a mentor," Regina Granger said.

"We worked together on many cases—even risked our lives on a few. But nobody is above the law. These are capital crimes. And they deserve the ultimate penalty. When you get your copies of the indictment, you will see that we are asking for that."

Regina closed her eyes for a moment, and hands shot up. The five reporters sounded like twenty, but Regina, true to her word, wasn't taking any questions. She set her jaw and walked away from the podium.

"God have mercy," I said.

"I hope he gets the needle," whispered Mace.

ACKNOWLEDGMENTS

DURING MY YOUNGER and more abrasive days as a lawyer, I once wrote that an opponent's legal brief was "a parade of sentences vainly in search of an idea." I'm afraid that the same might be said of my stories without the help of the literary drum majors listed here.

I'll start with Lee Hough, who is both agent and friend, and who always gives great advice at the concept development stage. Thanks also to Michael Garnier, Mary Hartman, and my wife, Rhonda, who helped work on this story even before Tyndale did the heavy editing. I wouldn't even try to do this without you. On this book, I tapped the expertise of Andrew Hall, one of Georgia's finest criminal defense lawyers, who helped this Virginia attorney fill in the cavernous gaps in his understanding of Georgia criminal procedure. All of that is before the editing magicians at Tyndale take over.

Thank you, Karen Watson, for asking the tough and probing questions at the concept stage. (Have you ever considered law school?) As always, your insights (and encouragement) were invaluable. Thanks to Jeremy Taylor for bringing the story into sharper focus and the characters into another dimension. And thanks to Stephanie Broene, the third member of the Tyndale triumvirate, who provided reams of encouragement with just the right touch of constructive critique.

But that's not all. Sometimes, a book is inspired by real events, by people who are larger than life. That's the case here. And I need to thank them too.

Poison. The suspicious death of a spouse. The loss of a father. The pursuit of justice. These are the themes of *The Last Plea Bargain*. They did not come from thin air.

I am indebted to Ginger Somerville-Grant, Sara Somerville, and Alita Miller for allowing me to represent them in their nine-year quest to avenge their father's death. Your fight for justice inspired many of the themes I tried to capture in these pages. Thanks for never giving up. Sometimes, the good guys win.

"Do not be overcome by evil, but overcome evil with good."

ROMANS 12:21

ABOUT THE AUTHOR

RANDY SINGER is a critically acclaimed author and veteran trial attorney. He has penned eleven legal thrillers and was recently a finalist with John Grisham and Michael Connelly for the inaugural Harper Lee Prize for Legal Fiction sponsored by the University of Alabama School of Law and the *ABA Journal*. Randy runs his own law practice and has been named to *Virginia Business* magazine's select list of "Legal Elite" litigation attorneys. In addition to his law practice and writing, Randy serves as a teaching pastor for Trinity Church in Virginia Beach, Virginia. He calls it his "Jekyll and Hyde thing"—part lawyer, part pastor. He also teaches classes in advocacy and civil litigation at Regent Law School and, through his church, is involved with ministry opportunities in India. He and his wife, Rhonda, live in Virginia Beach. They have two grown children. Visit his website at www.randysinger.net.

ALSO BY RANDY SINGER

Fiction

Directed Verdict

Irreparable Harm

Dying Declaration

Self Incrimination

The Judge Who Stole Christmas

The Cross Examination of Oliver Finney

False Witness

By Reason of Insanity

The Justice Game

Fatal Convictions

The Last Plea Bargain

Nonfiction

Live Your Passion, Tell Your Story, Change Your World

Made to Count

The Cross Examination of Jesus Christ

www.randysinger.net

CP0232